The Wrath of Zar

The Demons of Destiny

Book One

THE WRATH OF ZAR

Book One
The Demons of Destiny

Shayne Eason

WestBank

Publishing

This is a work of fiction. All characters and events in this novel are fictional. Any resemblance to actual persons or events is coincidental.

The Wrath of Zar

All Rights Reserved © 2007 by Shayne Eason

No part of this book may be reproduced or transmitted in any form or by means, graphic, electronic, or mechanical, including photocopying, recording, taping, or by any information storage or retrieval system, without written permission except in the case of brief quotations embodied in critical articles or reviews.

Published by WestBank Publishing

For information address
4408 Bayou Des Familles,
Marrero, LA 70072

Cover by Nicole Cardiff

ISBN: 0-9789840-1-3
ISBN: 978-0-9789840-1-4

Printed in the United States of America

Dedication

I dedicate this novel to my wife Mandy.
She gave me everything I have.

Epigraph

*The threads of destiny are both intricate and delicate,
Woven through a world and time of ignorance,
Beating upon a door of death and despair,
Carrying the fortunes of souls they destroy.*

*Come Warrior, young and ignorant, determined yet misled,
Come Warrior, vigilant and caring, defeated yet pursuing,
Come Warrior, irritable and immature, torn yet loving,
Come Warrior, guardian and protector, powerful yet threatened,
Come Deceiver, intelligent and wicked, truthful yet lying.*

*As the enemy strengthens its hold,
Those who choose to fight will stand against it,
And when the glimmer of hope all but fades,
Destiny will awaken.*

Chapter 1

Gnith walked upon broken grass as he crept toward the mouth of the cave. The entrance waited at the base of the mountain, turned slightly from the rising sun. The effect caused an illusion that defended the entrance from those who pursued its secrets. He wheezed unsteadily through his stuffed nose, tried to catch a scent of his past. His eyes deceived him, yet painful memories of a horrible past flashed through his mind. It alerted him that the entrance was certainly there. Mirror bats flew along the edge of the mountain. They dove down into the meadow and flew in a single row barely above the ground. Their golden-tipped wings flickered through the tall grass like a river of fire. Gnith scratched his balding head with ragged fingernails as he watched them. The ground vibrated beneath his wrinkled toes. He gasped. They were coming.

The sun crept over the eastern horizon and warmed the open meadow at the base of the mountain. The outline of the cave flared with a powerful light that forced Gnith to shield his sensitive eyes. He stepped forward protecting his face from the bright light. The glow around the entrance softened. Afraid to lose his opportunity, he rushed forward and ran as fast as he could. The mirror bats shrieked and exploded into the sky. Gnith screamed and covered his head. He forced his eyes open and peered between his arms as he pushed through the cloud of bats. A sigh of relief escaped his sore throat. He loathed bats. He snapped his fingers and summoned a flame in his palm. A torch hung from a sconce on the cavern wall. He clutched it firmly and lit the bundled twigs. His shadow sprang onto the craggy wall. He looked out beyond the entrance. Seven riders sped across the swaying grass. Their mounts pointed straight at him and the forbidden cave. He smiled, licked his rotten teeth and ran deeper into the cave.

The walls closed together as he descended. Water leaked from the ceiling. Cobwebs stretched across his path. The smell of bitter air wrinkled his nose as the cavern tunnel twisted and turned as it descended into the Pales of Nothingness. Water seeped from the walls and turned into a flowing stream. Memories of the curse cast upon him ignited and reminded him of the torture he endured—water burned his feet like acid and fire. He moved quickly and attempted to ignore the pain.

    The voices of those who hunted him echoed down the tunnel. He listened intently as he focused on the path behind him. His pursuers were in the corridor now. One of them shouted orders to the others. They wanted to kill him; this he knew. His feet burned as he ran harder over gravel and water; pain shot into his thighs and chest. He groaned as his muscles tightened in response. The torch slipped from his fingers and fell into the water, the flame snuffed out. Water surged below, but the darkness kept its location a secret. It almost caused him to lose concentration. Whatever the circumstances, Gnith knew failure would never be forgiven. In pitch darkness, he cautiously continued his descent. Suddenly, the ground beneath him collapsed. Gnith screamed and plunged into a torrent of water. The current dragged him under. His skin erupted in boils; the water burned him like dragon's fire. The current swept him downstream. His fingernails broke as he tried to grab the bank, but the current pulled him back under the surface. His feet touched mud and gravel on the bottom. He thrust himself upward and kicked as he went. He shot out of the water and flung his arms onto the bank. For several moments he gasped and groaned from the horrible pain. Then he pulled himself onto dry land where he rested and waited for the pain to subside. His body convulsed as he crawled to his feet. He felt a root hanging from the cavern wall. He broke it off and snapped his fingers. He lit the makeshift torch and held it up over his head. Skin peeled off his charred body like cloth. Blood wept down his legs and slowly dripped to the floor. He staggered forward, exhausted. When he rounded the next bend he sighed with relief; he found the entrance.

    The Pales of Nothingness was a small island deep in the cavern. It was surrounded by a circle of raging water. Statues of great proportion stood on either side to form an aisle of temperament and courage. Six stood at both ends, each an exact replica of the other. They towered over him in height. They displayed frowns and eyes of deception. Long wavy hair fanned their backs. They wore helmets on their heads and armor on their bodies. Weapons of strength were held firmly within their grips. Gnith stumbled forward. He was almost frightened by the glower on their faces. Beyond the statues was the door he sought. It receded into a rock wall surrounded by a maze of intertwined weeds.

    The hunters closed in. He heard their voices followed by splashes into the raging water that encircled the island. Gnith lurched to the door. His pain became nothing more than the price demanded for success. He tore at the tangle of roots and moss that nearly covered the forbidden door. It revealed a picture that showed the sun centered between two moons. One was silver, the other red. Beneath them was a warning encryption. Gnith knew the warning by memory—he had recited it for years. He smiled with pleasure and stepped back.

Shouts of anger caught up with Gnith. He looked back over his shoulder, his eyes searching the darkness beyond. Flashes of blue light revealed his enemies' positions. They were very close now. He snuffed the flame and turned back to the door. His mind searched for emptiness. He looked within for the power bestowed upon him. Years of preparing soothed his nerves, calmed his anger long enough for him to achieve his goal. The future flashed through his mind. A smile formed on his hideous face. The Gods showed him the way. He snapped his fingers, and a long staff appeared in his hands. The power of the weapon pulsated, sending flashes of warmth through his body. He reeled back and slammed the end of the staff into the sun. It sank deep into the door; the moons exploded in bright light. Pain shot up into his arms. He had to hold on, or failure would follow.

The moons on the door orbited the sun in opposite directions. The door creaked and groaned as if it had a soul. It shook from the power of his staff. The cavern rumbled. Debris dropped from the ceiling above. Again he looked over his shoulder. The seven Warriors of Ches were nearly upon him. Their fearless leader stormed down the centre aisle. Weapons of death flashed through the dark. Screams of revenge threatened him. Gnith turned back to the door. The moons' orbit ceased when they were both directly over the sun causing an eclipse of the greatest power. White light burst outward from the sun. A mighty wind erupted from within and hurled Gnith back through the air.

The statues roared to life. Rock crumbled off their faces and hair. They brandished their weapons of stone and cried out with life. They replicated the image of the ancient god Faral, the one who cleansed their world of evil so many centuries ago. The Warriors of Ches yelled to one another and positioned their backs together. Gnith watched with eager anticipation for the outcome that would prove his victory. The ground shook as the twelve statues stepped off their pedestals. Flails and swords made of iron and stone rose high into the air. Pebbles rolled off their faces as their resounding war cries announced the battle. The twelve statues attacked the Warriors of Ches.

Gnith smiled and spun around to face the entrance. It stood wide open now, waiting for him to claim his prize. Holding his staff firm, he hurried into a dank room carved from sheer rock. It carried just enough light from an unknown source for him to see. The walls were blank and devoid of decor. For an instant Gnith worried that he made a mistake. He shivered at the thought of torture and death.

An ominous shadow formed. It grew larger and larger. It twisted and turned as it rolled from one side of the room to the other, hissing as it shifted. Gnith genuflected holding the staff out in front of him. It was the moment he had dreamed for years beyond years. His pain was pushed aside as his heart pounded. He savored his moment of glorious victory. The shadow settled in the middle of the room and transformed. It grew legs and arms on a skeletal frame. Rotten skin clung to its bones. Its eyes were swirls of red mist. Silver hair grew long and stringy from its cracked skull. "Welcome back, Master," Gnith murmured. His throat was raw; it hurt to speak.

The creature held his weapon in his skeletal hands. "Has the alignment begun?"

"Yes, Master, the alignment begins. It is why I have come."

"Then the Gods are awake?"

"Yes!" Gnith could no longer hold his excitement. "I bring a message, Master."

"What is it?"

"Seeds of evil must be planted in Wyndhaven and Corrona. We must recover the Dryden, and Granaz must be unleashed. The Set-thra has discovered his soul and soon he will be ready."

"Well done."

"The Warriors of Ches are fools, Master! They are here!" The creature stepped forward and placed his skeletal hand on Gnith's head. Warmth infiltrated his skull, trickled down his spine and wormed into the rest of his body. Gnith watched in amazement as the skin on his body healed. The constant burning stopped. Gnith sucked in a breath of air and said, "Thank you, Master."

They left the pungent room and returned to the Pales of Nothingness. The battle drew out in front of them. The Warriors of Ches clung to success, their lives hanging on the balance of victory.

"Master," Gnith began.

"Silence!" the creature hissed. "Do not speak my name. The Gods have resurrected me as a mere ghost; I'm no longer the warrior I once was. A time will come when I shall unveil my true identity, but until then, you will address me as Vayle."

Gnith bowed. "Yes, Master Vayle."

Demon Vayle extended a bony hand and pointed outward. "Kill the Warriors of Ches and destroy the guardians that held me for centuries past."

A flame appeared in Gnith's palm. A grin crept upon his lips.

"Yes, Master. Yes indeed."

Twenty-Three Years Later the Andar slid into his chair and stared coldly at the blank parchment in front of him. The candle on his desk gave little warmth, barely enough to warm the fading thread of hope from his dying soul. After all of these years it had come to this. He tugged his long beard. There were moments in his life that hinted of this terrible day, but the glimmer of hope always fueled his resolve. He realized now that there was no hope. His hands shook as he withdrew the pen from its cylinder. With slow, wheezing breaths and the movement of his pen, the words formed:

> It is today that I bid my farewell. I am defeated by my greatest enemy. I know now not to counter. My ambition dies with my body; I can no longer bear this pain. The Demons of Destiny will soon awaken. There is nothing more I can do. I pray that another will fight for Yannina's survival. The ignorance throughout Yannina disgusts me. Once again I fight alone. Even my faithful apprentice, after many years of training, discourages me. His own desires are frightening. His motives are kept secret. I can no longer weep of failure. I can no longer mourn the loss of my daughter. I can no longer try to save the people who abandoned me or those who betrayed me. The Demons of Destiny will rise to power. Who in this world can stop that now? It is the end of the world; I shall go first. Forgive me, Faral, for failing you.

The Andar shivered from the cold draft that blew in through the window. Visions of that dreadful day flashed in his mind; he shut the memory off, no longer interested in recalling the nightmare. He withdrew a silver knife from a wooden box. Tears trickled down the crags of his face as he held the blade in his withered fingers. He pointed the tip at his heart. The Andar sucked in a deep breath and clamped his eyes shut. The tip of the blade punctured his skin. *"Destiny awakens...."*

The Andar gasped. The words reverberated through his mind. He saw an image of a young man standing alone in a forest of elk trees. He put the knife down and turned in his chair to look around...to make certain no one was nearby. He bolted out of his chair and rushed to the door. He was overflowing with excitement and energy—there was hope after all.

Somewhere in Yannina, a young man was about to face his destiny. The Andar knew that Faral showed him the way. The depression that nearly swallowed his soul disappeared. It was replaced with a hope he'd only dreamed of.

Images of a village in chaos penetrated the Andar's brain. He was uncertain if what he saw was the past...or the future. He did know that the young man he needed to find was in very grave danger. He snatched up his cloak knowing his apprentice had to find the young man. He glanced at the knife. What seemed hopeless before was changed. Destiny had awakened.

Chapter 2

As Adan Caynne closed the large stable door, he stopped to check over his shoulder. A cold breeze brushed his hair and sent a shiver down his spine. He shifted his gaze back and forth through the night, watching the trees. Nothing moved, so he pushed the door closed and locked it tight. The moon hung in the middle of the sky untouched by clouds or tainted by nearby stars. He felt comforted as the moonlight washed over him.

The distant murmur of voices floated down the hill. Ruhln Fest had ended, but the celebrations were just beginning. Those who chose to stay would be drinking Marwin ale and singing around the fire pit. He felt guilty for leaving early. Maureen dressed beautifully. Their childhood friendship was transformed with feelings he never thought possible. Being with her made him nervous. A nagging feeling persisted that he might not be good enough for her. He knew Maureen could have any man she wanted. They weren't even together, and already he feared losing her. Something else troubled Adan, a feeling that gnawed at him since he first climbed out of bed, a feeling of being watched. His father often talked about a sixth sense, but he sloughed that off as nonsense. He thought that a night of good sleep would free his mind of it.

The moonlight enabled him to follow the path without difficulty. His house sat high and tight to a bank that dropped down to the creek. The creek flowed softly on his left as it snaked in and around the elk trees. He loved that; the movement of the creek told him he was home. Built by his father years ago, the house rested in front of the large custan tree. Custan trees were very rare in Ruhln. It was the reason his parents chose that spot to build their house when they first settled in Ruhln. Adan opened the door. He was tantalized by the smell of plum pudding and fresh bread. He pulled off his cloak. "Father, are you home?" he called.

Loud voices descended from the second floor warning Adan that his father and younger brother were arguing...again. Dex's rebellious attitude grew as the boy got older. Their father, stubborn in his own way, disciplined him by taking away his freedom. As punishment for disobedience, their father made Dex remain at his side and follow his orders—Dex hated that. The angry voices grew to shouts. Dex ran down the stairs with their father close behind. "Dex, listen to me!" his father shouted. The house seemed to vibrate with his every step.

Adan ducked into the corner next to the stove knowing it was best not to be involved. Dex found him hiding and shot him a look that made him feel like a cowering rat. "My brothers won't even stand up for me. Everyone hates me," he lamented. His bottom lip trembled.

Adan felt his heart sink as he stepped away from the corner. "Dex, don't speak of such things. You know it's not true."

Their frustrated father stood at the bottom of the stairs. He was about to speak when Dex shoved the door open, "I'm tired of everyone blaming me for their problems." He shook his head in bitter frustration and ran out the door.

"Should I go after him?" Adan asked.

His father shook his head. "No, let him go. I can't talk to him right now." He moved to the center of the room and sat at the table. "I've got a headache."

Adan had never heard his father sound so defeated. "What are we going to do about this?"

"Maybe it's time to tell him."

Adan froze. Memories of one terrible morning still haunted him. "About what?" he murmured. He felt nauseous at the lie...and the memory.

"About the day he disappeared, when you found him in the forest." His father raked his fingers through his thick beard. The last few years had taken their toll on Darren Caynne. He showed more grey in his hair and beard.

"I forgot about that," Adan lied again.

"I've often wondered if maybe we should have moved."

"Do you regret your decision?"

"I don't regret it. Your mother and I built this home. She gave birth to you here. Leaving this place would be like leaving your mother and all our memories together."

"When will you tell him?"

"He's old enough now. It's his reaction that worries me."

Adan thought about that. "I think he'll understand why you kept it a secret. We're lucky nobody else slipped it out."

His father glanced up with a weary look. "Everyone else has been too fearful about it to tell him. I've had many sleepless nights over it myself. I just wish he would settle down a little; his stubborn attitude always gets the better of him."

Adan pointed at his father. "That comes from you. You should be blaming yourself."

A knock sounded. His father nodded. "You get that."

Relieved he no longer had to carry the conversation; Adan opened the door to a warm surprise. Maureen stood with a smile on her face. She carried a basket with a small gift. He found her presence always pleasant, no matter when or where. She flipped her long dark hair over her shoulders and tugged on her blue dress. "Hello, Adan, I'm off to visit my grandfather. I was hoping you'd come along."

An excuse to leave his father's foul mood behind was what he needed. "I should search for Dex anyway," he said to his father as he donned his cloak.

"Good evening, Darren," Maureen said, stepping inside the door.

"Will you say hello to your grandfather for me? I haven't seen him for a while now," Darren said.

She smiled. "Of course I will."

Maureen entwined her arm with Adan's as they headed up the path together. "It seems late for a visit, doesn't it?" Adan hoped she might have something else in mind.

"Poppa Cadin never arrived at Ruhln Fest. We're all a little worried. I want to check on him and give him his gift."

"All right," he replied, disappointed. Her grandfather was a strong-hearted old man. He loved to tease and embarrass Adan. Maureen assured him that Cadin liked him. Adan doubted it. He believed Cadin's playful banters were warnings to keep his hands off Maureen. The trail was a steep climb with the path wending around the large elk trees. The tips of slender grass that grew along the sides of the path glowed softly from the moonlight. "Are you warm enough?" he asked her. She was only wearing a dress.

"Oh yes." She rubbed his arm and snuggled up to him. "You left the festival early."

He rubbed his face; a habit that accompanied a lie. "The horses had to be fed."

"Thank you for the necklace." She traced the fine jewels with her fingers and slid her hand around her neck.

He hadn't noticed her wearing it. It took months to find all the myir needed to piece it together. He flushed. "Thank you for wearing it."

She stopped him on their path and turned into him, "I love it." The moonlight reflecting off her eyes tugged at his heart. Her lips glowed softly. His chest tightened. "You left before I could give you mine," she scolded.

"You didn't have to get me anything," he replied with a smile.

She smiled just a little and pushed her body into his. "I didn't." Her arms slipped over his shoulders. Her skin felt soft and smooth on his neck. Warmth from her body seeped into his. The movement of her lips made his skin tingle. He felt her breasts push into his chest; he reached around her waist, pulled her in tight. The touch of her lips left him numb. Her breath slid by his mouth and warmed his soul. He kissed her as softly as he could; worried that he might hurt her. Not in his entire life had he experienced anything more powerful. Someone tapped his shoulder. Adan felt her body tense before she screamed. He spun around, almost too frightened to look. There loomed a huge man with a pointed hat holding a large axe up over his head. His bearded chin was a mass of tangled hair. Instinctively, Adan shoved Maureen behind him and threw his arms up in defence. The stranger lowered the axe and rocked with laughter. Adan relaxed when he realized they were victims of a terrible prank. There was only one man in Ruhln with that laugh.

Maureen stomped her foot. "Hunter Gorge! You should be ashamed."

Adan shook his head. "Hunter, you shouldn't do such things." He took a deep breath and smiled at Maureen. He couldn't wait to kiss her again.

"What a mean thing to do!" Maureen yelled. She smacked Hunter on the shoulder.

When Hunter's laughter finally subsided, he said, "I haven't had so much fun in years. You're the second couple I've scared tonight." He rubbed his beard and pointed back up the hill. "I found another young couple behind the Inn. I snuck in from behind, swinging my axe and screaming bloody murder. If they hadn't been naked at the time I would've scared the clothes right off them!"

Adan laughed. Maureen cast him a stern look. "Hunter, we have guests from all over Yannina. Ruhln Fest brings us a great amount of business. If you continue frightening people, the word will spread, and we'll lose customers. We welcome people to our village to give thanks...not to scare the wits out of them."

Hunter cleared his throat and nodded his head. He feigned remorse with a frown. Then laughing again he headed back up the hill. "Aren, tell your father to drop by for a pint."

Adan sighed. Hunter always had him confused with his twin brother. "I'm Adan."

Hunter stopped. They could barely hear him muttering to himself, "Bloody twins." Only Hunter Gorge would say such a thing.

"I'll tell him," Adan called out.

Hunter waved his hat. "Be sure to do that, Adan. I'm going back to Ruhln Fest. There's many a keg of Marwin ale to be enjoyed!"

Maureen took Adan's arm with hers as they watched him tread up the hill. She shivered. He pulled off his cloak and wrapped it around her shoulders. He wanted nothing more than to hold her and kiss her again, but it was getting late. "I suppose we better get to where we're going." They continued their journey arm-in-arm. Adan had to admit, as much as the strange feeling still bothered him, today turned into one of his best days. Nothing could ruin that now.

"I love the moon," she said, breaking the silence.

"It is beautiful."

"Everything about tonight has been perfect."

"Funny, I was just thinking the same thing."

The road dipped where it crossed the creek. A bridge was built over it when the creek washed out the road. Whenever Adan crossed the bridge he remembered that terrible summer. It was right after the washout that Dex disappeared. Adan would never forget that misty morning when he found his little brother...and all the death that surrounded him.

A horse appeared from the forest on the other side of the bridge. Its hooves stomped loudly on the bridge deck as it crossed. It carried two riders, their identity hidden in the shadows. Strange folk were not unusual in Ruhln during the festival, but for some reason Adan found their appearance frightening. Maureen must have felt it as well; she squeezed his hand as they approached. He soon distinguished a man and a woman. A long axe was haltered to the saddle, a bow swung over the man's shoulders and a large quiver of arrows tied off the saddle. There were no tournaments until the fall, and they were always held in Wyndhaven. It was wrong to carry weapons of such strength to the festival. Adan scrutinized them as they drew near. The man was huge with a short-trimmed beard and curly, dark hair. He wore thick leather coverings that reminded Adan of the clothes Aren used to wear during his training sessions with their father. The stranger didn't appear as ferocious as the weapons he carried. It was difficult to identify the girl as she hid behind her companion. "Can I help you?" Adan asked. With the amount of weapons holstered between the two, he felt foolish carrying nothing more than a small hunting knife. He didn't stand a chance if he was forced to protect Maureen.

The big man responded, "We're looking for an old friend." His deep voice sounded friendly enough. Searching for friends was better than looking for enemies. The girl behind him stared from beyond his shoulder. She smiled politely.

"I know almost everyone who lives here," Adan replied.

"I'm looking for Darren Ches. I don't know if he still lives here, but last time I came through he did."

Darren Ches. His father's name was Darren, but not Ches. There was no other Darren in town. The last thing his family needed right now was somebody from his past. His father hated to talk about that as it was. "I'm sorry, there's nobody here with that name."

"Drat. I suppose he changed his name again. It would be like him to do that. Have you heard of Darren Caynne?"

Maureen tightened her grip. Adan rubbed the side of his face, wishing he could tell the stranger that he'd never heard of Darren Caynne. It seemed the right thing to do. He whispered to Maureen. "Can you go on alone?"

She smiled. "Go ahead. I don't have much farther to go." She kissed him on the cheek and returned his cloak.

He watched her until she was safely away. To the strangers he said, "Follow me." Adan backtracked to town. He knew he wasn't going to take them directly to his doorstep, especially this man, armed to the teeth and tied to his father's past. He wasn't going to leave them where he'd met them, either. As soon as he felt they were a safe distance from Maureen, he intended to leave them on the road and find his father.

Adan hated how his father kept secrets from their family. As children their father told them not to ask questions about his past, but when Dex disappeared, he and Aren thought it was time for an explanation. As usual Darren refused and warned them not to question him about his past. He told them that ignorance would benefit them forever. That pronouncement frightened Adan. He remembered one night when he and Aren talked late into the night about what kind of person would keep secrets from his own family. They talked about Dex, and about how his odd behaviour along with the incident in the forest could be tied to their father's past. What they finally agreed upon was how caring and gentle their mother was. No woman like that would end up with a man uncaring and poor in heart. As mysterious as Darren was, they surmised that their father had their welfare in mind for shutting them out of his past. The brothers made a pact never to discuss the subject again because they loved their father. They also agreed to protect their little brother Dex.

Adan made a fist. He completely forgot about Dex. As soon as he told his father about his guests, he would make it a priority to find him. Hopefully, he was already home in bed. Adan didn't like the idea of Dex running around in the dark alone. He peered over his shoulder. The man was talking to the woman, their words muffled by the calm wind. The horse bobbed his head up and down to the beat of his walk. It was a powerful-looking horse. His neck was several hands higher than all of those back at the stables. He had heard about warhorses, but thought the stories were made up. The inn was farther down the road. A few townsfolk huddled around the fire drinking from a keg of Marwin ale.

Adan lifted his hand. The stranger tightened the reins and stopped beside him. He felt better knowing Maureen was probably safe inside Cadin's house with people close by.

"What's your name?" he asked them.

"I'm Hythe; this is Leahla." He patted his horse on the neck, "This is Firestreak."

Adan nodded. "Darren doesn't live far from here. I'll let him know you're waiting. I won't be long."

Hythe smiled and turned to Leahla. "Smart, for such a young fellow."

Adan thought it was an unusual comment. He said, "Ruhln Fest hasn't died yet. There's plenty of ale meant for travelers. Help yourself, if you like."

"I know what Ruhln Fest is, Lad. We're both fine, thank you."

Hythe seemed like a good person to Adan, but he couldn't shake the feeling that secrets meant to be stifled were about to be resurrected. Something bad was going to happen. The discomforting feeling at the back of his mind worsened. He left the road and followed the trail that would take him home. He checked behind him several times to make certain he wasn't being followed. He broke into a run and hurried home. Maureen and the kiss still lingered in the back of his mind.

Chapter 3

Adan slammed the door open. A candle burned in the middle of the table flickering softly like the fire in the hearth. He undid the top button of his cloak and rubbed the back of his neck. "Father?" he called. His boots thumped on the wooden floor as he approached the stairwell. The stairs creaked as he climbed. He wondered how his father would react to someone from his past. At the back of the hallway was his father's room, the door open only by a crack. To the left was Dex's room. His bed was empty. Adan was disappointed that his brother had not returned home. His father's bed and nightstand were visible through the small opening at the end of the hallway; Adan grabbed the wooden handle to open the door all the way, "Father?"

The door jerked open tearing the handle from Adan's grip. "How many times have I asked you to knock?" his father roared.

Adan noticed his father's closet unlocked with the door ajar. He quickly shifted his gaze pretending not to notice. "I'm sorry, but I called your name twice. I didn't know you were in here."

Darren shook his head and blocked the entrance to the room with his body. "What is it, then?"

"Some people came to the village. They're looking for you."

"Who?"

"The man's name is Hythe. He has a woman named Leahla."

Darren's eyes widened. "Are you sure that's his name?"

"Yes, and they're heavily armed." Adan stepped to the side hoping to catch a glimpse of the closet. His father kept that closet and its contents secret for years. He warned Adan and his brothers to keep out. Now it was open; Adan wanted to know why.

Darren stepped into the hallway and closed the door to his room. "Where is he?"

"I left them near the inn. They're waiting for you."

"Take me to them."

His father followed him down the stairs. "Who are they?" Adan asked.

"Hythe is an old acquaintance."

Darren's vague answer was what he expected. He thought maybe he could ask why they were here, or perhaps how he had known them. He also thought about the open door to his father's closet. For years he and Aren wondered what secret was kept in there.

Adan followed his father up the trail. Hythe and the woman were waiting near the inn where Adan left them. "Hythe," Darren called.

They hugged. "It's good to see you," Hythe said in his deep tone.

"After all these years I doubted that I would see you again."

Hythe smiled. "I had the same doubts. I want you to meet Leahla."

Darren smiled at her. "It's a pleasure." He slapped Adan on the back. "You've already met my son, Adan."

"We weren't formally introduced," Hythe said. He shook Adan's hand, his grip powerful and his hand huge. Adan glanced up at Leahla astride the horse; she smiled at him. He thought he would never find another woman more attractive than Maureen, but this one was perfect. Her hair hung halfway down her back. Her legs were partially bare. He found that strangely attractive. Her eyes amazed him more than anything. In the dark they appeared to be brown, but something told him the color was something much more beautiful. He turned away, ashamed, as if he had betrayed his feelings for Maureen. "When we first met, you reminded me of your father," Hythe said to Adan. "I'll never forget the look in your eyes when I asked to see him."

"It's not often strangers arrive in the middle of the night armed with weapons and searching for my father."

Darren stepped around them and took the reins to the horse. "Let's go home. Leahla looks tired. She can sleep while we get caught up on old times." Hythe agreed.

"I have to find Dex," Adan said.

Darren turned to him. "You know where to look. He's probably run off to Whistle Rock again. Bring him back as soon as you can. We'll be up for awhile."

Adan turned down the road. Not once had his father mentioned Hythe. Obviously this stranger was part of that past he wasn't supposed to know about. Adan tightened his cloak and looked up at the stars remembering his mother. She once told him a story he would never forget: The stars were the guardians of their world. When a person died, and if their aura was strong enough, they would be chosen as a guardian and placed in the heavens. He recalled the night after her death. Crushed with sorrow, he climbed to Whistle Rock and sat on top of the world. He watched the sky waiting for a new star to be born. Adan smiled. He was cold that night too. Nearing sunrise, with not a shred of hope left, a glorious shooting star streaked across the dark sky and magically stopped in the middle—his mother's star. He remembered that as he stared with tear-filled eyes that glistened in the moonlight. "I miss you," he whispered. Now as he remembered that cold night he drew his cloak tighter. The night seemed quiet even with the inn only around the corner. The celebrating had subsided.

Maureen appeared from around the corner just as he crossed the bridge. She rushed to him. "I can't find him."

"You can't find Cadin?"

"It's not like him, Adan. He and Father are always arguing over something, he wouldn't deliberately disappear. I'm worried."

"Come home with me. Maybe my father has seen him." At that moment Adan's gaze was pulled into the forest. The night wind rolled through the trees twisting the undergrowth toward the forest floor. The black of night engulfed them as the moonlight disappeared behind a cloud.

"What's wrong?" she asked him.

A shiver slid down his spine; the feeling of being watched returned far more powerful and demanding than ever. He leaned into Maureen and whispered, "We should move."

"What?"

He motioned her to follow him and took her hand. A figure lurched out from the bush. Maureen screamed. It was difficult to see what it was. The raspy breaths gurgled as if it weren't human at all. Adan shoved Maureen behind him and unsheathed his knife. He desperately tried to keep hold of his courage. "What is it?" Maureen asked in a trembling voice.

"Maure-e-e-n . . ." a raspy voice called out.

Adan lowered his knife as he recognized the voice. Maureen cried out, "Poppa, what happened to you?"

The moon reappeared. Adan watched Maureen as she cradled her grandfather in her arms. He was bathed in blood from terrible gashes across his back and through his stomach. A shredded robe barely covered his frail body. Adan's stomach heaved when he saw Cadin's bloody eye socket.

"You must run," Cadin rasped. Adan watched the forest as closely as he could. He sensed that whatever attacked Cadin was still close. The thrumming of his heartbeat was matched by the rapid thoughts that flashed through his mind. Adan knelt to pick Cadin up, but the old man batted his hands away. "Run," he urged, "get away!" Blood pooled on the ground around him.

Between sobs Maureen cried, "You must come with us."

"No! Run! Don't stop! They're coming!" Cadin shook as if he were having a seizure.

"Who's coming?" Adan demanded.

Cadin reached out and slapped Adan across his face. The smell of his blood hurt more than the sting of the blow. "Foolish boy, run!"

"We can't leave you here to die!" Adan shouted back.

"I'm already dead. Go. There's no time." With shaking hands, Cadin grabbed Adan by his shoulder and hissed an urgent whisper. "Protect her for me." Adan sucked in his breath and fought back tears, worried about the task; he wasn't a warrior.

Maureen kissed her grandfather on his forehead. "I love you," she whispered.

Adan grabbed her by the wrist and they sprinted down the road. He ran as fast as Maureen would let him. Frightening images flashed through his mind. He listened for the splashing of the creek with every stride knowing it would announce the safety of his home. He glanced at Maureen and swore silently that he would lead her home to safety. In the distance they heard Cadin's agonizing scream. When it stopped they knew the old man's pain was over. Maureen stumbled and shook uncontrollably as she collapsed against Adan's chest. He forced her to calm down. "Maureen, we must run."

"I'm afraid, Adan. Who would do such a thing?" she sobbed.

Adan urged her to run knowing his house was nearby. They raced along the trail lit by moonlight. He was familiar with the way it switched back and forth across the rock bluff. The silhouette of a horse waited near the bridge, its long neck down toward the water. Dim light seeped through the closed shutters. Candlelight flickered outside. It told Adan that someone was between them and their safety. He stopped and whispered to Maureen to remain silent. The horse whipped its head out of the creek and uttered a loud whinny. Something crept around the house. The door opened and his father stepped out with Hythe behind him. Adan yelled. "Father, get back inside; there's something there!"

"It's only me, Adan," Aren called out.

Adan took Maureen by her hand and led her down the hill. Having his brother close to him brought comfort. If anyone could help him protect Maureen, it would be Aren.

"Did you scare the horse?" his father asked, looking at Aren.

"Yes," Aren replied. "I surprised him when I crossed the bridge."

His father nodded. "All right, just making sure it wasn't something else." He noticed that Maureen was covered with blood. "Maureen? Are you all right?"

Adan answered. "Something attacked Cadin on the trail." He didn't want to say that he was dead; not with Maureen still shocked by it all. Aren combed back his hair with his fingers and turned away. Adan sensed that his brother was bothered by something.

"Come quickly," Darren motioned them inside. Maureen slumped. Adan caught her. He carried her inside and put her in a chair in front of the fire. "Tell me what happened," Darren said.

"There's not much to tell. We were on our way back here when Cadin staggered out of the forest. Something attacked him; he insisted that we run away. He wouldn't come with us. We heard him scream shortly after leaving him."

"Did Cadin say what it was that attacked him?"

For the first time, Adan realized he was trembling. "He only said, 'they are coming.'"

Darren asked Hythe, "Did you see or hear anything suspicious when you came into town?"

"No, I didn't."

Darren scowled. "We must find Cadin immediately."

"Dex is gone," Aren said. His eyes glistened in the candlelight with unshed tears. "Myron and I ran into him on the road on our way back from Ruhln Fest." For Adan it was like looking in a mirror, except that now his identical brother stood with his face set in a powerful frown, his golden brown hair hung in wisps over his bloodshot eyes. "I said something . . . I uh I didn't know he was there." Adan knew he must have said something terrible; to see tears welling in Aren's eyes was a rarity.

"Precisely, what did you say?" Darren asked with an edge. There were times that Darren would become so angry and release a rage so inhumanly powerful, it was doubtful even Faral could stand against him. Adan watched now as that anger sparked in his father's eyes.

Aren stepped back from his approaching father. "I was talking to Myron about Mother. I told him how much I miss her. I said that if Dex had not been born, Mother would still be alive. I didn't know Dex was behind me. Dex heard me and ran away."

Darren stared at him a long moment, then rubbed his face with both hands. It's what he did when he was upset or angry, or perhaps it was his way to calm himself. He shook his head. "I can't believe that you, of all people, would say something like that."

"I didn't mean it as it sounds, I swear. I just miss her. That's all. I miss her."

Darren abruptly turned away and shouted, "We all miss her!"

Hythe walked forward. "I'm so sorry...."

"Now is not the time."

Hythe nodded, "Of course."

Aren wiped his face with his sleeve. "I didn't mean it."

"It doesn't matter anymore," Darren replied. "It's late, dark, and whatever it was that attacked Cadin is out there; so is Dex. Let's bring him home. We can discuss everything else after that."

"I need to go home," Maureen pleaded.

"You'll stay here," Darren said in a no nonsense tone. "I'll run by your house and let your parents know what happened. I'll take your father and find Cadin. You two," he said, pointing to Adan and Aren, "I want you searching for your brother on horseback. Stay mounted."

Adan looked at Darren square on and boldly said, "I won't leave Maureen."

Darren, shocked, stared at Adan for only a moment. "Stay then and pray that Dex returns. Don't let him out of your sight if he does." He turned to Aren, "Take your swords." Aren nodded and ran up the stairs.

"I'm coming with you," Hythe said. "Leahla can look after these two."

Darren said, "Thanks," and followed Aren up the stairs. "I'll be back in a moment."

Hythe hugged Leahla. "Protect them." She nodded and kissed his cheek. "Adan," Hythe quietly asked, "How did your mother die?" Adan took a deep breath. He didn't know what to think. He thought it was an odd question. Before he could reply, Darren came down the stairs. Hythe said, "Never mind, I'll ask your father." Adan was tempted to tell Hythe that it wasn't any of his concern.

Darren carried an unusual sword that Adan never saw before; it was difficult to get a good look at it in the dying candlelight. His father noticed him trying to view it and turned it away. "Hythe, I'm ready," he announced.

Aren came down behind his father. Two swords hung from the belt above his waist. They were secured within a scabbard made of wood. His face showed his determination. His hair was combed straight back like he did at Wyndhaven when he competed for the honor of Dal-Varr. A line drawn with black stone crossed his left temple to the bottom of his nose. It was the mark he used during tournament competition. Adan had never been so proud. His father urged them both to take up the sport when they were young, but only Aren showed an interest in the tournaments. Adan wanted nothing to do with swords or fighting. His father trained and practiced with Aren every day for years. Eventually Aren became a champion. With Maureen trembling in fear, Adan regretted that he didn't show an interest in it: he, too, might be a warrior. Protecting Maureen was what mattered most to him now. Without training he couldn't do that as well as his brother.

"Aren, what are you doing?" Darren asked with a touch of irritation.

"What do you mean?"

"You're not going to war; you're looking for your brother."

Aren nodded. "I know."

Darren shook his head. "Don't feel guilty about what happened. Just find him and bring him home. Hythe and I will find out who attacked Cadin."

Leahla stood beside Adan as they left. She stared at the door with her arms crossed over her stomach, expressionless. "Thank you for letting us into your home," she said to Adan.

Adan sighed. "Both of you are welcome here." He noticed her eyes then and stared. Her pupils were silver instead of black.

She smiled. "Thank you." Her voice was quietly soothing.

Maureen rubbed her forehead. "Adan, I need to lie down."

"Come on." He would give her his bed. She still trembled as he led her up the stairs. Leahla stayed by the fire. "I won't be long," he told her. He thought about Cadin and Dex. The thought of his little brother out there with a murderer on the loose left an uneasy feeling in the pit of his stomach. He prayed that Aren would find Dex before anything happened.

Chapter 4

Darren waited for Aren to arrive safely at the stalls before heading up the trail. "Why don't we take our horses?" Hythe asked from behind.

"I want Aren to ride. If he finds trouble he'll be able to get away easier. We can fight our way out. If we find Cadin, I don't want horses spooking anything off. I want to catch the scum who did this."

"Who do you think it was?"

"I wish I knew."

"Darren, I'm sorry about Catherine. What happened?"

The last thing Darren wanted was Hythe meddling in his affairs again. "She died during the birth of my third son."

"That is Dex?" Darren nodded. Hythe touched his shoulder "I'm sorry."

"It's been difficult, Hythe. Dex is rebellious and temperamental. I try to understand him, but I get so frustrated with his attitude."

"Darren, do you think it could be from the warning?"

"I want no part of what you're thinking. I thought you put that behind you. I won't have that fight again."

Hythe didn't back down. "Faral warned you not to have more than two children."

Darren's anger smoldered. "Don't you dare speak about that," he rasped.

"It's important." Hythe stood his ground. "How could you push away such a threat? How could you do that to your wife?"

Darren's pain and rage, locked away for so many years, burst forth with a hammer-blow to Hythe's face. "Don't talk about that curse!" he shouted.

Hythe hit the ground. He rose rubbing his jaw. "Faral warned you about a third child. Now they all may suffer."

Darren backed away. "Enough!"

"You don't understand. I want to help you."

"I told you once that I would not succumb to Faral or his preaching. He betrayed us that day; I shall never forgive him."

"He did not betray us!" Hythe emphasized each word. "We lost the battle. We failed him."

"No!" Darren turned back up the hill.

Hythe followed him. "Why didn't you tell your sons who I really am?"

Darren stopped. He felt a touch of guilt for hitting him. "I don't know."

With a concerted effort to control his own emotions, Hythe spoke slowly. "I return home seeking the forgiveness of my brother. I find I have nephews, yet you didn't introduce me as their uncle."

Darren rubbed his face with his hands. "I'm sorry. I didn't do that on purpose. It's just that, after you left, you were dead to me."

"You fool! I'm your brother! I wanted you to accept the truth."

Darren looked up at the moon. "I hate what that man did to us."

"As you should, but that's no reason to ignore the truth. Have you told them? Do they know at least?"

"Adan is the smartest. He knows that something isn't right, but he also knows when to keep his mouth shut. Aren is interested in other things; I don't think he cares so much." Darren smiled. "Hythe, you should see that boy with his swords. He's unbelievable."

"What about Dex?"

Darren felt his hatred resurface as he spoke. "When Faral ordered me not to have more than two children, I wouldn't accept that. When we were betrayed and ambushed, I lost all trust in him. I refused to let my history affect the family I wanted. I wanted my children to grow strong and healthy; never to worry about the life I endured. For twenty-one years we've lived in peace. You must understand that I won't allow that curse to ruin our lives."

"Your conviction deceives you. Something has already happened."

To stop the shaking of his hands, Darren clenched them into fists. He dreaded telling Hythe that he was right. His brother warned him, but he and Catherine wouldn't listen. "Dex was an infant," he said quietly. "He couldn't even turn himself over. We woke one morning and found his basket empty. We couldn't find him anywhere. At first I thought Faral took him as revenge. Everyone in Ruhln searched. It started in the village and proceeded to the forest." Darren took a deep breath as he tried to block the memory of that day. "It was Adan who found him."

"What happened?"

"Adan found him alone and naked in an open clearing." Darren stopped and closed his eyes. "There were dead animals everywhere. I can't even begin to explain what I saw. Deer, rabbits, birds, squirrels, you name it. They were torn apart, their carcasses shredded and their eyes stolen. There was blood everywhere. Dex lay in the middle of it all, completely unscathed. The only marks on him were drops of blood beneath his eyes."

Hythe shuddered. "Darren—"

"I know, Hythe. We never left Ruhln after that, but perhaps we should have. Nothing like that has happened since. There is hatred in that boy I don't understand. I know I made a mistake, but after everything we did for Faral, I feel as though our faithfulness was betrayed." He stepped closer to Hythe. "Do you remember the day we fought in the Pales of Nothingness? The demon tricked us and released something behind that door. We lost the fight that day, remember?"

"I remember. How could I forget? My body is covered in scars that remind me every day."

"Whatever that was, it got away."

"No, it didn't," Hythe said.

Darren nodded. "Yes, it did. After we failed there, and after Gragg Creek—that was when Faral cursed me. As the leader, he condemned me for our failure."

"That's not possible! We fought and bled for him. He knighted us to secure our loyalty to him and his goals. Remember hard what we sacrificed for him. Our lives, our meaningless and petty lives were his to command, but he was just as loyal to us as we were to him. We were the Warriors of Ches…remember? Faral would not lie to us!"

"He lied. Something isn't right about what happened back then. We were used for something. I can't put my finger on it."

Hythe was shocked. "So that's it. You're questioning his motives now?"

"I won't let Faral win. Pretending that nothing ever happened is the only weapon I have. I want all of my children to live productive lives, especially Dex."

"I'm truly sorry. I wish I had never run away. But now, please, listen to me." Hythe put his hand on Darren's shoulder. "You must accept the truth and tell the twins about our past; they need to know for their own safety. When we find Dex, you should tell him the truth, too. Faral cursed him for a particular reason, and though we don't know what that might be, he needs to be protected more than anybody. His safety hangs by a thread."

Darren pulled Hythe into a powerful hug. "Forgive me for hitting you."

Hythe smiled. "It's forgotten; it brought back some memories."

"I'm pleased you're home." Darren turned back up the hill. "I need you. Once we take care of this mess, you and I can finally talk about better things. I would like to get to know Leahla."

Hythe tensed. "Darren, there's something else I need to tell you."

"Do you mean about her?" Hythe had a troubled history with women that often lead to mischief. For some reason when he had first met Leahla, Darren thought his brother had finally found someone to settle him down.

Hythe stammered, "I have to explain something that happened."

"We have all the time in the world now. Let's find out what attacked Cadin and get Dex home and into bed; then we can talk as long as we want."

"Of course, we'll talk later."

Darren felt some of the stress diminish as he climbed the steep trail. Years ago they had the same argument, but their youth and stubbornness blew it out of control. In the end, Hythe gave up and left. Darren knew that Hythe was right, too. As much as he wanted to defy Faral, he shouldn't have ignored such threats. He believed once that his punishment was losing his beloved Catherine—now he knew he was wrong. Maybe it was time to leave Ruhln. Maybe starting a life elsewhere would help. He thrust the thoughts from his mind and focused on the path ahead of him. They ran as quietly as they could, twisting through the tall trees. Once they arrived on the road, Darren turned north and watched for signs of Cadin. Hythe tapped his shoulder and pointed to the ground. Blood splotched the ground like puddles caused by a rainstorm. "If this is where it happened, then whatever it was took the body," Hythe whispered.

Darren shook his head. "I don't think so. We better find him. I don't think he went to Michael's for help, but we should let him know what's going on anyway."

"Why wouldn't Cadin go to his son for help?"

"They haven't been getting along lately," Darren said. He motioned his brother to follow and moved on. "I hope that old man is safe."

Demon Vayle waited within the shadows, hiding on the outskirts of Ruhln. Gnith stood impatiently at his side as he picked at his teeth with a rusty blade. Vayle dragged his bony fingers across Gnith's scalp. Shadows approached them with gleaming red eyes; the body of Cadin Dalton was thrown at their feet. "This is the one who discovered our arrival?" Vayle hissed.

"Yes, Master," Gnith replied.

"Slice him open. Let them feast."

"Yes, Master."

Vayle turned to his army of demons as Gnith began his work. They gathered along the river and waited for his signal to send them to victory. Their red eyes blinked with excitement and their bodies twitched. The sing-song growling from their jowls was their chant of death. When the time arrived, they would finish their song and charge deep into the night.

Beyond the wretched creatures waited two of Vayle's most beloved Dryden. The Dryden were his warriors and servants, trained to kill without compassion. Both of them were recruited long ago. The time for their deeds of glory was about to begin. They were not his only Dryden; he planted more in various settlements across Yannina over years past. They waited for his call and time of redemption. The two Dryden bowed as he approached them. "The time is upon us," Vayle said. Behind him the demons continued to growl and feast on Cadin's corpse. Vayle pointed to Demon Stihl. "Our Dryden in Ruhln gave me the information I asked for. Kill the Warrior of Ches and his family. Kill everyone."

Vayle turned to the other. "Demon Myra, find the boy and bring him to me alive."

Together Stihl and Myra bowed and said in unison, "Yes, Master Vayle."

Vayle raised his arms high above his head. The clouds rolled aimlessly through the night sky. The red moon rose over the far mountains and pushed back the light of the silver moon. The forest around them glowed with a blood-red hue, tantalizing those eager to spill it. "Our master guides us," Vayle said. Once he had the boy, the revenge he longed for would spin into reality. He lowered his arms. The demon army charged forth.

Chapter 5

Darren pounded on the door with his fist. "Michael!" Hythe stood away from the porch and looked out over the meadow in front of the house. The distant tree line was calm and silent. "The sudden appearance of that moon bothers me," Darren muttered, "It was never a good omen in the past." He pounded on the door again and checked to make sure his sword was still secured to his back. It was a long time since he wore it there.

Hythe said, "I hope Aren found Dex."

"He will. We need to find out who attacked Cadin."

The door finally opened. Michael held a candle and peered out at them. "Darren? Why are you here so late?"

"Let me in."

A hint of shock seeped into his sleepy eyes as he shot a cold look at Hythe. "Well, hello, Hythe. I haven't seen you around in a while." He opened the door wide and stepped back.

Darren told Hythe, "Stay here and keep your eyes open." He grasped Michael by the upper arm and escorted him deeper into his house.

"What's he doing here?"

"Don't worry about him right now. There's been some trouble."

Michael lit the lantern on the table and sat down. The room flared to life and Darren sat next to him. "What did Myron do now?"

"This isn't about him; it's about your father."

Michael frowned. "So what did *he* do now?"

"Maureen went to visit him not long ago."

Michael noticed the fear on Darren's face. He pulled his nightcap off and threw it on the table. "Where's my daughter?"

"She's at my place. She's safe for now."

"What happened?" Michael asked, almost whispering.

"Earlier tonight, Adan and Maureen came upon Cadin in the forest. Somebody attacked him."

Michael bolted out of his chair. "What! How can you act so calm?"

"I didn't want to alarm you," Darren admitted.

"Maureen's safe? Where's my father?"

"I don't know. I'm on my way to find out. I came to get you."

Suddenly, Myron appeared from the dark corner startling Darren. The boy had a knack for appearing out of nowhere. "Where's my grandfather?" he asked.

"We don't know."

Myron shook his head and frowned. "Where's Maureen?" Darren didn't approve of the look in his eyes, the boy was thinking foolishly.

Michael rose from his seat and walked over to his son. "She's at Darren's; she's safe." He looked out the window. "What on —-?"

"Darren!" Hythe shouted. Darren bolted from his chair and rushed out the door. Hythe pointed to the sky. A massive dragon flew over their heads and skimmed the treetops with its outstretched wings. Its black body glistened from the red moonlight. "That was never a good omen either," Hythe muttered as they watched the dragon disappear beyond their sight. Moments later, a red light spread across the meadow and into the forest. It grew brighter and brighter as it moved over the forest canopy. Darren unsheathed his sword. Hythe reached behind his back and undid a clip, letting his battleaxe fall from the strap.

Something invaded Ruhln. Darren thought of the dragon, but his instincts warned him it was something else. Cadin wasn't attacked by a dragon. He looked back at Michael and said, "Stay here; protect your family. Don't leave your house."

Michael stood on the porch trembling with fear. "What's going on?" A horse protested loudly from behind the house. Michael spun. "Where's Myron?"

Darren ran to the side of the house. Myron raced off with his crossbow in hand as he urged the horse to run faster.

"Myron, stop!" Darren yelled.

"Myron!" Michael moved himself in front of the horse with his arms in the air, but Myron yanked the reins to the left, and the horse turned. Myron disappeared into the forest.

"This is bad," Darren muttered.

Michael started back to the house and fell to his knees. "What do I do?" Michael asked, his voice quavering, his body shaking.

"I'll find him, Michael, I promise. Get inside." Darren pulled him to his feet. "Myron can look after himself. When I find him, I'll send him home." He forced Michael onto the porch. "Get inside, lock the doors." His friend was losing his mind, obviously horrified by what was happening in

Ruhln, and knowing that his father and children were in the middle of it. "Do it!" Darren shouted. He forced Michael into the house. "I swear on my life I'll bring them both home safely! Protect Ann; she needs you here."

Michael finally appeared to understand. "Thank you."

Screams and cries for help echoed through the forest. The red glow soared high over the tree line. It was near the inn where Ruhln Fest was held.

"What's happening?" Hythe asked.

"That's not dragon's fire," Darren said. "Something else is attacking the villagers."

They broke into a run. "I see that, but what could it be?"

Darren ground his teeth together as he held back the fear rising in the pit of his stomach. "We're about to find that out." He prayed for the safety of his children and ran toward the screams of death.

Chapter 6

Adan covered Maureen with a blanket, tucked in her slender body and kissed her on the forehead. She smiled at him. She was still shaking under the covers. "Don't kiss me there," she said.

For a moment he forgot about everything that happened. He was alone with her, with nobody to interrupt them. "I'm sorry I left you alone tonight," he whispered.

"It isn't your fault."

"My father will find out what's going on. You'll see."

Maureen nodded. She reached up with her hand and spread her fingers through his hair. "I feel much better now that I have you watching over me."

Adan felt guilty. He could never protect her as well as Aren or Myron could. "I won't leave you." That was a promise he knew he could keep.

She pulled his head down toward her. His lips trembled. A crash shattered the quiet from downstairs. "What was that?" Maureen asked, her voice quavering with fear.

Leahla screamed. Adan rushed out of the bedroom, vaguely aware that Maureen followed. Nausea and worry for Leahla enveloped him as he sprinted for the stairs. He reached back for Maureen and took her hand just as the ceiling collapsed in a cloud of wood and dust. Maureen screamed at the same time Adan lost his grip on her hand. Something hissed and lashed out at him through the darkness and debris.

Adan yelled when something grabbed him by the arm and threw him away as if he were lighter than air. He crashed through a wall and hit something hard. Gasping for air, he tried to focus as everything spun around him. Maureen screamed; the fear in her voice forced him to his knees. His lungs ached, but he finally managed to force some air into them.

"Get down, Adan!" He dropped to the floor and saw Leahla unsheathe a short sword hidden beneath her dark hair. She ran at him and lifted the blade high over her head. Something hissed and shrieked. It was followed by Leahla's war cry. Something fell to the floor. He looked as lifeless red eyes stared back at him from a severed head spurting blood where it had once been fastened to its neck. Adan grimaced at its greenish-brown skin and jagged teeth. Black hair was soaked in green blood. Behind him the body slumped to the floor.

Maureen screamed for help. She was halfway down the stairs face-to-face with one of the creatures. Leahla helped him to his feet and reached inside her shirt. "Maureen!" Adan yelled. She muttered for help, her face ghastly white. In that instant, Leahla threw her knife and struck the creature in the neck. Maureen screamed and shoved it down the stairs. Adan ran to her. She came down the stairs and threw her arms around him.

Leahla pulled her knife out of the creature's neck and said, "Demons."

"What?" Adan asked with an incredulous look. Demons didn't exist.

Leahla ushered them into the middle of the room. She put her back to them while she held her sword. "There's more. Be ready to fight," she warned.

Adan held Maureen as she cried and stared at the demons lying on the floor. They had claws on their wrists and knees with another extending from each elbow. White venom oozed from the tips. The slime on their naked bodies glistened in the candlelight. The smell of them turned his stomach. "How many more?" he whispered.

Leahla shook her head. "I don't know," she whispered.

The shutters in the front window were broken where the first one came through. He heard more of the demons outside; their shrieks and vile cries echoing in the night. They pounded on the ceiling and shook the house so violently it seemed the walls would collapse. Dust and dirt fell from above. The floor seemed to crawl under their feet. Maureen moaned in fear. The shrieking grew louder and louder. Adan could no longer think; fear had a grip on his mind—soon they would come and surely they would die. Leahla looked back. "This is what they do when they know they have you. They're trying to scare us!" He swallowed and held Maureen as tight as he could. He smelled her hair and thought about their first kiss. Her beautiful green eyes were soaked in tears; it tore his heart in half.

The remaining windows blew open. The demons hurled themselves in one at a time. Leahla charged. She spun and kicked. Her sword lopped off a head and she stabbed another. More came. They busted through the walls. A crash at the front door warned Adan there were demons on the other side. They were trapped. Four demons jumped at Leahla. Adan hugged Maureen, waiting for the moment they would die. From every direction demons rushed in for the kill. The door to the house flew open, followed by an undulating war cry. Myron rushed in, his crossbow aimed their way. He fired; the arrow ripped into a demon's head. Its body dropped to the floor with a thud. "Maureen!" Myron yelled as he reloaded.

Aren rushed in behind Myron with both swords drawn cutting down their foes. As Adan and Maureen moved closer for protection, Leahla struggled in the corner. Myron moved in front of Maureen and Adan while Aren leapt behind them and saved their backs. Leahla killed another and she joined them by the door.

Adan counted six more demons. They charged Aren at the same time, hissing and screaming with their claws pointed at his neck. "Aren!" Aden yelled. But his brother was a marvel as heads were severed, arms and claws hacked off. Leahla moved in next to Aren. Together, they slaughtered the last of the demons.

Aren, breathing hard, sheathed his swords. "Are you two all right?" he asked Adan and Maureen. Blood streamed down the side if his face. Adan nodded and took Maureen by her hand.

"We have to get out of here," Myron said. "They're everywhere."

Leahla cleaned her sword on a torn curtain. "We should find your father, Adan."

Adan tried to regain his courage. "Leahla, what's happening here? What are these creatures?"

"I've never seen one before, but I know they're demons."

"Where are they from?" Aren asked.

"From a place far away and for now we should leave it at that." Leahla walked to the door and stared out into the forest. "There are more of them up the hill. We should find Darren and Hythe."

"Maureen," Myron said, motioning her to take his hand. "Come with me."

Maureen hesitated slightly before reaching for her brother. Adan knew what she was thinking. He wasn't going to leave her. "I'm right behind you."

The cold air of the night wrapped itself around them. An orange light tainted the shadowed sky above the hill. The distant screams of a battle sent shivers down Adan's spine. He worried about the danger of leaving the safety of their home, the risk of going out into the night, but surely there was no other option. His family and friends were in danger. Perhaps they were dying. The feeling that bothered him the entire day pulsated, warning him the worst was yet to come.

Aren ran to retrieve the horses. Myron's horse wandered the creek, and he and Maureen chased it to the house. Leahla mounted Firestreak and waited for them to gather. Adan waited as Aren brought up his horse. He took the reins from his brother. "I suppose you never found Dex?"

Aren shook his head, a sad look on his face. "I heard the demons on my way to town. As soon as I saw them I came home as fast as I could. I ran into Myron along the way."

"I'm extremely grateful you did."

Aren tried to smile. "I noticed. Perhaps now you might be interested in a sword lesson or two?"

Maureen sat behind her brother on his horse and hugged him tightly. Adan watched her, guilt engulfing him. When the demons came close to killing them he acted as if death was inevitable, lacking the courage to fight when it mattered most. He knew he had to change or live his life without her.

"Where do you think father is?" Adan asked Aren.

"Myron told me he was at their place when he left to get Maureen, so that's where we should go."

They rode in single file, with Adan trailing. Far above them a glow filtered into the sky. The red moon had mysteriously appeared, hanging low in the sky, intensifying the glow throughout the forest. The distant screams pulsated. The stench of blood was in the wind. As much as Adan wanted it to stop, he never received his wish. One after the other, he knew a scream of pain was another life stolen. A demon leapt onto the trail in front of them, but Myron shot it dead instantly. Adan felt his horse tense up underneath him. He searched for more but it seemed to be the only one.

"We must go faster," Leahla said. "Aren, lead the way quickly."

They forced their horses into a canter, followed the trail easily through the red moonlight. When they came onto the road, demons swarmed the bridge. Their motions revealed they had someone trapped on the middle. Each of the demons forced its way toward the center of the bridge, red eyes flickering with hate.

Aren unsheathed one of his swords and said, "Someone is trapped in the middle; I'll help him."

"I'm going with you," Leahla replied.

So far none of the demons had noticed them. "Don't do it. We have to find father," Adan hissed.

Aren shot him a disgusted look, "That could be one of our friends. You wait here. If the demons charge…run. Myron, I need you to cover us."

Myron nodded. His crossbow was still loaded from their last encounter. He locked the crossbow into position and stretched out his arm. Aren and Leahla rode hard into the pack of demons. The moon disappeared behind a cloud and darkness slipped over. Myron was forced to hold his shot. Adan knew that once the demons noticed them waiting, there would be nothing he could do but run, leaving the fate of his brother in his own hands.

The clouds uncovered the moon and showed Aren battling as the demons swarmed around him. Adan felt a flash of fear when his brother was pulled off his horse and Leahla fell. He let out a loud yell as Myron fired his crossbow again and again. The demons heard Adan's voice. The outline of their bodies was no more than a shadow, but the venom dripping from their claws glowed in the night. Several of the demons hissed at the sight of Adan and Myron and screamed the alarm. The demons on the bridge broke apart their attack. In the pit of the battle, a bloodied Aren mounted his horse. The horse was difficult to hold steady, but Aren controlled it as he climbed into the saddle. And it was then that Adan saw who the demons had surrounded—his father. Aren helped Darren onto the horse behind him. Hythe and Leahla returned on Firestreak as the massive horse helped them in their battle by using his body to shield them.

Adan felt overwhelmed with guilt when he understood that his cowardly request to move on could have killed his father. He felt so ashamed that he would never be the man his brother was.

"Move out!" Aren yelled. Demons leapt out of his way as his horse roared through them.

Adan cracked the reins as his brother caught up to him. They sped away, leaving the screeching demons behind them. Aren turned off the road into the bush. Adan followed, making certain Maureen was still safely behind Myron. It wasn't far up the hill when Aren stopped. They crowded in together under a large elk tree, hiding from the light of the red moon.

"Are you all right?" Adan asked his father and Hythe.

His father nodded. Blood drizzled down his face, soaking his beard and torn clothes. Hythe was in better shape, though his arms were bleeding from the demons' claws.

"Where are these creatures coming from?" Aren asked.

"We don't have time to explain," Darren said. "Myron, take your sister home. Stay off the trails. Most of the demons are down at the inn. You should be safe." He looked at Adan. "You should go with him."

The red glow hovering over the distant tree line soared higher and higher. Adan didn't want to run this time. He wanted to stand up and gain some courage. Maybe it was time to fight. "What are you doing?" he asked his father.

"Before we were ambushed on the bridge, we ran into Hunter Gorge. He's countering the attack with the survivors. We must help them."

Adan wasn't a warrior like his brother, but he couldn't let them rush off to battle while he retreated to safety. He wouldn't make that mistake twice. He smiled at Maureen. Leaving her was the last thing he wanted, but the time had come for him to take his place beside his family. He tried to show her his feelings by the shape of his smile, and then he turned to his father and said, "I'm going with you."

At first it appeared that his father would discourage the idea, but then he nodded in approval. The warmth in his eyes was something Adan never witnessed; he had no idea if it was concern for his safety…or gratitude for his help.

"Be careful, all of you," Myron said. He flicked the reins to his horse. He and Maureen sped off through the trees. Adan watched and promised himself he would see her again.

Aren passed Adan one of his swords. "Take this."

Adan took the sword, surprised at its weight; it was heavier than it looked. It was steel cold to the touch and reeked of demon.

"Let's move," Darren said.

Leahla took the lead. Hythe sat behind her gripping his axe. They rode down the hill and onto the road that led to the Inn. Their presence startled a number of townsfolk gathered on the corner. The bulk of the demon force huddled in front of the burning inn.

Hunter waited amongst the gathering. When he noticed their arrival, he guided them to the rear of the crowd. "I'm grateful to find you've all survived."

"If we hit them hard and fast, they'll retreat back to the river. They'll be trapped there, and we'll be able to finish them off," Darren said.

Hunter nodded in agreement. "Yes, that's our plan."

Adan watched the crowd. It was too dark to see who they were. He could recognize a few people by the outline of their body, but he knew it was unimportant. They were all willing to fight together, and that was all that mattered.

His father reached for his shoulder and squeezed. "I want you to know that I'm very proud of both of you." Adan was surprised. Praise from their father was rare. "I've kept too many secrets from you. I promise after tonight that I'll let them go." He pointed at Hythe. "This is my younger brother. He's your uncle." Adan was so shocked, he almost dropped his sword. "I'm sorry I held back the truth when he first arrived. First thing in the morning, we're all having a long talk."

Adan guided his horse closer to Hythe. "I had no idea. Father never mentioned you."

Hythe nodded and smiled. Adan could see the resemblance now that he knew. If his father cropped his mangled hair and trimmed his beard, they'd have an uncanny resemblance. He was amazed he'd not seen it sooner.

"Why . . .?" Aren began before trailing off. He took a deep breath, "First thing in the morning then."

"Before we go into battle," Darren continued, "I wanted you both to know who he is and that I'm sorry. Tomorrow we'll clean the slate and begin a new life."

"Darren, I have to tell you something," Hythe said. "It's about Leahla." He rode Firestreak closer to Darren. Adan noticed that Hythe appeared unsettled.

"Not now, Brother, we'll deal with everything in the morning."

"It cannot wait; I must tell you now."

The crowd readied to advance. "Then tell me quickly if you must," Darren replied.

Adan couldn't understand why Hythe felt it so important that he would have to tell his brother before they rode into battle.

Hythe bit his lip. The sudden tension in the air pulled tightly with the wind.

"Well," Darren said with a touch of impatience, "tell me what you must."

"I found Leahla on the western shore. She doesn't remember who she is or anything about her past."

Darren shook his head. "And…?"

Hythe lowered his gaze. "That's it."

"That couldn't have waited 'til morning? I'm sorry, Leahla, but for now I must finish these bloody demons and find my son."

Hythe nodded, but his face was shrouded with guilt. Leahla eyed him suspiciously.

Hunter Gorge shouted the charge and the crowd surged ahead. Adan wasn't ready to fight, he needed more time. They charged the road together yelling in unison as they pushed ahead. The inn appeared before them where the enemy gathered their forces.

The demons backed one another. Their eerie and shrill cries were nothing compared to the intimidation of their claws. Their rotting teeth glistened red in the moonlight.

Adan held onto the reins as tightly as he could. He stayed at the back near his brother, as the front of the crowd dove into the demons. Within moments Adan was amidst the brutality. Demons and allies shrieked and died before his eyes; every moment another dead body hit the ground. Aren fought next to him, Darren and Hythe a short distance away. Demons were everywhere. Adan thought he was going to die, and those who loved him were going to die trying to save him. A slime-covered hand reached out in front of him and snagged his face. He panicked and couldn't breathe. It pulled him back. He tried to stab behind him, but his sword was ripped away from his fingers. He hit the hard ground on his back. His horse bolted. A demon jumped him, gashed his chest and dove for his neck. Adan screamed in pain, wincing at the claws rushing for him. A gush of wind split the air and the demon fell atop him, dead. He pushed it off and saw Myron reloading his crossbow. At that moment Adan felt grateful that Myron rarely did as he was told. Myron sighted another demon and fired. It took the shot in the chest and slumped to the ground. Myron never missed. Adan found his sword lying on the ground and picked it up. The fight thinned out. Hunter Gorge fought two demons at once. His uncle chased three demons farther into the bush. Victory was within reach. They were going to win.

Next to him a demon swung a wooden cudgel. The blow caught Adan in the back of the head and knocked him to the ground. He dropped his sword as he fell, but rolled just as the cudgel came down again. Adan whipped his legs around knocking the demon down. He jumped to his feet and found himself eye-to-eye with another one. He turned and ran. A demon appeared in front of him and swiped at him with its claws.

Adan ducked and turned, jumping off the road and into the forest, his mind racing—what to do? Terrible shrieks told him demons were pursuing. His chest burned with every breath. The demons stayed with him no matter what way he turned. Branches whipped back at his foes, almost slowing them down. He tripped and smacked his face into the dirt. When he looked up he found a house set back in the dark. The demons howled behind him. He jumped to his feet and sprinted for the house. He pounded on the door and checked behind him. Red eyes flickered in the darkness. Nobody answered. Adan kicked the door open and dove inside. He turned and slammed it shut. The broken lock clanged on the floor just as a demon leapt through the window, shutters smashing to pieces from the impact. Another demon slammed through the door colliding with Adan. He hit a table and slid across it to the other side. Both demons lunged for him. He picked up the side of the table and threw it at the demons, knocking them back by the blow. A third demon entered through the open door. Adan turned and ran into another room, slamming the door shut. It had no lock. He screamed for help and glanced around. There was a desk in the corner of the room with a burning oil lantern; the small flame sputtering in the draft. A few shelves were stocked with old books. It had a window that had been boarded tight—He was trapped.

The demons rammed the door from the other side. Adan pushed back as hard as he could. They slammed into it again and again. His strength was giving out. He let go of the door and sprinted for the burning lantern. He was there in four strides and grabbed the handle. He turned back to the door and lifted the lantern into the air.

The demons stumbled into the room. Adan threw the lantern as hard as he could. The lantern struck the first demon and exploded into flames. It twisted and roared, grabbing its comrade for help. The second demon pushed it to the floor and charged Adan at the desk. The third was fast on its heels. Adan reached behind the bookshelf and pulled it over. The first demon was crushed to the floor. Books dropped to the floor fuelling the fire. The third demon leapt out of the way with a guttural sound, almost as if it were laughing and sliced Adan across the side of his face with its claws. Adan cried out in pain and fell back. He covered the wound with his hand as blood spilled from the side of his face. Adan retreated to the far wall. The room was ablaze. The demon charged again.

A vision of his mother flashed in his mind and dared him to gather his courage. Then a second vision of Dex shattered the first. Adan pictured his little brother alone, frightened and shivering at the base of a tree. He reached for the wooden leg at the corner of the burning desk and ripped it off. Swinging the wooden leg like a sword, he screamed with newfound strength and thrust it hard into the demon. It toppled head over heels. Adan catapulted off his enemy and sprinted for the door. Flames surrounded him making it difficult to breathe or see; his face throbbed in pain. He tripped over one of the burning corpses.

Another demon charged into the burning room impervious to the danger. Adan tackled it throwing them both out of the flaming room. He reached for its neck as they rolled across the floor. The demon backhanded Adan across the open wound rolling him onto his back. He nearly passed out from the excruciating pain. The creature lunged into the air and landed on Adan; it raked his face again.

"*Adan . . .*"

A powerful and vibrating blue light burst from Adan's chest ripping through the demon. Shards of bone and slime exploded through the smoke pouring in from the other room. Adan coughed blood. He pulled himself to his knees and crawled back to the forest. He fought to block out the pain as he searched for an explanation for the voice that called out his name and the blue light that burst from his chest. His legs quivered as he climbed to his feet. The house crackled and fell apart. Waves of heat whipped outward. He pressed his cloak to his face, disturbed by what had occurred. He didn't know what to think as he staggered off.

The screams and sounds of battle turned his attention back to the inn. Fire had spread throughout the forest as if it chased the villagers who ran away in frantic desperation. He thought of his father and brother and broke into a run, dodging the fire through the forest, charging up the hill, swearing now that he would no longer be a hindrance, that now was the time to gather courage to face these wretched creatures. At the crest of the hill the inn struggled to hold, but the fire ate away at the foundation. A cloud of sparks spat at him. Adan threw his arms over his head and circled around back to the road. A demon fell dead at his feet. When Adan looked, he grimaced—two people he had known from town lay next to it.

"Adan! Run!" Aren shouted. His brother held both of his swords in the air. Blood streamed down his face from a wound on his forehead, but it was the simple fear in his gaze that caused Adan concern. A demon attacked Aren. He countered and warned Adan. "Look out behind you!"

Adan's mind moved in slow motion. He wanted to flee, he knew he had to, but curiosity forced him to peer behind him, wanting to discover this danger that Aren warned him of. As he turned on his feet, a sword was careening down on his neck. The man driving the blade wore glossy black armour, so black he could have been part of the night itself; his eyes as red as the moon. The sword was unexpectedly deflected away and Adan dropped to the ground. There stood his father, sword in hand, blood and sweat soaking him from the head down.

The man in black turned to face Darren. "The time has come for all to die."

"Who are you?!" Darren shouted.

Adan stood as another figure emerged from the dim forest. A red cloak covered his identity, though its intensive red eyes gleamed brighter than the cloak itself. As it moved, it seemed to float above the ground.

"Who are you?!" Darren shouted again.

Adan paced, too horrified to do anything else. He'd lost sight of Aren. He thought of Myron and Hythe. The battle had thinned out; only the dead covered the road, but now his father needed help. Darren charged at the man in black. Adan searched for a weapon and found a blade covered in slime. By the time he'd picked it up and turned to his father, it was too late: The man in black armour stripped Darren of his sword and kicked him to the ground. Adan screamed and rushed forward as the dark stranger lifted his own sword high into the air. The man in black looked straight into his eyes and leered. The sword pierced his father straight through the heart. Blood gushed from his chest, body twitched in death. Adan staggered backward; worried the worst was yet to come.

Aren rushed in, war cry echoing, swords drawn. He kicked the man in black and sliced him across a shoulder. The stranger turned and retaliated. Aren parried the blow, forcing his second sword into the stranger's neck. The man snatched the blade from the air in time to save himself. He held the blade within his gloves, squeezing the sharp edge of the sword within his palm. He ripped the sword from Aren's grip and tossed it behind him. Aren charged again. The stranger countered and slashed Aren across the legs.

Aren skidded into the ground head first and rolled.

Adan saw it all, but he was too stunned and too frightened to even move.

The man in black lifted Aren into the air and tossed him toward the figure in red. The figure in red glided above the ground. Long, skeletal fingers snatched Aren up by his hair. Aren twisted in the air cursing his attacker. Blood ran down his legs and splashed on the ground below. The demon flipped him into the raging fire as if he was a pebble. Then it raised a hand. Lightning arced form its fingertips and bolts blasted the inn. The lightning exploded on impact destroying the building, fragments raining into the air. The blast slammed Adan to the ground, but he was back on his feet instantly. "No-o-o-o," he screamed. Blinded by rage he charged the demon in red. Something hit him from behind—his world went black.

Dex ran as fast and as hard as he could. He followed a game trail along the bank of the Delilah River. Fear drove him away from home; all he thought to do was escape. He ran and ran from the foul beast. It first appeared after his encounter with Aren and Myron. Dex had sprinted for his usual hideout at the caves of Whistle Rock hoping to lose his hunter. But terrible creatures cut him off, forced him deep into the forest. Now he just wanted to escape. His energy was failing. He glanced to the sky. The flying beast with its huge wingspan still circled above him. It waited for the moment to try again. Dex heard it screech and flap its wings as it dove for another try at him. He tripped and fell, but it saved him from the beast. Its claws nicked his back below his neck. The creature soared back into the sky, wings red in the moonlight. It cawed as an eagle, loud and piercing, sending shivers across his skin.

Dex climbed to his feet and heard a low, growling chuckle behind him. He turned as another creature emerged from the darkness, its scaly and dark skin reflecting in the moonlight. It stepped forward, drool dripping from its mouth. Long claws extended from its wrists. Above the forest canopy the flying menace screeched again. Dex's lips quivered. He wanted to tell his father he was sorry. He wanted to tell Aren that he understood. The creature lunged and swiped at him. Dex ran. From above the tree line came his hunter, claws extended for the catch. The Delilah Falls waited.

The great river rolled over the cliff and into a deep canyon where it continued on to the ocean. Mist rolled through the air far below hiding the mysteries within. Dex ran as hard as he could, no longer worried about the consequences of what the leap would do to him; he threw himself over the cliff's edge to freedom. The flying beast dropped swiftly into a power dive and snatched Dex by his shirt. It opened its wings and flew out of the mist. Dex dangled high in the sky at the end of the creature's claws. It turned north to the mountains. Dex wept quietly and mumbled farewell.

Chapter 7

Maureen straightened her back and rubbed her tense muscles. It had been too long since Adan's last sign of life. There were moments she thought he would awaken when he moaned and winced in pain. He was found by Hunter sprawled face down in the dirt. At first Hunter thought he was dead like those around him. Maureen sighed and reached down to a bucket of water next to the bed and removed a cloth. She wrung it out and draped it over the three long and deep cuts that seeped blood down the side of his face, even though her mother did her best to sew them together. She kissed his chin. As long as he lived, she didn't care what he looked like. As much as she prayed for him to recover, she dreaded it equally. He would have to be told what happened, and the news would surely break his heart.

Myron knocked on the bedroom door. It creaked as he pushed it all the way open. Then he stepped over to the bed and placed his hand on Adan's forehead. "The fever broke. He's recovering."

Maureen tried to reassure herself with a smile. "Have you found Dex?"

He shook his head. "We searched everywhere. We might have to accept that he's gone."

"You must find him. He's all Adan has left."

Myron pulled her to her feet and held her tight. "I'm so sorry."

"Why did this have to happen?"

He held her for a bit before letting go. "I have to get back. Father needs my help. Let me know if his condition changes."

She nodded. "I'm going to stay here. I'll be along shortly." She wiped the tears from her eyes. When Myron left, she rinsed the cloth in the bucket of water. He flinched when she placed it back on his face, but she held her excitement; she saw him do that before. She bit her lip in frustration. In one night all of their lives had been changed forever. Why? Demons were a myth, mere stories told to children, stories of the era when Faral first arrived with his beautiful bride Yannina and his brother Faris to rid the world of demons. He'd named the world after Yannina upon his victory. Demons were not part of common history; they were nothing more than a myth. Why then did the demons come? Now history was changed forever. Maureen collapsed onto the bed beside Adan and burst into tears. Nothing would ever be the same again.

Adan awoke. He screamed, body shaking from head to toe. He calmed down as he realized he was safe. Adan touched the deep cuts. "It really aches." His voice sounded dry.

Maureen reached for his hand. "Everything's going to be fine."

"Has Dex come home? Where are Aren and my father?"

She tried to remain calm. "We can't find Dex. Myron and others have looked everywhere. I'm so sorry."

"What about my Father?"

"We found him in front of the inn. It was a bad wound, Adan, nobody could've survived it."

"What about Aren? Where is he?"

Maureen shook her head, wondering why life was so brutal. "Your brother was found inside the inn . . . ."

Adan's eyes widened. "Is he alive?"

"The inn burned to the ground. Aren didn't have a chance."

"No!" Adan turned away. She reached for him. He pushed her away.

"I'm sorry," Maureen whispered to him.

"Please…leave me alone for awhile. I just want to be alone."

Maureen nodded. "I'll return at sunset." Adan had already fallen asleep.

It was dark when Adan awoke to a cold breeze coming through his window. The shutters banged against the outside wall. He pulled his quilt over his head and breathed the warm air underneath. The quilt reminded him of his mother. She made it for him before Dex was born. It was such a distant memory. The side of his face stung. Horrifying visions flashed though his mind and with them came a wave of nausea. He flung the quilt away and inhaled fresh air. His muscles were sore. He touched the side of his face feeling the wet and ragged cuts; three wounds to forever remind him of the night that changed his life. He stared at his brother's empty bed in the corner knowing Aren would never sleep in it again, knowing nearly everyone close to him was dead.

He lifted his head and swung his legs over the side of the bed. His head throbbed in rhythm to the pain in his cheek. He was careful when he stood, grasping the edge of the bed for balance before he tried to stand on his own. He felt flimsy and weak, worried that a large gust of wind would carry him away. He struggled to the door, taking each step as if he were learning to walk all over again. He gradually made his way down the stairs. The fire at the back of the house was burning high. The walls and ceiling had been patched where the demons broke through. The back door was open slightly, which he found awkward. They rarely used that entrance. There was mud on the floor. He turned as Maureen walked in the front door. "You're awake," she said.

The sight of her made him uneasy. He didn't know how he was supposed to feel anymore. He staggered to a chair and grimaced at the broken table. Maureen rushed to help him. He pointed to the mud. "Who did that?"

"I don't know. I never noticed it." She walked to the back door and closed it tight.

Lightheaded, he struggled to keep his wits around him. "How long have I slept?"

"Three days. You need to drink some water right away."

"No, I don't want water." Usually Aren would be sitting across from him. His father would sit on his right arguing with Dex about something that didn't matter. He stared at the broken table wondering if there was any point in living. "Where are they?" He asked.

She sat next to him. "My father buried them both next to your mother."

His eyes welled with tears. "This isn't fair . . . ."

Maureen hugged him. "I know. I'm so sorry."

"I didn't get to say goodbye."

"I promise everything will be fine."

Adan had a fleeting urge to push her away. Instead he held onto her as hard as he could, grateful that she was there.

The next morning Adan gathered enough courage to leave the house, surprised at how good the sun felt on his face. The sound of the creek running down the side of the hill brought back pleasant memories. He was pleased there was still comfort in that. He wanted to thank Michael for everything he had done and visit the graves, so he followed the creek down the hill as it rolled away from the stables. It twisted and turned down some rock and flowed into a small pool. There were two new graves on the other side of the pool. He was shocked at the impact the graves had on him. He wanted to believe they would find their place in the heavens, just as his mother had. The thought lifted his spirits. His family could be together again. One day, they would all be together. He smiled and said, "I love you." He turned around when he heard somebody coming down the hill behind him. The sunlight hid the visitor's face, although the long beard and pointed hat explained it couldn't be anyone but Hunter Gorge.

"I see you're alive, Boy. Looks like you'll be just fine. A scar builds character, remember that." Hunter smiled. He carried a sword that Adan didn't recognize.

"Thank you for taking me home."

"You're welcome; I came to give you this." Hunter handed him the sword.

"What is this?"

"It belonged to your father. I wanted to make sure you got it, so I held onto it until you got back on your feet. It's a Dragon Sword…very rare."

Adan removed the sword partly from its scabbard and admired the blade. He remembered watching his father descend the stairs with it. He'd blocked the weapon with his body so Adan couldn't get a good look at it. He glanced at Hunter Gorge. "Why is it called a Dragon sword?"

"I don't know anything more than that. Your father was a man with a questionable past. All that mattered to me was his good heart."

"Thank you very much, Hunter…for everything."

"Not a problem." Hunter turned and stopped. "Adan, I'm real sorry about what happened; both your father and Aren were good people and didn't deserve what they got. If there is anything I can ever do for you, don't hesitate to ask."

Adan stared at the old man, astonished. Not in his entire life had Hunter called him by his proper name. Hunter winked and headed up the trail. Adan pulled the sword completely out of the scabbard. The handle looked like a short tusk covered in scales. It thinned out near the base of the blade where the color was almost completely white. The color changed once more at the tip, shifting into polished silver. He put the sword away and wondered why his father had ended up with such an oddly named and rare item.

He wandered up the trail, past his home and toward the road. As he made his way, he studied the houses damaged in the demon attack. He remembered the terrifying incident where he was trapped inside someone's home, and how it burned to the ground just after his escape. He stopped on the trail when he remembered the strange blast that came from him to save his life. Even though he was grateful, he didn't want to think about it. In the last two days he had thought too much about what happened that night. He moved on and came to the trail that led from the road to the farms. Maureen approached him, holding her dress above the ground. Her beauty nearly made him forget everything that happened. She wore the same blue dress that she wore at Ruhln Fest. The necklace around her neck sparkled in the sunlight as she moved through the trees. He loved her long, dark hair. Her appearance brought relief to his heart. Perhaps there was a reason to live after all. When she saw him, she smiled, "Adan! I was coming to find you."

"Is your father home?"

"No. He and the others are working on the inn today. I think Myron is with him."

"I wanted to thank him," Adan replied.

"You can thank him later." She took his arm. "You look much better today."

He moved his arm away. "Maureen, I wanted to talk to you as well."

"About what?" she asked with a touch of alarm.

"I need to thank you."

She smiled. "We'll get through this together." She touched the cuts on his face. Her touch was feathery soft. "Don't worry about those. Your face will heal." Adan's appearance was the last thing on his mind, though he found comfort knowing Maureen wasn't horrified of them. She took his hand and motioned him along. Around the bend of the road the bridge appeared. A stream of memories flooded through his mind.

"Where are Hythe and Leahla? Did they survive the attack?"

"We don't know. They disappeared, Adan. My father told me they vanished after the attack."

Adan didn't know what to think about that. Hythe was his uncle. Why would he run away? Wouldn't he want to see his brother buried? "Are you certain?"

She nodded. "There are many speculating they had something to do with the attack. Their arrival was a strange coincidence. After they disappeared it only made those accusations worse."

"I doubt that. He was my father's brother."

She took his arm. "Let's not worry about it." It did bother him, though. Why would the two leave so suddenly?

"Hunter sent two riders for help, one to Corrona and one to Wyndhaven. Once they hear what's happened they'll send help. Hopefully we'll find out what's going on. I'd like to know if I can feel safe again."

Adan listened to her but his mind was elsewhere. Something wasn't right. It didn't make sense. Why would Hythe run away? "Please take me home," he said.

She smiled and rested her head on his shoulder as they walked.

Chapter 8

A week passed and Adan regained his strength. The sun had already set by the time he returned home after spending the day helping Hunter and the others lift walls at the inn. His aching body longed for a solid night of rest. He climbed into bed and thought of Maureen. He hadn't seen much of her over the past few days. Ruhln was busy and hard at work. Everybody pitched in. Tomorrow he would try to spend time with her. He saw more of Myron since they worked together at the inn. It was difficult at times. He respected Myron and his help, though he wished his friend would stop talking about what happened. He didn't want to relive that terrible night over and over again. His thoughts quickly faded as sleep took him. The nightmare began.

A prisoner breathed with a wheeze and rattle as he hung from the wall, hands chained and feet dangling. Blood dripped from his head and bloodied what was left of his clothes. His body was scarred and raked with welts. Adan stared at him as he stepped closer; with each step his fear heightened. "Help me, Adan," a raspy voice whispered. Adan studied the prisoner's face and noticed tears of blood.

Adan screamed and bolted from his sheets, touching his eyes as if he expected to find blood of his own. He dressed quickly, stuffed a blanket and sweater into a shoulder bag and charged out of his room and down the stairs. In the kitchen were two loaves of bread that Maureen dropped off earlier in the day. He put them into the bag. His father's sword caught Adan's attention. He strapped the sword and scabbard to his back and covered it with his green cloak. There was one more thing to attend to before he left Ruhln. He went upstairs to his father's room and set his pack on the bed. His heart raced as he pulled on the closet handle. At long last he would see what his father hid all of those years—it was empty. Adan stared into it as he surmised that the closet was used to keep the Dragon Sword locked away, but why was that such a big secret? It didn't make sense.

"Adan," Maureen called.

He closed the closet door before answering her. "I'm here."

"I'm sorry to startle you. I haven't seen much of you lately." She noticed the pack. He was certain her eyes had found the sword hiding under his cloak. "Going somewhere?"

Adan reached for his gear. "You shouldn't be wandering around in the middle of the night; there could be demons about."

"We have people on lookout now. What's going on?"

"Dex is alive."

She smiled and raced to embrace him. "He's here?"

"No, I must find him." He stepped around her and went down the stairs.

"What?" she asked, following him down into the living area.

"It's hard to explain. I know he's alive and I have to find him."

"You're going to leave right now in the middle of the night?"

Adan walked past her and opened the door. "I'll be back, I promise." He turned to leave.

She rushed over and grabbed him by the arm. "Adan, please, please don't go."

"I must. He needs me."

She cried, "I can't believe you're leaving after everything that's happened, and after we've become so close."

He gently brushed away the tears trickling down her face. "He's my little brother, all the family I have left. I'll find him and bring him home. I promise."

"You're going alone?"

Adan nodded as he closed the door. He locked the latch. "Will you watch this place for me?"

"Yes," she replied, but she shook her head no.

Adan swung his pack over his shoulder and pulled her close. He gave her a lingering kiss. "I promise to return."

Her beautiful green eyes glistened with tears, "Swear it. Swear you'll come back to me. I almost lost you once already."

Adan smiled. He loved her. He knew he did, though he couldn't tell her now. "I swear it."

As he climbed the path away from home, he heard her soft sobs. It broke his heart, but Dex needed him more. He walked slowly along the outskirts of town. He said his farewells when he passed the inn. Now he must find the courage to leave. He sighed. It *had* only been a nightmare. Yet it was so real. The person in it was certainly Dex, but what bothered Adan the most was how much his little brother had aged. It had him worried.

He heard footsteps. Maureen, he thought, she just wasn't going to let him go without another try.

"Adan," Myron called.

"What are you doing?"

"Maureen . . . told me you left," Myron gasped out, trying to catch his breath.

"Why did she do that?"

"She cares about you, of course! I'm coming with you."

"No, your family needs you at home."

"My father would be quite displeased if he knew I let you head out on your own. I'm your friend. I'm coming."

Adan was in no mood to argue. Fighting with Myron was like kicking a dead horse. "Fine, just remember it's your doing…not mine."

Myron had his wind back, and he walked at his side. "Where are we going?"

"I don't know."

Myron sighed. "Maureen said that you're looking for Dex."

"He *is* alive. I won't stop searching until I bring him home. I pledge my life to it."

Myron swung his crossbow over his shoulders and tied a pack to his waist. A quiver of arrows swung back and forth across his back. "How do you know he's alive?"

Adan stopped and looked at him. He knew Myron would probably think of him as a fool, but he told him anyway. Myron could think what he wished. "It was a nightmare. Dex called out to me."

Myron nodded with understanding. "Well then, let's go find him."

Surprised by his friend's reaction, Adan smiled, suddenly grateful to have him there. "Thank you. I hope I'm not getting you into trouble."

Myron glanced to the stars. "Whatever. I'm ready for anything." Together they stepped out of Ruhln and into the unknown.

Chapter 9

He approached the City of Corrona in darkness, hiding himself from the soft light of the moon. The wind carried the smell of the distant ocean as it brushed back the weeping branches of the scattered trees. He hid himself within the shadows of the brush, waiting for his moment to advance. As he stood unmoving, his eyes studied his charge. A solid wall of white marble circled the city's perimeter, leaning outward to keep their enemies from gaining entrance. It was as wide as it was tall, with ragged steel cable hanging off the upper ledge. With every turn of the wall, a long wooden pole jetted outward at an angle, flying a long banner sewn with the symbol of Corrona. Knights of the First Guard paced back and forth as they patrolled the wall. Their predictable movement showed him they believed nothing could harm them. That was the weakest of flaws, one he would certainly use to his advantage. He licked his dry lips, wishing they were wet with blood. It was too long since he tasted his enemy, too long since he killed. Years of preparation forced him to retire, but now that the time was finally here, his patience was no longer necessary.

Both moons were radiantly bright, and though the silver moon was larger in appearance, the red moon overpowered it almost completely. He was grateful for their presence; it eased his task. He scanned side-to-side, mapped the wall as it faded into darkness. To enter through the front gate involved a long walk and an incredible amount of time. There was little time to spare. Surely Ruhln was crushed; the second phase of the assault must begin immediately. If Corrona discovered the attack on Ruhln, their chance of surprise would falter. He watched as the knights continued to pace, shouting idiotic comments between them. Their impressive attire glistened in the moonlight, but not even that could save them from their approaching deaths. The myir in their armor was hidden by the dark of the night, but soon blood would strike the crimson haze, and the intruder felt certain the combination would glimmer.

His fingers tingled with excitement as he sprinted from beyond his shadow, charging for the bottom of the wall. Claws sprang from underneath his fingernails. He shoved them into the white marble and pulled himself upward. He climbed faster than he remembered he could. Memories of war and death came back to him, the days when he had been allowed to run and conquer. His hands clasped the top of the wall and the intruder sprang into the air. One of the knights saw him and charged, calling out at him to stop. Before his feet landed on the top of the wall, he released the weapon from within his cloak so fast it snapped like a whip as it slashed the knight through the neck. Blood rained through the air, sprayed backward like a gushing stream.

The intruder turned west. The remaining two knights rushed him with brandished weapons, their faces fearful. He was disgusted with their stupidity. He had expected at least one of them to run for help. He grasped a cold steel handle. He released his anger, spun, hissed and plunged his weapon deep into the body of a knight. In his next attack, he rotated the weapon above his head, screeching into the night. The second knight lost his head. The knights were sprawled at his feet in a pool of their own blood.

The intruder secured his weapon and turned to look upon the City of Corrona. His cloak flapped in the night wind. The red moonlight warmed his soul, reminding him of the feel of death. In the background the Palace of Ionia rose from the depths of the city, towering high into the low-hanging clouds. As he stood on the edge of the great wall, he could barely see the other side. Smoke billowed from chimneys in long, twisting tunnels. Candlelight sparkled from thousands of windows, though they appeared dim to the street lanterns that swung high through the air. The Palace of Ionia watched over the city like its protector, reaching around with arms of solid wall. The very sight of it all was pure strength, and within that strength was false encouragement. The intruder was well aware that somewhere deep within that dominance of power were two worms eating away at the foundation of trust. The people of Corrona were fools, all of them led by their dimwitted king and his pathetic queen. Soon that would change, and then the Dryden would extract their revenge.

He leapt off of the wall. The buildings around him were rundown and weathered. He traversed an older section of the city. People stood in small groups in the darkness of the alleyways, as if they were waiting for something to happen. The Palace of Ionia stood tall over the buildings, helped show the course. As he continued toward the palace, the buildings around him brightened with life. More and more people appeared. He made certain his cloak hid his face as he entered a busy street. Lanterns hung high on poles, burning bright with light and clouded with insects. Men and women on horses rode in different directions as beggars pleaded for gold. He struggled through a crowd that gathered on the side of the street. A man on stilts entertained a small crowd as he juggled several flaming torches. At the same time his sidekicks tried to knock him off his wooden legs. The crowd laughed when the man wobbled precariously. The intruder slipped a knife from his robe as he pushed through the crowd. He slit a neck. The body slumped to the ground and before anyone noticed what happened, he was away from the crowd and on his way. When the screaming started, he smiled and tucked his knife away.

There had been a time, long ago, when the city had been magnificent. Now it was old, rustic and overpopulated. The city could not expand with the growing population while the outside walls held them trapped. The people of Corrona had no other choice other than to build upward. The newer, poorly built buildings were several stories high; some of them seemed to tilt away from the wind. The people of Corrona did what they could, but the city was not structured for so many people. That was evident with the smell of garbage and urine that came with every shift of the wind.

The street that circled in front of the palace had long silver poles with lanterns staggered along the sides. It illuminated the palace's front gate. A balcony above it had been built since his last visit. Banners hung off the balcony, edges shimmered in the lantern light. He couldn't see what was on the banner, but he assumed it was Corrona's symbol. Corrona's shield was the oddest out of all those in Yannina: it was a newborn babe in fetal position. From the infant's back two silver wings curled high above his head. There had been a time in his life when the intruder was interested in such things. Now he didn't care. Corrona's past belonged to the people living inside its walls. When they were all dead, the emblem would have no more value than the dirt he walked on. The palace rose into the sky above the balcony. Several different towers expanded in height over the main structure. Windows and balconies littered the outside walls. An enormous flag of Corrona was draped down the eastern side. A middle-aged man stepped up on his left, peering at him through the corner of his eyes. The intruder reached out and grabbed the man by his throat. He snapped his neck and watched the man fall dead. He moved on to the palace. He eyed the moons casually, the red one in particular, and thanked his god for the powers he held.

The entry to the palace stood before him and three knights approached with their weapons drawn. He was amused. They were about to die without glory. Chances were that the knights stationed farther down the street would not hear their pleas for help.

"Who approaches?" one of the knights shouted.

"My name is Aramaz. I have come to rid Corrona of its king," he said softly, barely above a whisper. The knight moved forward to hear him better. Aramaz snatched him by the neck and released his power; the knight fell. The second knight brandished his sword while the other bolted for the door. Aramaz released his weapon and struck the knight running for the door. It killed him instantly. With a flick of his wrist he disarmed the other and released his power at the same time. The last knight hit the ground dead. Killing exhilarated him. He shivered as he looked at the blood and gore. He dipped his finger into the blood and tasted it with his blood-thirsty lips. The sun rose; its light brushed the tips of the tallest towers. Today would be a day sewn into history books. It would be his pleasure to hand them the needle of blood. The Gods would be proud of him this day...for the time was at hand to kill the king.

Chapter 10

King Oland hung his lantern above his desk before he settled into his chair. His tired bones creaked as he sat. He cursed his old age and remembered a time when he was young and alive, a time when little could scare him. As his body aged so did his worries. He recalled a battle of long ago, a battle that stole the life of one of his dearest friends. Oland would never forget that tragic night. It was the beginning of the end. Faral warned them that their defeat in that battle would haunt them forever. And it had. The rumblings of a war north of the mountains rustled in the wind, battles rumored to have begun from a fictitious motive. Merchants were found dead on the road to Wyndhaven. There were whispers that the black dragon known as Zar had awoken. Oland tightened his robe from the chill of his thoughts. He could almost smell the blood in the air even though he was certain it was only his mind relaying horrific prophecies, but evil forces were growing in strength, of this he was certain. He removed a pen and blank parchment from his desk and placed them in front of him. His thoughts were snuffed away as if a blanket fell over his mind. When there were times he could think of nothing, he chose to think of his son, Riordan. It was unfair that he would pass the young man his legacy at such a troubled time, but there was no other choice. Riordan needed to be king now. The people of Corrona truly loved the prince, and for that Riordan would make a grand king. His thoughts slowly came back to him. He dipped his quill in ink. As he touched the tip to his parchment, his thoughts came to life:

My dearest friend,
    I'm certain you're well aware of what has been happening around our land and surrounding areas. Battles are raging in the far north for no apparent cause; the hatred between Akhran and Terrace sends a dark cloud toward us carrying unspeakable power. We can no longer ignore such threats. We were once warned of the Demons of Destiny. I must admit that I was skeptical about such a thing, but I fear now that our ignorance may become our downfall. We swore never to raise our weapons to fight another battle, but

my dear friend; I feel that if we stay to our oath any longer, Yannina will perish.

I understand your feelings regarding Faral. The curse bestowed upon you is heartfelt, and I swear to you that I, even after so many years, still feel our failure on my shoulders. This time we do not fight for Faral. This time we will fight for Yannina.

Please, forward my letter to the others. We must seek answers immediately.

Your friend always,
Oland

A tear slipped down his cheek; he brushed it away with an aging hand. He folded the letter and closed it with hot wax and the royal seal. Behind him, Assandra stirred in her sleep. At fifty-three years she was still beautiful in his eyes. She was an excellent wife, a good mother and a grand queen. She was the world to him and he would treasure her forever.

He moved quickly and quietly, taking with him a lantern to help him cross the dim room. The door squeaked as he pushed it open. He whispered to the knight standing guard. "Deliver this to Ruhln. The man you seek is Darren Caynne."

The First Guard bowed, "Yes, Your Majesty."

As Oland returned to the bedroom, Assandra awakened. She rubbed the sleep from her eyes. "Oland, return to bed. You promised me that today we would rest well into the morning."

Oland smiled. It was their mornings together that Assandra loved and looked forward to the most. Too often they would be separated from the burdens of their kingship, and on most days they would not see one another until it was time to return to bed. Only in the mornings did they have their precious time together. He turned the handle on the lantern and the light faded to nothing.

A smiling Assandra waited for him in bed. She held the covers back so he could join her.

"You seem disturbed, is there something wrong?" she asked him.

"No, there's nothing wrong." Assandra snuggled into him, wrapping her arms around him as tight as she could. He thought about the letter on its way to Ruhln. He wondered what she would think if she knew what he was doing.

"I love you," Assandra said.

Oland kissed her forehead. "And I love you."

The First Guard hurried down the spiral stairwell. His nerves floated on air, though he was proud he had been chosen for such a task. The knight knew it was of an important nature to be handed a message at the break of dawn from the king himself and with strict orders to carry it to Ruhln. He tucked the message behind his breastplate. The palace was dimly lit as the sun topped the horizon; its rays peeked through the palace windows as he passed. He stopped at the bottom of the stairs to reclaim his breath. Dancing shadows cast from candlelight flickered across the stained-glass windows. He wiped sweat from his brow and hurried on. The light dimmed to almost black. He heard footsteps on the stone floor at the far end of the hall. "Who goes there?" he shouted. The sound drew nearer. The First Guard searched through the darkness, but all he could see were flickers of flame. He released his sword. "Who are you!" he thundered. Whoever it was sprang alive and rushed at him. The First Guard held his sword up in defense. He hollered for help wondering why he was the only knight in the main hall of the Palace of Ionia. He heard the crack of a whip, though it sounded of metal. The last thing he was aware of was his own blood spraying through the air.

Chapter 11

Prince Riordan Adynall silently admired the sunrise. His gaze shifted to the City of Corrona as it came alive with the new day. Every morning he watched his people begin their day, as a way to understand them. Eventually Corrona would be his to rule. As his father advised, it was necessary to understand them completely. The people of Corrona and their king required a relationship of trust. Riordan admired the bond his father had with the citizens of Corrona. They trusted him and never questioned his decisions. They knew under his rule their best interests were secure. The morning sun washed over his face. He closed his eyes and wished for courage to accept his future. Riordan felt but a shadow compared to his father. There was tremendous responsibility in becoming king; Riordan was unsure if he was fit to the task. He knew that one day his father would pass him those duties. When that time came, he knew he would embrace it and hold the responsibility close to his heart because his father expected that from him. He took in a deep breath of air and left the tower.

Riordan returned to his room and pulled a black vest with silver buttons over his shirt. Several small knives were neatly concealed inside the vest. They were tools of a defense method taught to him by his father. Riordan was quick with knives; his throwing accuracy was unmatched by any in the kingdom. He brushed his thick hair with his fingers hoping the silver strands wouldn't fall out. The silver strands marked royalty. To him they were foolish, but his father refused to end the customs of their family that dated back for generations.

A knock came at the door. Riordan smiled and turned to the door, hoping it was breakfast. "You may enter."

The door groaned as it opened. Jannen stepped inside holding a large silver platter of assorted fruit. "Prince Riordan, how are you this morning?"

Riordan grinned. "Are you preparing to become one of the servants? I thought training with the First Guard would have been enough."

Jannen almost laughed. "I intercepted Erissa on my way to see you this morning. I offered to bring you your breakfast."

Riordan took the platter to the balcony. "I'll never be able to eat all of this. You'd think after so many years of leftover food the cooks would figure it out. Are you hungry?"

"I ate with the other knights this morning."

Riordan pulled up a chair for his friend. "Then you may offer some conversation. After I eat, I plan to visit the city."

Jannen sat across from him. "What's the occasion?"

"My father decided I haven't spent enough time outside the palace walls. I find that oddly humorous since as you and I spent our entire childhood trying to escape."

"Why did he decide that?"

As Riordan cut a slice of prism he wondered if it would be his last. The warm season was ending and there would be a shortage of his favorite fruit. "My father told me a good king must first earn the friendship and trust of those he rules."

"Everyone I've spoken with anticipates the day you will become king. They believe your capabilities will equal your father's," Jannen assured him.

Riordan eyed him with a serious look. "You speak kindly this morning."

Jannen shifted in his chair. "I speak the truth, Your Highness."

Riordan threw a grape at him, hitting him in the jaw. "Don't be so formal. You know that's unnecessary when it's only the two of us."

Jannen smiled. Riordan wondered if his friend would throw the grape back at him. When they were young it was common for them to skirmish. Jannen retrieved the grape and set it back on the platter. "Times are different now, Riordan. You will become King of Corrona. I must respect you for that. One day I will be the commander of the First Guard; I want to earn that role because I deserve it... not because you and I are friends."

It was a special trait that Riordan admired in his friend. Jannen took everything with great seriousness. He would succeed in his goals. Riordan wished there were more days when he didn't have to be formal all the time. "I will never give you something you haven't earned. Remember that." Riordan cleared his throat and sipped his morning drink. "How are things in the First Guard?"

Jannen frowned. "There is tenseness among them I don't

understand." He paused and rubbed his cheek. "Sheldhan is grumpy."

Riordan picked at a melon. "Sheldhan is always grumpy. He's overworked. There are many duties to a man in his position, more so than just running the First Guard. The man is responsible for the safety of the entire city."

"No," Jannen disagreed, "There's something more to it. Lately I haven't been able to speak with him. It almost seems to me that he completely disregards me, as if I'm no longer needed. I never thought much of it until Oban mentioned the same thing to me. He feels the same way, almost as if Sheldhan favors the other knights."

Riordan frowned, "I'll speak with him. I know he's overworked. He may be unaware that his mood affects some of you."

"It's nothing, Riordan. Forget I mentioned it."

"Nonsense, I want to know these things, *especially* when I become king." Riordan stood. "Come, I've had enough to eat. I'm ready to visit the city." When Riordan entered the hall, Jannen fell back, stayed several steps behind. Riordan hated the procedure; it always made him feel as if he were being shadowed. He never understood why people weren't permitted to walk at his side. Riordan trekked through the open halls. The arched ceilings were supported with white columns. Banners hung off the walls. The higher towers of the palace were visible though skylights; the colored glass filtered the brightness of the sun. Riordan watched the dust as it sparkled in the air, floated as if hung by invisible thread as it twisted and turned with the gentle breeze. The metallic silver floor was polished as smooth as a mirror. The empty hall echoed with the sound of their footsteps. The entire level was reserved for him alone. It was still early. Soon the palace staff would flood the place. Riordan went down the steps to another level. Something black brushed by the outside of one of the windows. "Jannen, what was that?" he asked.

"Where, what did you see?"

A wave of nausea rattled Riordan's stomach. "I saw something on the balcony."

Jannen was unconcerned. "I saw nothing." His armor creaked as he stepped up to the window. He leaned over the ledge to look up and down. "There's nothing to see."

Riordan stared at the window "I know what I saw."

"I'll mention it to the others. We'll keep our eyes open."

Riordan shook it off. "Forget it." He thought that Jannen didn't believe him, because the evidence had vanished. The incident chilled him, though. Riordan always believed in his instincts. Something warned him to be cautious.

Jannen eyed him with a concerned look. "What's the matter, Riordan?"

"It's nothing." He turned and headed down the stairs. Voices rose as they descended down the twisted stairwell. A group of knights were clustered together at the palace entrance. Sheldhan stood in the center of the group pointing and shouting orders to each of the knights. The tone of Sheldhan's voice hinted at trouble. Riordan rushed into the group of knights, pushing them out of his way so that he could get to Sheldhan. A dead knight was lying on the floor. "What happened to him?" Riordan demanded.

Sheldhan responded. "There must be an intruder in the palace, Sire."

Riordan covered his mouth. The sight of the dead knight was something new to him. The man's blood was splattered across the stone floor, reaching high up the wall. The killer had walked through this blood, and his footprints clearly led into the palace. "How did this happen?"

Sheldhan shook his head. "I don't know." He pointed to Jannen. "Protect Prince Riordan. Take one of these knights with you."

Jannen nodded. "I'll take Oban." The young, clean shaven knight moved next to Jannen.

Sheldhan told the others, "Search in pairs. As you come across more of our men, recruit them to our aide. I'll return to the barracks and send out the alert. It is imperative that every able man search throughout the palace."

"My parents," Riordan whispered to himself. He almost buckled, realizing that the intruder could be an assassin after his father. "My parents!" he screamed. Without thinking he turned and ran. Sheldhan yelled at him to stop, but Riordan ignored the call and ran as fast as he could. The sound of heavy footsteps chased him up the stairs. As Riordan entered his floor he recalled the black cloak he thought he had seen, and he derided himself for not taking it seriously. The thought that he could have apprehended the intruder at that point made his sickness crawl. His failure to investigate could very well be the death of his own parents. Riordan sprinted up the next set of stairs, aware that he was leaving the knights behind him. It was impossible for them to keep up the pace with their armor.

Riordan pushed servants out of his way at the top of the stairs. They yelled as he hit them from behind; the clang of platters on the floor drowned the noise of the knights chasing him. His parents' chamber was at the end of the long hall. Riordan sprinted at full speed, reaching into his vest to grip one of his many knives. He threw his shoulder into the middle of the bedroom door. It crashed open. Knife in hand, he searched the dimly lit room for his parents.

"Riordan?" Oland asked. The king and queen were eating breakfast in bed. The curtains were drawn across the window to hide the glare of sunlight.

Riordan almost fell with exhaustion, overwhelmed with relief. "There's an intruder in the palace."

Oland straightened. "What?"

"Someone killed a knight inside the palace."

The knights of the First Guard staggered in behind him gasping for breath. Sheldhan glared at Riordan and shook his head in disproval. "That was foolish, Prince Riordan. I can't protect you when you run from me."

Riordan snapped back. "When I found you ordering the knights to search the palace, there was not one word of protecting the king. That should have been the first priority."

Oland climbed out of bed and covered himself with a gold-colored robe that hung from the bedpost. "There's no time to argue. Find this intruder immediately." He waved at Sheldhan, "Go now."

Sheldhan stepped toward the king and handed him a crumpled note. The king appeared shocked. "What is this?"

"A letter I found on the knight."

Riordan wondered why his father reacted so to the letter. Oland took the parchment. "Thank you, Sheldhan." Sheldhan nodded and stepped through the broken door.

Riordan sat at the bench next to his father's desk and realized he still held the knife, his knuckles white from his firm grip. He forced himself to relax. "When I saw what happened downstairs, I immediately feared the worse." He tucked the knife inside his vest.

Assandra stood next to Oland. "We're both fine. Sheldhan will find this person and then we will discover his motive." She glanced at Oland. "What is this letter in your hands?"

Oland whispered into her ear. Assandra smiled and kissed him on his cheek. She moved to the window and drew open the curtains. The sunlight flowed into the room, warming the air instantly. The king sat at his desk. "Son, I'm grateful you thought of your mother and me, but you must remember your own safety foremost. You are the future of Corrona." Oland took a deep breath. For a moment Riordan thought his father might cry. "You are their king now."

Stunned, Riordan said, "What?"

"My days on the throne are limited, Riordan. You have your entire life in front of you. Your life is much more valuable than mine."

"Don't speak as if you don't exist, Father. I will accept the duties of king when my time comes and not a moment sooner."

Oland scratched at his grey beard. He appeared deep in thought, perhaps even troubled. "Riordan, your time is upon you. I no longer wish to be king."

Riordan pounced to his feet. "I'm not ready to be king!" he nearly shouted.

Oland motioned him to sit. "Calm yourself, Son, keep your voice down. This incident this morning has awakened my senses." He rolled the parchment between his fingers. "I must tell you something before it's too late." He checked on Assandra, as if confirming that she would not be able to hear him. "I have a past that you and your mother know nothing of." Riordan never saw this look of worry on his father's face before. Oland always carried a commanding presence with authority and confidence, but now there was sadness in his eyes. "Years ago, I was asked to join the Warriors of Ches who fought for Faral."

Riordan held his breath. The Warriors of Ches were recruited by Faral to defend Yannina from his wicked brother, Faris. The stories told to him as a child had been a fairy tale, based on legends and lore of Yannina's complicated history. At first he thought perhaps his father had told him a cruel joke, but the seriousness in his voice could not be mistaken. "How is that possible?" he finally asked.

"When you were a child, I was invited to join a group of men on a mission to find an ancient artifact. We were told this artifact must be retrieved, otherwise something known as Granaz would awaken. From its ashes the Demons of Destiny would rise. This would lead to the destruction of our world."

Riordan felt a chill at the mention of demons. "What are the Demons of Destiny?"

"Perhaps the real question is, 'What is Granaz?' I was never able to clarify that." He looked directly at Riordan. "We failed in our search to find the artifact."

"Why are you telling me this now? Why after all of these years and only after an intruder threatens our livelihood?"

"I'm worried that our failure twenty-three years ago is the cause of these mysterious events that are happening throughout Yannina. I'm worried that Faral's warning is upon us; that we are in danger of witnessing these terrible events." Oland stared into empty space. "We were all ignorant back then. Some of us didn't believe in the gods…or our cause. We were betrayed and one of my close friends was killed. We were angry. A few of us decided that we would no longer fight for Faral, but some stayed the course. I was one who decided our mission was useless. I returned to Corrona. Over the years this past has haunted me. I'm no longer aware of the condition of my friends, save for two. I won't tell you their identities yet, but one lives in Ruhln. I must contact him immediately. I fear the worse for Yannina. That is why your time is upon you. I need you to be king, so that I may take my leave. I'm telling you this now because I'm certain this intruder is part of the mystery I need to solve. If he has come to kill me, there is less time than I hope."

Riordan's mind felt thick and complicated. "Does Mother know about this?"

Oland frowned and shook his head. "When I left on my journey all those years ago, she thought I was on a peace mission with Akhran and Terrace. I dread telling her now, but I know I must."

Riordan always believed strongly in Faral, as most of the people in Yannina. Faral was the savior of their world, and now he protected them as a guardian shadow. Riordan was awestruck that the mighty god had recruited his father to be a Warrior of Ches. "I'm not ready to be king, and you are older than you pretend. I'm not sure I should allow you to run away to finish some battle started years ago."

Oland was quick to explain. "I won't fight, Riordan. I need to gather information. I will use the First Guard to fight this round."

"Why not remain as king, then?"

"No one must know of what is happening. Understand this, Riordan, we fight for Faral, but there are those in this world who fight for Faris. I'm living proof that a Warrior of Ches existed. Surely, too, there are Dryden among us."

"What are Dryden?"

"As Faral commands the Warriors of Ches, Faris leads the Dryden, evil mercenaries recruited to do his bidding." His father stared deep into his eyes. "Do not trust anyone."

"What is our next strategy?"

"For you…nothing, you'll wait until I've announced my retirement. Then we will prepare you to take over as king. Before I do that, I must have a long chat with your mother and come up with an excuse for the High Council because they will disapprove of my decision. I will declare your succession at the High Council this morning."

"Father, I'm not ready to become king."

"You won't be alone. I'll be here to help you…remember that. I'm doing this to allow me to investigate without the entire city watching me. I will still be with you."

Riordan had many questions to ask, but he noticed his mother growing restless at the window. "I'll return to my room for now. I would appreciate it if we can speak about this after I have had time to soak it all in."

Oland rose to his feet, "Of course."

Riordan smiled at his mother. "I'm assuming both of you will remain guarded in your room?"

Oland nodded. "I have faith that Sheldhan will find the intruder quickly."

Riordan agreed and stepped through the broken door. Knights on guard saluted him. Jannen and Oban stood to the side waiting to escort him through the palace. Jannen said, "Sheldhan told us that should you leave your parents, we were to escort you back to your room and nowhere else."

Riordan replayed the conversation with is father over and over again. One sentence stood out the strongest. *Do not trust anyone.* Riordan sighed and nodded to Jannen. "Off we go, then."

Chapter 12

As Riordan reached the entrance to his room a knight approached and said, "Prince Riordan, I have good news. Sheldhan captured the intruder."

"Where is the intruder now?"

"Sheldhan sent him to the holding room. There is some unrest with the First Guard due to the lives lost this morning. Sheldhan is trying to calm everyone down."

"Of course," Riordan replied. Both Jannen and Oban appeared as relieved as he felt. He nodded at his protectors. "I wish to speak with this intruder. I want to know why he came here; he has much to explain." Riordan turned back to the knight. "Thank you for the information. Please continue and let my parents know." The knight saluted Riordan and pressed on.

Jannen said, "Riordan, I don't like the idea of you confronting the intruder until we know more about him. I'm not comfortable taking you to a threat that we know nothing of, whether we have him in custody or not."

"Nonsense, I'm certain Sheldhan has him well contained."

"Will you at least speak with Sheldhan before you do this?"

Riordan still felt the chill of his father's daunting words. *Do not trust anyone.* "Fine," he said and headed for the stairs.

During the day, commoners were allowed to venture into the main floor of the palace. Obviously the threat had been contained; otherwise, Sheldhan would not have allowed so many people wander the palace. Still, Riordan felt uneasy. The only way into the higher levels of the palace was through strict security, but obviously they were not as safe as they once thought. The First Guard handled the large crowds, ushering them through to the main hall.

Riordan addressed the closest knight. "Have you seen Sheldhan?"

"He's in the garden, Your Highness."

Only the royal family and the First Guard were allowed to enter the Garden of Ches. It was the only place where Riordan and his parents could venture with peace of mind. The First Guard had stations around the perimeter built above the trees on the outside wall. Because of the level of security within the garden, Riordan knew he could leave Jannen and Oban at the entrance. "Please wait here," he told them. He followed the stone path deep into the garden. Trees were spaced evenly apart, with flowers planted on either side of the path. Fountains pushed water high into the air in an arc reaching over to the other side of the path. The main monument was in the center of the garden. The statue of Faral Ches was larger than life and depicted him in action. Faral held his staff above his head. The details of his face suggested he was casting a spell. His stance portrayed him holding steady from heavy wind with his cloak sweeping out behind him. Faral Ches was the god who cleansed their world of demons. Since his death, he'd protected Yannina in spirit helping them in troubled times. During the Dragon Wars, Faral chose the fabled warrior known as Anemenitty to lead the people against those who sought to destroy Yannina. Anemenitty was the first Warrior of Ches recorded in history. It was said that Anemenitty saved their world…just as Faral had. Riordan found it hard to believe that his father fought for Faral. He believed those stories were myths. Now it was as if his entire world was flipped over. As he studied the statue, he marveled that the god was truly real.

"Riordan," Sheldhan said from behind him.

Sheldhan saluted as Riordan greeted him. "I was told that you apprehended the intruder."

"Yes, we arrested him near the kitchens." Sheldhan shifted his feet.

Riordan wondered why he was nervous. "What is his name? Did he tell you his motive for killing those guards?"

"He hasn't told us his name yet, but he admitted to the crime. I've moved him to the dungeon. Perhaps a few days in our most unpleasant cell will change his perception on things."

"Good. I would speak with him."

"That is risky, Your Highness. We don't know anything about him."

"If he's contained, then I should be fine."

Sheldhan rubbed his chin with his thumb, spoke hesitantly. "Very well…but I'm not certain your father would approve. Would you mind if I cleared it with him first?"

Something was amiss. "Sheldhan, are you ill?"

"No, no not at all, I'm just concerned."

"I am the Prince of Corrona. Have you forgotten?"

Sheldhan turned away, unable to look Riordan in the eye. "Of course not, I beg your pardon."

"You will do as I ask. Where is the prisoner now?"

"He's on his way to the dungeon."

"Good, when he is secured with chains, I will speak with him."

"Brutus has first watch; I'll let him know you'll be coming."

"Thank you."

When Sheldhan saluted and left, Riordan massaged his temples with his fingers, soothing a headache that started in his father's chamber. He couldn't recall a headache coming so swift and hard. There was no time to worry over it. He wanted to look into the eyes of the man who killed his men. His actions were punishable by death. Riordan wanted to be certain that this murderer was fully aware of it. Riordan retrieved Jannen and Oban and together they went to confront the intruder.

The lower levels of the palace were occupied by the First Guard and servants to the palace. The large kitchen used to facilitate so many men always produced meals for the knights rotating shifts. Attendants tripped over the maids in the narrow hallways; all of them were overworked with little time to complete their tasks. Knights of the First Guard were either on duty or off, and those who had time of their own made their fun by chasing women. It wasn't often Riordan ventured below the main floor of the palace. He was fascinated by the architecture. The Palace of Ionia was well crafted. The engineers designed the lighting for the lower levels by placing long cylinders inside the walls that deflected sunlight into the hallways. It looked as if the sun shined straight through the stone in areas that should be completely dark. Many of the chamber walls were built with colored glass cut with symbols pertaining to the City of Corrona. Outlines of the kitchen staff moved about on the other side, the tone of their voices suggesting they enjoyed their work. Riordan followed Jannen through a hallway to a stairwell that led down to the next level. A handful of knights climbed up toward them.

Sheldhan led the pack. When he saw Riordan, he held up his hand for his knights to halt. Riordan glanced at the five knights behind him; the only one he identified was Brutus.

"Prince Riordan, the intruder was moved to a holding room on the ninth level by request of the High Council. They asked to speak with him."

Riordan felt annoyed. "Why would the High Council ask to speak with him?"

"It is because four knights were murdered. I do not disregard orders from the High Council."

Riordan's headache raced across the back of his eyes. "I'll go there, too."

Sheldhan nodded. "You may visit with the prisoner in the holding room. I'll be there shortly." Sheldhan stepped around him and his knights followed.

Riordan watched him disappear and murmured, "Something's strange." He wondered if Sheldhan lied. The notion seemed ridiculous; he was the family's loyal friend.

"There's unrest amongst the First Guard," Oban said. "I've felt it for some time, almost as if the force is divided into two factions."

Riordan frowned at him. "What?" The young knight clearly misunderstood his worries.

Jannen shook his head. "He means nothing. What do you want to do?"

Riordan wished more than anything that his headache would go away. "I suppose we better make our way to the holding cell."

Brutus reappeared around the corner, his brow furrowed with worry. "Prince Riordan, may I speak with you?"

"Of course, what's wrong?"

Brutus glanced over his shoulder. The big man was obviously tense. "Something is wrong with Sheldhan."

"I beg your pardon?"

Brutus shuffled his feet nervously. "I'm certain something is amiss regarding this intruder. Those I've spoken with have not seen this person. I haven't seen him either. I was asked to guard a cell that held him, and then I'm told he was moved to the ninth level holding cell."

The pain pulsating in his head was almost enough to render him unconscious. The thought of Sheldhan betraying him hardened his anger. "Thank you, Brutus, your concern and honesty is much appreciated. I want you to return to that cell and remain there."

A glimmer of understanding replaced the concern in his eyes. "Yes, My Prince."

Riordan turned to Jannen. "Find out what Sheldhan is up to."

"Where are you going?" Jannen asked him.

"I must speak with my father immediately."

Oban asked, "What do you wish of me?"

Riordan didn't want him trailing Jannen. It was best his friend handled Sheldhan on his own, yet the last thing he wanted was to endanger the young knight. "I want you to find out more about the unrest in the First Guard and report to me what you find."

The young knight smiled an eager grin. "Yes, My Prince."

"Go," Riordan ordered.

Jannen stared at Riordan "Be careful."

"I will," Riordan said. "You mind Sheldhan. Keep a close eye on him. If he does anything suspicious, report to me or my father. Understood?"

Jannen nodded. "I'll speak with you shortly." He turned and hurried down the hallway with an eager Oban on his trail.

Riordan struggled to step forward from the fierce headache and gasped for breath.

"Riordan..."

The voice that came from inside his head erased the pain. He stood tall and cleared his thoughts. An image of an old man appeared before him, pointing down the hallway.

"Run to your father ... Go...."

Riordan ran down the hallway terrified for his father.

Jannen felt the sweat drip off his chin as he held his breath. With sword in hand he quietly lifted the shield on his helmet. He peered around the corner with his back tight to the wall. When he heard voices, he pulled back hoping he wasn't seen.

"Welcome to Corrona, Demon Aramaz."

Jannen's heartbeat quickened. The voice belonged to Sheldhan. He cautiously peeked around the corner. He watched as Sheldhan drew the curtains from a large window to reveal someone draped in weeping black cloth. The stranger said, "Your dedication will be honored, Sheldhan. Your debt is fulfilled. You'll be rewarded as promised."

"The king is waiting for you," Sheldhan replied.

"Excellent."

Jannen sheathed his sword and ran. He dove through an open door and down a set of stairs. It was imperative he find either Prince Riordan or the king immediately. He darted to the left at the bottom of the stairs. Something dark came at him from the side, caught him by surprise. It struck him in the back of the head. Pain raced down his spine. When his armor struck the floor, he vaguely hoped the noise would echo so someone would hear it. The pain in the back of his head throbbed to the front. His efforts to scream failed; he couldn't even lift his tongue. It terrified him that he couldn't move. Lying on his stomach, all he could see were two boots as someone stepped over him. Whoever it was dropped a mace on the floor in front of him, and then disappeared around the corner. Jannen fought to stay conscious as he stared into the twisting stairwell. His eyes fell heavy; all he could think of was Riordan…and the events about to unfold.

Chapter 13

The king and queen waited before a closed door. The symbol of Corrona was etched into the metal, and white glass was inserted into the frame for the child's wings. When the doors opened it appeared as if the child unfolded its wings. Oland took Assandra's arm with his and stepped up a short set of stairs and into the throne room. The members of the High Council rose from their seats and stood quietly as they entered. Statues of the First Guard were situated between each member. They held shields tight to their chests and swords pointed at the ceiling. The statues, dressed in the armor worn by the First Guard themselves, glimmered bright from the sunlight cast down through the wooden rafters. Banners of red and black spiraled across the walls, twisting around one another as they hung over the High Council. The throne consisted of double seats with arched white wings as back support. The wings spanned out across the width of the throne room, the outer ends painted gold. Behind the throne were a few short steps that led to the highest balcony in the entire palace. It overlooked the city on one side and the Garden of Ches on the other.

Oland waited as Assandra took her seat. He turned to acknowledge the High Council, smiled at them and waited for them to take their seats. When Oland sat, their session would begin. Whispering broke out among them. Oland lifted his hand for silence and squeezed Assandra's thigh with the other for reassurance. He said, "Before we begin our daily tasks, I wish to make a declaration. I've ruled Corrona for almost thirty years. A few of you were part of the High Council when I succeeded my father."

A few members grew restless, especially Sarek who was the newest member with just under twenty years on the Council. Lately Sarek was more vocal on many matters. Oland found his attitude annoying.

Oland continued. "I've served as king long enough. Prince Riordan's time is upon him. I choose to step down as king and spend more time with my wife." Assandra squeezed his hand.
"My decision is final and immediate." Mumbled comments floated around the throne room. "Riordan will assume his birthright—He *will* serve you well."

Nathen rose from his seat. "Why? Are you ill?" The murmuring continued.

"My health is fine. There will be no further discussion on this matter. My word is final." Assandra squeezed his hand again. She still displayed a regal beauty with her long silver hair.

Sarek rose from his chair, "Permission to speak freely, My King?" Oland nodded. "With all due respect, it is unwise that you step down at this moment. This could be construed as a bad omen along with wars in the north, and unheard creatures stalking our lands. If you are capable of leading us…you should."

"We've been through this before, Sarek. I've told you more than once that we will not participate in the war between Akhran and Terrace. Whatever their reasons for war is their own problem. These monsters you speak of are nothing more than rumors."

Sarek gasped. "People are turning up dead! It has even reached the palace! It was only this early morning that we lost four precious knights, perhaps even more."

"That is of a different nature. I'm certain Sheldhan has already resolved the situation. Let it rest."

Sarek approached him. "Riordan is not ready to be king."

Oland nodded. "Neither was I when I first assumed the role. I've taught Prince Riordan well. You all know this. I'll still be here to assist him."

An obviously irritated Sarek shook his head and turned back to the High Council. "How many of you support this decision?"

A member said, "It's his decision, Sarek. We all love Riordan. There's nothing to fear since King Oland is willing to help him through these troubled times."

Sarek turned back to the king, emotion erased from his face. "I strongly disapprove."

Oland wondered why Sarek disapproved. His persistence appeared as if he had a separate agenda. "The High Council's duty is to help and support the king. Corrona is too large for one man to rule; that's why all of you are here. Remember, it is not only my duty, but yours to help Riordan." For the first time, Oland felt the impact of his decision. His era was over. "I choose to spend the winter of my life in peace with my wife." He looked intently at all of them. "Don't I deserve this? Riordan is quite capable; surely you understand that." Sarek fumed in silence. Oland looked at Assandra. She smiled and moved her lips; he read them perfectly. "I love you, too," he whispered.

In the meantime, the intruder crept slowly up the stairs that led to the throne room. His thirst for blood overcame his patience. The time to kill was at hand. He transformed into the shadow of death and oozed into the throne room, a silhouette forming across the light of the air. He stretched out with blood lust; excitement pulsated through his being.

Oland watched quietly as the members of the High Council spoke among each other and shifted uncomfortably on their chairs. There was something about change that frightened people—Oland was never able to understand it. Suddenly, the lighting went dim. He glanced up startled that the sun glared so brightly. Assandra gasped and tugged at his arm. Oland turned back to the High Council. Some were slumped in their chairs, others sprawled on the floor unconscious. A man dressed in a black robe appeared at the entrance to the throne room. He stood still as if he waited for something.

Panic consumed Oland. He moved in front of Assandra to protect her. The man in black glided across the throne room at incredible speed.

Oland gasped and Assandra screamed his name.

Chapter 14

Riordan staggered into the throne room and fell to one knee as he entered, sucking in air as deeply as he could, almost dizzy from the long run up the spiral stairway.

"Is there something wrong, Riordan?" Nathen asked him. He was a long time friend of his father. He sat in a seat in the High Council, tapping his fingers on the armrest.

Riordan ignored him and climbed to his feet. When he found his parents looking at him, he nearly collapsed in relief. Sarek waited next to them, watching Riordan with an icy glare. The High Council glowered from shadowed eyes, hands gripped their chairs. His father mumbled something. As his lips moved, the color in his face drained away. Riordan wondered why everyone stared at him as if he were some kind of stranger. Sheldhan entered the room from the far stairwell and ordered Riordan to stand aside.

When Oland attempted to speak blood spurted from his lips. Riordan yelled, "Father!" He rushed to Oland and placed his hand on his chest. He screamed again when he felt the knife burrowed deep into his ribcage. He lunged for Sarek with his own knife in hand. He had him by the throat when his father fell from the throne.

His mother lurched out of her chair, a look of utter shock on her face. "Riordan! What have you done?"

Riordan applied pressure to the underside of Sarek's chin. "Tell me what happened or you die." He ignored his mother's words.

"He's dead!" Sheldhan announced, closing Oland's eyes.

In unison the members of the High Council rose from their seats screaming for answers.

"What happened here?" Riordan shouted again.

"He's trying to kill Sarek!" someone shouted.

Sheldhan reached for Riordan and forced him to release his hold on Sarek. His feet were kicked out from under him. Sheldhan slammed him to the floor. His mother stepped over and scowled down at him. "It was by the hand of his son," she said with utter disgust. She shook her head. Her eyes flashed with hate. "Take him down to the lowest part of the palace and throw him in the darkest cell."

Sheldhan bound Riordan's hands. "What are the charges, My Queen?"

"For the murder of our king," she hissed.

Riordan was shattered. Surely she didn't think he would kill his own father. He managed a glimpse at Sarek and saw a hint of a smile. Riordan twisted away from Sheldhan and dove for Sarek. "It was you! You killed my father!" Sheldhan forced him to his knees.

"The prince is mad!" Sarek yelled.

"Take him away!" his mother shouted again.

Riordan couldn't understaind. Everyone stared with conviction in their eyes. "Mother, what happened here? What's wrong with you?" When Sheldhan forced him away, he shouted, "I'll find out and I'll kill the man responsible myself. I swear on my life!"

Sheldhan punched him hard in the side. "Keep your mouth shut!"

His mother's look of hatred stung the love in his heart. The pool of blood from the hole in his father's chest spread across the floor. "I swear it."

The taste of his own blood woke him. Groaning in pain, Jannen managed to crawl to his knees. He forced his helmet off of his head. Relief from the pain was instant. He frowned at the large dent on the back of it and threw it over his shoulder. He spat blood from his bitten lip. The pain in his head was still daunting, but there was a bit of relief when he stood. He staggered into the hallway.

"Stand aside, Jannen."

When Jannen looked up, he stared in shock. Sheldhan propelled Riordan down the stairs.

"Jannen, help me," Riordan pleaded.

"What are you doing, Sheldhan?" Jannen demanded.

"Riordan is under arrest for the murder of the king."

Jannen's first instinct was to confront Sheldhan, to accuse him of his crimes, but instead he held his calm. The Commander of the First Guard conspired with the intruder. The situation was dangerous. He knew Riordan didn't kill his father. Sheldhan was the real traitor, but Jannen's instinctively knew to be cautious, because the man had an intruder at his helm and the entire First Guard to help him.

The prince shook his head. "I didn't kill my father."

Sheldhan hit Riordan in the stomach, and the prince gagged at the pain.

In the brief moment that Sheldhan turned his head, Jannen gave Riordan a barely perceptible nod. It told Riordan not to worry; that he would be coming for him. Jannen remembered the First Guard's rule: never raise arms against a fellow comrade. He forced himself to inhale deeply, and as he exhaled he wrapped his fingers around the handle of his sword. He recalled a time when he and Riordan were children, and they'd promised they would be friends forever, no matter what happened in life. *Never raise arms against a fellow comrade*, he thought again. Jannen sighed. If he had to break that rule, then he would break it.

Chapter 15

Jannen kept Sheldhan in sight while he hid from view. Several other knights joined Sheldhan as Riordan fought back. They bound, gagged and dragged him along the floor, torturing him for fighting against them. It was difficult for Jannen to stay calm. The knights were loyal to Sheldhan because he was their commander; the possibility that he might have to challenge the entire First Guard frightened him. As they descended from the tower and into the main stairway, shouts of treachery and anger were directed at the prince. Word that the king was dead spread throughout the palace. Jannen was sickened that people believed the rumors were true. He pictured Riordan trapped inside one of the awful cells that he knew existed in the dungeon. He couldn't stomach the thought of his friend jailed for a crime he didn't commit.

Knights stationed at the entrances stared at him curiously; the confusion on his face was evident. Other knights forced the commoners back out into the city, motioning them to keep calm. Jannen was unsure what he should do, but he knew he required help.

"Are you Jannen?" a voice asked from behind.

An older man dressed in the white robes of the High Council smiled as Jannen turned to face him. Jannen recognized him, but was unsure of his name. "Who are you?"

"I'm Nathen."

"What do you want?"

"Please, I seek your help."

Jannen couldn't tell if the man was frightened or nervous. "Why do you come to me?"

Nathen opened his palms as if it was an offering of peace. "I come to you because Riordan is your friend. I saw that in your eyes."

"What is it that you want?" Jannen asked again, remembering now who Nathen was. He was known to be Oland's greatest ally within the High Council.

"I've known Prince Riordan all of his life. The love he has for his parents goes well beyond the normal family ties. This accusation has me confused and hurt."

This piqued Jannen's interest. "What do you know?"

"After Oland announced that Prince Riordan would be king, I began to feel faint. My mind is cloudy as I try to recall what happened, but I'm certain I fell out of my chair. In the next instant, I was back in my chair watching Riordan rush to his father. It appeared that he stabbed Oland, but my senses tell me otherwise, that perhaps I witnessed an illusion. As I recall the event, I believe the prince killed his father, but my heart tells me otherwise. The queen must have gone mad. It's impossible to believe she would sentence her son to death. Sheldhan is loyal to the queen and must obey her. I worry for the prince. We must get him out of the palace until we understand what has happened here. Riordan's life is in danger. Will you do this?"

"Is this an order from the High Council?"

"Think of it as an order from a friend of the king."

Jannen thought a moment. Nathen knew the importance of having someone he could trust. He looked at the old man and quietly said, "Sheldhan betrayed us. I caught him conspiring with the intruder who killed our men this morning. I'm certain it was the intruder who killed the king, not Riordan."

"May Faral protect us," Nathen whispered sadly. "Why would Sheldhan do such a thing? He was Oland's most trusted companion."

Jannen didn't care to understand his motives only that he needed to be stopped. "I was waiting for Sheldhan to secure Riordan in a cell and position his guards accordingly. I can handle two or three knights, but not the entire First Guard. That's what will happen if I don't do this carefully."

"You may be surprised. Riordan spent much of his time with many of those knights. He has more friends than you think. Remember that."

Oban ran up to them. "Jannen, have you heard what happened? Some of the knights are arresting the others. Fights broke out in the Garden of Ches."

"What?"

"This is terrible," Nathen said quietly, "I must return to the others and let them know what is happening. Save the prince, Jannen."

Oban nodded. "I did as Riordan asked. Eric was aware that some of the knights were acting strangely. We agreed to split up and continue investigating. Just as I was leaving Eric, they tried to arrest him, but I think he escaped into the palace."

"Oban, Sheldhan betrayed us. I need your help."

A knight of the First Guard approached them. The knight stopped when he recognized them. Jannen couldn't identify him with the shield closed on his helmet. The knight whistled. Many of the First Guard rushed in from the garden. "They're going to arrest us!" Oban shouted.

"We must save Riordan! Follow me!" Jannen shouted.

"Where is he?" Oban ran along beside him.

The sound of swords leaving their scabbards followed them as they rushed down the hall. Jannen came to one of several entrances to the lower levels of the palace, and ducked in knowing that particular entrance had a locking mechanism. Once he and Oban were through the door he turned and slammed it shut. The vibration of the door smashing into its frame dropped the lock bar. "He's somewhere downstairs."

They heard shouts to surrender from the other side of the door. "Jannen," Oban yelled as he followed him, "we won't succeed."

Eric cut them off just before they got to the kitchen. "Jannen, have you heard what's happening? They tried to arrest me!"

"I heard. Follow us, if you want to help."

They kept moving and Eric said, "I passed Brutus on the floor below. He's searching for Riordan."

"We must save our king," Jannen said. "Sheldhan betrayed us."

He led Oban and Eric with him into the hallway, aware that the First Guard would be coming for them. They marched swiftly, searching the doorways as they went, guided by the light shining down through the pillars. Jannen led them down a long, curved hallway. It circled around until it straightened, and Jannen knew they were at the northern edge of the palace. The walls were built with tempered glass, separating them from the kitchen. The glass was sectioned in different colors, pieced together in shapes that were revered in the Palace of Ionia. Jannen especially admired the images of the First Guard; he swelled with pride when the sunlight shined through the glass . . . until today.

"What are you doing?" an impatient Oban asked him. "They're coming after us!"

Jannen studied his uniform. It was made with pride and dignity, harnessed with myir imported from Ruhln. The redness in the metal was the color of heart and courage. To wear the uniform of the First Guard meant you were part of something great. To wear the black and red meant you were a protector to the king and its people, sworn into an oath of honor and loyalty. Jannen looked at his red sleeve. It was folded as it should be, covering his right shoulder. The day he received it was the best day of his life—now it was tainted. Jannen ripped the sleeve off and threw it on the floor. He turned back to his friends. "There is little honor amongst us. Sheldhan wears the gold sleeve because he is our commander, yet he betrays us. Everything the First Guard stands for is false."

Both Oban and Eric followed Jannen's lead and tore the banners from their shoulders.

Jannen nodded. "Now we shall save our king."

At that moment Sheldhan appeared behind them. He stopped abruptly when he saw them. A squad of the First Guard behind him slammed into each other. Sheldhan's eyed them with hatred. Then he shifted his gaze to the floor where their banners lay. "This is how you repay the respect I've given you?" Sheldhan asked, derision dripping from his tongue. "I know you and the prince are friends. I can understand the pain you must feel at his betrayal. I could have forgiven you for disobeying my orders, but"—he pointed at the banners—"this kind of treachery will not be forgiven."

Jannen shouted, "Riordan is innocent. You betrayed Corrona and everything it stands for. I saw you with the intruder. You are responsible for the deaths of those knights!"

Sheldhan thrust his blade forward and shouted, "Kill them!"

Jannen sprinted for the stairs, waiting for them several strides ahead. Oban grabbed his shoulder, "Get down!"

Sheldhan stood to the side as the knights of the First Guard drew their bows. Jannen turned and jumped into the glass wall. The glass shattered and splintered into a shower of shards. Arrows whizzed through the air. Jannen raced through the kitchen. Eric bled from his mouth, cut from the glass, but held the pace. Oban crashed into barrels of utensils scattering them across the floor. Jannen threw pots and ladles behind them. Another wave of arrows hammered into the kitchen wall. They went around the corner and back into the hallway, stopped when three guards cut them off from the front, swords drawn and pointed at Jannen.

"Your treachery ends here," one of them said.

Brutus appeared behind the three guards, unquestionably the biggest man in the First Guard, and the one with the biggest heart. He wielded a silver pole as a cudgel. In one smooth swing he knocked all three of them unconscious. He dropped the pole and smiled. "What took you so long to arrive?"

Jannen shook his head. "Where's Riordan?"

Brutus pulled his sword free. He noticed their missing banners and after a moment's reflection, he ripped his off, too. "Follow me; I think I know where he is." Jannen nodded and followed. They sprinted through the second floor and past the sleeping chambers for everyone who worked in the palace, including most of the First Guard. Brutus led them across the floor toward the third stairway. The sunlight disappeared at this level. Torches hung on the walls. Brutus snatched one and headed down to the third level. The air turned cold and stale.

Four knights heard their footfalls on the stairs and came to demand they leave. Jannen attacked with his sword. Brutus disarmed two and pounded his fist onto their heads rendering them unconscious. Oban wounded one and Jannen disarmed the last. Behind them the First Guard charged down the stairs with their weapons drawn. Brutus yelped as an arrow struck his shoulder. Oban snapped it off and motioned them all to run.

"Go!" Brutus ordered them. "Riordan is in the last cell at the very bottom. Set him free." He reached for Jannen and pushed him to the side. He handed him his torch. "Don't fail."

Brutus swung his sword and dove in front of Jannen and his friends; arrows sank into his body and Brutus fell back momentarily. Gathering his strength, he yelled again and rushed up the stairs, killing knights as he went. Bodies rolled down the stairs. Blood splattered the walls.

Jannen was horrified. "We must keep moving!" Oban called, running rapidly down the stairs.

More arrows sank into Brutus. Still he fought to hold them all back. "Free the king!" he yelled.

Jannen, Oban and Eric entered into a long corridor. Cell doors made of wood and steel staggered along the long hallway. The last cell was situated at the bottom of a short set of stairs. Jannen inserted his torch into a holder on the wall and yelled out to Riordan. The door was barred heavily with a large piece of wood, wrapped with a thick chain and lock. Without the key, he was going to have to break it open. Behind them the First Guard stormed down the hallway.

Jannen glanced at Oban and Eric, and then swung his sword at the door, taking a chunk out of the wooden bar. He swung again and again, screaming to Riordan on the other side. He didn't get an answer, so he assumed Sheldhan hadn't removed his gag, but in a moment that would change.

Behind him Oban and Eric faced the First Guard as it charged. Oban stabbed the first knight with his sword. A second knight attacked from the side and Oban pulled out a knife, thrusting it deep into his neck. Both guards fell to the floor as Oban retrieved his sword. Eric was disarmed and forced to the floor. Oban almost fell down the stairs, but he recovered mid-stride and leapt to Eric's aide.

Jannen watched the battle between hacks at the door; he was almost through. Several knights fell as Oban fought, but he was badly outnumbered. Jannen panicked. He swung his sword, missed the target, and connected with the steel chain. His hopes faded when his sword broke. He swore and cried out Riordan's name.

Oban killed the man on top of Eric and set him free, but then a First Guard attacked Oban from behind, stabbing him in the back. Oban fell to the ground facing upward, and the knight promptly shoved his sword in Oban's stomach. The knight pulled free his sword and Oban spat blood. Eric, beaten and bloody, cried out and swung his sword. The knight deflected the blow and struck Eric's neck. He fell back, his life drained away forever. Jannen stared in horror. He failed. He looked up the stairs and into Oban's young and hopeful eyes. Oban leaned against the wall still holding his sword. His other hand stayed the wound in his gut. "I'm so sorry," Jannen cried.

"*I'm* not . . . ." Oban replied. He used the rest of his strength to throw Jannen his sword.

Sheldhan charged over the dead bodies and down the stairs. Jannen swung the sword high and fast. The wooden bar split in half, chain hit the floor with a clang. He kicked the door open and dove inside just as Sheldhan caught up to him. The Commander of the First Guard used the blunt end of his sword and smashed it down over Jannen's head.

As Jannen hit the floor, a terrible realization that Riordan no longer had someone to save him came to his mind. "Riordan," Jannen mumbled, his eyes searching the dark cell. But when the call came unanswered, he feared the worse. *Faral save us all,* he thought as darkness engulfed him.

Chapter 16

Adan stretched, yawned and pushed away his damp blanket. The morning dew made him shiver. He missed his bed. Myron snored in his sleep. Adan smiled, knowing it kept the animals away. He climbed to his feet and brushed the moisture off. It was only their third night away from home, and he felt completely lost. He went to the bank of the Delilah River and splashed the sleep from his eyes. He stood, stretched and looked north up the river. He admired the majestic elk trees with branches drooped low over the river. The Ruhln was home. As long as he was in the forest he could have comfort in that.

Myron woke. "How long have you been awake?"

"Not long."

Myron sat up and rubbed his hands. "It was cold last night."

Adan returned to their shelter and leaned into the tree. "And wet."

"It's that time of year; blistering during the day and nippy at night."

"I don't know what we'll do through the winter."

Myron shot him a surprised look. "We'll be gone that long?"

"I'm not going home until I've found Dex."

"But, Adan, we could spend years looking. You may have to accept the fact that he's gone forever." Adan shrugged his shoulders and looked away. Myron would never be able to understand. He knew, deep down, that his brother was alive. "I promised you when we left that I was going to help you through this. I guess I'm in it for the long haul."

"Thank you."

Myron rolled up his blanket. "What are we having for breakfast?"

Adan reached down for his pack. "Nothing," he replied, hungry as well. He knew he should have better prepared.

"I have fishing gear. We could try to find a spot along the river if you want."

Adan nodded. "Let's move north, then."

Myron had his pack together. "Have you decided where we are going yet?"

"If we follow the river far enough, we'll come across the road to

Wyndhaven. I was thinking we could travel that for awhile. If we come across someone we can describe Dex. We might get lucky."

"Let's get moving then. I want to walk in the sunlight so I can dry off."

Adan strapped on his father's sword, already tired of carrying it. He knew that in the unlikely event he had to use it, he'd probably be unable to handle the weight. He swung his pack over his shoulder as they set out. Adan ignored his hunger. Myron would provide food as soon as they found somewhere they could catch fish. He could wait for that. They moved steadily along the river's edge. The ground was clear of brush and easy to follow. Massive branches swayed over their heads, shifting back and forth through the morning wind. As the day grew old the sun warmed the forest, but the elk trees provided the shade they wanted. A cool breeze shifted off the river.

Adan ached to hold Maureen in his arms. With every passing day those feelings grew. He hoped she understood why he had to leave. One day he would return home. If she truly loved him she would be waiting. It broke his heart to think of her with someone else. If Myron hadn't come along, he would already be lost. Adan understood the value of Myron's friendship. He was very grateful that Maureen sent her brother to travel with him.

A bend in the river cut the bank on the west side. A pool of water formed at the river's edge, separated by a strip of sand from the rest of the fast-moving current. A creek flowed out of the forest and trickled into the small pool. Fish were known to habit areas where creeks merged into the river. "Perfect," Myron said.

Adan was relieved to unload the weight of the sword from his back. He watched Myron dig at the side of the bank. "What are you doing?"

"I need bait."

Adan watched him uncover several worms and select the largest one. "I was hoping we'd stumble on a deer or something."

"It's eerie that we've seen no sign of wildlife."

Adan sipped from the creek. It didn't calm the hunger pangs as he'd hoped. "I know. The forest is very quiet today."

Myron stripped off his clothes and waded into the water. "A-a-ah!" he shuddered. "It's freezing." Adan sat at the bank and watched.

Myron smiled. "Stay there. I don't need you scaring the fish away." Myron hooked the worm and let his line sink into the water.

"You believe you're actually going to catch something?"

"Of course I will. Why wouldn't I?" Myron shook his head in disgust.

"Well," Adan said with a bit of skepticism, "I've seen you fish before."

"You can keep your comments to yourself. We'll be eating like kings before you know it."

Adan laughed. "Remember when you built that net?"

"That net was a great idea, and it stretched the entire creek."

"Yes, and you made the holes in the net too big and the fish swam through it."

Myron ground his teeth in mock insult. "I wasn't trying to catch the small fish!"

Adan smiled, Myron was as stubborn as anyone could get.

They waited in silence. When Myron started to shiver, he pretended it wasn't bothering him. "I'm somewhat nervous standing in this river."

"What are you talking about?"

"Do you remember when we were young? My grandfather told stories about Yannina."

Adan knew what he was getting at. "There was no truth to any of them."

"Well, since the demons attacked Ruhln…maybe there is."

Adan stretched out on his back. "You're talking about the demon in the river, aren't you?"

Myron nodded. "Yeah, was his name Xerrand?"

"I think so. To be honest, I've forgotten many of your grandfather's stories."

Myron watched the river flow. "Maybe it's true. Perhaps a demon sleeps somewhere deep in the river."

Adan shook his head. "I doubt it."

Myron pulled back on the line, "Got one!" Adan gathered wood for a fire while Myron caught more fish. The sun was nearly set when they finished their meal. Myron continued to fish into the late evening. "I wonder how my parents are," Myron said as he hooked another fish. The end of his line jerked and the fish jumped out of the water. Myron held his line and was able to pull in his catch. He waded out of the water and smacked the fish against a rock.

"I'm sure they're fine."

"With darkness setting in, I should stay out of the river. At least we have breakfast."

Adan fueled the fire with driftwood. The wood popped as flames danced in the air. Myron rested beside him and wrapped himself in his blanket. "I'll gut the fish in a moment. I'm cold."

"I'll do it," Adan offered.

"No. You'll make a mess. Better if I do it."

"Fine, you're the expert." There was never a point in arguing with Myron.

"May I ask you something?"

There was a tone in Myron's voice Adan hadn't heard before. "Of course you can."

"Why are you so certain Dex is alive? I searched everywhere after the attack. I tried to find a trace, anything that would offer some hope."

Adan took a deep breath, knowing sooner or later Myron was going to ask that question. "I had a dream."

"I know, you told me when we left Ruhln."

"I know what you're thinking, but this is different. It wasn't a dream where Dex was alive." He didn't know how to explain. "It began with this prisoner chained to a wall. I couldn't see his face. As I stepped toward him, the prisoner struggled to breathe, and then he asked for help. He was old, I mean, older than you or me. I reached for him and lifted his head, so I could see his face." Adan stopped explaining when he remembered the blood dripping from his eyes. "It was Dex."

"Older? How would you know it was really him?"

"I'll never forget the face. He stared at me with such hate, as if he intended to kill me."

Myron rubbed his back. "We'll find him before that happens. It was only a dream, try not to think too much of it. I was worried, though, Adan. I thought maybe you were out here running from something."

Adan shook his head. "What do I have to run from?"

"Maureen?"

Now Adan knew exactly what his friend was wondering. "I care for her more than you can imagine. After the attack, my renewed admiration for life made me realize that. She is my world; I miss her so much."

Myron smiled. "That's good to hear."

"Help me."

Adan shot Myron a look. "What did you just say?"

Myron looked puzzled. "Huh?"

"Please, help me," a voice said.

Adan jumped to his feet, thinking of Dex. "Can you hear that?"

Myron shook his head, clearly confused. "Hear what?"

"Go west, friend. Help me...please."

"You can't hear it? Someone is calling for help. There it is again!" Adan ran on instinct. He rushed into the woods away from the river.

"This way," the voice directed. The forest was dark. It was difficult for Adan to find his way. He let the words guide him.

"Adan, you must stop!" Myron yelled.

Adan thought only of Dex. He crossed a creek at the top of the hill. Across from that an open field waited in the moonlight. The voice came to him clearly, explaining to Adan that he was close now. He heard distant cries and the sound of wood snapping beyond the clearing. The trees trembled. A powerful roar ripped through the night air. Myron crashed into Adan from behind and they fell on the quivering ground. Another roar echoed across the open meadow. Adan stumbled to his feet, shaking from the ear-deafening noise.

"What have you gotten us into?" Myron muttered.

"Help me."

A dragon broke through the distant tree line into the clearing. Adan stood to his feet, awestruck by its size. The ground shook with its every step. It was hard to tell the color of its scales in the moonlight, but the yellow in its eyes couldn't be mistaken. Its head was flat, with long ears pointed back. Bony plates ran down its spine, growing larger as they descended down its back. Spiky thorns protected its mouth. Steam burst from its nostrils. The dragon spread out its wings and tried to take flight. "What's going on?" Myron muttered as he thrust Adan out of the moonlight.

Adan rubbed his face. Below his cheek, under the scars, an itch burned fierce. He gasped when he saw demons chase and attack the dragon from every angle, shrieking their terrible noise. Ropes had been thrown high over its back. The dragon shook and twisted, but the demons prevented him from flying away. They managed to clasp a steel collar around the dragon's ankle. It was attached to a long chain and clawed anchor that weighed him down. The anchor snagged on brush and trees preventing his escape.

"*Help me,*" he called.

"It's calling me for help, Myron. We have to do something!" Adan shouted.

"No!"

Adan pulled out his father's sword. Adrenaline surged through his body giving him the strength to lift it into the air. "Those things killed my family!"

"Don't be a fool! You'll die just like your brother did." Myron loaded his crossbow. "Worse yet, you're going to get me killed."

The dragon stumbled to the ground. Ropes were quickly fastened to the beast as the demons passed them from side-to-side. The dragon snarled and fought back, but the demons were clearly in control. Adan snuck toward a demon securing a rope to a tree. It had no idea Adan was there. The demon was only a few strides away. He could kill it easily. His arms were shaking. Myron's warning flashed through his mind. That combined with the sight of the demons crawling over the dragon's back made it hard to breathe. Deep down he knew what had to be done. It was important to stand up against the enemy. He wasn't Aren, but he knew what his brother would do in this very situation. At that moment, Myron pulled him back. He took aim with his crossbow and fired the shot. The demon fell dead. It started a chain reaction across the open meadow as every demon shifted their eyes toward them. The dragon roared. "Damn it, Adan!"

Myron pulled him by his arm and they ran. They sprinted up the side of the creek dodging deadfall and brush. The shrieking demons followed.

The dragon roared again. The sound was so loud and so demanding it rumbled the very ground they ran on. Three demons jumped out in front of them. Myron shot off an arrow, killing one instantly. Adan tripped and fell, dropping his sword. Myron yelled. A demon sprang into the air with its claws drawn, hissing as it fell. The ground vibrated. Adan flinched, certain that he would die. Suddenly the demon was snatched out of the air by the jaws of the dragon, saving him in time from the killing blow. Myron pulled him to his feet. They ducked as the dragon stepped over them, its tail barely missing their heads. Adan reached for his sword and they both took cover below the belly of the dragon. The demons were forced away but they continued to attack. They shot arrows with ropes attached back and forth, keeping the dragon from using its wings. Adan shook with fear, too afraid to even look at Myron.

Myron lashed into him. "You got us into this mess, now pull it together!"

Chaos ensued as the dragon charged through the forest and back into the clearing, the long chain and steel claw used as the anchor ricocheting through the forest around them as the dragon forced his way onward. Demons trailing them were ripped in half by the speed of the anchor tearing through the trees. Still the demons had them trapped. The dragon was pushed up into the end of the clearing, wedged in between two elk trees. Ropes flung through the air all around them.

Myron shot arrow after arrow. Demons dropped dead one after the other. "Cut the ropes!" Myron shouted.

Using Myron's voice as courage, Adan hacked and slashed his way through the ropes. The dragon protected them with his body. He kept the demons at bay as he snapped at them with his jaws. With some of the ropes cut away, the dragon managed to free a wing. Adan crawled under its belly, hoping the dragon knew he was there. Once he made it to the other side, he cut more ropes. Demons dropped only strides away as Myron shot them dead. Myron never missed; this gave Adan the confidence to concentrate on the ropes. Once the dragon was freed from the ropes, it snapped the chain with its teeth, stretched its wings and emitted a resounding roar. Adan and Myron ran for cover. The dragon stomped on the remaining demons that chased them. A moment later they were safely hidden in darkness.

"Thank you."

Each of the dragon's wings was as large as his body. Most of the clearing disappeared with the dragon stretched out. His scales were a silverfish blue. His belly was much darker. Sharp-bladed fins protected its tail. The dragon approached them. *"Thank you for coming to my aide."*

Adan stood with Myron at his side. He once heard that some dragons were peaceful. A long time ago they were thought to be the guardians that protected their world. As he tried to catch his breath he spoke. "Can we trust you?"

"Of course, we've been in battle together. We owe each other our lives."

Adan lowered his sword. "Why do I hear you in my mind?"

"I cannot communicate with my tongue, so I choose this method instead." The dragon shifted the sore leg that was anchored by the chain.

"My name is Zadryan."

Myron stared at Adan with a perplexed look. "You're talking to him?"

Adan nodded and turned to the dragon. "Zadryan, My name is Adan. This is my friend, Myron."

"Thank you for coming to my aide, Adan and Myron."

"Why were the demons attacking you?"

"Zar was hunting my mother and me. She told me to hide. The demons found me. I don't understand their motive."

"Who is Zar?"

"He's the powerful black dragon who has lived in Yannina for a very long time. Zar is threatened by my existence."

Myron elbowed him in the side. "Who is Zar?"

Adan sheathed his sword. He had heard once that a black dragon was hibernating somewhere in Yannina. "He has awakened then?"

"All evil creatures have awakened, Adan. Remember that." Zadryan stretched his back. *"Extend my regards to your friend and keep that sword close to you. It's how I found you."* Adan wondered if that was why Hunter called it a Dragon Sword. *"Demons are close. Somewhere near here I sense a man with great power; you're not safe."*

Adan felt the urgency. "Which direction should we travel?"

Zadryan lifted his head high into the air. *"Go north. Good luck, Adan."*

Wind pushed down on them as the dragon flapped its mighty wings and flew away. "Myron, we must run. He told me there is an enemy near with great power and there are more demons nearby." They ran back down the hill to the river bank. Adan kicked apart their fire as Myron packed his belongings. "Don't leave anything behind; grab the fish."

Myron grabbed his arm. "Don't ever run away from me like that again. Do you understand?"

"I'm sorry," Adan apologized. Together they ran north along the river.

Gnith waited impatiently. He stood by the carriage with his companions as they guarded the prisoner, his identity covered by a white cloth. Gnith watched the sheet rise up and down as the prisoner took slow, agonizing breaths. Demon Vayle emerged from the shadows of the forest. "Is the prisoner secure?" Vayle hissed.

"Yes, Master," Gnith replied.

"The dragon escaped us." Vayle said with displeasure. He loomed over the carriage and pulled away the sheet. The prisoner cowered before him. "Well done." Vayle threw the sheet back and glared at Gnith. "Don't let anything happen to him. I must speak with Zar."

"Yes, Master," Gnith said again. Vayle returned to the darkness of the forest.

Above the forest ceiling a creature flew, screeching like an eagle. Gnith glanced upward as he licked his cracked lips. After a moment of silence, he and his demons continued their journey down the long, empty road.

Chapter 17

The sun climbed the eastern horizon. It was nice to see light after fighting their way through the dark. Adan wondered what the day had planned for them. Exhaustion slowed them down. Adan felt numb below the waist. The brush grew denser as they traveled making it hard to walk. His shins suffered the worst of it; blood from the scratches soaked his torn pants. The terrain along the river bank was too difficult to traverse, so they journeyed further out where the terrain was steep, but clear of brush. Myron reached back for him and helped him climb over a fallen log. As Adan swung his leg over, movement at the bottom of the hill caught his eye. At first he thought it was the wind swaying the thick brush, but the rhythm was wrong. Fear gripped him. A man dressed in black battled through the thick brush.

"Myron!" Adan hissed in barely audible whisper. He pointed and ducked down on the other side of the log. The black figure struggled through the branches of brush. They were close enough to distinguish his form clearly, yet too far away to identify him.

"Is he following us?" Myron whispered.

The man in black broke through the last of the brush and headed up the hill with a slow and steady gait. Adan remembered what Zadryan had told him. The dragon warned him about a stranger nearby with great powers. This could be that stranger.

Myron readied his crossbow and quietly said, "I can hit him from here."

Adan pushed his weapon down. "Let's not forewarn him we're here, just in case. Maybe he hasn't seen us." Myron frowned, uncertain. Zadryan's warning echoed in Adan's mind, but he pushed it away. Myron motioned him up the hill. They ducked down and stayed out of sight. The terrain flattened at the top of the hill. To the west the forest was sparsely wooded. Only the long, tall grass separated the giant elk trees. There would be no cover if they went west. "We must keep parallel with the river," Adan said. He checked behind, but couldn't see the stranger he knew was there.

"I agree. We might have to move closer to the river bank. There's cover there." Adan was too exhausted to even think about fighting through the brush again. If they were being followed, it would be hard for the stranger to keep their trail. "Adan, we must run and keep running until we're as far from that man as possible." Adan knew not to argue. He slid his pant leg up to his knee and revealed a deep, bloody gash across his shin. "How did you do that?"

Adan couldn't remember. "It happened during the night." He pushed his pant leg down. "We don't have time to worry about it."

"We'll rest soon. Come, let's move."

They ran and followed the embankment as close as they could. Below them the river wrapped around a sharp bend splashing water high into the air as it rammed into rocks. The Delilah River was the greatest water system in Yannina. The more Adan traveled its edge, the more he respected its reputation. The width was incredible in certain areas. He remembered a map his father showed him. The river split into several systems that ran parallel with one another farther north, closer to the mountains. The Stag of Waters held the runoff from the mountains to feed the Delilah River.

They moved closer to the river's edge. The brush was as thick as before, yet the deeper they pushed through, the more confidence they gained. Adan worried with every step. His neck ached from checking over his shoulder. They both collapsed from heat and exhaustion when the sun was directly above them.

"Adan," Myron said in a raspy voice, "we need to rest."

"I know, but not too long."

They found a sandy opening. Adan lay back and Myron sat. "I don't know who that was earlier, Adan. I've been thinking that since we helped that dragon escape from those demons, it makes me wonder just what, precisely, we're doing."

"What do you mean?"

"Rest first, and then we'll talk."

Adan fell asleep almost instantly. When he awoke a bee buzzed near his ear. He swatted at the annoyance and sat up. "Myron?" A cool breeze from the river blew through his hair. "Myron?" A faded voice spoke to him. It was unlike before, different from the way the dragon called to him. Puzzled, Adan rose and walked into the brush away from the river. It was instinct that pushed him forward, curious to find the distant voice. He heard it again. It felt close, yet sounded so far away. The brush in front of him was thick. He pulled it out of the way. A decomposing Dex appeared straddled on the brush—throat slashed. Flies swarmed the stench and fed on the guts spilled from his insides. Adan stumbled back and screamed in rage and fear.

His own voice awakened him as he screamed his brother's name. He tried to focus, but everything was a blur.

"Adan…It's all right. Calm down. Everything's fine." Myron shook him lightly.

Adan stood in an attempt to forget the deadly images so vividly etched in his mind.

"What did you dream?" Myron asked.

Adan shook his head. It was so real. He felt the cool breeze and shivered.

"Your middle scar is bleeding."

Adan rubbed the scar. "I've fallen more than I can remember."

"Here," Myron said, tearing a strip of cloth from his shirt. Adan pressed it against his face and sat down on the sand, still trying to decipher his thoughts.

"Adan, I need to talk to you."

Adan looked at him as if seeing him for the first time and said, "What about?"

"We need to focus on an objective. We can't keep running hither and yon. We need direction." Adan only shook his head. Myron sat on the sand beside him. "You know that I'm here for you. I'll go to the end of the world and back with you. I'll put my life on the line to help you get your brother back, should it come to that. But I need direction. I need an objective. We're wandering around like a couple of river rats."

Adan took cloth from his face and noticed the blood stain; it reminded him of his dream. "What kind of direction do you need?"

"Direction is the wrong word, I think. I need to know that we have a plan in place, so we feel that we're accomplishing something. We must get away from this river. If we head west we'll find the road faster, and from there we could go to Wyndhaven. There are other towns on the way, like Palher. We should be searching there. If we provide descriptions of Dex, we may have some success. I believe in your dream, Adan, but we'll get nowhere trudging through brush. I don't think we'll have as many problems closer to Wyndhaven."

Adan thought Myron was right, though they were heading in the direction the dragon had told them. "What of Zadryan's warning?"

Myron shook his head, "I'm hoping the danger is behind us."

Adan sighed, worried it wasn't so. Still, he thought that traveling away from the river would distance them from the stranger and the demons. "Let's head west."

Myron stretched out on the sand. "Let me sleep some; then we'll continue."

Adan's face no longer bled. He pulled his pant leg up and wrapped the cloth around his leg. He stood and looked to the south. The river's noisy movement drowned out any other sounds. The remains of his dream diminished, he found comfort in Myron's presence once again, and he smiled. He would have been dead already had Myron remained in Ruhln.

"Adan, what happened in your dream?"

"I don't want to relive it by telling you."

"Have you always had nightmares?"

"No, they began after the attack on Ruhln."

"Do they differ?"

"Not really. They're always about Dex in one way or the other."

Myron lifted his head. "You said Dex acted as if he wanted to kill you?"

Adan would never forget the look in those eyes. "I won't let that happen."

Myron rested his head on the ground. "Me neither."

Chapter 18

Myron slept with a pleasant dream. He tried to stay asleep when something pinched him. It was a dream of him and Aren in their youth. Together they raced across the ridge of Whistle Rock with Adan and Maureen in tow. It felt good to laugh again with friends. An intense pain jarred him awake. "Bloody fool, Myron, wake up!"

Myron jolted up. "What's wrong?" He grappled with his bow and rubbed the sleep from his eyes at the same time.

Adan frowned, but with the hint of a smile. "Trying to wake you is like bringing back the dead. I kicked you. The sun is setting; we need find a safe camp for the night."

Myron sighed in relief. "You didn't have to kick me. You scared the wits right out of me." He yawned.

A full smile appeared on his scarred face as Adan strapped on the sword and scabbard. "What wits? Come, I'll lead."

Myron sensed a resurgence of confidence in Adan. Perhaps it was because they had a plan. Their destination was decided. It was possible that Dex would turn up. Obviously, Adan felt the same way. There was always hope.

The Delilah River sank into a small canyon, leaving a high embankment on both sides. Adan pointed to the top of the hill. "We should camp there."

Myron nodded. "Should we encounter trouble, we could jump into the river for a fast escape."

Adan shook his head. "Only you would think of something so idiotic. You don't even know how to swim."

Darkness fell over them, but the moonlight helped them reach their destination. Myron stared back from the top of the hill. He could see the river twist out of the narrow canyon and back toward the area where they'd stopped to catch fish. The thought made him hungry; however, lighting a fire would be foolish. A funnel of smoke would be easily sighted.

"I'll take first watch," Myron offered.

"Thank you. Don't fall asleep." Adan curled up between roots at the bottom of a looming elk tree. Its canopy stretched far out beyond like a natural shelter.

"I can't believe you'd say such a thing. After everything I've done." Myron shook his head.

Adan smiled. "Let me sleep."

Myron replied with a smile of his own and kept his remarks to himself. It was nice to hear Adan sound lighthearted. Since the attack on Ruhln, Adan was more subdued. Myron watched Adan as he slept. His friend carried grief and pain, always wearing it on his shoulders and reflected in the scars on his face.

When they were children, Myron's friendship with Aren was strongest. He was closer to Aren. Maureen and Adan spent most of their time together, while he and Aren explored mines, entered tournaments in Wyndhaven and traveled to Corrona to sell their myir. He and Aren were more alike. But that was all suddenly changed. Helping Adan made him feel like he was helping Aren. He took pride in that. He wished the pleasant dream that Adan woke him from was once again a reality. He would never turn back on Adan. He knew that Adan truly believed Dex was alive. They hadn't found a body. Until they did, there was a chance. Wyndhaven was about four days on foot. He was still worried about the man in black. His grandfather taught him to use his instincts to track game and to sense when he was the prey. His instincts kept him alert. He prayed to Faral for protection.

Adan stirred and murmured in his sleep. Myron cringed at the thought of anything hurting him. He would die before he let anything harm him. A whisper of wind brushed softly against his face. A feeling of warmth traveled through him. It was as if the wind spoke to him. The sensation that he felt left him completely confident and safe. He thought about his grandfather. Cadin was often in his thoughts and prayers, but this was different. With the wind circling him as he stared out over the river, he sensed that his grandfather was with him in spirit. "Poppa?" he said.

The wind whispered; *Guard Adan with your life.* Myron knew his grandfather's spirit spoke to him in the wind. His eyes welled with tears when he realized his family's prophecy was true. All his life, since he had been a boy, Myron wondered about it...about how the spirits of his departed family came alive in the wind to give courage to those left behind. The wind faded. Myron felt strangely rejuvenated. Courage was something he recognized within himself, but now that he knew his grandfather was with him—that courage felt ten-fold.

Adan twitched in his sleep, so quietly and in peace.

Myron yawned. He didn't need to be convinced to protect Adan. That was why he was with him. As long as he had a breath to breathe in his body, Adan would have that protection. He nudged him with his boot. The scars on Adan's face twitched as he woke.

"No nightmares this time?" Myron asked.

"I slept well."

"Good," Myron replied. "Now get out of there. It looks comfortable." They switched places, and Myron fell asleep with the feeling his Grandfather was nearby.

Adan kept watch as the Delilah River splashed and tumbled around the bend below. Then he searched the sky and smiled at his mother's star. The tone of Zadryan's voice startled him. *"My friend Adan, come to me."* Adan was hesitant to leave Myron. *"Your friend is safe. I'm not far."*

Myron was already snoring. Adan sensed the truth in Zadryan's voice. "All right, I'll let him sleep."

Zadryan directed him away from the river across a clearing into the trees. *"Thank you for coming. You look wounded, Adan."*

Adan reached up with his hand and felt the scar. "I'll be fine."

"Good."

"Why are you here?"

"I'm concerned for your safety; you saved my life."

"I appreciate that."

"What are you doing out here?"

Adan caught himself staring. The dragon appeared much larger than the previous night. The plates running down his neck and back were larger. The scales guarding his body appeared polished and redefined from before. He wondered if the excitement of the previous night had impacted his observation. "Wyndhaven," he finally answered.

"Why do you go through so much trouble to get there?"

"What do you mean?"

"Surely it would be easier to travel on the road instead of along the river."

"We just decided to travel to Wyndhaven to search for my brother."

"He is lost?"

Adan told him all the details about the attack on Ruhln and the disappearance of Dex. The dragon moved his head closer to Adan; his yellow eyes blinked repeatedly in interest.

"*I'm sorry for your family lost. How may I help?*"

"If you can help me find Dex, I would be grateful."

"*I will.*" Zadryan rubbed his side against an elk tree; his back brushed the canopy. "*There is honor in dragons, Adan. My mother said we're all unique...that we must work together to survive.*" Zadryan paused and lowered his head. Adan instinctively stepped back at the size of his teeth. "*I told her about you and what you did. What surprised her most was how I found you through your sword. What is your full name?*"

"Adan Caynne is my full name."

"*I must tell my mother. She called you friend. She wants to know more about you.*"

Adan nodded. "I feel the dragons are my friends as well."

Zadryan knocked Adan to the ground with a head thrust. For a brief instant, Adan thought Zadryan attacked him. "*We're not all alike, Adan! Tread carefully. There are dragons in this world with immense power that would crush you without a second thought. Zalphyna, my mother, taught me to value life and to help those who help me.*"

Adan said, "I understand."

"*I hope so.*" Zadryan walked past him into the clearing. He unfolded his wings and stretched. "*Return to your friend; he awakens.*"

"Will I see you again soon?"

"*I promised to help find your brother, did I not?*" Adan held himself steady against the downdraft as Zadryan took flight. "*You'll be safe tonight, Adan. Rest well.*"

When Adan returned to camp the sound of the raging river came back to life. Myron was curled up against the elk tree. The sun peeked over the horizon thrusting orange and red into the eastern sky. He glanced down the hill and dropped immediately to the ground. The man in black slowly trudged up the hill from the embankment. Adan watched in horror. Zadryan told him they would be safe tonight. He had failed Myron, left him unprotected while he slept. "Myron!" he hissed. As fast as Adan spoke his name Myron was on his feet. "Look!" Adan pointed down the hill.

Myron reached for his crossbow and loaded an arrow. Adan unsheathed his sword as Myron shot the arrow. It deflected off the rocks and missed the man in black. "Bloody luck," Myron rasped. He rarely missed his target.

Adan dropped his sword and ran to a boulder near the edge of the hill. Myron hurried over to help. Together they rolled it to the embankment and sent it down hill. It missed the stranger by a stride and bounded into the river. "There's another one!" Adan pointed. Again they missed. Their hopes of crushing their foe faded when the stranger took cover.

"Let's run, Adan."

"Away from the river this time," Adan said, "Let's go west as we planned. Maybe in the darkness we'll lose him." He glanced at the rising sun; they didn't have much time.

"Agreed," Myron hung the bow on his waist. "Grab your sword and let's get out of here."

As the sun shined light on their new day, darkness followed.

Chapter 19

They ran steadily. The soft, rolling hills and open, less dense stands of trees helped them gain distance on their pursuer. An eagle screeched as it passed over them. Its shrill cry startled Adan. His first thought was that the bird revealed their position to the man in black. Adan led the way as they weaved around trees and bushes. After what seemed like an eternity, the road finally appeared. The sight of the hard-packed trail felt like victory.

"We made it," Adan said. "With luck we'll run into someone who can help us."

Myron glanced over his shoulder. "Do you think we lost him?"

"I don't know, but I'm not interested in waiting around to find out." The brush on either side of the road was covered in dust. The dry air didn't help his thirst. Adan repositioned his pack and they trudged ahead. He limped as pain shot up his right thigh. Now that they were on track to Wyndhaven he wondered what he might find there. He doubted that Dex traveled all that way, but it wasn't impossible. The road to Wyndhaven was long and often steep. At one point there was a narrow stretch that followed the river bank. Beyond that was the crossroads where Adan must decide whether to take the road to Palher or turn west and continue to Wyndhaven. The short detour from Wyndhaven wouldn't slow them down too much.

Aren and their father journeyed to Wyndhaven every summer to compete. Usually Adan remained at home with Dex, but last summer they went as a family. Aren often spoke of its grandeur, of the thousands of friendly people, attractive women and amazing castle peaks. Adan was disappointed. Wyndhaven was a castle surrounded by small towns. Ancient stories said the castle was built for a special purpose. Adan never saw the inside of the castle. He heard there was a maze of tunnels and shafts within the castle walls. He remembered that day, how excited he and Dex were. Adan thought they would be allowed inside the castle. Dex was disappointed when it didn't happen. At least Adan finally watched Aren compete. His twin was well known amongst everyone who competed for the honor of Dal-Varr. He was younger and more competitive than most, a top winner every year. Myron competed in the archery contests. He'd never accomplished as much as Aren, but he certainly had his moments. The earlier incident was the first time Adan saw him miss a target. Myron *never* missed. He wondered if lack of sleep had anything to do with it.

As the afternoon dragged on, Adan felt a throbbing in his head. He yearned for water to wash the dust from his eyes, mouth and throat. He looked back. The road stretched out empty behind him and disappeared around a corner. He wondered who their pursuer was. Had Zadryan lied? The dragon told him they were safe from danger. Didn't he know the man in black was coming after them? Adan knew he would see Zadryan again, and ask him about it.

Adan raised his hand in warning when he heard a wagon. Myron quickly smiled and Adan hoped it would be someone who could help them. When they turned a corner they discovered a simple wagon pulled by two horses. Leading the horses were two figures dressed in red robes; an identical figure stood on the wagon. The wagon was clearly used for hauling material, and Adan wondered what they were doing. Behind the wagon came a fourth figure, this one wearing green and slightly taller than the others. As they approached, Adan noticed the limp. The scars on his face began to itch. Adan gently rubbed his face. He remembered the last time they itched like that. "Get off the road," he hissed.

"What?"

"Something's wrong." Adan grabbed Myron's tunic and hauled him off the road. He led him deep into the brush. "I want to have a safe look at them." They circled around. They found an embankment on the other side. They slithered through the brush like snakes and used the tall grass to hide. Below them the carriage slowly creaked into view. The three on foot hobbled along slowly. A white throw splotched with moisture covered the top of the carriage.

The walkers clutched wooden staffs in their hands to help them walk. The Red cloaks covered their identities. One of the walkers removed its hood—it was a demon. Adan scratched at his scars. "Stop that," Myron said. "What are they doing?"

"I don't know." It seemed odd for the demons to be seen in daylight. He thought they hid until dark. He remembered how the demons fought with inexplicable hatred and disregard for their own lives. It was difficult to fight an enemy that didn't fear death.

"There will be more of them nearby," Myron whispered.

The carriage was directly below them. "What do you think is beneath that cover?" Adan whispered.

"I know what you're thinking. It could be anything under that throw."

Adan wondered if Dex was underneath it. He shook his head. "Had they seen us, we would've been dead."

Myron nodded. "Someone else comes, quiet now."

Gnith moved slowly. He hung his head as the sun beat down on his back. The heat was difficult for him to bear, causing weakness in the bones and boils on his grey skin. The wagon creaked as the wheels turned in tune to the horses' steps. The prisoner was secured with rope, guarded by Gnith's demon ally. The white throw covered his identity from prying eyes.

The sunlight throbbed against his flowing red robes as Demon Vayle emerged from the forest. Gnith and his demons stopped and bowed before their master. "How is the prisoner?" Vayle demanded.

Gnith poked at the white blanket. "He's in much pain, Master."

Vayle hissed, "Don't let him weaken; we need him alive." Vayle removed the sheet. The prisoner stared in fear and pulled his legs into his chest. Vayle covered the prisoner and turned to Gnith. "I want you to come with me. My Dryden control Corrona. We will move into the next phase." Vayle pointed to the other demons. "Take him to the Temple of J'yradal. I will meet you there. Kill anyone who stands in your way."

"Yes, Master," The demons hissed.

Vayle headed into the forest with Gnith close behind.

Adan seethed with fury when he saw Vayle. "He killed my father and my brother!" he rasped.

"I know." Myron shoved his face to the ground. "Be silent or we'll suffer the same fate."

When Vayle approached the carriage, Adan and Myron were both surprised. They couldn't hear his conversation, but they both felt intense sympathy when he uncovered a prisoner. The sunlight hid the prisoner's identity, but Adan was convinced it was Dex. When the two demons disappeared into the forest, the wagon continued down the road and around a bend.

Adan stood and drew his sword, but Myron motioned him into the shadows of the forest. "Hold on. Use your head. Now is not the time."

Adan sheathed his sword. "We must save him."

Myron nodded. "We will, but we must wait. That demon in red is too powerful for us; if we charge them head on we'll be dead before we blink. Let's run north and find a location to set an ambush. If the demon in red is not with them, we'll attack. It's the only chance we have."

Myron was right. Adan remembered how the demon in red killed Aren so easily. "Yes." The thought of Dex back safely in his arms almost made him cry.

Myron locked his crossbow to his left arm. "Can you run?"

Adan no longer cared about the aches or pains he suffered. He wanted save his brother. They ran until they found an area farther north where the road passed through a meadow. Tall, weeping grass straddled either side of the ditch. The demons were far enough behind them. Adan rubbed his neck to calm himself. He must control his fear for the sake of his brother. They took cover in the grass. Myron loaded an arrow. "Adan, make certain the grass stays upright. Don't bend it or it will look suspicious to the demons."

Adan swallowed the bile his stomach pushed up. "Myron," he whispered, "thank you."

Myron gave a smile of confidence. "We'll get him back."

They heard creaking of wheels and the erratic cadence of demon footsteps. Myron used his hands to communicate. He gestured that there were only three demons and the one in red was not with them. Adan wiped sweat from his brow and whispered, "Protect me, Father." He was out of time to think it over. Adan knew if he wanted to save Dex, the time was now. They leapt onto the road.

The first demon shrieked at the sight of them. Adan rushed forward before the demon could protect itself, and thrust his sword deep into the demon's stomach. Myron fired an arrow into the neck of the second demon. The third demon slammed its wooden staff to the back of Myron's head. Myron hit the dirt, spitting blood. Adan swung the Dragon Sword over his head. The blade flared to life in a blue haze. The demon deflected the blow with his staff and struck Adan in the side. It knocked the wind from his lungs. The demon retreated to the carriage deck to guard its prisoner. The creature tore off its garments. Its gnarled body had jagged fins along its back. Large claws seeped white fluid from its knees and wrists. Long black hair contrasted with its red, beady eyes. The demon roared and beckoned Adan to start the battle.

Adan shoved his fear to the back of his mind—victory was within grasp. He leapt onto the wagon. The Dragon Sword flared to life with the blue light. Myron, recovered from the blow to his head, climbed onto the wagon with his loaded crossbow.

The demon blocked Adan's sword and swung his staff at Myron. It struck Myron's shoulder and made him lose balance. He fell against the wagon seat as his crossbow released the arrow. It stabbed the horse's rump and the wagon catapulted into full speed. Adan landed on the white throw that covered the prisoner. The demon charged him for the kill. Myron tackled the demon. They sprawled across the wagon bed beside Adan. The demon tried to ram its claws into Myron's chest. Adan climbed back to his feet. The demon backhanded Myron rolling him to the rear of the wagon. The demon climbed back to its feet and once again deflected Adan's sword. Adan screamed and swung again. He felt the power of the sword infuse strength and courage into him. The demon's staff shattered. The demon fell. Adan slammed the Dragon Sword through the demon's chest. The sword erupted in blue as it ripped the demon in half, green blood surging into the air.

Myron climbed to his knees, grabbed the reins and brought the wagon to a stop. Adan lifted the shroud from the prisoner, excited to see his brother. He stared with stunned disappointment. It wasn't Dex. The prisoner was Prince Riordan of Corrona. There was no mistaking his identity. Adan knew too well what the silver strands in his hair represented.

"I don't believe my eyes," Myron finally said.

Chapter 20

It was close to midnight when Darych Shade leaned against a building. He longed for his bed. There was a time when he found it exciting to patrol the streets, but the repetition in his work wore him down. Commanding the Wyndhaven Force demanded all of his time; he couldn't recall the last time he took an extended break. Darych found it odd that so many people wandered Ebury Street so late. Ebury was a long and dusty road and normally quieter in the late evening. A wagon rumbled by in front of him. When the driver noticed the crest on Darych's breastplate, he nodded in recognition. Laughter resounded from the building and Darych stepped away from the wall. A sign rattled over his head. He smiled; the cold taste of ale would ease his weary bones. The Tooth and Tavern was his favorite place to wash away an old day.

The wood porch creaked with his footsteps. The swinging doors pushed outward and a drunk crashed into him. The man fell to the porch and vomited. The stench of sour ale hung in the air with the haze of smoke. Sputtering oil lanterns hung low off the ceiling, centered over the tables. Darych recognized many rabble-rousers from his patrols crowded around several tables. Tension grew with his presence. Several patrons left. Others remained seated as they waited for Darych to make a move. All he wanted was to relax with a pint of his favorite ale. When he pretended none of them existed, the tension settled and people resumed their conversation.

Dancers kicked up their skirts at the back. Drunken fools stood by the stage and yelled bawdy comments to accompany the bawdy music. The tavern wasn't popular for its music. It was the ale that brought the business. Marwin ale was the finest. A special delivery arrangement with ale producers in Ruhin guaranteed a plentiful supply. Darych found Ray, the ale keeper, working at the back. His old, one-eyed friend waved him over. "Darych, you look like a hairy beast." Ray said as he poured the ale. "You need to shave that beard of yours."

"How are you, old friend?"

Ray smiled and winked his only eye. "Better these days, I suppose." He slid a large bronze cup across the wooden counter. "First one is on the house. I doubt you'll find a seat to enjoy it. We're very busy tonight."

Darych swigged the ale. "I don't need a seat to enjoy this." He motioned toward the crowds. "I've never seen you this busy."

Ray spoke while he served another customer. "The rooms upstairs are reserved for a month. Strangers continue to ask, but I've had to turn them down. Some offer a lot of money. It's hard to say no." He shook his head. "People are afraid to venture far from the major settlements."

"I've noticed the crowded streets lately."

"My shipment from Ruhln is two weeks late. I sent my boy to investigate. That mug you have is from the last barrel."

Darych frowned. "Has Ruhln ever missed a shipment?"

"Until now, Ruhln has never been late or missed a shipment."

Darych swigged his ale and wondered if he should check into it. "Keep me informed."

Ray nodded, "I will."

Darych wended his way through the crowded tables. One of the women deliberately pushed her cleavage up against his armor. Darych was appalled at the sight of her; someone had knocked out her teeth. It was less crowded at the back corner and he needed to get off his feet. He noticed a cloaked and hooded fellow sitting by himself. His table had a few empty chairs. "Mind if I share a table with you, friend?" he asked.

The stranger's eyes were dark like his hair and beard. The muscles in his face were distinguished when he moved his jaw. A tattoo of the letter *f* was written below his ear. His broad shoulders hinted at the power beneath his cloak. The stranger responded in a deep voice, "I could use some conversation."

"My name is Darych Shade."

The other man removed his hood. "I'm Larnen." He pointed to the crest on Darych's breastplate. "You're a general."

Darych sat across from him. "Not at the moment. I'm finished for the night."

"I admire the Wyndhaven crest. What do the eagle and spear represent?"

Obviously Larnen was neither from Wyndhaven nor from southern Yannina. "There's an ancient legend that says the Castle of Wyndhaven was built in the heavens and lowered down through the sky by an ancient race. Some say the eagle is the symbol of this ancient race and the spear represents courage. The gold in the back is my symbol of rank."

"The rank color is the same in every settlement."

"Where are you from?"

"Have you heard of Akhran?"

Darych smiled and nodded. He knew exactly where Akhran was and everything else that belonged with it. "Our Princess Karyna is engaged to Prince Rowen of Akhran."

Larnen raised his brows. "That's unusual. How did this come about?"

"The two of them met a few years ago in Akhran. Princess Karyna went there to act as emissary for her father."

Larnen swallowed his ale. "That's about the time the war started."

Darych nodded. "Lord Valhun of Akhran requested a meeting with our King Mel to discuss the possibility of war with Terrace. King Mel was sick, so he sent Karyna in his place to decline an alliance with them. She was only seventeen when she fell in love with Rowen. King Mel was devastated with the news our kingdoms would unite through marriage. While trying to avoid war, he'd accidentally forced us into it." Darych shifted his weight. He contemplated removing his armor but decided against it. "To prevent that King Mel forbade her to marry until the war ends."

"The war rages, much like the day it began."

Darych nodded. "And Karyna still wishes to wed Rowen."

"You know, Darych, I left Akhran only two years ago. I never heard any announcement of their engagement, and I was enrolled in their army at the time."

For a brief moment Darych wondered if the stranger thought he lied. "That's very odd."

Larnen shrugged his shoulders. "Perhaps they decided to keep matters quiet until the war ended. Maybe I heard but didn't care." He laughed out loud.

Darych smiled. "Why did the war start between Akhran and Terrace?"

Larnen frowned. "We never really knew. Our nations enjoyed a peaceful existence for years. One day the devastating war started, and neither side looked back. Now they fight with hatred we cannot comprehend."

Darych sighed. That was exactly what he'd been told, and that was why King Mel wished to be left out of it. The thought of Karyna married to that chaos sickened him. Larnen finished his drink. "I have worse news, my friend."

Darych looked directly into his dark eyes. "What do you mean?"

"The last few years I traveled throughout Yannina. I've met new people in new places, like you, and I hear their stories."

"What kind of stories?" he asked with heightened interest. Darych always enjoyed listening to tales woven from travelers.

"It's not one story in particular; it's when I string them together. Something is going on in Yannina. I'm not sure what that is, but I'm certain it isn't for the good."

Darych leaned back in his chair. "I don't understand." He wished they would stop singing that awful bawdy music.

"Have you heard of demons?"

"Of course, every child is told the story of Faral and his brother Faris; the legend of how Faral overcame his brother's betrayal and saved the world from demons."

Larnen appeared tense and shook his head. "There's another story, one that is not as common. Have you heard of the Demons of Destiny?"

"No."

Larnen leaned across the table. "Rumors are spreading like dragon's fire, friend. The Demons of Destiny are awakening. When they do, the little war in the north will be child's play."

Darych laughed. "What exactly are the Demons of Destiny?"

"I don't have the slightest idea…yet."

"Larnen, I'm a man of faith. I don't believe in fairy tales and ghost stories. Demons are nothing more than myth."

Larnen smiled. "You may believe in them soon." Darych finished his ale and slid his mug across the table. "I heard something unusual tonight, some rumblings of an attack."

Darych realized he liked Larnen even though he believed in superstition. "An attack where?" he asked.

"I heard that a town named Ruhln was destroyed."

Darych froze. He knew people in Ruhln, the king had friends there. Ray told him he was missing a shipment of ale. "By whom?" he demanded.

"I suppose by superstition, if you believe in such things." Darych frowned. He was not about to believe that demons destroyed Ruhln. "War is coming to Wyndhaven. You can count on it."

"I have to go." Darych rose from his seat. He didn't know what to think. There would be no reason for anybody to invade Ruhln. It had to be nothing more than a ridiculous rumor. He politely shook hands with Larnen and stepped away from the table. Darych waved farewell to Ray, but his old friend was shaking his head at a customer. The Tooth and Tavern was out of ale. Even if what Larnen had told him were only rumors, the king would appreciate a conversation with him. Darych turned around, ready to offer Larnen a night in the castle. He glanced back and forth, wondering if his eyes played tricks on him. Larnen had disappeared.

Chapter 21

Princess Karyna stared out through the open window. The moonlight brightened the street of Ebury as it reflected off the buildings along the rolling hills. Every day her concerns for Rowen intensified. She tried to remember the last time she heard from him. She shuddered to think he was hurt…or worse. If she received the approval from her father to marry, Karyna was uncertain if she should continue the engagement. Their relationship the last two years proved difficult. Rowen was pressured further into his duties. Months passed before she heard from him, and when she did, his notes were always curt. They didn't sound like the man she fell in love with.

She remembered the shock and pain on her father's face when she told him. Her relationship with her father turned sour; she believed she would never forgive him for making her wait to wed. Yet now, almost three years later, she thought he might have been right, but before she could really believe that, Karyna knew she had to see Rowen again. Only then would she really know. Love was too complicated. Maybe Rowan drifted away from her and fell in love with someone else. She cringed at the thought and smiled. Maybe she still loved him after all. She closed the window, rubbed her bare arms with her hands and crossed her room. Her divan was in front of the fire. She sank into the soft suede and burrowed under the blanket. As she drifted off to sleep, she remembered the first time she met him.

Karyna awakened as the carriage bumped loosely down the road. She yawned and stretched. The Wyndhaven Armaments, Sheilna and Frenna, were sitting together by the window. "Good morning," Sheilna said.

Karyna sat up and peered out the window, relieved to find the mountains had disappeared with the night. "Are we close to Akhran yet?"

"Yes," Frenna replied. "Lieutenant Race said we should arrive soon."

"I'm a little nervous," Karyna said. "I've never done anything of such magnitude before."

"They are the duties of a princess," Sheilna reminded her. "You'll be fine."

"No, this is my father's duty…not mine." The carriage had little room to move. Frenna offered to take Karyna's hand as she stood. Sheilna lifted the bottom of the bed folding it tight to a niche in the carriage wall. A bench swung out with the underside.

Frenna helped her sit and combed her thick, unruly hair. "We need to get you dressed."

Sheilna reached up onto a shelf and removed a gown. "I know you've been waiting for an occasion to wear this dress."

Karyna smiled. "Thank you."

Karyna hated her thick hair. Every morning she sat in pain as Frenna tugged on her scalp. "I envy you two," she said.

Frenna laughed. "Why?"

"You two always appear at your best. I love how you manage your hair keeping it long and straight. I don't know how either of you do it when much of your time is spent working with me."

It warmed Karyna to see Sheilna smile. "As the Wyndhaven Armaments we must appear at our best in your presence. It isn't difficult to brush our hair and dress." Their garments were simple. Karyna admired the white outfit they wore and appreciated its simplicity. Sheilna and Frenna wore white pants and a white vest over a long sleeved shirt with a flowered pattern around the cuffs of their sleeves. The symbol of Wyndhaven was displayed proudly on their backs. Sheilna and Frenna were beautiful women. Even dressed in her own gown, Karyna felt inferior.

Frenna finally loosened the knots and tapped her shoulder. "It's finished. Your thick red hair is unique." Sheilna motioned her to drop her nightgown and lift her arms. Karyna slipped on the dress and stood in front of the mirror. It was her favorite dress, a long, silver gown with the front cut low, one strap over her left shoulder to her right backside. Sheilna secured the strap. "Your hair comes from your mother," Frenna reminded her.

Karyna knew she was right about that. Her mother had the fullest head of red hair that anyone could have imagined. "I miss her."

Frenna glanced at Sheilna. "We all do, Karyna."

"You two became my closest friends when mother died. I don't know how I would have made it through all these years without you. Thank you."

"There's no need to thank us," Sheilna said.

The carriage wheels squealed as they slowed. The horses guiding the carriage whinnied and someone approached. "Princess Karyna, we're at the outer limits of Akhran," Race called from outside. "You should sit up front as we ride through the city."

Sheilna opened the door to the carriage and Karyna stepped out. She gasped at the sight of Akhran. She never imagined such a magnificent sight. The city stood before her backed by the clear morning sky and seagulls flying high overhead. From the outskirts of the city to the rising palace in the back, from the ocean to the rolling hills in the east, the landscape was awash with beauty. The air was brisk and reminded her of the spiced tea her mother drank every night. She grimaced when the homely Race blocked her view with his receding hair line and pathetic features. "You should ride up front, Your Highness," he repeated. He pointed to a man seated on his horse on the road ahead of them. "That man ahead is a general. He's waiting for us."

"Understood," she replied. Karyna climbed up high to the front end of the carriage. When Sheilna and Frenna took their positions on either side of her, the driver snapped the reins. The knights of the Wyndhaven Forces split to protect both sides of the carriage. She reviewed the statement her father wanted her to give to Lord Valhun. For the first time in her life she must conduct her actions like a princess. She would not disappoint her father.

The general approached them as they drew near. "Akhran awaits your arrival, Your Majesty." The general bowed before her.

"Thank you. It's been a long journey. I'm excited to be here."

The general smiled. "I'm General Mammond. It is my honor to lead you to the palace."

"Thank you," Karyna replied. Sheilna reassured her with a smile.

As they rode through the outskirts, smells came to her one-by-one, some pleasant, some sickening. Vagabonds curled up in dark corners. The sidewalks were crowded with traders. As Karyna's carriage passed, they sought her attention. Some threw garbage, to her intense dislike, while others tempted her with gifts. A beggar spread his lips and spat a seed at her from the melon he was eating. She found the constant bickering of traders, squawking of chickens and barking dogs annoying. Dirty children chased each other with wooden swords and poles. They laughed at Karyna as she rode by. Race's request that she sit up front was dim-witted. The road inclined slowly; the palace was built on the crest of the hill. Karyna felt relieved to find the city brightened as they neared the palace gates. Normal people lived closer to the outskirts of the palace.

On the higher ground Karyna viewed the ocean. The crisp blue waves washed up on a white beach. Ships were moored along the loading docks. Some were anchored farther out. She never saw a ship before. Her father told her the tale of Faral coming to Yannina on a ship. The thought that people still used them was a mystery to her. She began to find the lifestyle of Akhran intriguing.

Mammond motioned the palace guards standing at the gatehouse. The portcullis groaned with life as it was raised. Mammond led them inside. They entered a garden decorated with trees and shrubs trimmed in different shapes. The path they rode was made of interlocking brick, the color as unusual as some of the flowers. The walls that surrounded the area were covered in yellow moss. Red clovers poked through the stone.

An older man with gray hair and neatly trimmed beard approached her. He wore a long, blue robe stitched in gold. "Welcome to Akhran, Princess Karyna." He bowed before he continued, "I am Aldred, the Lord's advisor. I shall guide you to your room."

"Thank you."

"You must be exhausted after such a lengthy trip. I'll take you to your room immediately so you may rest. Lord Valhun is eager to speak with you. Rest now, so you may speak with him this evening."

"I'm eager to meet him," she said, though she still felt nervous. Karyna stepped off the carriage and waited for the Armaments to follow. Race and his men unloaded her trunks from the back of the carriage.

Aldred led them deep into the palace. Other than its size, the palace itself was nothing spectacular. She weighed it against the Palace of Ionia in Corrona, and this one poorly compared. It was large, but boring with the usual stone walls, red carpet and guards. Aldred guided them up one flight of stairs after another. Karyna was eager to arrive at her room. It would be pleasant to lie in an unmoving bed. "We're here, Your Highness." Aldred pushed open a door and walked into a large room. Windows that opened to the ocean were spaced along the outside wall. White lace hanging from the ceiling draped across the windows. Karyna felt comfortable the moment she walked in. Aldred opened a second door across from them. "The knights may use this room; it should suit the seven of you well. There are enough beds for everyone. There is another room across the hall for the ladies, but if you prefer you may use this room as well." Sheilna whispered to Frenna. Karyna didn't need to read minds to understand what they were discussing.

"Yes, Aldred, that would be appreciated. Sheilna and Frenna do not leave my side."

Aldred smiled, "Of course. Refreshments will be brought in immediately. Lord Valhun wishes you enjoyment in your stay."

"Thank you, Aldred."

"I'm off to let Lord Valhun know of your arrival. When it's time to meet with him I shall return." Aldred bowed politely and closed the door with his exit.

Race and his men unloaded her trunks at the end of her bed and went into the adjoining room. Karyna pulled away the white lace at one of the windows and watched the ocean fade into the horizon. "I feel overwhelmed."

"There's no need for that, Karyna." Frenna said. "You can deliver the message from your father, and we'll be off in the morning."

Karyna tapped the stone wall with her nails. "I do hope my father has recovered."

"King Mel is a strong man," Sheilna replied. "I'm sure he has."

Karyna climbed into bed and sank into the soft mattress. "This feels unbelievable. I didn't realize how tired I am."

Frenna sat beside her. "Sleep, if you're needed, we'll wake you."

"Thank you," Karyna murmured as sleep overtook her.

It was later that afternoon when the knock sounded. Karyna remained dressed in her favorite gown, and her hair had been done as she liked. Strings of hair hung above her eyes, hiding the imperfection of her fat forehead. She wore a necklace of pearls dipped in gold that belonged to her mother. It comforted her. Race entered the room. He also heard the knock and knew it was time to leave. "Are you coming as well?" Karyna asked. She wasn't particularly fond of Race, but she understood why he was with them. There were only several people her father trusted to accompany her on such a trip; Race was one of them. Darych would have been her choice, but he was too important to leave Wyndhaven for such an extended time.

"The king ordered that I must remain with you at all times, Your Highness."

Karyna nodded and opened the door. "You're stunning, Princess Karyna," Aldred said as he greeted her.

"Why thank you, Aldred. I assume Lord Valhun is ready for our meeting?"

"Yes. His excitement grows with the hope of good news."

Karyna smiled and followed him down a flight of stairs and into another room. People watched her through hooded eyes. She checked over her shoulder to verify Sheilna and Frenna were behind her. Cold and nervousness threatened to overtake her. Two large doors remained closed at the end of the hall. Aldred motioned the guards on duty to open them. She entered the throne room and approached a man sitting high above the rest. Strangers stood in rows on either side with their hands behind their backs, watching her with inquisitive eyes from veiled faces. They wore black robes. Necklaces with the symbol of Akhran hung from their necks. The symbol reminded Karyna of the half-moon, but the exaggerated form appeared immoral.

Lord Valhun was also dressed in black with a red jacket and a crown of gold. Jewelry decorated his hands and shoes. The back of his chair rose high over his head with the chilling half moon carved in detail. To each side of him a woman waved a fan over his head. Karyna was shocked and disgusted with their skimpy attire. She approached Lord Valhun as close as she dared and knelt before him. Her companions followed suit.

"Rise, Princess Karyna; there is no need of that here." Her nerves threatened her speech. Lord Valhun was godlike as he looked down with intense eyes. It was unlike anything she'd ever seen. "Welcome to Akhran. I'm sorry about your father's ill health. Mel is strong. He will recover."

"Thank you, Lord Valhun." Karyna rose. His kindly tone made her feel more comfortable.

"What word do you bring for your father?"

She remembered her words. She took a deep breath and spoke as a princess should. "My father must decline." Lord Valhun bowed his head in disappointment. Karyna continued, "With all due respect, my father does not understand the commitment of war. Terrace is another beloved city to Wyndhaven. It has never threatened us. For this reason alone, my father will not raise our weapons against them. We deeply apologize for your struggles and pray your conflict will soon be resolved."

Lord Valhun shook his head. "This is bad news, Karyna. With your support it would be resolved sooner."

"I'm sorry this news upsets you, Lord Valhun. There is nothing I can do." Her father warned her they would try to convince her. Her reply was exactly what he told her to say. They would be defenseless against it. Karyna watched Lord Valhun groan in frustration. How could he even think that Wyndhaven would jump to their aide?

"Karyna, will you speak with me in private?"

Sheilna cleared her throat in warning. Karyna said, "The Wyndhaven Armaments will not leave my side."

Lord Valhun nodded in approval. "Very well, then."

In an urgent tone, Race whispered, "Your Highness!"

Karyna turned back to him. "Wait here."

Race disapproved and shook his head, but stepped back as ordered.

Karyna, Sheilna and Frenna followed Lord Valhun through a narrow door behind the throne. They passed two guards as they entered a library packed with shelves and books. Comfortable chairs faced different directions. The door slammed shut behind them. Karyna spun in panic at the sound of Sheilna and Frenna's swords sliding from their scabbards. The two Akhran guards stationed at the door had their swords drawn, but Sheilna and Frenna held their blades to their necks. Karyna shot Lord Valhun a look. "You said we would be alone."

"Very impressive," Lord Valhun admitted. "I admire women who know how to fight. I especially appreciate how well you hid your weapons with your hair."

Sheilna nodded to a chair turned away from them. "You told Karyna you would speak with her in private, though someone sits in that chair."

Karyna turned to Lord Valhun, "Why did you lie to me?"

Lord Valhun raised his hands, palms out. "I apologize. I meant no harm. I wanted you to meet my son."

The stranger rose to greet her. Karyna felt her face flush at the sight of him. She wondered if she still appeared her best. His short-clipped hair complimented his dark eyes. He wore a brown tunic that boasted broad shoulders beneath it. As he approached her, he stretched out a hand. "My name is Rowen Wilde. I am honored to meet you, Your Highness."

"I apologize if my guards startled you, Karyna." Lord Valhun said. "I should have asked you to meet with my son instead as I intended. I offer my deepest apologies."

She was tenser now than when she heard the sounds of swords drawn into the air. She nodded to Sheilna and Frenna, and the Armaments withdrew their weapons. The tension in the air eased as the weapons were sheathed. Rowen offered to take her hand. He gently kissed it and bowed to her. He was the handsomest man she had ever met.

"Please sit, Karyna." Lord Valhun motioned her over to a chair. "Rowen has been commanding my army for some time now, heading the advancements against Terrace. I thought you should listen to what he told me last night." She nodded and did as she was asked while trying to hide her trembling. She still felt his lips on the back of her hand, the warmth of his breath as it caressed her skin. Once settled into the seat, she made certain the Armaments remained close to her.

Rowen sat in the chair across from her. "Our camp was invaded a week ago by two individuals. Together they slaughtered almost a hundred of us."

"Two men?" she asked with disbelief.

"One was definitely human; I killed him myself."

Karyna looked away from his eyes. It bothered her that he had killed someone.

"The other was not human at all."

Karyna glanced back and forth between father and son. "What do you mean?"

"It was a demon. The creature was massive. My forces paled in comparison. By the time we brought the creature down, casualties were very high." It was Rowen who seemed to shake now, "I've never been so afraid."

Lord Valhun spoke, "Karyna, you must make your father believe. Terrace is controlled by evil. Its army is strengthened by these fowl demons. It leaves us little chance for survival. With Wyndhaven aiding us, we would have a chance to succeed."

Karyna shook her head in disapproval. "My father will not partake in this war. I'm sorry."

Rowen continued, "Karyna, what do you think will happen when Terrace has destroyed us? They will move their forces on Wyndhaven, and then to Corrona. Don't you understand? Your father is in this war whether he approves it or not."

Karyna had her orders. "I'm truly sorry. Until Terrace threatens our livelihood we cannot offer you our support."

Rowen shook his head in disappointment. "Then that is the way it is to be."

"I fear that our land will be destroyed and our freedom raped from our existence." Lord Valhun muttered and strode back to the throne room.

It was like a dagger to her heart. Mel warned her not to succumb to their feelings, but these were real people on hard times. Rowen started after his father and turned. "Please, return to your room."

Karyna rose from her seat. "I'm sorry."

"We will find a way to win this war. Akhran will not fall to demons."

After he left, Karyna stood silently thinking. She wondered if Sheilna and Frenna were thinking the same thing. Demons were a myth. She returned to find Race standing next to her bed. He tapped his boot on the floor. His stern look proclaimed his disappointment in her ability to follow orders. "I'm only here to protect you, Princess Karyna. We don't know these people. How do you know they can be trusted?" He was almost shouting. "Sheilna and Frenna cannot protect you by themselves!" Karyna ignored the warning. She sat down and pretended he wasn't there. A frustrated Race stormed off into the adjacent room and slammed the door behind him.

"I must admit I was a little worried at one point," Frenna admitted.

"I'm sorry," Karyna said. Sheilna mentioned something, but Karyna didn't hear; her thoughts fixed on Rowen. She lay on her back and thought about him. She fell in love with him the moment she met him. His kiss on her hand made her tingle with excitement. It was difficult to keep her emotions in check while attempting to keep her nation's interest at heart. Yet she did just that. She was proud of the way she handled it.

Karyna looked up when Frenna called her name. She held the door to the corridor open. Rowen stood in the frame with his hands behind his back. Karyna walked to greet him.

He said, "I apologize if our attitude was uncomfortable this evening. You must understand we are a country at war, and our minds are quite stressed. I hope you may find it in your heart to forgive us."

"Of course I understand."

Rowen smiled. "Thank you."

"Is there anything else?" she asked. Though careful not to show it, she hoped there was.

"Yes. I wish to re-introduce myself."

"I beg your pardon?"

Rowen bowed. "My name is Rowen Wilde, Prince of Akhran. May I have the honor of escorting you to dinner?"

Karyna's heart skipped a beat. "What is this?" she asked with a grin.

"I'm afraid we got off on the wrong foot, and I would like to make amends. Will you accompany me?"

Karyna lifted her hand and he caressed her palm with his. "I would be honored to be escorted by you." With her Armaments following, Rowen led her out of her room and down the stairs.

Karyna slept soundly in her own quarters when someone knocked at the door. She lifted her head. "Who's there?" She rubbed her eyes, unhappy to be interrupted from her pleasant dream.

"It's Race, Your Highness. I brought you something."

Karyna grunted. She rose from the divan and made certain she was properly covered. She opened the door wondering why he bothered her so late. Race appeared distraught as he acknowledged her. "Your Highness, a messenger arrived from Akhran, carrying a message for you."

She felt a tightening in her stomach from the troubled look on his face. "What news does he bring?"

Race kept his focus on the floor. "I brought you the letter immediately. Your father hasn't seen it."

"Thank you." He handed her a small parchment. Hidden inside she could see red. Race backed away and Karyna closed the door. She was flushed as she unrolled the parchment. Her hands trembled and she felt faint at the two simple words written in blood. She dropped the note and covered her mouth. Unsure, she shouted for Frenna and Sheilna. They barged into her room with worried expressions.

"What is it?" they both asked.

"Something awful has happened to Rowen."

Chapter 22

Darych exited onto Ebury Street, slightly confused. The sudden disappearance of Larnen contradicted everything he believed in. He replayed their conversation over in his mind and hoped he wasn't losing his mind. He moved swiftly. The king must be told of the attack on Ruhln…even if he harbored doubts. Demons were a myth. Still, when he compared the information of Larnen and Ray, he wasn't quite so sure.

Wyndhaven waited at the end of the street with the steep mountain range known as the Angled Spine appearing like a shadow from behind the castle's keep. There were shops, ale houses and trade booths on either side. A scream startled Darych. From the depths of the alleyway came the figure of a skinny little man, his arms loaded with an assortment of items. He stumbled against the side of a building and dropped several of the items. He regained his balance, muttered something about a clumsy wall, hiked up his pants and ran. He was thin and short, his clothing barely covered his privates. A large woman with an angry red face swung a broom in the air as she chased him out of the alleyway shrieking, "Thief! Thief! Stop him!"

Darych cut the thief off with his outstretched arm. The thief landed on the ground in a grunt. Darych yanked him to his feet. "I didn't do it!" The thief's fiery, red hair was a tangled mess that shot out in every direction.

"Who are you trying to fool?" Darych asked.

The large woman still screamed and swung her broom hitting the thief and Darych. The fat lady spluttered, "People like you are the reason why good folk have to work twice as hard to make a living." She whacked the thief again and gathered her belongings. Once she had them all she popped him again and marched back the way she came.

"What do you have to say for yourself?" Darych asked him.

The thief reeked of onion. "I swear I didn't do it." He lisped through missing teeth.

Darych scowled. "I'm not a fool! I saw what happened."

"I told the truth!" The thief tried to squirm away, but he was no match for Darych.

"Then tell me who did."

"It was my dog Scruff!" he shouted. "Come here, Scruff. There he is.

Come on, Boy!"

There wasn't a dog in sight. "Get out of here. If I ever see you around again I'll run my sword through you." Darych pushed him away.

The thief smiled with gratitude and raced down the road calling his invisible dog. Darych hoped he would never see the little thief again, but he had the feeling he wouldn't be so lucky. Darych had no time to deal with thieves. The king needed to hear what had been spoken this night on Ebury Street.

Knights of the Wyndhaven Forces waited for him at the castle gate. Four of them guarded the entrance. Darych checked the towers to see if the beacons were lit. It was a sign that all was well within. Should trouble arise, the torches were snuffed out. "Commander Darych, you're late coming in for the night," one of the knights said to him.

Darych recognized the voice. "Evening, Rhyus. I spent some time studying the bottom of a glass." He winked at the knight and his comrade smiled.

"Well done, Sir. We appreciate it when you take some time for yourself."

Darych took a relaxing breath as he checked over his shoulder. Wyndhaven had lived in peace for years. Because of the war between Akhran and Terrace, Darych didn't let the guard at Wyndhaven falter at any time. As long as there was a war in Yannina, it was crucial to keep a close eye on their surroundings. "Was there anything unusual tonight?" he asked.

Rhyus shook his head. "There hasn't been a chirp. Somewhat boring, if you ask."

Darych frowned. "You should be grateful for boring." As he mentioned it, he remembered feeling the same way only a short time ago. "Open the gate; I must speak with the king and get to bed."

"Yes, Commander," Rhyus replied.

The gates swung open and Darych entered the courtyard. The stables were on the west end near the stairs that rose up to the outer wall. Two knights would be stationed there. Darych knew David and Haryld had the duty. A narrow moat circled the castle walls. The drawbridge was lowered for him. Two knights approached him from the inside. "Welcome home, Commander Darych."

"Anything happen while I was out?" he asked Lyle. There wasn't any other way into the castle other than through the front gates, and they wouldn't be likely to tell him any different than the four guarding the outside walls, but he thought it was important to interrogate everyone since one man's opinion of a quiet evening may differ from another.

"It was another quiet night in the Castle of Wyndhaven."

Darych patted him on the shoulder. "Good work. Enjoy your night."

"Thank you, Commander."

Darych loosened his breast plate as he walked into the main hall. It was empty except for two knights standing guard at the entrance to the throne room. The room was poorly lit because the source of light in the main hall was dependant on the sun. Only a few candles were lit in wall sconces to help him navigate. The distant sounds of wind traversing through the hollow shafts of the castle seemed to echo through the ceiling. Darych never liked the sound. He remembered when he was young and crawled into one of the shafts. They were the size of a carriage wheel and perfectly round. All of them were located high on the walls, accessible only with a ladder. After crawling a short distance, the wind was so unbearable he had to turn away. He chose several others and tried to explore, but with every one he found the same thing. Where the wind came from is what baffled him most.

His curiosity about the wind in the shafts died with his parents. He would never forget finding their bodies torn apart on the kitchen floor. He was just a child, and it took years for him to recover. News about it reached the king and Mel took Darych under his protection. After a few years living under his care, Darych decided to train with the Wyndhaven Forces. He adapted so well that he moved up the ranks faster than anyone in their history. He used the death of his parents as inspiration, swearing that once he was commander, no child would ever have to worry about violence in their kingdom. It was a large task to uphold, but Darych pledged to do his best.

The Wyndhaven Forces never solved the murder of his parents. A year after it happened, a similar event took place with a child called Race. Just as Mel took Darych under his care, he did the same with Race. Darych was older than Race. They didn't become close friends as the king wished. However, they respected one another. Darych admired Race in many ways, but off duty the man always seemed displaced and distant.

There were a string of murders after that. It was believed to be the work of the same evil person because of similarities between the gruesome killings. The Wyndhaven Forces failed to apprehend the killer. Eventually, the murders stopped. There was unfinished business there, and Darych always hoped he could solve the mystery.

"Darych," someone said from behind him.

Darych closed his thoughts. Karyna and the Armaments approached him. "Where's Race?" she asked him.

Of all the things he expected to hear from her, this was not it. She was known to dislike Race. His suspicions were roused. "What are you up to?"

"Have you seen him?" Karyna asked him again, keeping something hidden in her hands.

"What is that?"

She tucked it behind her back. "Have you seen Race or not?"

"No, what do you have?"

She handed him a small parchment. On it were two words written in blood. "Where did you get this?"

"Race gave it to me. He said a messenger brought it from Akhran."

That made no sense to Darych. None of his knights spoke of a messenger. "When did you get this?"

"Not long ago. I must speak with this messenger right away."

Darych took a deep breath. This was not what he needed right now. Surely she planned to run after Rowen now. "Return to your room and I will search this out."

Sheilna and Frenna stared at one another, and offered a hint of approval to Karyna.

"No, I must speak with this messenger. I need to know what this is about."

"This is my job, Karyna, not yours. I will locate Race immediately and ask him why he thought he should take this to you without consulting the king. I promise to speak to the messenger and give you any information I gather."

The stress of the situation was eating at her. "Thank you," she said quietly. "Please let me know as soon as you find out something." She turned and the Armaments followed her back through the dark hall.

Darych couldn't help but feel trouble was at hand with rumors that Ruhln had fallen, along with this mysterious letter. First he would speak to the king. He headed for the king's chambers and knocked on the door.

"Who's there?" asked the king from the other side of the door.

"It is Darych, My Lord."

"Come in, then."

The king was in bed reading notes from the lone candle on his night stand. "I apologize for disturbing you so late, My Lord."

"What brings you to my room so late at night?"

"I have some worries."

Mel straightened himself and pushed his back into several pillows. "Explain them to me."

"I heard a rumor that the town of Ruhln was invaded and destroyed."

Mel gasped. "Are you certain? Who invaded Ruhln?"

"It is rumored to be a demon army. Demons don't exist."

The king placed his hand over his heart. "Any idea when this might have happened?"

"I'm not certain. My source on this isn't strong, as it's only a rumor."

Mel closed his eyes and sank into his bed. For a moment he lay there in silence. Then he said, "I have friends in Ruhln, Darych. One in particular is a very close friend." He opened his eyes and motioned for Darych to sit on the bed. "You mentioned your source, what was it?"

"I shared a drink with a traveler at the Tooth and Tavern. He told me he was from northern Yannina. During his travels he heard about the attack on Ruhln. His tale caused me concern because the owner of the inn just told me his shipments from Ruhln were late…for the first time."

Mel wrinkled his brow. "Where is this man now?"

Darych found it difficult to explain to the King of Wyndhaven that the man they spoke of had simply disappeared. "I don't know. I stood and when I turned to him, he was gone."

Mel leaned forward. "I beg your pardon?"

"This is the very reason I'm not sure if the source is reliable. I remember the conversation with this man perfectly, but his disappearance troubles me. I almost wonder if I dreamed the whole thing."

"Nonsense, were there any distinguishing marks on this man?"

Darych tried to remember. "He was a big man named Larnen." He took a breath of air and scratched his itchy beard. "He had an *f* tattooed on his neck."

Mel reached for his shoulder, and whispered, "Tell me that again."

Darych glanced at the king, and wondered why he suddenly seemed so tense. "There was a tattoo on his neck of the letter *f*."

Mel placed his hand over his heart. "That man, Darych, was a messenger from God."

"I don't believe that. Faral doesn't exist."

"That is blasphemy. Don't hate Faral for the murder of your parents. He can't save us all."

Darych focused on the door to the hall. The image of his parents torn apart on their kitchen floor flashed through his mind. "Please don't remind me of that."

"Forgive me, Darych. The man who spoke with you was sent by Faral to inform you of what has happened in Ruhln. You must go there. Take some of your men. Find my friend and assist him in any way possible. Will you do this for me?"

Darych tried to clear his mind. Faral didn't exist. It's what he believed, and though he never questioned others and their beliefs, he always thought he deserved the respect to have his ideals left well enough alone. The king always preached of Faral, but Darych wanted nothing to do with it. He forced himself to concentrate on the matters at hand, hoping the king would leave the subject of Faral alone. "Of course I will. Do you honestly believe that Ruhln was invaded by demons?"

Mel cleared his throat. "Not necessarily, but Faral works in mysterious ways. Take the men that are closest to you. That way, should you encounter trouble, you will have the strength to prevail."

"What if an attack comes on Wyndhaven in my absence?"

"There are thousands of knights in our reserves. We'll be fine."

"I'll leave Race here in my place while I'm away."

"Good," Mel said. "When you arrive in Ruhln, and if it was attacked, send word immediately."

"I will." Darych remembered two reasons to speak with the king. "There's something else. I must talk to Race to find out exactly what happened, but somehow he received a parchment from Akhran and gave it to Karyna. It is written in blood." He handed the king the note.

The king read it. "What has that girl gotten into?"

Darych frowned. "I ran into Karyna on my way to see you. She was looking to speak with this messenger herself."

"Where is the messenger?"

"My knights reported nothing out of the ordinary tonight. Something isn't right."

"I'll speak to Karyna in the morning. We must use caution. Something feels bad about this." He tucked the note into his pocket. "Let me handle this. I want you to concentrate on getting to Ruhln."

"What are you going to do with her?"

"I'm not sure what to do with her. Her hatred for me seems to increase daily."

"It isn't hatred, only frustration." Darych reassured him.

"Perhaps I made a mistake when I forbad her to marry. I may have sacrificed our relationship forever. I wish her mother were alive."

"She's just stubborn. One day she'll grow out of it."

Mel sighed. "Thank you, Darych, your service and friendship is deeply appreciated."

Darych smiled. "Thank you."

"Don't worry about Karyna and this note, I can handle that. You find my friend."

Darych walked to the door. "I'll leave first thing in the morning, and I'll have Race report to you regarding this letter. Rest well, My Lord." He reached for the handle. "Oh," he said, "you haven't told me the name of your friend."

"His name is Darren Caynne."

Chapter 23

Karyna sat at the end of her divan, basking in the morning sunlight. Her doubts and worries about Rowen left her depressed. She wished she had her mother. Sheilna and Frenna would always be there for her, and for that she was eternally grateful, but their love would never be the same as a mother's love. It bothered her that she could barely remember what her mother looked like. She would never forget her smile or her red hair, but it was all her memory could surface. The void that grew between her and her father didn't help. She didn't want to talk to him. It was a long time since she had a real conversation with him that didn't progress into an argument. As soon as they were in the same room together, both of them tensed up and searched for an excuse to leave.

Before she received the letter, there was hope that Rowen would take her away from Wyndhaven to begin a life with him in Akhran. Sometimes she wondered if her feelings for him stemmed from her need to be rescued. She sometimes admitted that her love for him was dead, and the only reason she hung onto it was to find a way out of Wyndhaven. That all changed when she read the message. Deep down her love for Rowen was still there. The fact that he needed her rekindled those feelings. She remembered that first night they dined together when they sat across from each other on a balcony that overlooked the ocean.

"Tell me about Wyndhaven," Rowen asked her.

"Wyndhaven is rather boring."

Rowen smiled. "I don't know much about southern Yannina, but I've heard that Corrona is spectacular."

Karyna nodded, "It is, actually. I've traveled there often. The Palace of Ionia is amazingly high, built with white marble and tempered glass. The rest of southern Yannina is a bit of a bore. There are many small villages scattered through eastern Ruhln."

Rowen smiled. "What about Wyndhaven?"

"There is nothing unusual about Wyndhaven."

"I've heard stories about Wyndhaven since childhood. I assure you, they were very interesting."

She looked skeptical. "You heard stories about Wyndhaven?"

"I heard that Wyndhaven has strange walls filled with tunnels and shafts. Nobody understands what they were used for."

Karyna knew what he spoke of, but she wasn't interested in discussing it. She wanted to know more about him. "I've never learned anything of interest about Wyndhaven."

The meal was some of the best food she had eaten. She sipped her wine wondering how her father would feel if he knew she was drinking wine.

"Karyna, would you come for a walk with me?"

Karyna felt giddy from the wine. "I would like that."

Rowen rose from his seat took her hand. Karyna remembered grasping that firm hand when she first met him. "Will your ladies be accompanying us?" he asked.

Sheilna and Frenna stood farther back on the balcony. Both had looks of concern. "I'm sorry, Rowen, but they must remain with me at all times. We won't even know they're around."

Rowen took her arm with his and led them off the balcony. She felt the flush and knew it was the same color as the setting sun. The sound of the ocean waves crashed against a cliff wall as they climbed another set of stairs. An arched opening waited at the highest step with the colored sky as a backdrop from the other side. The jagged rooftops of the palace were higher behind them, and Karyna almost felt lost on the edge of the world. There were others who walked the wall enjoying the view. Karyna loved the orange and red in the sky as the sun sank into the ocean. The breeze brought the taste of the ocean with it.

"Tell me about your guards," Rowen asked her as they walked. "I was very impressed with their quickness."

Karyna made certain her ladies were still following them. Sheilna and Frenna held their distance. They smiled when she checked on them. "Sheilna and Frenna belong to a faction known as the Wyndhaven Armaments. The Armaments were started long ago by my ancestors. They are the sole protectors of the queen and her children. They are widely respected in Wyndhaven. They train with the Wyndhaven Forces. They have the capability to protect me. Neither of them leaves my side. Their quarters are next to mine. They are my dear friends, and since my mother passed away, they have been so much more."

"You are fortunate to have people around you with such commitment. You won't find that kind of dedication in Akhran."

Karyna smiled. "They are everything to me."

"Look at this." Rowen pointed down to the ocean. "This happens almost every night."

Karyna peered down at the ocean waves. Thousands of red canaries skimmed over the ocean flying at full speed toward the bottom of the wall. Just as she thought they were going to collide with the rock, they dipped their wings and swirled upward. Karyna shouted with awe as they soared far above the wall. The sunlight sparkled through the clouds of wings as the canaries danced in the sky. She glanced at Rowen and laughed with joy. The little birds flew up and up as if pushed by a current of wind. They spun and spiraled back down to the ocean waves. Before plummeting into the water they pulled up and flew back the way they came.

"They're so beautiful!" she exclaimed.

"Akhran has its treasures," he replied.

Karyna realized she was clinging to his midsection and pulled away, embarrassed. Rowen smiled and moved his arm around her shoulders. They followed the wall around to the eastern side of the palace where she could view the shores of northern Yannina. Off in the horizon, a cloud of smoke strung into the sky.

"What is that?" she asked when she felt his body tense.

At first he remained silent. "That smoke comes from Faradawn, a small town near the mouth of Bile'd Canyon. I think Garret has attacked it."

Even though she knew a war was in progress, it was no part of her life. Now, as she saw the smoke billow into the sky, reality struck. The smoke was forever away, yet the sight made her sick to her stomach. War was something she didn't want to experience. "Who is Garret?"

"Garret Landen is the leader of the Terrace army and my fiercest enemy."

Karyna disliked the angry tone of his voice. "I'm sorry, Rowen."

"Don't be sorry, it isn't your problem."

She didn't know what to say. "I could speak with my father upon my return."

"No," he quickly replied. "I don't want you part of this war anymore.

My father and I will try other methods to win the battle. We are building a fleet of airships to give us the upper hand if they're finished in time."

"What are airships?" Karyna asked. She had never heard of such a thing.

"It's a ship that flies," Rowen said. "I would love to show you one, but I must report to my father. We must retaliate immediately. Garret must not get away with this so close to our capital."

Karyna pulled away from his arm, upset that their night was over. "If you must go, be safe."

"Karyna, maybe if . . . ." He touched her arm. "You're shaking."

"I know." She didn't know if it was because he was running back to his war, or if it was because she had to say goodbye. "Is there something wrong?"

"Yes."

Rowen caressed her face and kissed her. She kissed him back. His lips were everything she dreamed of.

"Is that better?" he whispered.

"Yes."

The sound of a sword whooshing through the air grew in volume before it stopped abruptly. Karyna turned to see a man dressed in unusual clothing with a sword in his chest.

Rowen ushered her toward a palace door. "Run!"

Shouting erupted as intruders climbed over the wall, weapons drawn as they charged. The clothing they wore flickered in the sunlight, almost like a ghost weaving through darkness. Sheilna retrieved her weapon from the intruder's chest and joined Rowen and Karyna. More men dropped from the roof to block the door they ran for. Frenna arrived in time to take them on. Neither of them had a chance as she cut them in half. Sheilna dove behind them, deflecting a knife as it whistled through the air.

"Get into the palace!" Sheilna shouted.

When they passed one of the dead men, Rowen took his sword. He kicked the door open and shoved Karyna inside. They were in a large room with windows opening out to the outside wall. Glass shattered as intruders leapt into the room. "Rowen!" she screamed. He pulled her back and charged the two men. The first one ducked and rushed to Karyna. She screamed, raising her arms to shield her face. The man raised his weapon just as Frenna struck him down. She rushed to Rowen's aid.

Sheilna stood at Karyna's side. "Are you all right?"

Rowen yelped as the other intruder cut his shoulder with a knife, and before Frenna could do it, Rowen stabbed the man through his chest.

"Who are these people?" Sheilna demanded.

"They must be assassins sent from Terrace," Rowen said. "They're wearing clothing sewn with some sort of craft or spell. It must be how they managed to infiltrate our guards. I believe we killed them all."

Frenna sheathed her sword. "Karyna, we must return to Wyndhaven first thing in the morning."

Karyna was appalled at the sight of blood, but grateful it wasn't hers. "Yes, we must."

"I'm dreadfully sorry, Karyna." Rowen covered his shoulder wound with his hand.

Before she could reply, Sheilna and Frenna took her by each arm and led her back into the palace. Later that night, she stared out at the ocean's white breakers in the moonlight, listening to them crash onto the banks. It had been a beautiful night until they were attacked. Their kiss would be a memory she cherished forever. Now she was depressed. Rowen had surely run back to his army, and tomorrow she would return home.

Race was extremely upset when he found out what happened. Sheilna told her they would not be leaving her room until their departure. Lord Valhun personally apologized, but it didn't make amends with those who protected her.

A shooting star split the sky. Karyna made a wish.

"Wasn't that beautiful?" someone whispered.

Karyna looked around. She heard Race and his knight's muffled voices in the opposite room. Sheilna was asleep on her bed while Frenna kept watch near the exit.

"Over here," she heard.

Karyna peered out the window and saw Rowen. "How did you get there?"

He sat far on the left with his legs dangling over the edge. It was a three-story drop to the courtyard. "Come out here."

Karyna shook her head. "They won't allow it."

"Just for a moment," Rowen pleaded. "I pledge on my life you will be safe."

She hesitated, knowing she would love to spend more time with him.

"You have until they realize I'm missing. It won't be long."

"Here, I'll help you." The roof line was the same height as the bottom of the window, so it wasn't as difficult as she thought. She followed Rowen down to the ledge and sat next to him. "I'm sorry about what happened earlier."

"I'm fine," she replied. "How is your shoulder?"

He touched his shoulder. "Good as new."

"I had a wonderful night until they tried to kill us."

"So did I," he said with a smile.

"I thought you left to join your army."

"Father sent Mammond when he found out about the attack on Faradawn. Mammond is a good general; he'll be able to handle things until I arrive."

"When are you leaving?"

"I won't leave until tomorrow. I've been away too long already. I only meant to stay overnight, but I was held back."

"Held back? What do you mean?"

Rowen stared into her eyes. She loved it when he did that. "I mean you." He kissed her. He held her in his arms and let her head rest comfortably on his chest.

"I don't want you to go back to war, especially now that I've experienced it first hand. I couldn't imagine what it would be like to be in the middle of a terrible battle."

"It's my obligation, Karyna. Be assured that I'm safe at all times. I am not permitted to fight. I'm there to direct the battle stratagem, not to fight."

"Still, your life is in danger as it was tonight."

"That's what bothers me most. I let my guard down tonight."

She sighed. "When will I see you again?"

"Soon, I think." He paused and said, "Karyna?"

"Yes?"

"You're having an effect on me." Karyna smiled. She hoped that she did. She trembled, but it didn't register. She had been trembling with excitement…or fear most of the day. Rowen placed her hand over his heart. "Do you feel that?"

She felt his steady heartbeat, "Yes."

"I give it to you, Karyna—for tonight—for tomorrow—forever. What you decide to do with it is your decision. I hope you will never break it."

Her eyes glistened with tears. She felt his lips on hers once again. "I won't break it," she whispered to him after their kiss. They sat together in silence and watched the stars.

"Maybe I won't go back tomorrow," Rowen finally said. "Will you stay in Akhran for another day?"

"I would love that," she replied. "Though Sheilna and Frenna will take some convincing." She glanced over at the window. Frenna stood at the window with her back to them as if she wasn't listening. Karyna would thank her for not interrupting them, or forcing her to return to the room. She rested her head on his shoulder and wished the sun would never rise.

Karyna was jarred back to reality when a cold draft gave her a chill. She pulled a blanket over her legs. She continued to think about those days she spent with Rowen. She had stayed two more days after the assassination attempt. Rowen learned that the Terrace army withdrew into Bile'd Canyon, so he didn't have to leave as soon. Those days with him were the sweetest of her life. Rowen proposed to her the night before she left. Karyna, too, felt they were meant to be together. When she left the following day, her heart was torn. She didn't want to return to Wyndhaven.

Now; however, enough was enough. Her father repeatedly scorned her relationship as nothing more than a foolish child's infatuation. Not permitting her to wed was ridiculous. She thought it blind stupidity for him to tell everyone he was not part of the war. She knew Rowen spoke the truth. The last time she heard from him, they were trying to stop the Terrace army from advancing south. Still, her father would not render aide. And now the mysterious message arrived. She recognized his writing and prayed the blood was not his own. She had to do something about it. Even though the strangeness of the message hinted that she could be riding to trouble, she knew she would be safe. She knew Rowen was alive and would protect her. A knock sounded and she opened the door. Her father poked his head in. "How are you this morning?"

"I haven't slept all night." She didn't believe he cared.

King Mel walked into her room and cleared his throat. "I come to speak with you about this message you received."

"Did Darych give it to you? He told me he was going to find the messenger and speak with him."

"I sent Darych to Ruhln, so I told him I would handle the letter." King Mel handed her the wrinkled parchment. "It is troubling indeed."

"I have to find him. You know I must go."

He shook his head. "It's a trap, Karyna. It must be a trap."

Karyna paced the cold floor. "That is why I wanted to speak with the messenger. I might know who he is. Rowen would only send a message like this with someone I knew. I became acquainted with several of his military officers, Father."

"I can't let you speak with him. Your judgment may be impaired by your feelings. You must remain at the castle."

Karyna slammed the parchment against his chest. "You imprison me in this castle. You know this is authentic. You distort the truth and keep me from the messenger. Farewell, Father." She withdrew her hand from his chest; the note slipped to the floor. The door from the adjacent room opened. Sheilna and Frenna entered with concern on their faces. Karyna was grateful for the thin wall that separated her room with theirs. She needed their support now more than ever.

"Karyna, please . . . ." Mel said.

She ignored the heartbreak on his face, because she thought it was just another ploy. Her gaze shifted to the note on the floor. The words *help me* beckoned her. It was time to speak with the messenger herself.

Chapter 24

Karyna entered the stables and searched the stalls for the messenger's horse. The few horses there all wore the Wyndhaven brand. The feeling that someone she trusted might hide information from her darkened her mood. "Most of the stalls are empty. The rest are our horses," Frenna announced.

Karyna almost snapped at her, but caught herself before she did. It wasn't their fault others in the castle tried to deceive her. "I see that. Where are all the horses?"

"Darych may have taken them for his trip to Ruhln," Sheilna said as she opened the top gate to one of the stalls. A brown mare greeted her and Sheilna petted the horse's long neck. "He would have used all of these horses before taking them from their reserves outside of the castle."

Karyna never felt more frustrated. "I suppose the messenger walked here from Akhran."

Sheilna glanced at Frenna. "We should speak with Race."

Again Karyna bit back a sharp retort. She reminded herself they were there to help. "Is there anywhere we haven't searched that we might find him?"

A knight of the Wyndhaven Forces came into the stables and removed his helmet.

Karyna recognized him at once. "Race, where have you been?"

"I spoke with your father," he answered.

"Where is the messenger?" Karyna demanded.

Race frowned. "He left. He told me he had to return to Akhran immediately."

"Didn't anyone tell you I wanted to speak with him?" She felt like pulling out her hair.

Race scratched his chin. "He only left a few moments ago. You could catch him. He went east, but said he was in a hurry, so he may try to cut through the forest."

"I don't believe this," she said. "All I wanted was to speak with him. If I lose that opportunity, I'll be quite upset."

"Karyna," Sheilna began, "I'm not certain leaving the castle would be wise."

"Then stay," she said bluntly. "Rowen sent a message asking for my help. Something is amiss about this whole thing; all I want is to speak with this messenger. I'll get to the bottom of this myself." She marched down the stalls until she found her horse. She lifted the saddle onto the horse's back, something she never did before. Frenna helped strap it on.

"Are you going to ride in a dress?" Sheilna asked with a crooked grin.

"There's no time to change." Karyna led her horse down the center row of the stables. She wasn't about to trek halfway though the castle and back so that she could wear the proper attire.

"We're coming with you," Frenna said.

"Then get ready," Karyna responded. She pointed at Race. "Tell my father what I'm doing, and have him prepared to send help to Akhran."

"I'll deliver the message." Race slid his helmet on and walked out the door.

Karyna nudged her heels and flicked the reins. Sheilna and Frenna scrambled to mount their horses; they yelled at her to wait. There was no time to lose. She must catch that elusive messenger before he was lost to her forever. She was relieved to find the castle gates swung open. There were many horse-mounted knights around the entrance. They had three wagons loaded with supplies. Karyna slowed and guided her horse through the crowded entrance. A few of the knights cast her confused looks, but moved out of her way. Sheilna and Frenna caught up with her; together they passed through the gate.

Ebury Street was crowded. Karyna snapped the reins and turned down an alleyway. The smell of foul meat made her gag. She rarely visited the towns outside of the castle. She followed the alleyway as it turned through the back end of the town. Clothes hung out windows to dry. The houses and shops were rundown, their exteriors dark with excessive rot. Karyna thought she made good progress when they exited the alleyway. The distant tree line of the Ruhln Forest was in clear sight, and she knew the road would be farther south. She pulled her gelding to halt and pondered her course.

"What are you thinking?" Sheilna asked her.

"I don't know which way to go. The messenger either took the road or tried to save time by cutting through the forest."

"No matter what he does, he will eventually have to pass through Palher. It is the only route into the Angled Spine."

"Then we'll travel the forest. Maybe we can catch up to him by then."

"We'll find him," Frenna assured her.

Sheilna said. "Let's go."

"Wait," Karyna said. "I want to thank you both for coming with me."

There was always something warm about Sheilna's smile that Karyna found comforting. "We'll always be here for you," she said.

Frenna nodded.

Karyna repeated, "Thank you."

Sheilna rode her horse in front of her, offering her a grin of support. "Karyna, it's an honor to serve you." She swung her horse around. "Now come, if we want to be home by nightfall, we best be moving."

Sheilna and Frenna sent their steeds into a full gallop. Karyna watched them ride with an astonished smile, wondering what her life would have been like had it not been for them. She snapped the reins, eager to catch the others.

Chapter 25

Rhyus handed Darych Shade the reins of his horse. "We're ready to depart on your word. Chad will ride point. He's anxious as always."

"We can be off then." Darych mounted his horse and shifted his sword once he was in the saddle. He loved how the great blade flashed in the sunlight. Rhyus moved to the front of the line. Darych quickly counted twenty-seven. They were some of his best men. He knew if they found trouble along the way he would need them. He thought it was smarter to take a few of his best men, instead of those who needed time to develop their skills. It seemed foolish to send him to Ruhln on the basis of a mysterious rumor. The king believed Larnen was a messenger of God, that Faral sent him to inform them of an attack. Darych thought it made more sense to send a messenger to Ruhln first to confirm it. If the rumor was true, they could send aide immediately. Instead, Mel insisted he leave immediately with his most loyal knights. It was no secret that Mel strongly believed in Faral, but the whole thing felt absurd.

After his conversation with Larnen, he didn't know what to believe. It almost made sense when he placed the appropriate facts in order, although he just couldn't consider that demons attacked small villages. Darych suspected they would travel all the way to Ruhln, and find it business as normal, proving Larnen was not a messenger sent by Faral; just a normal man who managed to duck out of sight quickly. It was the most logical explanation.

The knights of the Wyndhaven Forces rode in single file with the three supply wagons at the rear. Darych waited for them to pass, nodding to them as they saluted him. They were his close friends, some of them much like family. He recruited and trained most of them. Darych never knew war in his lifetime because Wyndhaven was blessed with peace.

His thoughts were diverted when he noticed Karyna and her Armaments pass through the castle gate. He found it slightly disturbing; she should never ride a horse in a gown, especially one that appeared to be used for special occasions. He scratched at his beard, trying to understand what she was up to. Quite often she did things that made him shake his head at her, but this was different. Something wasn't right. It had to do with the note and the mystery of the messenger, who according to his men, didn't exist.

Lieutenant Race approached him as the rest of his men exited through the gates. "Darych, I've re-scheduled the shifts to accommodate the men you're taking and added posts throughout the villages as requested."

"Good."

"Is there anything else I need to do in your absence?"

Darych continued to stare after Princess Karyna as Race awaited his answer. "Race, did you speak with the king as I asked?"

"Yes. After our conversation, King Mel left to speak with Karyna." Darych tapped his fingers on the handle of his sword. "Why do you ask?"

"I'm worried. Princess Karyna stormed out of the castle on her horse wearing only a dress."

Race pointed after her. "I mentioned to her that the messenger left. She wants to catch him."

"What!" Darych gasped; astounded that Race would allow such a thing. "We've tried so hard to keep her out of trouble, and you let her run off to seek it first hand? I can't believe you permitted her to do that."

"My apologies, I don't know what I was thinking."

"When did this messenger arrive last night?"

David and Haryld greeted the messenger and helped him to the stables. I took the messenger to a guestroom."

Darych remembered his return to the castle that night. David and Haryld were the only two guards he didn't speak to. It was possible they welcomed a messenger during the shift change. He needed to pursue the matter a little more. "You took an unknown soldier into the castle?"

Race nodded. "The look on your face implies that I made another mistake. I left him heavily guarded and went to find Karyna."

Darych respected Race, but his actions made him rethink that Race was ready for command. "There is war in Yannina. As long as that war exists, we must always be cautious. If anything happens out of the ordinary while I'm away, take immediate action. Don't second guess anything."

Race repeated, "My apologies."

"I will go after Karyna and ask her to return home, and then I will question the messenger. After that I'll join my men on their journey to Ruhln. If Ruhln was invaded, I'll send word to you first. You must inform the king. Most important, I want you to send word to Corrona. King Oland is a great ally."

"Consider it done. Have a safe journey, Commander Shade." Race saluted him. His expression showed the stress of his errors.

Darych said, "Forget your mistakes, just be certain not to make them again."

Race appeared on the watchtower and waved farewell as the Wyndhaven Forces slowly descended Ebury Street. Darych saw him and fought his suspicions. He snapped the reins and sped to the front of the line. "Chad, something requires my attention; I will catch up to you by nightfall."

"Is everything all right?"

Darych smiled. "I need to find Princess Karyna and set her course straight."

"Good luck."

Darych left his knights behind and headed into the crowded villages of Ebury Street. King Mel trusted the knights to protect his daughter. He would fail his king, and his friend, should something happen to Karyna. Race let her leave the castle without a hint of concern. What concerned him the most was that in the worst situation, the Armaments wouldn't be enough to protect her. Karyna didn't understand the brutalities of war. Terrace would kill her just to spite their enemy. When Karyna fell in love with Rowen, she unknowingly put herself in grave danger. The histories of their world stated as much, and history had a way of repeating itself. Karyna failed to recognize that the message might be a ploy from the enemy. No, he thought, he had to give Karyna the benefit of the doubt. She wasn't as naïve as many thought her to be. Perhaps she only wanted to recognize the truth. King Mel never believed Karyna's feelings were true love for Rowen. He was convinced that her feelings resulted from the devastating loss of her mother. It always seemed ridiculous to Darych, but it was a possibility. He would insist that Karyna return home, and if he had time, he would search for the messenger to ease his suspicions of Race. Then it would be off to Ruhln to find a man named Darren Caynne.

Chapter 26

Karyna and the Armaments rode east through Ruhln Forest. The trees were evenly spaced as if someone from long ago had planted them perfectly. It created a mirror effect that caused her to keep watch on the mountains, to be certain they stayed their course. Suddenly, Frenna yelled, "Stop!" and slowed her horse. "Something's wrong."

Sheilna's horse pranced and snorted as she pulled back the reins, "What is it?"

"It's colder, but the sun still shines. Can you feel it?"

Karyna felt the chill and was confused why they felt it was a problem.

"I feel it," Sheilna said. "The breeze is cold. It could be a wind off the mountain."

Frenna shook her head. "In the afternoon the wind changes direction. This wind comes from the south."

Karyna felt the cold strengthen. "What does it mean?"

All three horses were skittish. Frenna's horse spun in a fuss and nearly threw her. "They're nervous," she said.

Karyna held her breath. "Perhaps we've caught up with the messenger."

Sheilna unsheathed her sword. "I don't think that's it."

Karyna felt her heart gain speed. "You're frightening me."

Frenna motioned her horse ahead. "Look there."

Karyna stared through the open forest. The sun felt hot on her neck but the wind brushing up against her legs felt cold. Tall grass wept toward the ground, and as the wind bobbed it up and down they all saw a red object hidden within. It was far enough away they couldn't identify it completely. Karyna's peripheral vision caught movement. When she turned to search the area, there was nothing. "What do you think it is?" she asked.

"I feel like we're being watched," Frenna said.

"I don't like this," Sheilna added. "We should return to Wyndhaven."

"No," Karyna insisted. "I must speak with that messenger."

Sheilna nodded and turned her horse. "Frenna, stay here with her. I'm going to find out what that is."

"Be careful."

Sheilna rode toward the red object. Karyna watched intently, staring around them as she nudged her horse closer to Frenna. The cold wind fell calm. Silence sifted through the trees. Sheilna alit from the horse and knelt down at the red object. "It's a young man. He's dead," she called out.

"Is it the messenger?" Karyna yelled back.

Sheilna shook her head. "I don't believe so. He doesn't appear to be a knight at all." She rose and mounted her horse. Suddenly, darkness rained down from above. Dark, ugly, deformed creatures screeched and hissed as they dropped from the treetops thudding onto the soft ground. Karyna screamed. She lost count as more and more appeared. Her terrified horse rose to its hind legs inadvertently bucking her off. She slid off the saddle and landed flat on her back. Frenna yelled encouragement to Sheilna and dismounted her horse. Their attacker's grotesque bodies were slouched forward; they wielded long claws that seeped fluid from the tips. Their red eyes resembled burning flames hiding behind long straggly hair. Sheilna was surrounded by the vile creatures but she fought them off.

"Sheilna," Karyna screamed. The creatures charged Karyna where she'd backed up against the trunk of a tree. Frenna moved in front of her to cut them off. She slammed her sword into those closest. The creatures bunched together claws extended. Frenna was forced to fight many at the same time. Sheilna ran toward them screaming at Karyna to take cover. One of the creatures jumped high into the air and landed on Sheilna's back. The impact knocked her to the ground. A second creature joined its comrade; together they sunk their claws into her body.

Frenna took a blow in her midsection. She screamed in agony, but continued to fight. Karyna moaned in disbelief as the creatures outnumbered the Armaments. Many of the vile things were all over Sheilna, mutilating her poor body. Blood sprayed the air as one of the creatures sliced through her leg. Before she fell, she killed another. She managed to kill two more and regain her balance. Frenna shrieked in a mix of fury and agony as the remaining creatures attacked at once. Sheilna, her body covered in blood, crawled through the grass on her belly. She used every ounce of strength to slither forward, crying out to Karyna. Karyna shivered at the sight of her. An instant later, the tops of Karyna's wrists exploded in fiery pain. She fell from the agony. Frenna swung her sword and cleaved a head from its spine. Sheilna threw her sword. The handle landed at Karyna's feet.

The pain in Karyna's wrists subsided. She turned at Frenna's agonizing scream. Another creature, this one different than the rest, had its claws deep in her guts. Karyna stared in horror, pupils frozen in disbelief. The creature released her. Frenna fell without breath as her body hit the soft grass. The creature stepped toward Karyna. "Master will be proud," the creature hissed.

Survival instinct kicked in. Karyna grabbed the sword and lifted it into the air. She tripped on her dress as she stepped backward. The creature took another step toward her. This one was taller, its body not as slouched or as green, but its eyes were as red as the rest. Its long hair descended below its waist. A long robe covered most of its body. Long pointed ears angled forward. They quivered as the creature hissed, "Your life has come to an end, Your Highness." From behind the rest of the creatures gathered. One-by-one they circled Karyna with murderous anticipation.

Darych Shade held the reins steady as the horrid scene came into view. He feared the worst as the dark, shifting forms circled their target. The closer he got, the tighter the knot in his stomach became, though he had precious little time to worry. As his horse closed the distance, Darych climbed up and crouched on the saddle. His war cry erupted when he saw Karyna surrounded by the hideous creatures. His horse charged through them. He leapt off the saddle and tackled one of the creatures. He thrust a knife deep into its neck. He was on his feet instantly. He unsheathed his great sword and slammed it into another. Six remained.

The creatures attacked at once. Claws slid harmlessly off his armor and Darych kicked them back. He retaliated with strength and used the length of his sword to hold them back. With each attack he killed another. All the time his war cry echoed through the forest. Just as he thought it would soon end, his feet were flipped out below him. He landed on his back. The weight of his armor slowed him from reacting. The last of the vile creatures sprang onto his chest, cackling as it brought up its claws. White venom gushed from the tips of the claws. The creature taunted him, allowing venom to drip onto the side of his face. Darych screamed when it burned and tried to lift his sword. Suddenly, the creature jerked and howled as a blade poked through its chest from behind. Karyna stood behind thrusting the sword deeper into its chest. Darych threw it off and climbed to his feet. "Are you all right?" he asked.

She rushed to him and sobbed uncontrollably. When there were no more tears, she looked up at him and said, "It's my fault they're dead, Darych. Everything is my fault."

"Tell me what happened," he said as he attempted to ignore the vile stench that reeked from the creatures. Their existence meant there was truth behind the attack on Ruhln.

"Sheilna stopped us and told us that we should return to Wyndhaven. There was something red in the grass ahead of us. Sheilna went to investigate. She found a man, but he was already dead."

Darych saw the red that she spoke off. "Is it the messenger?" he asked her.

Karyna ignored him as she closed Frenna's eyes. "Their death will haunt me forever. I don't deserve to live."

He didn't have time to worry over Karyna's sense of guilt. "I must return you to the castle immediately, but even if we leave now, I'm afraid we won't make it by dark."

Karyna looked around at all of the dead creatures. "One of them is missing." He shot her a puzzled look. "One of them was dressed in a green robe; it spoke to me."

He tried to recall everything from the beginning when he rode in to save her; all he thought of was her safety. He couldn't remember one clothed at all. Darych studied the forest, and when he heard a groan he spun about nervously. It came from the direction of the man in red. "I thought you said that man was dead?" He motioned Karyna to stay close. With sword in hand, he approached the injured man cautiously. They found a young man lying on his back; his chest gashed open. Darych knelt at his side. "He's alive." The man rolled his head and tried to speak. He was young and wore the markings of an Andar. "I can't leave him here; we'll have to take him with us."

"What of Sheilna and Frenna?"

"We must leave them, but when we return, I'll send someone to retrieve the bodies." Karyna caused him some concern when she shook her head in disproval. "Karyna, I promise we'll return for them. Now is not the time to grieve. If what you said is true there will be more of these nearby. We must get out of here as quickly as possible." Darych looked into the young man's eyes and asked, "Can you ride?" The man nodded. "Karyna, come help." He tore and wrapped a strip of blanket from his saddle bag around the man's chest. Together they hoisted him onto Darych's horse. Darych climbed up behind him. The stranger in red groaned in obvious pain.

Karyna's horse had disappeared during the ambush, but circling the trees not far from them was Sheilna's. "They didn't want to follow me out here," she told him, "but they did anyway. They were the only true friends I've ever had. I'll never be able to forgive myself."

"You'll be able to grieve their deaths soon…but not now. I need you on that horse. We don't want their sacrifice to be in vain. They died to save you. You have to respect that. Now come."

Karyna surprised him when she seemed to shove aside her grief. She wiped the tears and dirt from her face and ran to claim Sheilna's horse. She climbed into the saddle and motioned the horse to run. Darych pointed in the direction he thought was west and together they rode.

Darych could feel the slow heartbeat within the stranger. He found it odd that a man so young carried the markings of an Andar. He didn't know much about them. An Andar was a highly educated scholar, taught by handing down information and knowledge from generation to generation. As far as he knew, there was only one Andar alive in Yannina, but perhaps this man was a younger generation, learning the ways of the Andar. He heard rumors once that an Andar could wield unbelievable powers. As he cradled the stranger in his arms, he doubted it was true. Maybe it had been true once, but he was certain now that an Andar was nothing more than keepers of knowledge.

As the sky glazed over with shades of gray and black, Darych realized they were lost. They never found the road to Wyndhaven. As darkness fully descended, he knew they had no choice but to set camp. Riding during nightfall would make their situation worse. He found a large elk tree with a thick ceiling. Darych didn't think it would rain. The canopy would offer a little protection in case it did. He had nothing but the one blanket for gear. His belongings were packed onto one of the supply wagons. Karyna was worse off; she wore a shredded gown. The night would be cool. He withdrew the blanket and knelt beside Karyna who was slumped against the base of the tree. He covered her with it and turned to the young man who fought for every breath. He leaned back against the trunk to think. If demons were following their trail, they could sneak into their camp. If they scented blood, they were in grave danger. He thought about his men and wondered if they would be searching for him. He hoped Chad would sense something was wrong. Even if he was smart enough to send a messenger back to Wyndhaven, than the king would send out reinforcements. Come morning, they may be discovered. Karyna remained wrapped in the blanket. "We should get some rest, Karyna." She barely nodded. Clearly her thoughts were somewhere else. He could relate to how she felt by the traumatic event of his childhood when he'd found his parents. She was handling it well, but chances were she was still in shock. There would come a time when their deaths would really hit her. He hoped someone would be there to console her. His thoughts were interrupted when she spoke with a tremulous voice.

"Rowen told me there were demons in our world. As soon as I saw them, I knew I had let him down. In the three years I've known him, he warned me of the danger. I ignored him, and now my friends have paid for it." Darych moved to sit next to her. As he put his arm around her, she broke down and cried.

Chad waited at the tent door. He watched the knights complete their duties. Camp was prepared. It was almost time to set the watch.

Haryld approached him from the road, "We can't find Darych anywhere."

Chad sighed, disappointed. He was worried. He hoped Rhyus was having better luck. "Continue looking."

"Is there anything else I can do to help?" Haryld asked.

"No," Chad replied. He sipped water from a tin. "What can we do? I've sent Rhyus back to Wyndhaven in case Darych returned there, but we won't know until tomorrow. We'll have to move slowly and hope for the best."

A terrible screech thundered through the night. Chad turned in a rush and reached for his sword. Down from the sky a massive creature came—its black scales glistened in the moonlight. The knights readied for battle.

The great dragon Zar with wings stretched out and neck pointed down swooped into the unsuspecting camp. His belly burned for death and he released his fire. Wicked blue flames ripped through the camp engulfing knights as they ran for their lives. Their bodies disintegrated on impact; only their charred armor remained as the pieces fell to the ground. Zar flapped his wings and returned to the sky. He came down for another pass. He released his fire and destroyed the camp with ease. He tipped his wings to break his speed and landed in the chaos. The remaining knights attacked. Zar smelled their fear. He lurched down with his jaws and snapped up a few with his teeth; he felt their bones snap as he chewed and swallowed. He lifted one of his great paws and crushed more of them into the ground. His tail, jagged with sharp fins and claws, whirled around, destroying the surrounding forest. Trees collapsed around him, crushing the knights who retreated for their lives. He released his fire and burned others to death. He sensed where any remaining life was, and that's where he attacked.

When they were all dead, he screeched with victory at the moonlight, flapped his wings and returned to the sky.

Chapter 27

Adan stared in disbelief, wondering how it was possible. At first he thought he was mistaken, but the prisoner was surely him. He remembered the prince vividly from his last visit to Corrona. The prisoner truly was the Prince of Corrona. Myron watched as Adan used his sword to cut the ropes. The prince groaned in relief when Adan removed the gag from his mouth.

"Water," Riordan murmured in a weak and raspy voice. "Please, I need water." He struggled to his knees. His long, dark hair was matted in blood; the silver strands in his hair were torn and wild.

"We have no water with us," Adan told him. He hated himself for being so foolish. When he left home he didn't take anything useful.

"We crossed a creek not long ago," Myron offered.

"No, Myron," Adan said, "we can't go back the way we came. We must get as far away from here as possible. It can't be far to Windhaven."

"No!" Riordan gasped, "I must . . . return home." The prince attempted to stand, but stumbled over the side of the carriage when he collapsed.

Together Myron and Adan moved him to the ground. Welts and bruises darkened his otherwise pale skin. His breathing came in rasps.

Adan eyed him with worry. "What are we going to do?"

"We must find him water," Myron replied as he untied the horses from the carriage. Adan helped him free the horses. They pushed the wagon off the road and down a steep bank. It caromed off the elk trees and finally broke apart near the bottom. "Let's lift him onto a horse," Myron said. "Up ahead, the road meets with the river. We'll follow it until we get him water. After that we should travel in the forest. Demons will come after us when they discover what happened." Adan nodded. With their help, Riordan struggled to his feet. They hoisted him onto the wounded horse. "This horse is hurt. They need water too."

"Let's get out of here, Myron; it was too easy to rescue him. He's the Prince of Corrona. This could be a trap."

"You ride with the prince and help hold him steady. I'll ride this one." Myron turned to pull the arrow from the horse's hide.

"Don't," Adan warned him. "Leave it alone. I was told that unless an arrow is removed properly, it's better left alone."

Myron stopped and rubbed the horse's hide. "We'll find the river as fast as we can."

Riordan collapsed onto the horse's mane, almost falling off. "Please . . . I must . . ."

"Don't worry. We're going to find water," Myron replied reassuringly.

Adan climbed onto the horse. He felt comfortable without a saddle. His father taught him to ride bareback.

Myron mounted the horse; it huffed and snorted in pain. "We'll have to save the horses' strength," he said. "We can only ask them to run if we're in dire need."

Adan glanced behind him one last time. When the demons discovered that the prince was no longer their captive they would come after them; it was a terrifying thought. His encounter with them haunted him. It was the first time he killed anything with the Dragon Sword. The blade came alive in his hands. He felt the force when the sword ripped the demon in half, and remembered the sting in his eyes from the powerful light.

"Please . . . I must return home," Riordan pleaded.

Myron glanced at him. "He's in bad shape, Adan. Once he has water his senses may return. We'll explain our situation then."

"Do you have an idea about how they captured him?"

"Maybe Corrona was been invaded like Ruhln."

"I hope not," Adan replied. The magnitude of demons needed for such an evasion was a frightful image.

They rode into the day. Adan couldn't help but continue checking over his shoulder. Riordan slept most of the time, straddling the horse's neck and dreaming in his sleep. His eyelids shook and his face flinched as if he were being tortured.

"Finally," Myron said. "I can hear the river." The road turned a sharp corner, and then straightened out as it ran parallel to the river. It was a long stretch of road that faded into the distance. The overhang of the elk trees provided a ceiling, their branches thick with dust from the well-traveled road. Adan and Myron helped Riordan to dismount and carried him to the water. "We've found water, Prince Riordan. You must find the strength to drink."

Riordan's hands shook as he drank slowly for a moment. He whispered, "Thank you," and rolled onto his back, eyes closed.

Myron said, "I should try to catch some fish. I don't know if I'll have any success, but it's worth the effort."

"I don't think we have time for that," a worried Adan said.

"Yes, but we should eat something. Take Riordan and the horses west from here. I'll spear some fish and catch up to you."

"That's too risky. I think we should stay together."

"I'll be fine. Don't forget I was taught by the best tracker in Ruhln—my grandfather. I won't lose you. If I find trouble, I'll lead it away before catching up."

Adan had a bad feeling. "I don't know, Myron."

Myron was insistent. "Trust me. We don't have a choice about it anyway. We need food. It's not safe for all of us to stay here while I fish, so you two can move ahead where it will be harder for the demons to find you; I'll catch up shortly."

"I hate arguing with you."

"What's to argue?" Myron smiled and added, "Just do as you're told."

They lifted Riordan to his feet; already the prince showed signs of recovery. His skin, at least the areas without bruises, had a bit more color. Back on the horse, he once again slumped onto the horse's mane. Myron said, "Go west. If I don't catch up by nightfall, find a good place to camp, but don't start a fire."

"Make sure you find us by nightfall. I don't need to worry about you too." Adan took the reins of both horses and led them up the small slope onto the road. He still harbored a bad feeling about leaving Myron behind. Instead of climbing up behind Riordan, he mounted the other horse and kept them at a slow walk so the sleeping Riordan wouldn't fall. The sound of rushing water faded until it was gone completely. The forest was quiet and abandoned, but he watched his surroundings carefully.

After traveling for a while, Riordan surprised him when he sat up and looked around. He slid his gaze toward Adan. "Who are you?"

"My name is Adan."

Riordan rubbed his eyes. "Where are they?"

Adan assumed he meant the demons. "My friend and I saved you from three demons."

"Where did he go?" Riordan searched side to side, seemingly confused.

"He's catching fish. He'll join us later."

Riordan rubbed his arm, "Three demons?"

"Yes."

"There were many more than that, I assure you."

Adan nodded in agreement. "I know. How do you feel?"

"I'm a little lightheaded and hungry."

"Myron's a good fisherman. He'll catch us something to eat."

The prince seemed more coherent, but his eyes appeared lost, as if they faded into another world. "Thank you for saving me. May I ask why you did such a thing?"

"I thought you were my brother," he replied. Adan felt the disappointment gather back into his heart.

"Was your brother taken prisoner by these demons as well?"

Adan had never really thought about that. "I don't know. He disappeared during the attack on Ruhln."

Riordan gasped. "Ruhln was invaded?"

The surprise in his voice startled Adan. "Yes. We lost many lives. My father and brother were killed."

"It's bloody insanity! Why would Faral let such a thing happen?"

Adan didn't think much of Faral anymore. He was supposed to be the God that protected them from such things. "Perhaps Faral has forgotten us."

"I am so sorry, Adan. I promise when we return to Corrona, I'll send aid immediately. You and your friend will be rewarded as well."

Adan didn't want to tell Riordan that Corrona was not where they were headed. "Your Highness . . ."

"Riordan is my name. Please use it."

Adan nodded, "Riordan, we're not going to Corrona."

"I must return home as soon as possible."

"No, you'll head straight into the demons that captured you. Something else has been following us for the past couple of days. You don't need a battle with that as well."

Riordan cursed. "I must get home." Tears glistened in his eyes.

Adan didn't know what to tell him. Heading back to Corrona would bring disaster. "May I ask what happened that brought you so far from home, and into the hands of demons?"

"My family was betrayed. I believe a member of the High Council attacked my father, killing him as he sat on his throne. My mother," Riordan stopped and dried the tears from his eyes, "my mother accused me of killing my own father. I was betrayed and taken prisoner by the leader of the First Guard." Adan knew what the High Council was, and had heard of the First Guard. The First Guard protected the city. Their loyalty to their king was unmatched. "Something happened." Riordan shook as he recalled the event. "As Sheldhan led me down the stairs, he hit me. I collapsed and blacked out. I was blindfolded when I came to. I heard a conversation between Sheldhan and another. He offered me to the other person and said he would cause a distraction so I would be taken from the palace unnoticed. When we were away from the palace, they removed my blindfold. It was the first time I saw the demons. I fought the battle of my life, but one demon in particular was very strong. There was nothing I could do."

Adan assumed Sheldhan was the leader of the First Guard. "So you were betrayed by this Sheldhan as well?"

"I was betrayed by Sarek, Sheldhan, some of the First Guard and members of the High Council who witnessed the entire event. What hurts me the most is the vision of my mother standing over my father and accusing me of killing him."

Adan felt his tongue empty of words. It was difficult to believe that the prince was the victim of such treason. Then again, after the attack on Ruhln, Adan knew that anything was possible. "Riordan, journey with us to Wyndhaven and tell the king there what happened. He might help you."

"I must return to Corrona and set things right. I can't stop thinking about what might be happening back there."

"I know it must be hard, Riordan, but consider what is at stake. You were powerless the first time. Without support you will undoubtedly end up in the same situation. Come with us."

"How far is it to Wyndhaven?"

"Not far now, a day or two at the most." Riordan appeared undecided.

Adan sensed an opportunity to pressure him. The thought of a third companion during their trek to Wyndhaven comforted him. "It would be a wise decision. If Wyndhaven turns out to be a mistake, at least you will have more time to heal before you return."

"Let's get there quickly, then."

Myron felt relieved that Adan was ignorant about fishing. The river was much too fast to catch fish, not like the small overflow they found a couple of days back. He threw his pack over his shoulder and ran onto the road. His intentions were to backtrack and make sure they lost their enemies. Myron thought they were still being followed by the man in black. He ran south through the forest. He stayed close to the side of the road keeping cover from tree to tree. His crossbow was locked, loaded and ready to fire should he have to use it. After they rescued Riordan from the demons, Myron sensed a shadow that moved through the trees. He didn't tell Adan because he feared Adan would overreact and run the horses. Those horses were weak and exhausted. They would need them if they encountered more demons. He hoped the water they drank would give them strength.

 Myron was confident in his tracking. If he put his mind to it he could cover their own tracks, lose whoever trailed them forever. He would have to start acting like his grandfather taught him. Their lives might depend on it. He wished he could convince Adan to return home. Now that they had rescued Riordan they were in deeper trouble than he had ever imagined. Adan dragged them into the middle of something he wanted no part of.

 The demons practically handed them Riordan. Adan was right about that. Somewhere in the forest the demon in red waited, hiding as he and Adan took his prisoner. Perhaps it was only luck but the worst possibility must be considered. The river rushed in the distance. The trees were tall and spaced evenly, yet the tops spanned out hiding most of the sky. Rays of sunlight poked through the ceiling, shimmering through the tall grass. Adan and Riordan were north of him now. He knew exactly where they were, and how far they traveled since leaving him. His instincts told him something else was close. A gray rabbit appeared from behind a tree. Myron watched it, shocked by its appearance. The rabbit stared back; the whiskers on its nose twitching. Then it suddenly snapped its head the other way. Myron held his breath. A breeze lifted the hair on his neck. The rabbit tore away and disappeared into the tall grass. Myron stared intently at an elk tree.

 A man stepped into view from behind the tree. It was him. The man was far enough away that Myron felt comfortable, knowing he could shoot him dead before he had a chance to harm him. He lifted his crossbow and took him in his sights. The stranger wrapped his face with a black cloth; a sword hung on his hip. Myron held his fear. There was a familiarity about the man, the way he stared with his dark eyes. The man stepped forward with a limp. One shot and Myron knew it would be over. He never missed. As a cool breeze caressed his nerves, Myron squeezed the trigger. With one quick motion the man in black snatched the arrow from out of the air with his hand. Myron let his crossbow down in horror. There was only one man Myron knew who could do such a thing, but that was impossible. Myron swallowed the bile rising at the back of his throat from the insanity. He had the courage to fight him, but if he failed, the man in black would pursue Adan. There would be nothing his friend could do to protect himself. He turned and ran. The stranger didn't chase. He merely followed, limping with every stride.

Myron would leave a false trail. It was their best chance. Until they reached Wyndhaven, Myron knew they would never be safe.

Chapter 28

Adan worried as darkness fell over them, irritated that he agreed to leave Myron behind. He led the horses down a small hill. The undergrowth throughout the forest thickened as they descended into a small valley. A soft rumble in the distance announced fresh water. Massive branches from the elk trees touched the forest floor engulfing them as they treaded through. Adan found the creek at the bottom of the hill. The water flowed off a small rock bluff and formed a pool of water. The horses stomped and snorted at the sight of it.

Riordan nearly fell when he dismounted. "I'm afraid I still don't have my strength."

"Don't waste what strength you have. You should rest." Adan watched the forest with a look of concern.

Riordan leaned against the rock bluff and emitted a soft moan. "I've always had good health. Faral always watched over me. I didn't have to deal with pain." Riordan often spoke of Faral. The prince was much more into the god than anyone else Adan had known.

"I'm hungry," Adan said. The bush rustled behind them and Myron staggered out with his crossbow in hand. "Myron!"

"Sorry I'm late." Myron tossed a skinned rabbit at his feet. "I've never seen so many rabbits. They're all over the place."

"Where were you?" Adan demanded.

"I ran into an old friend."

Adan raised his brows, "Who?"

"I met up with the man in black."

"He still follows us?"

Myron knelt at the pond. He sipped water from his palms and smiled at Riordan. "He was. I believe I left a trail that will confuse him. We should be safe for the night."

Adan turned the dead rabbit with his boot. "What am I to do with this?"

"Nothing, we can't cook it here. A fire will waste all of my efforts today. I'll take it up the hill as far away as I can and cook it there. You two wait here."

Adan admired his intelligence. "Thank you."

"Just remember you would be lost without me." Myron took the rabbit and headed up the hill, following the creek as he went. Adan hid his smile. He undid the scabbard and removed the sword from his back. He rested beside Riordan and leaned against the smooth rock wall.

Riordan said, "You and Myron are good people. I'm sorry you've been through so much."

Adan smiled. "It's not your fault. I worry how these strange events may be tied together. I worry for Yannina."

"I agree. I was told about demons in ancient stories. I never knew they really existed. I would like to know where they come from."

Adan thought of his father. The strange events before his tragic death rolled through his mind, and he wondered if he knew about the demons. "Perhaps in Wyndhaven we'll meet someone who does," he suggested.

The silver moon crept into the sky. Adan didn't think much of the moon anymore. It reminded him of death. At least the sound of the creek still soothed him. It brought back memories of home, of his house and the stables built nearby. It seemed so far away now.

Riordan shifted to ease his aching. "I hope Myron returns soon. I am very hungry."

Adan smiled. "He will."

"Are you two good friends?"

Adan nodded. "I tried to leave Ruhln on my own, but Myron followed me. Had I left on my own, I'd probably be dead."

Riordan smiled. "I have a good friend back home. Our friendship was strong when we were younger, but as we grew older it became difficult because I am the Prince of Corrona. He drafted himself into the First Guard so that we could remain friends." He paused for a moment and closed his eyes. "I fear for his life. I know he would have tried to save me."

"What about your mother?"

Riordan lowered his head and his body shook. "My mother betrayed me as well."

Adan was unfamiliar with Riordan's family, but the notion made little sense. What mother would betray her son? "Riordan, there must an explanation. Do you really believe that your mother betrayed you? These demons have strange powers. Perhaps she was cursed."

A glimmer of hope sprang into his eyes, "Do you believe that?"

"We must hold onto any hope that we can grasp. I have to believe that my brother is alive. I must believe that I can find him; otherwise I would have to ask myself what I'm doing out here. I will not do that." Adan thought again of Myron. "That's why Myron is so special. I know he questions my motives, yet he supports me anyway. I owe him my life."

Riordan sat silently for a moment. "You're a very special person, too, Adan. I'm grateful for everything you've done for me. You've given me a chance to fight back, and I'll never forget that. When you saved me from those demons you gained another friend. Like Myron, I will do anything for you."

Adan didn't know what to say. It seemed odd to hear something like that from royalty. He assumed they didn't really care about those lower than them. It was a pleasant surprise to learn otherwise. He smiled and shook his head.

Myron returned with his charred rabbit. He insisted the fault belonged to Adan, who failed to bring the proper utensils. Adan felt grateful regardless. The little bit of meat that he ate felt like an entire meal. He washed it down with plenty of water and thanked Myron. Later that night they huddled together below the rock buff hidden from the light of the moon. Adan told Riordan everything he and Myron had been through. It struck the prince with awe when he spoke of the dragon. Riordan thought there might have been only three demons guarding him because the rest were trying to capture a dragon. The notion almost made sense.

Adan was aghast when Riordan explained in detail what happened to him. Adan hadn't realized the gravity of what happened. Corrona was in the hands of the enemy. "The longer I stray from Corrona, the more I fear for the safety of my people. I cannot imagine what is happening there."

Myron picked at his teeth. "It seems to me that the events throughout Yannina are patterned. It worries me that someone powerful is guiding this force of destruction."

"What about Wyndhaven? Do you believe something may have happened there?" Adan asked.

"I hope not," Myron replied. "Otherwise our efforts are futile. If Wyndhaven has fallen, then we are in more trouble than we can imagine."

Riordan threw a pebble at the pond. "Wyndhaven and Corrona are the two largest settlements south of the mountains. If they have fallen, we have no way to fight back at the enemy. Only Terrace and Akhran have a large enough force to help defend against these demons, but they are too busy fighting each other. If Wyndhaven has fallen, our hope is lost."

"We must get there as soon as possible," Adan said. "If it has not been attacked, we must warn the king."

"Agreed," Myron said and stretched out on his back. "When the sun rises in the morning, we'll ride as fast as the horses can carry us."

"You two rest," Adan told them. "I'll take first watch."

Myron didn't argue. Riordan stared back through the darkness. "I could take first watch, Adan. After everything you two have done for me, I would like to see you rest."

"You need your sleep more than I do. Get some rest now." Before Riordan could reply, Adan stood and walked down to the creek. For a while he stared at the stars thinking about his mother and father. The silver moon glowed. He shivered from a cold breeze.

"Adan," Zadryan called.

Adan smiled. He could no longer mistake the peculiar deep voice that sounded in his mind.

"Adan, please come to me."

He didn't want to leave his friends alone.

"Trust me, Adan, they're safe. I flew the area. There's nothing to fear."

Adan remembered when he returned from their previous encounter the night before. The man in black almost caught them.

Zadryan read his mind. *"I didn't fail you last night, Adan. I swear there is nothing nearby that will harm your friends."* Was he implying that the man in black was not a danger? *"I cannot say for sure, Adan. Please, trust me. I must speak with you. I'm not far."* If anything happened to Myron or Riordan while he was away, he would never forgive himself. He didn't want to put too much faith in the dragon. *"I promise, Adan, that if harm comes to them, I will defend them myself."*

Adan was agitated. "We must keep our conversation short, Friend," he said softly, aware that the dragon would hear him. After securing the Dragon Sword on his back, Adan quietly left camp. He climbed out of the small valley. At the top of the hill, Zadryan waited. Adan was taken by surprise again. Zadyran was much bigger than the previous night. His height remained the same, yet his body was larger and heavier. The plates on his back had grown, and now there were more of them. Claws sprouted from the tips of the wings and hind legs. The tip of his tail bulged at the end, almost as if something was inside ready to burst out.

"I'm growing, Adan. I'm at a stage in my lifetime where I cross over to adulthood. The process is very painful."

"Is this normal?" Adan asked. "It's happening so quickly."

"Yes, it's normal for a dragon. It is known as the stage of makara. *I shall become one of the strongest dragons in Yannina."*

"That's incredible."

"I ask you to journey with me."

"Why?"

"My mother wants to meet with you."

Adan was hesitant. "Then your mother can come here. I can't abandon my friends."

Zadryan lifted his head over top of the trees. *"These are dangerous times, Adan. My mother can no longer fly this area. Zar has awakened. He hunts my mother and me. Zar doesn't know my scent. I can hide from him, but he would easily find my mother. Please, come with me."*

Adan was emphatic. "I will not leave my friends."

"You drew ancient power from the sword, Adan. My mother's name is Zalphyna. She knew your father. Please, she must meet with you. There are important issues to discuss."

"Issues—ancient power—what are you talking about? How did your mother know my father?"

Zadryan moved his large head toward Adan. His yellow eyes blinked behind scaly eyelids. *"How is it possible? How is it that you and I are now friends, Adan? Anything is possible."*

"Zadryan, promise me that my friends will be safe. Promise me on your mother's life. Tell me why you are certain they will be safe."

"I know this because part of my instincts as a dragon helps me hunt food. I can sense life. There is nothing that will hurt them, I promise. I swear they will be fine."

Adan thought for a moment. "What about Zar? Can he sense life as well as you? What happens when he flies over our camp? He will discover my friends and kill them."

"That is a fair question, Adan. The explanation is the same answer I gave you when you noticed how quickly I was growing. Makara *is more than a stage of growth; it is the power that makes us, the heartbeat of our*

soul. It is a power inside me. Once I come into age, my makara *will grow in strength and change me physically. I may also use* makara *to shield us. I don't sense life with scent. I sense it with my* makara. *Because Zar has not yet discovered my* makara, *I am safe from him. When you are with me, you will be protected. Zar has discovered my mother's* makara, *and that is why she is not safe."*

Adan glanced into the darkness of the forest, in the direction of Myron and Riordan. "What will protect them while we're gone?"

"*I cast my* makara *shield on them as well. They are safe."*

"If you're telling the truth, and your mother truly knows my father, then what was his name?"

"*His name was Darren."*

To hear his father's name through the mind of the dragon was overwhelming. The intriguing idea that he was about to learn the truth erased his concerns. "How long will we be gone?"

"*Not long"*. Zadryan lowered to the ground. "*Climb on, friend."* As Adan approached the dragon, his blue scales reflected the moonlight into his eyes. Adan grabbed onto a scale, placed his foot on the dragon's leg and climbed to the top of his back. There were crevices within his scales that fit like a saddle. Using his legs like a catapult, Zadryan lurched into the air. The sound of his wings erupted with power.

The wind ripped across Adan's back. He was filled with worry and regret. Had he not wanted to learn more about his father, he would have told Zadryan to return him to his friends. But he held on, frightened that the wind might blow him away. Even though he resented the moon, he was amazed how its light shined down onto the forest, emitting a powerful glow that soared for an eternity. Zadryan took him higher. Adan howled in fear. Zadryan took him higher yet. The air turned extremely cold. "Lower!" he shouted.

Zadryan groaned and dove back down toward the forest ceiling.

Adan saw Wyndhaven. The castle sat against the Angled Spine; a mountain wall of ice from east to west, stretching across the entire continent, the very backbone of Yannina.

He could see Corrona far to the south. The wall guarding the city circled around in an arc, backing the Palace of Ionia with incredible strength. Corrona truly was a marvel to behold, and yet, it had fallen. Adan thought he could see the ocean far to the west. He smiled; he had never seen the ocean before.

Suddenly, Zadryan tipped back his wings to slow his speed and dropped into the forest. As they fell through the branches, Adan tightened his grip, worried that he would get snagged and ripped away. "Is there something wrong?" he asked in a loud voice.

"Be silent, Adan, don't speak another word until I say." Zadryan landed on the forest floor, and then shifted himself until he was up tight against a tree.

They waited. It felt like a lifetime. Adan continued to shift uncomfortably, sweating with nervousness. His sword was heavy. Sweat ran into his eyes, but he was too afraid to move…too afraid to wipe it away.

Zadryan held his breath when a shadow, dark and forbidding, cast itself over them. It slid overhead blocking the rays of the silver moon. Adan choked back his fear and swallowed a whimper below his breath. He felt the tension in Zadryan's body. The ominous shadow passed by and the moonlight returned. Still, they waited. The strides of time felt like an eternity. It was so hard for Adan to contain the fear he felt.

Finally, Zadryan moved away from the tree. The dragon stretched out his wings and flew back to the sky. Adan searched in every direction, but all he saw was moonlight and treetops. Zadryan returned him to his camp. Adan jumped to the ground, confused. "What happened, Zadryan?"

"It is not safe. My request for you to meet my mother almost killed us. Return to your camp. Stay hidden in the darkness."

Before Adan could reply, Zadryan unfolded his wings and flew into the sky. Adan ran to camp, relieved to find his friends asleep. Another shadow flew above him. Adan stared as another dragon, much larger than Zadryan, soared above the forest canopy. Its shadow weaved fear through the forest as small creatures trembled with fear. A cold wind brushed back his hair. Overtaken by immeasurable fear, Adan tried to meld with the trunk of an elk tree. The shadow disappeared. There was not a sound in the dark forest. Adan collapsed to the ground and wiped the sweat from his forehead, hoping Zadryan escaped undetected.

Chapter 29

Darych struggled to lift the stranger on his horse. He mounted behind him and supported him with his arms. His horse snorted at the extra weight. The young man opened his eyes a little and his mouth moved. "Easy now," Darych said. "There's no need to waste your effort." He tightened his grip on the stranger and said to Karyna. "Let's head south."

Karyna's spirit died with Sheilna and Frenna. Her red, swollen eyes betrayed her grief. Darych spent nearly the whole night keeping watch. He knew Karyna hadn't slept either. Darych understood her grief and shock. It was the most devastating event she ever witnessed. Darych was impressed that she held her composure as well as she was. She mounted Sheilna's horse and scratched at her wrists. "We came from that way."

Above him the forest ceiling came alive as a flock of birds flew from one branch to another. The sun shined down from the east; he was certain he had pointed south. "We'll reach the road and catch up with my men. We'll treat this man's wounds and escort both of you to Wyndhaven. I'm convinced the rumors of Ruhln are true. The faster we get there the better." The stranger lifted his head and muttered something. It was the first time he tried to speak, although Darych couldn't understand why he wasted so much effort in doing so. "Keep quiet," Darych commanded. "Don't waste what strength you have. You're going to need every bit of it." He found it remarkable that the stranger healed quite well during the course of the night. The gash across his chest closed together enough to stop bleeding, a remarkable feat from the size of the cut. His fever broke with the night and his heart rate sounded much better. He even seemed to have enough strength to sit upright as they rode, an amazing accomplishment considering he was near death only a day earlier.

The morning passed into the afternoon. Darych felt confident with their location as the sun moved overhead. It was unnaturally hot for the time of year. The late end of summer normally brought cool winds and lower temperatures as winter approached. Karyna didn't offer much in conversation, not that he expected her to. Darych turned back to look at her and noticed that she scratched at her wrists again. He saw her do that more and more as the day pressed on. The road finally appeared on the low side of a gentle hill. He was filled with relief. "We made it; I recognize this part of the road. We're much farther east than I thought."

"Finally," she replied, scratching at her wrists again.

"Are you all right?"

"No, I don't know what it is that bothers me." Karyna moved her fingers up her arm and let out a groan when she hit her elbows. "It started during the fight with the demons."

Darych shifted uncomfortably in the saddle. He rubbed his chin. His beard bothered him where the creature spilled its venom.

"Your beard has a streak of white," Karyna told him.

"It must be a reaction from that fluid the creature dropped on me. At first it burned, but then it went away. It was bound to turn gray sooner or later." Darych thought it would be best to change the subject. "My men passed through here," he said as he watched the terrain along the road. "I don't think they're too far ahead of us." Again, the young man tried to say something. "What do you think he's trying to tell us?" Darych asked curiously.

"I don't know."

"Well, once we treat him, he'll heal faster, and then we'll know. Come, we must keep moving."

Adan sat behind Myron and admired the intensity in Riordan's eyes. The prince showed a real determination in their quest to get to Wyndhaven and he voiced his opinion on several matters. For instance, Myron was not going to be running off on his own again. Adan felt close to Riordan. There was something about their situations that seemed connected.

Adan noticed the peaks of the Angled Spine, a sign they were closing in on Wyndhaven. The castle was built at the base of the mountains where it overlooked the towns surrounding it. Riordan steered his horse between two trees. His horse bit at the grass as they walked. He smiled at Adan. "How are you feeling?" Adan asked him.

The prince rubbed a mark on his chin. "Bruised and beaten, but I'll survive."

"That's good," Myron said. "I think we're getting close to the road again."

Riordan nodded. "My patience is thin. I must return home as quickly as possible."

It would be difficult for Riordan, being so far from home and helpless against events that might be happening there. Adan had confidence that Wyndhaven would aide him. Wyndhaven and Corrona were the two strongest allies in all of Yannina.

"There's the road now." Myron pointed ahead to a clearing.

Adan didn't want to travel on the road again. Danger stalked it in the form of demons. As they rode onto the dusty road, an overwhelming stench made him gag. He pulled his tunic up over his nose to escape the wind that carried the awful smell.

"Oh my," Riordan said. He pointed ahead. Broken and shredded trees scattered the area in front of them. Long strips of blackness laid the ground barren and empty. Puffs of smoke filtered up into the air. "We should have a closer look," Riordan suggested. "Prepare yourselves."

Myron stared at him. "Prepare for what? I'm not going anywhere near there. It smells like rotten meat."

"We have to get around it anyway. Wyndhaven is in that direction."

Adan tightened his grip. He closed his eyes and tried to think of something other than the horrifying smell. "Just follow him," Adan said to Myron. "The faster we get through it the better."

The stench worsened. Black smoke corroded the air. Fallen trees halted them at the ridge of destruction. Riordan was the first to witness the massacre. From the look on his face, Adan knew there would be no other word to describe it better. Blood soaked the ground. Bodies were flung haphazardly about. Body parts were tangled with the fallen brush. Tents were shredded. The putrefied stench reeked of smoke and death.

"It must have been a dragon," Riordan whispered.

Myron pinched his nose to ward off the odor. "I hope it wasn't the dragon we rescued." Adan doubted that. Zadryan didn't have a killer personality. It wasn't in his nature.

"Let's get out of here. These are Wyndhaven guards. King Mel will want to know about this." Riordan said. Adan tried hard not to think about the terror these men faced. His fears for Dex intensified. He prayed for his little brother and hoped that he still lived.

"Did you hear something?" Darych asked Karyna. He stopped his horse.

"Someone approaches," Karyna replied. "It sounds like horses and wagons."

The sound of horses' hooves clapping on the hard trail grew louder. Six horses came around the corner pulling a flat deck wagon. As the wagon drew closer, Darych almost fell off his horse. It was one of the flat decks he helped load with supplies for Ruhln. Tarps used to cover the supplies were shredded and trailed the wagon. Most of the supplies were destroyed. Blood covered the wagon and horses like a coat of red paint. "No!" Darych yelled. He leapt off his horse and rushed to the wagon. The horses were startled when he jumped out in front of them. They whinnied in fear and backed up trying to get away. The smell of blood rolled away from the top of the wagon. Darych climbed onto the long deck and grabbed his face in a gesture of utter horror. The supplies were destroyed and covered with blood. Among the remains, Darych found a battered arm, its hand still clutching a sword. The blade was perfectly clean, as if the knight had no chance to defend himself.

The stranger in red slouched forward onto the horse's mane and almost fell. Karyna dismounted and rushed to his aide. She helped him dismount and eased him to the road where he lay on his back.

Darych drew his sword from its scabbard; the urge to strike something overwhelmed him.
The uncertainty of what transpired left him confused and hurt. He let out a piercing war cry.

Karyna approached him. "Darych, you must calm down."

"Not until I know who did this," he growled. He thrust his sword into the scabbard, jumped off the deck and began untying the horses. His mind moved in more ways than one, desperately conceiving a plan. First, he unfastened the tracks from the deck so the horses were free. Once finished, he motioned Karyna to help him. Together they turned the long flat deck around. He pulled the horses back to the front where he reconnected them to the tracks. He tethered his horse to a side post so it could walk without any weight. The horse was tired from carrying him and the young stranger.

Karyna stared at the mangled arm; her face set in a powerful frown, disgusted by the shredded tissue and clots of blood. Darych lifted the arm out of the wagon with great respect. He didn't know who it belonged to, but one of his men died while serving Wyndhaven. He placed it carefully in the ditch against the road. He didn't have time for a death service or burial, but he gave what value he could. He only had time for revenge. Darych was furious with himself for leaving them. His mood darkened. Who would dare attack the Wyndhaven Forces?

Together they brushed off the deck and managed to salvage some of the supplies. They found a water cask and bandages. Darych lifted the stranger onto the deck and propped up his head with torn clothing. The young man managed to swallow some water. Darych took the reins and sat at the front. He feared for Karyna; he was getting her involved with something terrible. He thought about sending her back to Wyndhaven, but discarded the idea immediately. She shouldn't ride alone. "Let's go," he said. Karyna climbed into her saddle and followed Darych down the road.

Demon Stihl watched within the shadows of the forest with Gnith at his side. The demon glanced at him with curious, beady eyes. "Let us attack," Gnith hissed. "Our master gives us speed."

"Wait," Stihl said as he pulled a glove over his right hand, black and armed with metal teeth. "We cannot fail a second time. Where are the others?"

"They left the destroyed encampment."

"Wait until our forces are all in place."

"Yes, Master," Gnith hissed again. "Master Vayle will be proud."

Vayle was not the one they needed to impress. Stihl peered up at the clear blue sky. Demon Myra watched them through the flying deamlon. "Let her watch, then," he muttered from beneath his breath.

Demon Stihl turned to his army of demons. It had been too long since he killed, too long since he'd pierced the heart of his enemies. Killing the Warrior of Ches was a memory he loved to remember. Watching Darren's son burn into oblivion was a pleasure he would never forget. Now it was a prince and princess. They were stumbling into each other; they could be killed together. It was perfect and almost too easy. Oh yes. Let that stupid wench watch from above.

Demon Myra waited high within the Angled Spine, looking out over the Ruhln Forest, waiting for her pet to return. Her eyes were black and shadowed. Her mind echoed across the Ruhln Forest and watched as her pet carried her vision. She watched as the prince and princess approached one another, watched as Demon Stihl waited to advance. Her long, golden hair blew out in front of her face and she brushed it out of her way. Her pupils turned back to gray, and now her vision was her own. The deamlon soared above the forest, gaining speed and elevation. She waited patiently and lifted her arm high into the air. The silver clip remained embedded into her wrist, put there permanently by Demon Vayle. The deamlon came to her with wondrous outstretched wings. It settled onto the silver clip with its razor-sharp talons. She pulled down her pet to look into its beady red eyes. She turned back toward the mountain cliffs, down into the depths of the J'yradal. Vayle would arrive soon and begin their quest for freedom. The boy will be down there, waiting, alone and frightened. Her lungs exploded with excitement, thrilled that the time had arrived. Her voice echoed down the spiraling tower toward the boy and his prison. She had time to play. The boy was secure and wouldn't be going anywhere too soon.

She whispered to her pet, "Take me to the battle." The woman reached down and grasped her whip, a movement to confirm it was still there. Her pet spread its wings, its talons still clasped to the silver clip. The deamlon lifted her into the air. Together they flew to the battle that was about to begin.

At first, Riordan was reluctant to pass through the camp. Then, for peace of mind, he changed his direction and searched the camp for survivors. Adan and Myron agreed, but both admitted neither had the stomach for it. Riordan searched the area himself while Adan and Myron waited on the perimeter. They were both ashamed; however, Riordan assured them they had already shown him great courage. He told them both to wait outside of the camp. Once he finished searching the area, he returned to them. His search was unsuccessful, though Riordan settled his conscious knowing he did what he could. They rode in silence after that. Death was on the mind now, and none of them wanted to discuss it.

Something deadly and destructive threatened Yannina, Riordan was certain. Every time he looked at Adan and saw the scars on his face he was reminded of it. The remains of that encampment raised many concerns for Wyndhaven. It was quite possible that demons invaded the castle as they did Ruhln, or perhaps something as sinister as their attack on Corrona. Riordan heard the sound of horses' hooves and the squeaky wheels of a wagon.

They all stopped and waited to see who approached. "I think we should get off of the road," Myron said.

"Let's hide. I don't think I want to be seen," Adan said.

Riordan nodded in approval, "I agree." He led them off the road and back into the forest.

From the opposite direction, Darych pulled back on the reins when he saw something dart into the bush around the tip of the bend.

Karyna pulled up beside him. "What is it?"

"There's something ahead. I don't know what it was, but there were only two." Darych drew out his sword. "I'm going to have a look." He took a deep breath. "Stay back; if something goes wrong ride as fast as you can back home. Don't stop for anything." She nodded. He flicked the reins. He was not afraid—he was ready for revenge.

Off the road ahead, Riordan whispered, "He saw us." His horse was difficult to hold steady.

"The man on the deck is holding a sword," Adan whispered, trying to look over Myron's shoulder.

"A big sword," Myron added.

Riordan peered over his shoulder, and a hundred pairs of gleaming red eyes were staring at him. He almost hesitated from the fear of what was about to happen, but he managed to scream. "Run!"

Myron spun their horse around. He muttered aloud and Adan scratched his scars.

The demon army charged. They swarmed through the trees, spreading their forces out as they ran. All of them were identical in appearance, save those that carried bows. Their naked green bodies were accented by the claws on their arms and knees. Their red eyes flickered with gleeful pleasure. Behind them arrows flew. Two slammed into the horse underneath Adan and Myron. An arrow nicked Adan's neck. The horse collapsed, sending Adan and Myron sprawling to avoid being caught under it. At the same time, the stranger on the flat deck wagon was upon them. He jumped into the air as if he wanted to strike them down. More arrows flew.

Riordan gasped and shouted. "We're not your enemy!"

The man stopped dead in his tracks and ducked from a cloud of arrows. "What's happening here?"

"I'm the Prince of Corrona! We're under attack!" Riordan screamed. His horse spun out of control. The man with the great sword staggered. He wore the blue and white armor of the Wyndhaven Forces, his gold seal indicated he was a general.

Adan pressed his hand against his neck as he and Myron scrambled to their feet. A girl rode off on her own as she cracked the reins of her horse and screamed for it to go faster. Demons chased her. They were everywhere. The road back to Corrona was their only path of escape.

"Get on!" the man on the flat deck hollered to Adan and Myron. They watched in horror as the demons closed in.

"Do it!" Riordan screamed. His looked back at the girl on the horse. Unless his eyes deceived him, she was Karyna of Wyndhaven.

Adan and Myron climbed onto the deck with the stranger. Another person in a red cloak was stretched across on his back with his head propped up. He lay there as if he were dead.

The general flicked the reins and the carriage roared ahead. Riordan rode beside them and prayed they had the speed to outrun them.

Behind them came the army of demons.

Chapter 30

The demons were fast. They continued to give chase, running at the same speed as the horses' gallop. They swarmed down onto the road from left and right as they charged and shrieked. Arrows rained down from the sky.

Adan held his neck in an attempt to stop the bleeding. The sting of the wound raced up and down his arms. He confronted the man who at first was going to attack them. "Who are you?" He pulled out the Dragon Sword. Behind him he could see Myron bending over the man who lay motionless on the deck. Riordan and the girl rode close behind them.

"Darych Shade," he said as he looked around behind him. A portion of his beard was white in contrast to his black hair. "The woman is Karyna Vannon, Princess of Wyndhaven."

Adan shook his head. "Princess Karyna? And he's the Prince of Corrona!"

"I heard him," Darych said. "Can you handle this thing?" Darych passed him the reins.

"I can try."

Darych lurched to his feet and let out a long and undulating war cry that reverberated through the air unleashing courage.

Adan held the reins and positioned himself in front. He thrust the sword under his legs so it would be there if he needed it. The road came quickly before him. The horses were making the turns accordingly, so he simply hung on. Myron came up and yelled into his ear. "You don't know how to drive this thing. Are you crazy?"

"No!"

Myron was nervous as he loaded his crossbow. "I don't know how we're getting out of this one." He tried to speak to Darych, but the general waved him away.

"Sit down, Boy," Darych told him. "I don't have the time."

The demons were on top of them. The first jumped high into the air and landed on Karyna's back. She screamed and tried to push it off. It was Riordan who saved her, knocking the demon to the ground before it had a chance to kill her. Another demon tackled Riordan and his horse swayed hard to the side.

Darych swore and cursed. Adan watched in disbelief as the carriage roared forward with demons running alongside the deck. Three jumped on the wagon. Darych killed two of them in a single swing of his sword and kicked the third off. He saved Myron who struggled to shoot his weapon. Two more landed on top of the man in red. Darych attacked. Their ghastly shapes were split in half by the power of his sword. Green blood sprayed through the wind.

Riordan finally had hold of the demon on top of him and threw it off. He pointed to Karyna. Adan heard him yelling over the noise of the battle. "Get on the deck with the others."

Another demon jumped into the air but missed the target, landing in front of Riordan's horse, and stomped into the dirt. Karyna sped alongside the deck. An arrow ripped through her hair as it fanned out behind her. Darych killed another demon and attempted to reach Karyna, but missed. A demon landed on Adan, pushing him onto his back. The creature lifted up its long claws and dove for his neck. It was Myron who saved him, slamming his crossbow over the creature's head. Adan pushed the demon up and off the deck.

Darych reached out for Karyna again. "Give me your hand!" he shouted. She grabbed his hand with hers, but before he could pull her off the horse and onto the deck, Adan screamed. The left wheels hit a hole in the road, and the entire flat deck jerked abruptly. Myron fell into Darych and knocked them both back. Darych grabbed Myron by his tunic and saved him from falling over the edge.

Adan watched the front left wheel peel apart. Darych turned back to him with an angry look, "Pay attention!" he shouted.

Adan repositioned himself at the helm of the deck and watched the road ahead of them closely; worried they didn't have much time before the wheel broke off completely. He grimaced as the road led them though the devastation they found earlier. The stench of death returned. From the corner of his eyes he saw Darych turn with a look of utter horror. He howled in protest. He stood with his sword in his hands as they passed through the destroyed encampment. His eyes welled and he howled again.

"Karyna!" Darych cried out to her. Karyna rode in close and reached with her hand. They clasped hands and they embraced as her feet landed on the deck. Darych spoke into her ear.   Karyna nodded to Darych and reached for the man in red, as if she was checking to see if he still lived.

Adan continued to hold on to the reins. He watched over his shoulder every chance he had. The demons fell back. Ahead of them the crossroads came into view. "Which way should we go?" Adan yelled out.

Darych knelt at his side. "I don't want to go either way."

"I agree," Adan shouted.

Another wall of demons blocked the road north. "We don't have much choice," Darych yelled. "Turn us south, hopefully we can outrun them."

Adan didn't want to go south. That would make them backtrack the way they had come, back toward Ruhln and Corrona, back toward the man stalking them. The horses shrieked when the demons tried to cut them off. They veered to the right galloping southward on the open road as it lay parallel to the Delilah River. The horses had no choice but to follow the twisting path, so Adan tied the reins off and climbed to his feet.

Three demons landed on Riordan and his horse, almost dragging the prince down on impact. Myron took aim with his crossbow and pulled the trigger. The tip of the arrow connected, spinning one of the demons into the air. "Get on the deck!" Darych shouted at Riordan. Riordan continued to struggle. The demons were swinging their claws. Riordan threw his hands over his head in protection. Myron had another arrow in place and fired it. It struck a demon in the face; it screeched in pain and dropped away. Riordan thrust his knife into the heart of the last one. Then he leapt onto the deck. He was covered with a mixture of red and green blood.

Karyna bled from a cut on her arm. Darych urged her to sit next to the man in red.

The demons swarmed them from everywhere now.

At the lowest part of the river, in the darkest corner, a heartbeat awakened. Amid the slow-moving currents and the freezing water, another stirred—Death. The ancient legend moved with its awakening—Death. Its long massive body jerked. It could feel the battle taking place. Blood from its ancestors cried for help. It roared and stretched. It rushed upward to the river's surface, gaining incredible speed as it went.

When Adan saw the creature blast out from the river, he was certain life itself had stopped. He watched it soar into the air, higher than the trees and up into the sky. Adan thought it wasn't going to stop, but then it came crashing down onto the road in front of them. Green and black scales armored its body. It stood on two legs with a long fin down its back. It looked at them through red eyes from a head that held level with the treetops. It opened its jaws and roared, revealing a long tongue and vicious teeth. Gills covered its chest, flapping from the torture of breathing air. It stepped forward and raised one of its massive arms.

Adan had once been told the tale of the Lord of the River, an ancient demon named Xerrand that patrolled the icy depths of the Delilah River. This had to be that demon. They were going to die. It was impossible to fight such a creature. Adan was stunned into inaction, incapable of deciding what to do. The ancient demon stood with its legs spread wide arching over the road as it raised its massive arm high into the air. Adan numbly waited to be smashed into nothingness.

Xerrand let them pass under his arched legs. Adan turned back, shocked that the monster didn't crush them when it had the chance. Bile rose from his stomach when he watched Xerrand snatch up demons and crush them like dried leaves. Those on the wagon finally regained their senses. They cheered in unison and applauded their new ally. Xerrand used his arm like a sword, striking down demons from every direction. The smaller demons leapt onto Xerrand's chest. The greater demon slaughtered them with impunity flinging them into the air as he pulled them away from his body. Then Xerrand soared higher than the trees and plunged with a mighty splash into the depths of the Delilah River.

Still, the demons came. Now they waited up ahead on the road, waiting for the deck to get to them. Adan fought to hold his courage. He swung the Dragon Sword back and forth with a mechanical effort. The sword came alive with a blue flare. Demons landed on the deck like insects. Amidst the chaos, a voice from within his mind told Adan to fight for his life.

Xerrand resurfaced and jumped onto the shore next to the road. Its tongue whipped out from its mouth and wrapped itself around a demon and pulled it back into its maw. He stomped with his feet and smashed with his long arms as he crushed most of the demons into the ground.

Darych fought off the last of the demons. Riordan protected Karyna and the stranger in red. Adan watched the surviving demons withdraw into the forest. Xerrand scared them away and dove back in the water. When Xerrand resurfaced, the stranger dressed in red, rose from where he lay and stretched his hands out toward the greater demon. The wind rushing over them stilled. The air transformed into a thick cloud. Blue lightning exploded from the stranger's fingertips. It reached for Xerrand amongst the fast-moving waves. The demon howled. As the lighting caught him, it sucked life out of the water using it to fuel its power. Xerrand roared and jerked amongst the lightning and waves. "No!" Adan shouted. He tackled the stranger slamming him onto the deck. "That demon helped us you fool!" At the back of his mind Adan wondered how someone could attain so much power and not use it against the demons that attacked them.

Several demons landed on the deck, taking them by surprise as distracted as they'd been with the unexpected attack on Xerrand. Darych fought to reach Karyna. A demon attacked her. As the tip of the claws were about to stab her neck, a flash of blue light engulfed and blasted the demon into the air. Karyna, stunned by the strange blast, threw her arms over her head and lost her balance. She slipped off the deck and hit the dirt road.

Darych cried out as he failed to help her. Adan knew with every stride they left the princess farther and farther behind. The demons came and came.

"I need you to hold them off!" Darych cried to Adan.

Adan nodded. He hoped he was fit for the task. Darych slid his sword into its scabbard and leapt onto the horses in front. Darych hobbled his way from horse to horse, almost falling as he finally reached the lead. He moved quickly to unbolt the horse from the rest of them. Adan watched in admiration as Darych broke free, halted his horse, and swung it around the other direction.

Adan screamed. A wall of demons stood ahead of them in the road. In front of them all was the one who murdered Adan's father. The front left wheel snapped. The deck jerked hard to the left, toward the river and a steep embankment. As the deck hit the ditch everyone was thrown off. Adan hit the ground and rolled to a stop. He gasped for breath and the scars on his face throbbed. Though his vision was blurred from pain, he saw the current of the river drag the remains of the wagon away. A demon attacked him. He swung his sword. The blade erupted in a blue flare and burned the demon to

ashes.
Myron and Riordan were nowhere to be seen. The river's edge was at his feet, and the man who killed his father approached him.

Karyna lay stretched out on the road unconscious. An image of an old man bending over her appeared in her mind. *"My daughter,"* a voice whispered. She jolted back to consciousness. Still the image came. *"My daughter,"* the voice whispered again.   She spat blood. Her teeth felt as if they were about to fall out. Her head throbbed in a rhythm that matched the pain throughout her body. Her wrists burned like fire. Her elbows stung. She knew the demons had her in sight. She pushed to her knees. Her stomach heaved. The old man flashed through her mind once more, whispering the words that haunted her, *"My daughter."*

The demons were upon her. Before she knew what was happening, long claws broke through her skin above her wrists and another at her elbows. She jumped to her feet and thrust her claws through a demons neck. A demon leapt onto her back, and she dug her left elbow into its gut. The tip of the claw penetrated its back. More demons came. One by one they fell at her feet. One after the other, Karyna battled them with her claws. The strength of their mystery ran through her blood. A demon lurched ahead, swinging its claws down at her face. She forced her left hand upward, their claws connecting on impact. The demon shrieked as she shattered its claws. She thrust her right hand into the demon and finished it off. They were all dead. Karyna slumped to the ground, consciousness slipping away. The last thing she heard was the whisper, *"My Daughter."* The claws disappeared.

Darych found her alive, but unconscious among the bodies of slaughtered demons. Except for the wounds on her hands she appeared fine. He positioned her atop the horse. He didn't have time to wonder what happened or how she survived. All that mattered was that she was alive. He mounted the horse and snapped the reins. Those that were in battle required his help.

Adan stepped back, afraid and uncertain about what he should do as the demon approached him in his thick black amour. His long black hair flared out behind him like a dark cape. Adan shielded his eyes from the glare of the silver breastplate. "Who are you?" the demon demanded. He lifted his long, powerful sword and pointed it directly at him. Adan felt his tongue twist with empty words. He took another step back and tripped over a log. He landed on his back and his hair brushed the river. "Tell me where you got that sword?" the demon insisted in his deep and demanding voice.

Adan looked down at the Dragon Sword, still settled in his firm grip. The sun beat down into his eyes, forcing him to squint. Thoughts rolled through his mind. He saw Dex and shot to his feet bringing the Dragon Sword up in front of him. "Where is my brother?" The demon attacked.

Darych Shade charged at them from the side deflecting the blow that would have killed Adan. "Get into the river!" Darych shouted. He and the demon became locked in a battle of swords.

Karyna stumbled down the bank behind Darych. Adan rushed to support her weight. The scent of demon was thick in her presence; the blood dripping from her wrists was thicker and darker than normal. Together they waded into the cold water and fought the current trying to claim their legs. Adan watched Darych battle the demon that killed his father. He felt like a coward and a failure. Adan searched the riverbank. Myron and Riordan were still missing; so was the man in red.

Darych stood his ground. Most of his efforts seemed to be blocking the demon's attacks. They moved in circles between thrusts, grinning at one another as they contemplated their next attack. The demon thrust his sword toward Darych's chest. Darych managed to turn in time, letting his armor deflect the attack. The demon raised his elbow and Darych took the blow to his nose and he tripped on a stone. The demon shrieked with triumph and plunged his sword down. Darych's arm was trapped between his back and the ground, but he managed to deflect the blow with his foot. He kicked again and shoved the demon away from him. He was back on his feet in an instant. The demon regained his balance, Darych attacked. The demon parried and swung. Darych dodged and the sword whistled over his head. Both of them were tired. With every blow Darych struck, Adan wanted it to kill.

"Darych!" Karyna yelled.

Darych shouted his war cry and struck again, forcing the demon to turn and counter. With his free hand Darych punched the demon square in the jaw. Then he turned and ran to Adan and Karyna. Karyna reached for his hand and together they pushed out into the river. Adan went down when the current grabbed him. He lost his grip on Karyna and was pulled away. Water stung his eyes. His lungs begged for air. The current pulled him far into the depths of the bone chilling river. Adan felt himself snagged by a whirlpool and around he went, trapped by the twisting eddy.

The demons fired their arrows into the water. Demon Stihl watched helplessly as his prey disappeared down the river. He raised his hand to stop his army from wasting arrows. The sting in his jaw faded as he massaged his skin with his fingers.

Demon Myra came down from the sky, hanging from the deamlon's talons. She landed on the ground in front of him; her face already mocking him. "I'm too late; you've already failed."

"They had help."

She shook her head at him, "Excuses."

Stihl shouted, "Enough!" He pointed out into the river. "Who is that boy?"

She frowned with a puzzled look. "What…boy?"

"The boy who resembles the one we killed at Ruhln. There is no way he could survive such a blaze. Vayle destroyed him with his fire."

Demon Myra appeared distraught. "I don't know what you're talking about. We have the younger one. Vayle is on his way to speak with him."

"No," Stihl hissed, "there was a twin."

"That's impossible."

"He has to be. This boy is identical to the one we killed at Ruhln."

She started to panic, "But that would mean—."

Stihl was annoyed. "Yes."

"I must tell Vayle."

"That also means our Dryden in Ruhln lied to us." Stihl told her. "I will have him terminated quickly."

"Do what you must." Demon Myra lifted her pet above her head, motioning the deamlon to take flight. "Once I return to the tower," Myra nodded to the deamlon, "Ashera will be your guide. Find and kill them. If a son of Darren Ches still lives, he must be destroyed. He cannot survive."

Stihl nodded and watched her fly away. He looked back to the river.

How he yearned for a true opponent. The Commander of the Wyndhaven Forces gave him a good fight, but it was not the battle he longed for. This boy, wielding a Dragon Sword, could very well do that.

Adan dozed in and out of consciousness. His mind drifted from place to place, straying across his deepest thoughts. His dreams returned; haunting nightmares that mocked him. He visualized his enemy standing before him with his deadly sword. The demon laughed—laughed at his cowardly behavior. "Fight me, you coward!" the demon taunted.

"No!" Adan cried. He held the Dragon Sword like a child in his arms. "Leave me alone!"

Dex entered his mind then. The image of the demon and his sword faded away. His brother hung chained to a wall. His feet dangled above the floor. "Help me."

"Dex," Adan cried.

At the bottom of the river Adan continued to spin around helplessly. Something cradled his back and reached around him. He felt himself lifted out of the water. Adan forced his eyes open and stared at the clear blue sky. He coughed up water. The breeze bit his wet skin. He shivered from the cold. Xerrand cradled him protectively in his slime-covered arms. He carried Adan to the bank and gently laid him on the grass. He groaned farewell and returned to the river depths. Adan's last thoughts danced around death as his exhausted and bruised body absorbed the soothing warmth of the sun.

Chapter 31

He shivered searching for warmth. He felt blood run down his neck and wondered why it felt so cold. Adan opened his eyes. He was on his side staring into a fire beneath the moonlight. Myron sat beside him talking to Darych. Riordan was next to him tending to a wound on his leg. Karyna was there, too. Everyone survived, even the man in red who lay across from him. Adan grunted with displeasure when he saw him. Adan felt uneasy with the presence of the man in red. He attacked Xerrand instead of the demons that were trying to kill them.

"Adan, you're awake." It was Myron, bending over him and leaning into his face.

"Yes." He coughed. His lungs ached.

"We're fortunate, Adan. Xerrand saved us all. We watched you disappear below the surface for a long time."

Adan asked the man in red. "Why did you attack him?"

Myron intervened. "His name is Talin. He already explained it to us."

"We know everything, Adan." Darych said to him. "Talin was sent from his master to find you. He believes that your family is somehow tied into these strange events. He also explains that you could be our only hope."

Adan stared at him confused. "What do you mean?"

Darych flashed Myron a smile. "Normally, I wouldn't believe such things. However, I was sent from the king to find an old friend of his in Ruhln. From what Myron tells me, that man was your father. That makes you a very important person, Adan. I will do everything in my power to keep you safe."

"My father was an old friend of the king?" Adan's words were slurred. He rolled over on his back. As he drifted away, he heard Myron explain how they saved a dragon.

He awakened in the morning next to a smothered fire. Adan understood that a fire was necessary to keep him alive, but they may have revealed their position to the demons. He remembered how the demon that killed his father approached him and asked Adan who he was. The tone of his voice hinted that he already knew. He trembled from the thought and tightened his cloak.

Talin slept in a sitting position against a tree. His chest heaved slowly with each breath. Myron and Karyna were both awake whispering to each other a few strides from camp. "How do you feel?" Myron asked when he noticed Adan was awake.

Karyna smiled. Her long red hair was wrapped around her neck and stopped above her breasts. It was her luminous blue eyes that held Adan's tongue. He had heard that the Princess of Wyndhaven was beautiful, but her presence was truly regal. He thought about Maureen and the comfort of his home. Perhaps leaving Ruhln was as foolish as Myron secretly thought.

"How do you feel, Adan," Myron repeated.

"I'm fine. Where are Darych and Riordan?"

Myron pointed to the water. "They're scouting up and down the river bank to find the best route for us."

"What do you mean?" Adan felt dizzy when he stood so he leaned against an elk tree. It was then that he saw that Xerrand placed them on the eastern side of the river. If they attempted to continue to Wyndhaven, they must cross the river.

Myron approached him. "Last night we decided to stay together. I hope you don't get upset, but I spoke on your behalf. I told them you wouldn't have a problem with that. It is necessary to go to Wyndhaven before something happens. Karyna promised to send guard units back to Corrona with Riordan. They will also send units to Ruhln. Darych will help search for Dex."

Adan rubbed the wound on his neck, wondering why anyone would want to help him. "I'm glad to hear that." His lungs were sore. Though it was early in the day the temperature was climbing rapidly. He was tired of being cold at night and extremely hot during the day. Karyna smiled at him. He wasn't sure how to act in her presence. Riordan was easier to speak with. With Karyna he felt the need to be cautious when addressing her. "Thank you for your help, Karyna," he said to her. She nodded and walked off rubbing her wrists.

"You're alive," Darych said as he and Riordan walked into camp.

"Yes."

"You worried us, Adan." Riordan said. The back of his neck showed damage from the demons claws.

Adan peered at the wounds. "How are you?" he asked Riordan.

"I'll live. We went for a pretty good spill down the river."

"We're all fortunate to be alive," Darych told them. "Confidence should be gained from that. We have a long trek back to Wyndhaven, and once we cross the river we're going to have it tough trying to get past that demon army."

"You know which way we're going then?" Myron asked.

"North," Darych said. "If I remember correctly, we should be able to cross the river near the Stag of Waters." He looked at Riordan. "We think the demons went south. I doubt they've given up on us, more than likely they're searching for a crossing themselves." He looked at Adan. "Can you walk?"

"Yes."

"Good. Talin is still in rough shape. How he managed to survive the river is anyone's guess. We need to help him."

Myron said that Talin explained his actions against Xerrand. Even though his friend sounded comfortable with the explanation, Adan wanted to hear it first hand. Darych nudged Talin awake and helped him to his feet. Talin's gray eyes were steely. Most of his blond hair was hidden by the hood of his cloak. Tattoos scribed the base of his neck. These odd markings reminded Adan of writing he saw once while visiting Cadin with Maureen. He asked, "Why did you attack Xerrand?"

Talin glanced at him. "Ah, the young man known as Adan Caynne is awake." He replied, speaking as if it pained him. "I'm sorry for my actions, Adan. Let us begin our journey, and I will tell you on the way."

"Keep your strength, Talin. I'll tell him what you told us last night." Darych pulled Talin's arm over his neck. He held him by the waist and together they began to walk.

They had nothing else to take with them, except their weapons. Adan was stunned to find his father's sword lying on the ground next to him. How he managed to hang onto it during his trip down the river amazed him. He picked it up and tied the scabbard to his back. Myron squeezed his shoulder, "You gave me a good scare yesterday. You don't know how relieved I am to see you back on your feet."

Adan nodded, "You as well, Friend." Adan's muscles tightened against his sore bones as he walked. The thought of struggling all day was tiresome. Adan knew it was best not to complain. He wasn't the only one in discomfort. He walked next to Darych and Talin hoping to get the explanation he longed for. The rest of the group trailed them as they followed the river north. The deadfall on the eastern side of the river forced them farther from the river than they wanted. He positioned Talin's arm around his neck. With Darych on the other side they helped him along. Adan waited eagerly for Talin's explanation.

"Thank you, Adan." Talin's voice sounded appreciative. Adan replied with a nod in his direction. Talin continued, "You slept through our conversation last night. I finally found strength to talk. I explained to everyone who I am and how I got here."

"He also explained how he managed to heal so quickly," Darych added.

Talin smiled. "I'm an apprentice, Adan. I'm in training to become an Andar, like my mentor, Jayntil."

Adan shot him an appraising look. "You are an Andar?"

"Yes. A short while ago my master had a vision. I later found that it was of you. At first we didn't know where you were, only that you were in great danger. I was sent to find you."

"How did you find out it was me he sought?"

"My master is highly adept in the abilities of an Andar. I do not question his capabilities; I do as I'm told. That would be a question you may have to ask him yourself. I would even suggest asking yourself that question first, and perhaps you might already know the answer."

Adan shook his head. "That makes little sense to me. My father's life was a mystery. Maybe the answer lies within his past, but it is not a question I can answer on my own."

"Jayntil told me to travel to Ruhln and find a young man named Adan. That's all I knew. It is possible that he was somehow able to connect with you mentally." Adan's memory drifted back to the night demons attacked Ruhln. When he was in a life-and-death struggle with a demon, a voice spoke within his mind just before a blast from within killed the demon. He relayed his story to the Andar apprentice. "The answer comes," Talin replied. "Before I could explain to you exactly how Jayntil was able to do that, there would be so much more to explain first."

Adan wanted to know how that was possible, and why Jayntil found it necessary to send his apprentice after him. His mind circled around the events and he found himself confused. "Why me?" he asked.

"I don't know. I do what I'm told. Once we arrive at Wyndhaven, I'll send word to my master. He'll want to meet with you right away."

The sun felt warm so Adan loosened his cloak. Talin was heavier than he appeared and Adan wondered how Darych managed to carry him so long on his own.

Adan had heard some things about Andars and their magical powers, but he didn't know what there purpose was. "What exactly is an Andar?" Adan asked.

Talin smiled. "Historians, if you prefer to call us that. We study every type of ancestry, different kinds of power and strength. Yannina is a world full of mysteries, especially ones of religion." Talin coughed.

"Save your strength, Talin, let me explain it to him." Darych offered.

"That's fine, Darych, speaking helps my strength return." He cleared his throat. "We are also much more than that. With certain beings comes a certain aura, their life force, if you will. As an Andar, I'm trained to draw on that power. I can also amplify it. The six of us combined provides a powerful aura. You see, Adan, right now I'm drawing on that power. I bring it into my body to contain and make it stronger. Once I've done that, I can send the energy back into us. How are you feeling now? Better I hope."

Adan realized that the Andar apprentice was correct. His muscles had loosened; he felt stronger; his lungs no longer pained him when he took a deep breath. "Yes, I do."

"If it were not for me, we would all be back at the river lying there near death."

Adan thought he understood. "That's what you were doing during the battle then...drawing on our life force to summon your powers?"

"Actually, Adan, I was drawing power from the enemy." A smile formed on the corner of his lips. "That was how my master found you on that dreadful night. You see, every living being in Yannina has an aura. Andars use the auras of those who live as a guide. They travel from one to the other until we find those we seek. Jayntil found you. That is how he was able to use your aura to kill that demon."

Adan was intrigued and wanted to know more. "Do you and your master always do this?"

"No, only when we must. When Darych and Karyna found me, I was barely alive. I used their combined aura until I could sense my own; that is when I began to heal quickly by using the three of us together. When the battle began, I drew power from the enemy."

"Why would you do that? Why not keep using Darych and Karyna?"

"When using this life force there is a price. Our aura will fade as I draw from it, becoming weaker and weaker. If I were to use it completely, we would all become fragile."

"We would be weak?" It was Darych who asked. He obviously had not gone as deep into Talin's explanation the night before.

"No, you wouldn't be weak; you would be fragile. There is a difference. Once the life force is depleted we crave more. It's hard for me to describe. My mentor is much better at it than I." Talin paused as he tried to form the right words to explain. "Our aura protects us, keeps us from harm. Do you know that feeling you get when you think somebody is watching you? That feeling you get when you're certain that danger is nearby? That is your aura warning you of the danger. If I were to use it completely, it would slowly return; however, you will be left without it for quite some time. It affects our built-in warning system, our survival wisdom."

"Shouldn't you stop drawing on it, then?" a worried Darych asked.

Talin laughed between fits of coughing. "No, I've barely scratched the surface. I've taken only what we need to move on, enough to give us strength to keep walking. Unless we become involved in another battle, we should be fine."

"That's strange to me. I had not heard much about an Andar before," Adan admitted.

"That could be your father's doing, Adan," Darych offered.

Adan knew that was true, now more than ever. "Talin, do you know where these demons are coming from?"

The Andar apprentice nodded slowly. "In the past few years, during our studies, my master and I stumbled upon something. I'm going to explain some history to you first, and though I'm certain you've heard this story many times; I will explain it to you as it was meant to be told." He cleared his throat, "Centuries ago, Faral, along with his bride and his brother Faris, discovered a world overrun with demons. Faral decided to rid the world of this evil. His first battle was on the northern shores. It was upon his first victory when he named the new world after his beautiful bride, Yannina. After several years of dreadful battles, Faral controlled northern Yannina. At that time he was betrayed by his brother who stole his bride and fled south of the mountains. Here Faris managed to ally with the demon hordes. Thus began the eternal conflict between Faral and Faris. Faral found his forces diminishing as he fought his wicked brother, so he searched for an alternative to defeat Faris. In his search, he stumbled upon a portal that could only be opened during an alignment of the moons. Knowing he had only one chance to succeed, he staged a final battle between himself and his brother. History proves that Faral won that battle, thus sending the demons through the portal. Yannina was killed during that fight; it is said that Faral took revenge by murdering his brother. Now"—a smile spread on Talin's lips—"this is where it becomes interesting. This part of the story is not as well known as the rest of it. In death Faris managed to claim a power so undeniably powerful it thrust him to a completely new level. Beyond the grave, Faris summoned select demons from beyond the portal, ones of strong aura and determination. He named them Dryden. The Dryden became his servants, and Faris promised to reward them for their loyalty. The Dryden's first task was to seek out and kill Faral Ches—and they succeeded. In his death, Faral also obtained this power. He chose those from Yannina who showed greatness and loyalty. He named them the Warriors of Ches. And the legend continues even today, Adan. Whenever the Dryden surface, Faral chooses those worthy enough to become Warriors of Ches to foil their evil schemes."

Adan nodded. "What power could both Faral and Faris find in death?"

Talin shook his head. "That is one answer I think all of us seek. I have always wondered one thing: Their hatred for another could have been something unlike any of us could ponder, to fight each other even after death, after all these years."

"But why are the demons returning now? Has Faris sent the Dryden out again?"

Talin lifted his finger, motioning him to wait for his answer. "The moons, Adan, are also an important part of Yannina's history. As I mentioned, Faral used a portal during an alignment to seal off the demons. Jayntil has studied the pattern of the moons and their rotation around our world. Sometime during the next year, the moons will align once again. As this alignment comes closer in time, the demons are appearing in heavier numbers and their strength increases. I believe these evil Dryden are in our world even now, preparing for this event. My master believes this is the sole reason why Yannina is in grave danger."

Adan felt uncomfortable with the thought that the worse was yet to come. Everything Talin explained to him made sense, but it didn't explain to him why he'd attacked Xerrand. "So, why did you attack Xerrand?"

"There is a myth. I read a book once that was from the time of Faral. The pages were brittle and faded, but I managed to piece together some of the information. Whoever wrote the book explained that there were three greater demons that guarded certain water landmarks within Yannina. The exact locations weren't mentioned. I was only able to decipher two of the names, Xerrand and Xerros." Talin took a nervous breath. "Xerrand protect us, Xerros destroy us. When I was lying on the carriage deck, I recalled that passage. I was terrified that it was Xerros attacking us. I didn't know it was Xerrand, or that he helped us."

Adan eyed him suspiciously. "Are you always able to call on that kind of power when you're near death?"

Talin appeared as if he were about to laugh. "As I already explained, I drew power from the aura of the enemy and amplified my powers."

Adan shook his head in uncertainty. There was something he didn't approve of. Everything the Andar apprentice told him made sense, he simply chose not to believe it. His explanations seemed . . . simple. "Why do you think Xerrand helped us?"

"I wish I knew," Talin replied, though he glanced at Karyna. "But there is something strange in the air."

A tree blocked their path, and instead of walking all the way around the elk tree, Darych climbed up and reached back for Talin. Adan helped push Talin up, then motioned the others to follow. Karyna needed a boost to help herself up, and then Myron and Riordan followed.

"One thing I have noticed since we encountered one another is that your aura is especially strong," Talin said to Adan.

Adan didn't know what to think about that. He was no longer in the mood to discuss the issue. He wanted more answers, but for now he felt they were better off left alone.

They continued their journey into the late afternoon. Adan could no longer help carry the extra weight and Myron relieved him. Riordan eventually took over for Darych and they pressed forward. Adan trailed behind them, and Darych joined him. "I want to thank you for helping us yesterday," Adan said to him.

"Well, it's not like I had much of a choice, now is it?"

"You saved my life, thank you."

"Do you know who that demon was?" Darych asked him.

"I don't know who he is, but he's the one who killed my father."

Darych shook his head. "Should I have fought him any longer, I don't think I would have survived. He was by far my greatest opponent."

"I have never been so afraid in my life." Adan kicked at a stick lying on the ground.

"You acted bravely. I recall a moment where you challenged the enemy when it was necessary. Where did you get that sword of yours?"

"It belonged to my father. I don't know anything about it."

"It appeared to be very powerful. I would hang onto that."

Adan watched the man in red. "Do you trust the Andar apprentice?"

Darych nodded, "As much as I trust any of you. My father said something to me once that stays with me: Always give the benefit of the doubt until you are proven wrong."

"You mean I should trust Talin until he proves otherwise?"

"You do what you feel is best. Never forget that. If you choose my advice, make it your decision." Adan smiled. He liked Darych. He hoped that once they made it to Wyndhaven Darych would keep his promise and help him find Dex. "I was sorry to hear what happened in Ruhln. I wish we had known and sent help to your village. Apparently your father was a good friend to the king. I know he would've done everything in his power."

"Thank you."

"Is your mother alive?"

"No. She died when Dex was born."

"Myron mentioned him last night. He's your missing brother, correct?"

"Yes. I know he's alive and I know I'm going to find him."

Darych grabbed Adan's shoulder firmly with his hand. "That's a strong attitude. You make sure you stick with it, no matter what. I'll do whatever I can to help you. I feel I owe that to you."

Adan found comfort in his words. "I would very much like to speak to the king in regards to my father."

"Consider it done."

Adan dreaded the truth about his father's past. It was a mystery to him his entire life. His father never wanted him to know anything about it. Who was he to intrude on that? He remembered the anxiety he'd felt when he'd found out that his father had befriended a dragon. Before he and Zadryan encountered Zar on that night, Adan actually wanted to know more about his father. When it didn't happen he assumed it wasn't meant to be. It reminded him of home when he found his father's closet empty.

Darych seemed distraught. He only noticed it now as they crossed a creek. Through their entire conversation Adan hadn't noticed, but now as he recalled, he could remember Darych talking to him, but his mind had obviously been elsewhere. "Darych, I'm truly sorry about what happened to your men."

Darych turned his eyes away from him, looking out into the forest. "I haven't dealt with that yet, and don't know if I ever will. Those were my friends. Now I realize we are entering a time of war. They were among the first victims of this war. I can understand that fate has spared my life, so that I might avenge them." He turned to Adan with wet eyes. "And avenge them I will."

They walked in silence after that, leaving Adan pondering what he meant when he mentioned fate. He pieced together the information he gathered, but came short of a reasonable explanation. He finally concluded that it didn't really matter. They were all together in a terrible mess and that's all he needed to be concerned with. He still wasn't sure about Talin. If the Andar apprentice spoke the truth he could become a great ally. Adan thought of Karyna as well. Other than a brief conversation with Myron, he hadn't heard her speak. She walked alone and never offered any conversation to anybody. He thought about trying to talk to her, but there was something about her mood that told him to leave her alone.

Their search for a crossing failed. The river was swift. None of them had any idea how deep the water was. Adan mentioned that the demons could be waiting for them and everyone agreed it was a possibility. By nightfall everyone was hungry and exhausted. They found a suitable camp in a small clearing near the river. Darych wanted to be able to keep a watch on the other side. He wanted to know if the demons were patrolling the western bank. After they settled into a camp, Myron offered to hunt something for dinner, but Darych considered a fire too risky.

Adan settled against the trunk of an elk tree, studying Talin closely as Riordan helped the Andar apprentice down beside him. Adan questioned the abilities of the apprentice once more, trying to understand him. It would be impossible to know if Talin was stealing his aura to strengthen himself. Adan remembered his explanation; that using an aura affected their wisdom, and again he felt the apprentice was not to be trusted. Adan eventually let the matter go. He knew there was nothing he could do about it…for now. He found it difficult to hold his eyes open and his stomach rumbled with hunger.

Darych offered to take first watch and Adan thanked him, but he chose to stay awake as his new friends settled next to each other around the base of a tree. The temperature was cooler now that the sun disappeared. He wrapped his cloak around him and prayed that Dex was more comfortable. He thought of Zadryan. His worry that Zar caught him that night grew. He hoped Zadryan returned safely to his den. Perhaps his dragon friend would find them and fly them back to Wyndhaven. Adan could only hope.

Myron snored. They had become closer friends since they had left Ruhln than they were their entire lives; Adan wanted nothing more than to see Myron safely home again. He almost laughed. He couldn't believe he'd tried to leave Ruhln without him. He had been so foolish that night. He thanked Maureen and wished her well. Riordan slept next to Myron. The prince was an interesting companion. Adan would never forget the moment when he and Myron pulled off that blanket. Riordan would make an excellent king. Karyna was difficult to understand with her mind off in some distant place. Darych, for some reason, always appeared unsteady around her. When he spoke to her, it was with great care not to upset her. Adan would never fail to appreciate how running into those two saved his life. Without Darych during their battle along the road, they would have perished. As he drifted to sleep, he thought one last time of Dex. "I'll find you, brother."

Karyna withdrew herself from the others as each of them fell asleep. Darych stood with his back to her, gazing out over the river. He heard the rustle of her boots on the dry ground and turned to face her. "How are you?"

She spoke quietly. "I've been better."

He nodded. "As have all of us, I'm sure."

Karyna didn't want him harassing her right now. "I need some time alone."

"I can't have you where I can't see you. Please stay here."

She approached the riverbank. She leaned down and felt the water with her fingers. The scars on the back of her wrists tormented her. She tried to remember what the old man had looked like, the one who'd come to her in her mind before the claws appeared. There was a familiarity with his appearance, as if she should know who he was.

Darych tried to comfort her. He placed his hand on her shoulder. "Tell me what happened."

"No, please, leave me be." She tried not to cry.

He nodded and left her alone. "I'm here if you need to talk to someone."

She found it difficult to believe that he was genuinely concerned. Only Sheilna and Frenna really cared for her, and now they were dead. She rubbed the scars on her wrist. She would never forget the feeling of the claws when they appeared. At the moment of battle she prized the power that flowed through her body, the excitement as she killed one demon after the other. She shivered. That was not who she was. She didn't enjoy killing. What would Rowen think when he discovered she was some sort of freak? She stared at the holes in her skin and cried. At the back of her mind, she almost hoped Darych would return to comfort her.

Chapter 32

Demon Myra waited for him at the prison door. She tapped her black boots on the cold, rock floor. She taunted the prisoner with her weapon as she wove the metal whip around her slender body. From behind her, Demon Vayle descended into the depths of J'yradal. The tower sank deep into the mountains with a staircase twirling around the outer rim. Above him the clouds were black as the night as they spun around in twisted eddies. "How is he?" Vayle asked her.

"Weak."

"Excellent. How did the battle fare?"

"Stihl failed you. Both Riordan and Karyna escaped."

"Argh! If I cannot have the prince I want him dead. He must be destroyed."

"There's more. One of Darren's sons survived the attack on Ruhln. There was a twin."

Vayle turned, his rage fuming from beneath his red cloak. "That's impossible."

She pointed into the prison. "His brother lives."

Vayle unleashed his power, tearing into the bars of the cage. The steel bent and twisted enough that Vayle could slip through. He dove for the boy dangling above the floor by chains on his wrists. Vayle reached around his neck with his skeletal hands and glared into his eyes. "What is your name, boy?"

"Dex," he whispered in a barely audible voice.

"How many brothers do you have?" Dex ground his teeth as he shivered in his grip. The boy kicked him, pushing Vayle backward. "Fool!" Vayle shouted. Lightning ripped from his fingers and shattered rock and stone to pieces. He reached for the boy again and in a dangerously soft voice that shouted his rage said, "Tell me." Dex spat at him. Vayle removed his hood slowly and revealed his features to the boy for the first time. The woman behind him backed away in fear. Dex shook with absolute terror as Vayle approached him. "How many brothers do you have?" Vale asked for the third time.

Dex swallowed and whispered "Two."

"What are their names?"

"Adan and Aren."

"There *were* two of them!" Vayle shouted with fury. He shook his skeletal fist. "I will go. I will kill him myself. Where is he?" he asked Myra.

"Riordan has allied with Karyna. The boy is with them. They are approaching the Stag of Waters."

Vayle pointed at her. "Gnith is on his way here to watch the boy. You will meet Aramaz as he approaches Wyndhaven. We must complete the final phase of our plan or our previous efforts are wasted. Do not fail me as Stihl failed me, or you will suffer a punishment so powerful you will hate that you ever lived."

Demon Myra nodded and knelt before him. "Yes, Master Vayle."

Vayle sped away, up the stairs and out of the tower, leaving her alone with the boy. His rage faded as he thought more and more of the situation. At least there was the second thrill of killing the son of Darren Ches. There was something about doing it twice that felt exhilarating. Waiting for him at the entrance to the underground tower was the black dragon Zar. "Take me to Stihl."

Chapter 33

Adan and his new allies continued their journey in the morning. They traveled north along the eastern side of the river. Darych led the way and helped Talin, followed closely by Karyna and Riordan. Adan and Myron came last and talked about their adventures. The sun was strong on this day. The sunlight always seemed to find gaps through the trees to heat the forest. The forest flattened and the river widened as they progressed. It forced them farther east. As evening approached the tired group found themselves standing at the edge of a swamp. "The Stag of Waters," Talin said, still holding onto Darych and wiping the sweat from his brow.

Myron glanced in his direction. "What?"

Talin turned, "The Stag of Waters. This is the beginning of a long series of swamps and drenches. We traveled too far to the east."

"I thought we would be able to cross the river here," Darych said. He rested while Talin sat on a stump. "Talin's right. The water is too deep. We are too far east."

"What do we do, then?" Riordan asked. "We must get to Wyndhaven. Perhaps we can turn west and get across the river."

"That depends," Talin answered. "Are we prepared for the difficulty of the journey?"

"Maybe we could turn back and regain our course," Karyna said.

"Then we will have to face the demons again." Everyone turned to Myron, standing next to Karyna. "What if they're following us on the other side?"

Talin smiled. "I think, Myron, we don't have to worry about that."

"What do you mean?" Karyna asked.

"I imagine the demons have already crossed the river and charge after us this very moment."

Demon Vayle backhanded Stihl with his bony fingers. "You incompetent fool!" Stihl wiped the blood from the corner of his lips. He stared back at Vayle with loathing. "Why did they escape?" Vayle demanded.

"Xerrand aided them."

Vayle reeled in disgust. He used his powers to drop Stihl to his knees. He shot lightning into his metal breastplate straight into his heart. "I will ask you only one more time. Why did they escape?"

Stihl screamed in agony. He ground his teeth together as he tried to break free and cried out, "Because I failed."

Vayle released his power and pushed Stihl to the ground. "Never fail me again." Zar waited behind him. Vayle turned to the dragon. "Fly my army across the river. Keep low as you are not to be seen."

"Yes, Master." Zar stretched out his wings, pitch black against the burning sun. The demons swarmed onto his massive back.

Vayle turned back to Stihl. "Go to Ruhln, find the Dryden that lied to us and kill him. I will kill the prince. I will kill the princess." He shook his skeletal hands in the air. "And I will kill Adan."

Zar flew to the other side of the river. A few more passes and the dragon would have moved his army of demons. Then they could hunt down the miserable humans. It was crucial to kill them all at once. Some weird twist of fate brought them together, but it served Vayle's needs precisely. He growled in anticipation. Kidnapping Riordan had been imperative. He admitted to his mistake of using his demons to kidnap the young dragon, so that he might use it as bait to capture the young dragon's mother. It was a mistake that cost him the prince. Now he would utilize other methods. Let the prince live his final moments with his new friends. He smiled and said, "Kill them all."

The group forced themselves through the murky water. A steady wind rippled the surface carrying the stagnant smell of still water with it. Their feet sank into the slime underneath pulling at their legs and slowing them down. Green moss floated on top of the knee-deep water. It clung to their clothes. Gilled swamp rats circled them and snapped at the leeches. Snakes with bladed fins as sharp as knives watched them with interest. Myron shot arrows at them to keep them at a distance. Stark and barren trees leaned awkwardly out of the water as if death pulled them down. Insects drilled holes into their ash-colored trunks. Riordan did his best to help Talin walk.

As the day went on, it appeared the prince pulled him through the water. It was exhausting to watch Darych struggle with his armor. Karyna threw fits of tearful rage as the leeches harassed her.

The Stag of Waters forced them even farther to the east. Their hopes of crossing were low. The swamps grew in depth and magnitude; islands of dry land were sparse. They found an island uphill from a long drench that ran east to west. It was hard to cross in the mud; it took the entire afternoon for them to reach the other side safely.

Adan collapsed on the dry land. The trees surrounding them were different from the deadwood that mostly inhabited the swamps. "These are marwin trees," Myron said.

"Like the ale?" Darych asked.

Adan had never seen a marwin tree before. It was a short tree without leaves. Instead it had vines with small flowers. "Willem in Ruhln uses marwin trees to flavor ale," he said.

Darych smiled. "So that's why it's called marwin ale."

Myron drew his knife from his belt and slammed it into the tree. As he worked he explained what he was doing. "A marwin tree has seven layers of bark. In the middle is the stem, or the core. That's what Willem uses to flavor the ale." He looked at them with a wide grin. "It's safe to eat and it tastes great." After Myron stripped away the layers of bark, he cut out a large piece from the stem. He walked over to Karyna and held it out to her. "Try it." Karyna scowled and hid behind Darych. Myron offered it to Riordan, but the prince humbly declined. "Darych?"

Darych shook his head. "You try it first."

Myron sliced a piece and handed it to Adan. He bit off a bite. Adan was surprised to find the texture soft, but the taste was potent with pitch.

Myron cut out another piece and handed it to Darych. He put it into his mouth and turned and spat nearly hitting Karyna.

Adan asked, "What's the matter?"

"That tastes terrible."

"It's not that bad," Adan defended.

Riordan held out his hand. "I'm hungry enough; let me try it." He took a bite and forced it down. "If it will help my strength return, than I will eat it."

Myron offered a piece to Talin. The Andar apprentice politely declined. Darych stood beside Myron and shook his head. "You two are ridiculous."

Adan smiled. "It's really not that bad."

Myron pointed west. "It would be nice to find the river, and wash down the flavor with some water."

Talin shook his head. "The Delilah River is unsafe to drink. The water that seeps from the Stag of Waters is poisonous."

Myron shot a look at Adan. "I told you not to drink the river water. You never listen to me."

Adan raised his brows. "You never said such a thing. It was your idea to drink out of the river, not mine."

Myron shook his head as if he were pleasantly displeased. "I remember trying to talk you out of it. You were persistent and drank it anyway." He pointed to the prince. "You even forced Riordan to drink it." Adan spat out the marwin stem and shook his head in disgust. When he noticed a twitch at the corner of Myron's mouth, he knew Myron was playing. He laughed and reached for another piece of marwin, the incident already forgotten.

Darych smirked and turned away from them. "We should try to get out of these swamps by nightfall."

"I agree," Riordan said. "The heat is keeping the insects away, but later it will cool off and they will come out of hiding. We'll never get any sleep."

Darych nodded. "We need that now more than ever." He pointed at Myron and Adan. "You two, stop messing around with that tree. We have to keep moving."

Myron was still hacking away at the insides to salvage what he could from the opening he created. Adan grabbed him by the shoulder as the rest of the group continued walking. "Don't eat too much," Adan warned him. "You haven't eaten much lately. It might upset your stomach."

Myron shoved some cuttings under his belt. "It tastes like the ale."

The Stag of Waters continued to be a difficult journey. Trees floated on the surface. Swamp vultures picked rats out of the water in front of them. The vultures were large and appeared brave enough to try to snatch even them as they waded through the water. Myron held them off with his crossbow. "The Stag of Waters has swallowed us," Talin said.

"What do we do?" Adan asked.

Karyna came up from behind them. Her face showed she was

depleted of strength.

"How are you, Karyna?" Talin asked her.

"I'm starving."

Myron handed her a piece of his marwin stem. "Trust me, you may not approve the taste but it will give you strength."

She sighed and nodded. She grimaced in distaste but managed to swallow.

The Angled Spine was clearly visible to the north as it rose straight out of the Stag of Waters. Dead trees stuck out of the water in every direction, as if the Stag of Waters had claimed them in one massive strike. They found a small knoll dry enough to keep warm. The insects flew over their heads in a cloud. "We will camp there for the night," Darych said. "Tomorrow we should be able to reach the other side."

Even though the ground was dry, water filled their footprints where they stepped. As long as Adan wasn't spending the night with water to his waist, he was grateful for what they had. They huddled close together and swatted at the blood flies. No one slept. Instead they spoke of their situation and for the first time Karyna joined the discussion. She told them all about Rowen who led the war against Terrace. It was strange to Adan to hear from somebody whose life was affected by events in northern Yannina. Akhran and Terrace were far away; they were no part of his life. Now, as he listened to Karyna, he felt as if her story was tied to theirs. Everything was part of the mystery of what was happening in their world. When she told them how Sheilna and Frenna died, Adan felt sorry for her. Just as he felt that he and Riordan had similarities in their quest, he began to feel that same connection with Karyna. She was just as affected by what was happening in Yannina as the rest of them. Yannina was no longer a safe place. They reminded each other of Wyndhaven and the importance of its power. Wyndhaven must not fall or they would lose hope of fighting back.

As darkness crept overhead, Adan offered to take first watch because he knew the last few days march depleted Darych's strength. Something told him they would need the general at his best. He settled himself on the bank of the island, where he could watch the swamps from nearly every direction. The dead trees became dark shadows in the night. The clouds blocked out the starlight.

"Adan, do you mind if I sit with you?"

It was the Andar apprentice. Adan had actually hoped for some time to himself, but perhaps the apprentice was hoping for some conversation.

Talin sat beside him and draped his hood over his head. "I was wondering if perhaps you could enlighten me on something."

"Me?" Adan asked in surprise. "What could I possibly understand that you wouldn't already know?"

Talin fixed his sight on him. "After our plight in the river, while you slept, Myron explained how the two of you saved a dragon."

"Yes, Myron spoke the truth. It was sheer coincidence how it came to happen."

"Would you mind telling me about it? Both my master and I have an immense knowledge of the history of Yannina, but the dragons remain a mystery. I was told once that they have been around since the time of Faral; that once they were the guardians of our world. However, neither of us has found any evidence to prove that theory. I must admit I'm fascinated. I wish to learn more about them."

Adan shook his head. "I don't believe I can help you with that. Zadryan hasn't said much to me. All I know is that he and his mother are hunted by Zar."

"Who is Zar?"

"He's another dragon. He's black as the night. I've seen him. He is one dragon you do not want to face."

Talin leaned forward. "You saw him?"

Adan nodded. "The last night I saw Zadryan, he left in a panic because Zar was close. Shortly after Zadryan left, Zar flew over our camp. I haven't heard from Zadryan since."

Talin sighed. "Would you let me speak with him, should that chance ever occur?"

Adan had his suspicions of Talin. "I suppose, but only if Zadryan allows it."

"There are many legends of dragons, but somehow their subsistence managed to clear the history books. There is of course the myth of Anemenitty Ches, and how he once fought off the impending attack of the dragon race and their fire, but as I hear your story, I can't imagine how it could be true."

"There are dragons that would kill us," Adan confirmed.

"Yes, I suppose that is true. Do you not find it odd that one dragon could be your friend, while another would be your enemy?"

Adan nodded. "Not anymore. How is it that a greater demon, which at one point I never believed existed, arose from the depths of the river to save our lives?" Adan tugged at some grass by his boots. "Yannina has become a confusing land to me."

Talin waited a moment in silence. "You do have a point."

Adan felt uncomfortable talking about Zadryan. It felt like betrayal. He decided to change the subject. "You mentioned Anemenitty Ches. Would you tell me about him?"

"It is written that the Dryden found a way to control the dragon's fire; there is a myth that dragons can release their soul into their flame, to give it life. Once the dragon's fire has life; it cannot be defeated. The Dryden gained control of this unique power and sought to destroy Yannina. Faral recruited a man by the name of Anemenitty to seek out the truth and defeat the Dryden. Anemenitty was the first Warrior of Ches recorded in history. There was a female Andar who fought alongside him. They fought together for several years." Talin pointed to the Angled Spine. "I was told the battle ended high within the mountains. And even though Anemenitty Ches perished, he succeeded in defeating the Dryden. Much damage was done by dragon's fire. In time Yannina recovered."

"I find Yannina's history interesting now, as most of it seems to be myths and legends, yet also fact," Adan said.

Talin agreed. "With the appearance of demons, I would think the legends are more truth than myth."

"Do you believe in Faral, Talin? Do you really believe that he watches over us in spirit… that he protects us?"

"Of course I believe in Faral. As an Andar I must believe in Faral. Our primary mission is to continue his story, to keep our history alive."

Adan thought of the Warriors of Ches. If Dryden lived among them in their world, where were the Warriors of Ches? "How does Faral choose someone to fight for him?"

"I'm uncertain, to be honest. I have not been chosen. My master would know. Jayntil was a Warrior of Ches."

That sparked Adan's interest; "Really?" he asked.

Talin nodded. "Jayntil told me that Faral came to him in a dream. Faral explained to Jayntil what had to be done. When he awakened, he remembered their conversation perfectly, as if it hadn't been a dream at all."

Adan was beginning to believe the Andar apprentice. "Is he a

Warrior of Ches now?"

"No, he's never told me why. I'm unaware if Faral has chosen anyone."

Adan tossed a bit of wood down the bank and into the water. "So much evil has happened lately. I feel lost."

"Don't fret, Adan. We are all together in this endeavor." Talin stood and groaned. "I still have little of my strength. I suppose I should rest. Thank you for offering first watch." Talin settled in with the others.

Adan rubbed his forehead. Suddenly, he felt light-headed. He rubbed his eyes and tried to focus as he fought the urge to fall asleep. He stood and staggered down to the bank. He grabbed shrubs to keep himself from falling into the water. It was almost as if there was fog inside his head, crowding his thoughts. It was then a memory surfaced: He remembered the words of Talin when he said; "Our aura protects us, keeps us from harm. Do you know that feeling you get when you think somebody is watching you? That feeling you get when you're certain that danger is nearby? That is your aura warning you of the danger. If I were to use it completely, it would slowly return; however, you will be left without it for quite some time. It affects our built-in warning system, our survival wisdom." Adan fought at his own mind. "One thing I have noticed since we encountered one another is that your aura is especially strong."

The possibility of Talin using his aura to help his own recovery was maddening. Adan raked his fingers through his hair. Slowly the dizziness disappeared. He took a deep breath to recover. Adan didn't have the proof, but the Andar apprentice was not to be trusted. He was certain of it.

Chapter 34

Riordan woke. "*Come to me.*" Raindrops trickled into his ear from his hair. How odd, he thought, he hadn't seen a rain cloud in days. In the great distance of the sky he heard thunder rumble through the clouds. "*Come to me.*" He shook his head, wiped the wet away from his face. Everyone slept. Nobody kept watch. "*Come to me.*" He stood. The rain chilled him. "*Come to me.*" He rubbed his ears. He was drawn to the strange voice that came from within his head. He stared out over the swamp. At his feet lay the beginning of a solid path of dirt that made its way over the murky water. He was certain it hadn't existed when he fell asleep. "*Come to me now.*" Riordan ran from his friends into the night. He followed the strange path as it twisted and turned through the darkness. He could barely see it, but he knew it was there. Above him lightning ripped through the sky. "*Come this way.*" He ran faster. Lightning shot down again. Thunder exploded in his ears. The voice continually guided him along the strange path. Riordan obeyed. He was eager to discover this voice that summoned him. The path led him onto a small hill. Lightning lit up the sky. A beautiful lone tree stood in the center of a small island. Riordan approached the massive tree that soared into the sky. He shivered from the cold rain, but the promise of warmth from a strange glow urged him on. A glowing knife waited for him at the tree. An unknown force held it in the air as it turned and shimmered along the long silver blade. "*Take me.*"

Riordan grasped the handle. Thunder exploded as he touched the blade. The force of the rain tripled. He could barely breathe through the falling rain. His instincts took over. Visions within told him what to do. He thrust the knife into the tree. Red liquid spurted back at him. He sliced down the trunk. The bark split away and revealed the clear wood within. At the bottom of the tree Riordan stopped and pulled out the knife. He raised it back to where he had started and thrust the knife into the tree. Again and again Riordan worked with the knife as the voice from within drove him to cut away. He stepped away when the voice stopped. The knife slipped from his hand and spun upward into the cold air where it faded silently into nothing.

Riordan held a staff that he carved from the tree; it glowed with a blue haze that warmed and shielded him from the rain. Excitement flowed through him. He struck the ground with it. The staff flared to life with an explosion of pure light. Rage boiled up inside him. With his rage the staff grew twice its size. Riordan screamed and slammed the staff back into the ground. Again, the staff exploded and its length continued to increase. It was four times taller than Riordan now, yet still carried the same weight. He could spin it over his head, to the right and back to the left. The power of the staff coursed through his body.

"*Riordan,*" a voice from above called.

The prince stared up into the rain. "Who is this that beckons me?"

"*I am Faral, Riordan. I have chosen you to fight for Yannina, but first I must test you.*" In the pouring rain an image gathered before him. It used the falling water to create its form. The liquid body glimmered colors like a rainbow. The beautiful figure pointed at him. "*Will you accept this glorious honor?*"

Prince Riordan was overwhelmed. His voice was tremulous. "I accept, Faral."

"*When you have proven yourself worthy, I shall return to you. Use your new weapon carefully, Prince Riordan.*"

The rage within Riordan slipped away. The staff shrank back to its normal state. The glow disappeared and the voice was gone.

"Riordan?" He opened his eyes. Myron shook him lightly by his shoulder. "Riordan, it's time to leave." Riordan shook the sleep from his head and stood up. The others were all awake and standing around. It wasn't raining; there wasn't a cloud in the sky. "Are you all right?" Myron asked.

Riordan shivered from the moisture of the night. "Yes, I'm fine."

"You slept well," Darych said. "I tried to wake you for your watch, but you wouldn't budge."

The memory of the night reminded him of a hangover. Everything about it felt so real. "Sorry, Darych, I didn't mean to . . . ."

"Don't stress over it. You needed the rest." Darych looked north. "Talin, how much farther do you think it is to the other side?"

"Not far. The mountains are close now."

Myron said, "Let's keep moving." He seemed anxious.

They left their camp. Riordan waited until they were all in front of him before he followed. It must have been a dream; he shook his head. And what an odd dream it was. But in his fingers, he could almost feel power pulsating, urging him to summon it forth.

Later that afternoon, Adan and the others were ready to give up and head back the way they'd come. They reached the north side of the Stag of Waters and stood together at the base of the mountains. The forest took a dangerously steep incline and the river dropped into a deep canyon. "What are we going to do?" Darych asked them.

They all looked at him with the same expression. Karyna's eyes betrayed her fear. Adan rubbed the scars on his face. Deep below the skin they itched. The demons were coming, and out on the horizon, there was a strange, powerful glow.

Chapter 35

Deep in her lair, Zalphyna woke. *"Zadryan?"* she called. Her son was missing. She unfolded her wings and roared toward the entrance. The mountain cliffs spewed downward, its surface smooth and clean in the brisk morning air. The Ruhln Forest stretched out for an eternity far below and covered southern Yannina with its thick canopy. She squinted against the burning sun. *"Zadryan? Where are you?"* Her instincts as a mother warned her of danger. Zalphyna lifted her wings and soared into the air.

Zadryan flew above the forest canopy, searching for Adan. He flew as low as possible, worried that Zar was in the area. After the incident with Zar, his mother forbade him from journeying on his own. Zar nearly caught him on that night. Whatever his motive was, Zadryan knew Zar would have ended his life. It was his friendship with Adan that forced him from his mother's directive. Demons were everywhere in great numbers. Adan and his friends were in the middle, and if he didn't help them, Adan would die. He searched along the river and saw what remained of an encampment. His senses picked up the scent of blood and smoke. Human life had been destroyed by a brutal attack. Only a dragon would destroy so much ground. He passed over the area once more. Moments later Zadryan saw where another battle took place. This time he found the remains of horses twisted together in a heap of blood on the side of the river bank. Nearby were bodies. He turned north, his thoughts focused on Adan.

A dark shadow sprang from the treetops below. Elk trees were shredded as Zar burst into the sunlight. His impressive jaws were wide open as he snapped at Zadryan's legs. Zadryan tipped his wings and the wind lifted him up; Zar missed by a stride. Zadryan pumped his wings. Zar remained on his tail. The sound of Zar's teeth snapping in the air drove him to fly as fast and as hard as he could. He heard the cracking of Zar's fire behind him and plummeted into the forest to escape it. Zadryan successfully dodged the infernal attack. He tilted his wings and flew back up above the trees. Zar shot flames again that forced Zadryan to veer to the left. The fire grazed his belly and he shrieked in fear and pain. He flew to the river and skimmed the water, flying low over the raging rapids. Zar closed in behind him. When Zadryan heard the crackle, he thrust his legs into the Delilah River. It created a powerful wake that blocked Zar's fire. Zar flew higher. The dragon's fire enfolded Zadryan. For a moment he was blinded by flame. Instinctively he lifted his legs and braced himself for the Delilah falls. A thick cloud of mist hung in the air.

At the point the river plunged over the ledge the water broke. Demon Xerrand rose from its depths. The greater demon turned his large head through the air and hissed. Zadryan veered to avoid a collision and miss the demon's attack. He collided into the elk trees and smashed into the ground.

Zar tipped back his wings in a futile attempt to avoid a collision with Xerrand. The blow sent them both careening over the raging falls. The mist sucked them in; they battled as they fell. They smashed against walls of water and rock as they spun through the air, spiraling downward faster than the river's current. Xerrand pinched the soft spot on Zar's neck with his razor claws. Zar snapped back with his sharp teeth and wrapped his long tail around Xerrand's chest to close off his gills. Zar flexed his tail until Xerrand released the grip on his neck.

Far below, the river fell onto jagged rocks. Xerrand landed first, softening the blow for Zar. The serrated rock rammed Xerrand's spine, causing him to release his hold on the dragon. Zar, thrilled with the battle, finished his foe. He snapped his back and ripped his chest open. He released his enemy from his grip. The current dragged the demon away, and Zar took flight.

Zar hid in the mist at the top of the falls, delighted to discover that a new enemy appeared. Finally, at long last, Zalphyna was before him; she hovered above the forest canopy. Zar had always admired the beauty of her silver scales in the glowing sun, but the thrill of battle and death was so much more pleasurable. Her beauty would soon be his trophy.

"*How dare you attack my child?*" Zalphyna roared.

"*Zalphyna, I welcome you.*" Zar waited in the air above the mist, eager for her to attack him.

"*You will die for this!*" Zalphyna charged. She rammed her head hard into Zar's underbelly. They spun almost out of control, though Zar escaped her and dove down over the Ruhln Forest. Zalphyna released her fire. The blaze struck his back. He careened into the forest. Elk trees blazed from the dragon's fire. Zar released his rage. He summoned his soul into his lungs and breathed life into his fire. The power exploded. Dragon's Fire roared with wild rage. Zalphyna retreated; shocked that he would release his soul. Zar batted his wings and charged. He gripped Zalphyna's head within his paws and sent her crashing into the ground. Zalphyna moaned and reached around with her tail. She managed to grip his neck and pull him off. She flew high up to the sky. Zar loved the challenge. He chased her higher and higher. Into the clouds they went where the air was thin and cool. Zalphyna flew higher still as she pumped her wings. Zar kept on her tail. The taste of blood lingered on the tip of his tongue. Suddenly, she flipped in the air, tucked her wings back and thrust her head into his chest. The blow stunned him. She lunged for his throat.

Together they fell, plummeting toward death. Zalphyna trapped him with her legs wrapped around him; it prevented his wings from opening wide. Zar was beneath her; she wanted to drive him into the next world. They twisted and turned but she held tight. She continued to hold him below her, hold him and point him to the ground. *"Nobody touches my son! Say farewell, old friend."* The ground approached them. Zalphyna roared. The wind howled. Zar felt the world of Yannina watch them as they spun out of control. Zalphyna motioned to open her wings, knowing that the time was upon her to release him. Zar opened his eyes and looked into hers. His black pupils leered. Hers showed fear. Zar flipped her just before they crashed. Zalphyna struck the trees first. She slammed head first into the ground. When the dust finally settled, Zalphyna lay alone in a mangled heap. Zar staggered until he stood on all fours. As the Dragon's Fire circled Zar, he craved death, and he sent his soul to seek his master.

Demon Vayle applauded. He witnessed this battle of a lifetime and loved every moment of it. His army of demons waited around him as they rested in the Stag of Waters. The Dragon's Fire approached him as it fed off the forest. The flames circled him, whispering into his ears, *"Master, what do you wish of me?"*

Demon Vayle smiled. "Search them out and kill them all. Destroy Adan Caynne."

The Dragon's Fire roared and tore away into the forest.

Chapter 36

The Dragon's Fire consumed everything in its path. Rampaging through the Ruhln Forest, it feasted upon the foliage of the great woodland. The scourging flames traveled faster than the wind could carry it.

Adan watched in horror as the fire roared toward them. He glanced at Myron and Riordan as they bravely held their stance. Beside them Darych stood tall. Karyna clung to him. "We must return to the swamps. It's our only chance," Darych yelled.

Talin removed his hood. He held back a sly grin that made Adan shiver. "Dragon's Fire will not stop until it has satisfied itself. There's no way to assume what damage it will cause. I have heard of legends that Dragon's Fire once destroyed our world." Talin returned his hood over his head, "Our only chance is to submerge ourselves in water, and pray to Faral for our survival."

"I agree," Adan replied, hardly sure if it would save them.

Myron pointed to Talin. "You're going to have to run."

"I will give everything I have."

Darych shook his head and lent his aide. "I'll help carry you."

Together Myron and Darych held Talin by each side.

Back through the forest they ran. The elk trees seemed to quiver in fear as they shook at the sound of the fire raging toward them. The Stag of Waters appeared at the bottom of the hill. Adan was the first to notice the flames screeching through the treetops, roaring toward them at unbelievable speed. The fire hammered through the forest canopy and sent flaming debris into the murky water. Its sound echoed around them and sang a song of death. Adan leapt into the water and dove deep below the surface as the flames raced overhead. He opened his eyes in hopes he could find his friends, then resurfaced and gasped for air. The water was deeper than he'd thought and he struggled to stay afloat. The forest around him burned fiercely. The heat of the blaze burned his scars. He watched his friends resurface, and he counted six to make sure they were all there.

Adan could hear other screams over the sound of the raging fire. Myron pointed west into the forest. The demon army advanced on them shrieking their battle cries. They waded into the water, untouched by the

Dragon's Fire. Their red eyes flickered like the fire around them. Adan choked back his fear. His feet found solid ground as he managed to climb a slope where the water came to his waist. The fire circled the swamp. He had no choice but to breathe the polluted air and draw his sword. Darych braced Talin against deadwood that floated above the surface. Riordan took a protective stance in front of the Andar apprentice. A blinding light erupted from Riordan's hands. Adan shielded his eyes from the glare.

"Riordan!" Adan screamed, worried that harm had befallen him. When he uncovered his eyes, he stared in shocked wonder. Riordan held a long wooden staff in his hands. A blue glow pulsated from Riordan's grip to the end of the staff. Even the prince seemed surprised. He almost fell in astonishment, then regained his balance and spun the staff over his head.

Darych drew his sword and called on the small band to stand together. The first wave of demons attacked. The prince and general countered. Both of them were marvels as they took the wretched creatures on. They slaughtered them by the dozens. Myron covered them with his crossbow. He shot demons before they had a chance to attack. Riordan's staff was like a sharpened blade as it cut through the demons. Darych's resounding war cry screamed strength and courage to them all.

A charred tree fell. Adan and Myron leapt out of the way. Another followed and Adan dove away again. This time he was separated from Myron. The burning branches forced Adan back. Demons swarmed in on him. He shook with fear as his life flashed in front of him. The water boiled around him. Murky waves rippled from the heat. It threatened to take his life should he escape the demons that advanced on him. A gilled rat crawled across his back to escape the fire. Adan shook it off. He checked across the fallen tree, still raging with flames, hoping to see Myron or the rest of them. Knowing they were there gave him a measure of strength. He closed his eyes from the smoke. Suddenly, the world around him stopped.

"*Adan,*" a voice spoke. He opened his eyes. "*Adan, you must fight. The will of a warrior is in your blood; take my sword and fight!*"

"Father!" Adan cried. The demons were almost upon him.

"*Fight, Adan! I'm with you. Fight or you're going to die.*"

Adan emitted a loud and undulated war cry. He lifted the Dragon Sword high over his head. The first demon leapt toward him, claws aimed at his head. Adan countered the blow with the sword. He expected the sword to flare to life as it had before…but it didn't. The blade barely scratched the demons tough hide. He stared in disbelief as the Dragon Sword failed him. The demon screeched and lashed out at him with its long claws. An arrow pierced the demon between its eyes. Myron hacked away at the burning branches and reloaded his bow once again. Adan gripped the sword with faded hope. The blade felt dead in his hands.

Down and off to the side, Riordan appeared with his long staff. He provoked the demons advancing on Adan into a fight. The prince charged and shouted his own battle cry. He smashed the disgusting creatures into the water. "Where did you get that staff?" Adan shouted.

"I'll explain later, we must regroup."

A shadow grew overhead. Another tree fell. Adan dove down into the water to avoid it. When he surfaced his eyes stung from the smoke. A demon jumped on his back and pushed him down. An arrow broke the water surface and hit the demon; it released Adan from its grip as it thrashed in its death throes. Adan resurfaced and Myron reloaded. A handful of demons attacked Riordan. Adan lost Myron from his sight as a burst of flames roared toward him. He dove below the surface.

Karyna supported Talin. She kept his head above the water. The Andar apprentice was unconscious. The run back to the Stag of Waters had depleted his strength. Her wrists ached and itched. She tried to ignore the threat of the claws appearing. She thought of Rowen, and wondered if she would ever know if she truly loved him. Darych protected the front of them by halting the demon advances, but he was badly outnumbered. Riordan had disappeared with Adan and Myron. A demon slipped through Darych's defense and charged. Karyna cowered in fear, expecting the worst. *"My daughter,"* a familiar voice called. It brought back a memory she hoped to forget. The claws extended from her wrists. She felt power surge through her blood. She released her hold on Talin and unleashed a furious attack on the demon. It fell into the swamp in several pieces. Karyna stared in bewilderment at what she'd done. She looked down at the claws dripping with green blood, and wondered what curse had befallen her. She looked back at the Andar apprentice.

Talin was conscious and stared with open and questioning eyes. "You!" he screamed. "You are one of them!"

She stared at him, confused. The claws tingled, hungry for blood. What was the apprentice implying? Talin held himself out of the water. She noticed Darych in dire need of help and she rushed to his aide. Across the swamp she saw that Adan was alone, outnumbered and overpowered. Behind him Myron fired arrows. Riordan appeared out of the smoke on her left and joined Darych in his battle. Darych watched her with open eyes. She ignored the astonishment and pointed to Adan and Myron. They were getting too far away.

As Myron worked to reach him, Adan resurfaced for air. He held the Dragon Sword in his hands, but he couldn't understand why the sword felt dead and powerless. The words that came from his father turned on the rage that flickered in his soul. A demon landed in front of him and Adan thrust the tip of the sword through its belly. Adan shouted with new strength. The sword felt dead, but it still had a sharp edge with the ability to kill. Another tree, ripe with flames, crashed down over him. It barely missed his head but one of the branches caught his leg. It dragged him below the water's surface. The demons crashed down around him.

Vayle paced with impatience through the flames. He watched in disgust as Riordan revealed his new weapon. He watched Karyna and her claws cut down one demon after the other. He watched the son of Darren Ches survive each onslaught. His demons fell against their weak attacks. Enough was enough. He reached for the sky with his skeletal hands. Words came chanting from his mouth in rhythmic rhymes, repeated over and over again. The swamp began to boil. Lightning formed at his fingertips and as he spread his hands the power burned.

Adan remained pinned to the swamp floor by a large branch. He was losing strength. The need for air overpowered everything else. He knew with one breath his pain would end. Above the water Myron rushed toward him. He knocked demons aside with his crossbow and dove into the water. Myron surfaced with his crossbow in hand, an arrow loaded and ready to fire. With his other hand he pulled Adan out of the water; he fired the arrow as Adan gasped for air. A demon fell into dead in the water. Adan took a deep breath. The air was poor and distasteful, but it was everything he imagined just moments ago. As Myron held him above the surface, he wondered why he deserved such a friend. From behind them a deep voice reverberated through the raging flames. Both of them turned to seek the source.

Demon Vayle stood back against the fire with his hands over his head. Pure lightning arced between his fingers. As he spread his arms apart the lightning bolted between his hands. The water boiled. Demon Vayle's voice resounded loud and clear. "Faris, our loyal master, bring me your servants of death! Rise, Xerros, kill those who oppose me!"

Xerros rose from the deeper end of the swamp. The massive creature that closely resembled Xerrand stood and howled. Adan mumbled incoherently in fear. Xerros dripped saliva from his teeth. Long thorns broke through the skin on his back until his entire spine was completely covered. His red eyes flashed with evil. The gills on its chest flapped in the smoky air. The horns that sprouted outward from his head were sharp and deadly.

"I must get you loose," Myron said. Adan couldn't reply. His leg felt dead and he couldn't budge it. The appearance of Xerros terrified him. They were all going to die. Numbness crept up to his thigh from where his leg was still pinned down. Myron took a deep breath and dove below the surface. He grabbed Adan by the waist and pulled with all his strength. Adan screamed and lost his grip on the Dragon Sword. It fell to the bottom of the swamp. Xerros locked his gaze on them and charged. Myron resurfaced. He held his crossbow outward with an arrow locked in position. He released the arrow. It pierced Xerros's in the head, barely missing an eye. The greater demon fell back. Myron dove again. This time he reached for Adan's leg. Adan watched as Xerros shook off the attack. The demon pulled the arrow from his forehead and tossed it to the water. Adan's leg was freed. He screamed in relief and horror. It was then Myron was grabbed from behind by a grip of scales and slime. Myron loaded his bow as Xerros lifted him from the water. Myron turned to face him and fired. The arrow screamed forth. It penetrated deep into the demon's shoulder.

Adan screamed and begged for mercy. He dove into the water to retrieve the Dragon Sword. He gripped the handle and rose to the surface just as Xerros tightened his grip. Myron shouted and tried to get a handle on another arrow. Xerros taunted Myron with a chuckle. Adan watched as Myron managed to lock an arrow into place and aim for the demon's head. It was his last chance to survive. He fired. At extremely close range, the arrow penetrated its entire length into the creature's head. The greater demon released Myron from his grip and reeled back in pain. Myron fell into the swamp and rushed for Adan. Xerros roared in rage and turned on Adan. He crashed through the water at full speed, arms raised in the air. The demon swung its claws down and Adan jumped out of the way. Adan thrust his sword around in an effort to counter, but missed terribly. The demon stared into Adan's eyes, as if promising not to miss him again. Xerros attacked. Adan brought his sword up in front of him to ward off the blow, the only thing he could think to do.

Blue lighting glided across the murky waves and wrapped itself around the greater demon. Xerros howled in agony. The sound resounded louder than an explosion. The smell of burning flesh permeated the air. The blast pushed Adan back into Myron and they embraced with relief. It was Talin who saved him. The Andar apprentice fell from exhaustion as the lightning faded. Enraged by the pain, Xerros regained his will as he roared and screeched with a determination to kill.

Adan pulled Myron through the water as Darych and the others finally made it to him. Riordan reached him first. Xerros zoned in, ready to kill them all in one last blow. Adan knew they were finished. He barely had the strength to wade through the swamp. To defeat such a demon was impossible. Surely it was over.

A loud screech cried down from the sky. It resounded over the raging flames and the growls from Demon Xerros. Down came their savior. With his wings tucked back for speed and his head locked down in line with its spine, the dragon known as Zadryan soared down at Xerros. Zadryan smashed Xerros square in the chest and they both flipped in the air. They rolled in the swamp water and their battle began.

Adan cheered. His friends could only stare in disbelief. As Zadryan battled Xerros, Adan and his allies pushed back toward the center of the swamp. They took down the lesser demons that stood in their way. Adan reached Talin and thanked him for saving their lives. The Andar apprentice breathed in ragged gasps.

In the meantime, Zadryan had Xerros tangled in his tail; he slowly crushed his enemy. Xerros fell and Zadryan rose victorious from the water's surface.

Another loud screech split the smoky air. The very sound of it vibrated through Adan, forcing him to turn to face it. Demon Vayle leapt high into the air. His red robe billowed. Red eyes focused on them from the confines of his hood. Vayle sailed through the air with his arms over his head. Lightning crackled from his fingertips. He glided through the air as if something propelled him. Adan braced himself. Demon Vayle's momentum was going to bring him down on top of them. He and his friends threw their backs together, waiting for Vayle to land among them.

A shining light materialized between them and Demon Vayle. It started small, but grew rapidly. From the center of the light a form appeared. "Master," Talin mumbled. The form was pure light. Streaky hair as long as his willowing robes flowed around him. His older face grimaced and he held up a staff of silver. Blue lightning burst from the tip of his staff and raced toward Vayle. The blow caught the demon square in the chest. Vayle was knocked away and the flames of the fire sucked him back. The fear and tension among the small group settled. The old man and the blinding light disappeared. Adan sighed in relief and called for Zadryan.

The dragon was behind him. *"Quickly, you and your friends must climb onto my back."*

"Get on the dragon," Adan screamed. He sheathed his sword, and they scrambled onto Zadryan's back. Zadryan lifted his wings and flew them to freedom.

As they left the black smoke Adan gratefully sucked in the clean air. The muscles in his body relaxed. Far below, the Dragon's Fire continued to destroy new ground as it raced to the east. Darych reached for his shoulder and squeezed. "Adan, you have much to explain about yourself."

"Adan, will the dragon fly us to Wyndhaven?" Myron asked him.

Adan shook his head, uncertain. "Did you hear that Zadryan?" he asked.

"It would be my honor to take you safely to Wyndhaven, Adan." The dragon flew west.

Vayle stood alone in the Dragon's Fire. The corpse that was Xerros floated above the water before him. His rage shook the burning trees around him. His ignorance whispered into the depths of his soul. Never again would he taste defeat—never.

Chapter 37

Hythe watched closely as the glow brightened. He watched since it first caught his attention. Leahla stood at his side and glanced at him with her silver eyes. "What is it, Hythe?"

"There's a forest fire," he said calmly.

She put her slender hand on his chest. "Are we in danger?"

"We might be."

Leahla grunted in frustration. "You haven't been the same since we left Ruhln. What is wrong with you?"

He stared into her silver eyes. He was filled with shame. His eyes misted. "I'm so sorry, Leahla, I cannot bear this pain."

She frowned. "What are you speaking of?"

"Guilt has plagued me all of my life. I can no longer pretend it doesn't exist."

Leahla stepped away from him. "You're frightening me. I'm aware of your past, Hythe. You've told me…remember?"

"No, I haven't told you everything."

She placed her hand over her heart. "Hythe, I love you. There is nothing you could have done that I would be ashamed of."

Hythe was not so certain. "I love you, Leahla. Please remember that."

The steady glow of fire on the horizon drew closer. "Then tell me about it. Clean your mind of guilt. I told you to tell Adan what happened before we left."

Hythe nodded. "I know." He fell silent a moment. He hoped what he was about to tell her would diminish some of the guilt. "Twenty-three years ago, I was one of the Warriors of Ches recruited by Faral to stop the Dryden from regaining an ancient power." He reached behind his back and found his battle axe. He wanted to hold it in his hands for awhile. "I did something terrible."

"I don't understand. You told me this story."

He shook his head. "Not all of it. There's more." It was the part he tried so hard to forget. "The reason I wanted to return to Ruhln was because I needed my brother's forgiveness. When we were reunited, I realized it was much worse than it was. I couldn't bring myself to tell him. I tried to explain my actions before the battle, but I was ashamed you would hear it."

She touched his hand, "Hythe."

"This artifact we tried to obtain was the same one that Faral and Faris used to give them the capability to resurrect after death. It was our job to find it before the Dryden did. If they found it they could use it to resurrect something known as the Demons of Destiny, which in turn would destroy our world."

She gently placed her hand on his shoulder. "Hythe, you've told me this before. I understand that you failed. It wasn't your fault."

He shook his head. "I lied to you. We didn't fail." He took a deep breath and pushed the words out. "I found it, Leahla; I found the power we'd sought." She looked at him with mix of shock and understanding in her eyes. He couldn't look at her. "You know now…don't you? It was you I found. You are the artifact the Gods are after."

Leahla didn't speak as she absorbed the news. Hythe could only wonder what was going through her mind. "What did this have to do with your brother?" she finally asked.

"Faral spoke of a prophecy, hinting that Darren's third unborn child would one day help the Dryden resurrect something known as Granaz. From its ashes the Demons of Destiny would rise. It would lead to the destruction of Yannina. Because we failed, the prophecy was evoked."

Leahla shook her head with disbelief. "How could you do such a thing? How could you hide the truth from your own brother?"

Hythe stepped in front of her, his look imploring. "Because I fell in love with the most beautiful woman I ever laid eyes on. I wanted you for myself."

She bit her lip. "You sacrificed our entire world so you could be with me?"

Hythe felt the tears slide down his face. "It sounds horrible, I know, but it didn't happen as easy as I explained. One of the Warriors of Ches betrayed us at the Pales of Nothingness. Faris had planted Dryden among us. Some I thought were friends plotted to destroy us. At the time I didn't know who it was. I even thought it could have been my brother. I didn't know who to trust. I did it to protect you."

Leahla's face was almost the same color as the horizon. The fire gained incredible speed, advancing on them like a stampede of angry horses. Leahla reached for the reins to hold Firestreak. The sound of the approaching storm frightened him. "I don't believe you, Hythe." He reached for her, and she pulled away from him. Hythe knew her well. The confusion in her eyes meant her feelings were damaged. "Who were the others?" she asked.

"The others who fought alongside my brother and I were King Oland from Corrona, King Mel of Wyndhaven, an Andar known as Jayntil and a woman named Aylynna. Later we recruited a seventh warrior." Hythe shook his head, unconcerned with the name, his thoughts still focused on Leahla and her state of mind. "I never believed in the prophecy, though I did warn my brother to take it seriously. Darren thought of it as a curse rather than a prophecy. He defied Faral. I wanted Darren to heed the warnings cast upon him, but he never listened to me. After a heated argument, I gave up on him."

Leahla mounted Firestreak. She watched the fire as it steadily approached. "You lied to me since the beginning. You lied about who I was. You told me I was found on the shores near Corrona. I was never able to remember my past, so I believed you. I don't know what to believe anymore, but humor me, Hythe. Who am I? What is it about me that the Gods want?"

The fire caught them both by surprise and Hythe leapt into the saddle. Firestreak charged ahead, but the fire was just as fast. It raced around them on both sides. The heat was inescapable. The fire seemed intelligent in the way it tried to surround them. For a moment Hythe thought it was over. Their path ended at the edge of a precipice. The ground disappeared. A lake waited far below. Firestreak drove them over the edge. The Dragon's Fire exploded behind them. They separated as they fell. Firestreak hit the water first. Hythe and Leahla splashed down close to him. Firestreak's lifeless body floated to the surface; the impact broke his neck. Hythe and Leahla clung to the dead horse. "Thank you for saving our lives, dear old friend," Hythe said.

Later when they rested along the lakeshore, Leahla said, "I want to know everything from the beginning. You can start by telling me more about the Warriors of Ches, about who betrayed you, and the name of the seventh warrior."

"He was a good friend to King Mel," Hythe replied. "And his name was Aramaz."

Chapter 38

Zadryan tilted his wings as Wyndhaven appeared below them. Karyna pointed to the castle, shouting over the howling wind. "Adan, tell the dragon to land inside the castle walls near the front gate. My father's throne is inside the main doors and up the stairs."

Adan nodded but he knew Zadryan heard her. The castle towered over the surrounding villages. Adan could only imagine the fear that would creep through the people as a dragon descended upon them. The last few days had felt like an eternity. Wyndhaven had seemed like a distant dream. Tears of joy filled his eyes. They finally made it. Now he could rest in safety and plan his next course of action to find his brother. Zadryan circled the castle. The towers of the castle were much taller than Adan remembered. There were many people standing upon the different bridges that connected each tower, pointing toward them as Zadryan descended. Adan studied the outside walls. Three watchtowers were spaced evenly apart, with the middle one sitting directly over the main gate. He was impressed with the amount of knights patrolling their posts. The dragon hovered over the ground before he landed. One by one Adan and the others slipped off his back. Knights of the Wyndhaven Forces approached them from every direction with their weapons drawn.

Darych waved at the knights approaching him. "Weapons down."

Adan helped lower Talin off the dragon's back. Myron jumped next to him. "We made it, Adan!"

After all they had been through Adan almost felt as if it was never meant to happen. Had it not been for Zadryan, then they would all be dead back at the Stag of Waters. *"I must leave, Adan, my mother fell in battle."*

"I'm sorry, Friend." Adan didn't know what else to say. "Thank you for saving our lives."

Zadryan blinked his yellow eyes. *"I'm grateful I found you when I did."* He stretched his wings.

Darych motioned to Adan, waving at him as he glanced around them. "Adan, hold on."

"Zadryan, wait a moment." Adan said as he ran to Darych. Karyna stared curiously. "What is it?" he asked Darych.

Darych scratched at his beard and pulled Karyna into them so she could hear. Riordan moved in behind them. "Something's wrong," Darych said. "I don't recognize some of these men." They all reeked of swamp and smoke.

Adan frowned. "But you're their general."

Darych frowned. "That's the problem."

Karyna shot him a sharp look. "What are you implying?"

"I'm not sure, Karyna. Riordan, Adan, come with us. Myron, please remain here with Talin."

Adan motioned to Zadryan. "I must ask a favor."

"I heard your conversation, Adan. I shall wait for your return."

"Thank you," Adan replied.

Talin crawled into a sitting position and rested his back against Zadryan's leg. "What's wrong, Adan?" the apprentice asked.

"I'm not certain. Darych is concerned."

Myron paced back and forth. "Don't be long."

"Myron, I have a bad feeling. Keep your eyes open for anything out of the ordinary."

Myron appeared unconcerned. "Just hurry."

Adan ran to catch Darych and the others.

Darych glanced from knight-to-knight. He counted those who appeared unfamiliar. It was possible the king called for reinforcements from the reserves, but he didn't think that was the case.

Race appeared behind a group of knights. "Darych, you don't know how relieved I am to see the two of you safe," Race said as they shook hands. "We found the destroyed encampment and feared the worse." He pointed to the smoke in the sky, "And then that fire started. I've never witnessed anything like it. From the east tower you can have a pretty good view at the damage it's causing."

"We're lucky to be alive. These are our new allies. Surely you know of Riordan, Prince of Corrona. This is Adan Caynne from Ruhln. We wouldn't be alive if it weren't for him."

Race shook Adan's hand. "Then I am truly grateful. My name is Race."

Darych asked, "Has anything happened in my absence?"

Race shook his head. "We have gone without an incident."

"Good, Corrona has fallen. Ruhln has been destroyed. I feared that

Wyndhaven had been attacked in my absence."

"Oh my, what happened?"

"You won't believe it until you see them with your own eyes. Race, we don't have much time. We must speak with the king immediately."

Race waved them onward, "Of course. When I saw that a dragon carried you and Karyna, I sent word to him right away. He will be pleased to know you are both safe."

Karyna stopped. "Darych, I'm going to my room. I don't want to speak to my father just yet." She rubbed her wrists.

Darych turned to her, whispering urgently, "Karyna, right now I need you to trust me more than ever. Do not leave my side."

She took a deep breath, "But Race said everything is fine."

Adan turned to Karyna. "I, too, have a bad feeling."

She frowned. "My father will not harm us. Surely you don't believe we're in danger?"

With each passing moment there seemed to be more and more knights coming out from inside the castle. Darych understood that a dragon flying down from the sky would cause alarm and curiosity. Had he been in charge, he probably would've done the same thing. "Of course I don't believe that."

"Then let me be on my way," she said.

Perhaps he was over-reacting. After all, they had only barely escaped from the Stag of Waters. He was exhausted. It could be hurting his judgment, but then again…maybe not. "Sir?" Race asked curiously.

"Please, Karyna," Darych implored, "you must trust me."

Karyna sighed, "Fine."

Darych turned back to Race. "Sorry."

Race had the castle doors opened and they stepped inside.

Myron studied the dragon. "So you're the one we saved. You're a whole lot bigger."

Talin groaned. "I need water."

"I'm sure we'll have all we can eat and drink soon enough." Myron rubbed his stomach. Food would certainly be nice. They waited next to the dragon between the outside walls and the front entrance to the castle. To help diminish the dust, the ground was padded with stone plates. There was a small moat in front of the door with a bridge leading into the castle. The rest of the area was wide open, except the stables in the back southern corner. Myron remembered the tournaments. During the competitions this was the area they used. Usually it was crowded with people. Battle arenas were built against the outside walls. Scaffolding would hang down off the walls where the majority of the people would watch. He never realized that each year they rebuilt the arenas. Myron assumed they left the equipment out year round. As he studied one of the watchtowers, he noticed three knights working on something at waist-level. He moved to sneak a closer look. The two other watchtowers were farther away, but there were several knights motioning to each other at both locations. He looked at the dragon and back to the castle. Several knights were positioned in a circle around them, but they kept their distance.

He hadn't even blinked at Adan's warning. They were in Wyndhaven now. They were safe. Myron walked casually toward the castle door. The doors were still open but several knights blocked the entrance. Myron wanted to reach for his bow, but his instincts warned him not to appear hostile. He spotted a set of stairs near the stables that circled back up onto the outside wall. He continued his walk as if out for a stroll. The knights watched him; he smiled and waved at those closest to him. He held onto his courage. He told himself there wasn't anything to worry about.

A knight guarded the bottom of the stairs. "It's a beautiful day," Myron said. The guard remained expressionless. He wore the same blue and silver armor as Darych's, only his was clean. The breastplate was the symbol of Wyndhaven; an eagle holding a spear. He wore his helmet crooked with the face shield down. A miniature flag hung off the top off his helmet. "Do you mind if I have a look around?" The knight stared forward with the same empty look. Myron figured that was permission and moved to step by. The knight stopped him. Myron nodded silently. He wondered if he should be concerned. He admired the castle's silver towers, and the vast blue flags that flapped in the wind. It was impossible that a stronghold such as Wyndhaven could have fallen. Myron shook his head. It was unfeasible. A breeze touched him. Myron suddenly thought of his grandfather. The way the wind tingled his skin warned Myron something was wrong. Moments later something on the watchtower reflected the sun into his eyes. He turned and almost dropped in horror. The knights had pushed a harpoon into the watchtower. The unit was on wheels. Loaded in its base was a long steel-tipped arrow. He only caught a glimpse of it, but there was no mistaking what it was…or their intentions to use it. They were going to aim it at the dragon. Myron cursed his luck. That meant Adan was in trouble. Worse yet, there were three watchtowers. Myron assumed there would be two more weapons.

After everything they had been through.

There was only one thing he knew to do. Myron reached for his bow.

Chapter 39

Adan trailed Riordan and Karyna as they followed Darych through the castle. They were led by one of the knights through the main hall and up stairs. Adan was mesmerized by the detail. The carpet was red and trimmed with gold. Blue and silver flags twirled down from a ceiling far above. Statues wearing the armor of the Wyndhaven Forces towered over them. They held shields tight to their chests. The symbol of Wyndhaven was carved with intricate detail on the face of the shields. Their weapons were lances that touched the ceiling.

Two more knights waited in front of a large oak door at the top of the stairs. They greeted Darych and Karyna and moved to open the doors. "The king is waiting at the throne," Race said.

"Thank you," Darych replied.

"I assume I can leave you alone with the king?" Race asked.

Darych shook his head. "No, you need to hear what has happened. The information is important. It will have heavy impact on the safety of our men." The oak doors were fully open and Darych entered. Race nodded and followed. Adan entered last, his nervousness growing with every step. He remembered in detail what happened to Riordan. As far as Adan was concerned, the moment Darych thought there was something wrong, their lives were in danger. Riordan felt the same way. Adan noticed how the prince studied every knight, almost if he memorized their positions.

The throne room was a long chamber with a set of stairs at the end. Pillars of white stone stood on either side of the red carpet. Smaller versions of the entry hall statues stood between the pillars. The lighting was powerful. Adan admired the flags of Wyndhaven that hung down between each skylight. The breathing of wind passed through the hall, echoing above their heads. Adan felt uncomfortable with the odd sound.

The king sat on his throne, two knights to either side. Adan watched carefully as several other guards moved around behind them. Darych shook his head and turned in a circle taking in everything within the room. He forced Karyna behind him as they approached the king.

Adan never met King Mel. He was older than Adan expected, but he kept his hair and beard trimmed sharp. The king wore a long blue robe with the symbol of Wyndhaven on the front.

Somehow, King Mel had known his father. "You have no idea what pleasure it brought to my heart when I found out that both of you were alive," King Mel said as he stood. His arms were open and welcoming. Race moved quickly up the short set of stairs and stood beside the king.

Darych stopped them at the bottom of the stairs. "We're lucky to be alive."

King Mel rubbed his face with his hands. "When I received word that the dragon had destroyed your camp, I was devastated. Then to find my own daughter missing, I didn't know what to do. We had several knights looking for you. Karyna, I am so relieved."

Adan raised his brows in interest. He pushed Riordan to the side and stepped in front of Darych. "How do you know it was a dragon that destroyed that camp?"

The king frowned and sat down. "Who is this?"

"This is Adan Caynne; he is the only reason we're alive," Darych answered.

The king gasped. "But that's impossible."

Karyna asked, "Father, what is going on here? Why are you acting so strange?"

"My dear, Karyna, I loved you so much, but you had to run away."

Karyna moved her hands to her waist. "What?"

"I'm sorry, Darych, you really were a true friend." Adan swallowed. The knights behind were pacing in impatience. "I had hoped," the king continued, "that over the years I could persuade you to believe in the gods as I have. It is disappointing, but at least there was Race to take over. He believes as I do. That will be necessary in Yannina's future. I'm sorry." King Mel stood once again. "Kill them."

"No!" Karyna screamed. The betrayal in her voice was of shock and denial.

Darych had his sword in his hands instantly. "What has happened here?"

Karyna cried out again. Adan removed the Dragon Sword from the scabbard on his back.

Race stepped down the stairs lifting his own sword into the air. "Karyna, you have no idea the pleasure your death will bring me. For years I've had to put up with the nonsense of your insolent behavior. Watching you die will be a triumph I shall cherish forever."

Darych's face twisted in betrayal. He uttered his war cry in pure frustration. He stepped up toward Race and cleaved his head straight off his shoulders. He pointed to the king. "Those who betray me will die!" Race's body slumped to the floor. Blood sprayed the red carpet. The king turned and ran.

Karyna stood in complete shock. She screamed again. "Father! Why?" The rest of the knights charged. Riordan's staff appeared out of nowhere, as if he had called it out of the air. He spun it over their heads and slammed it onto the floor. He did it again; the staff flared in length and power with every thrust. In one incredible swing Riordan took out half the knights. Darych killed two and reached for Karyna. She still screamed at her father, asking him why he would do such a thing. They ran for the door. It stood unguarded now, but the knights were close behind. Adan led the way, sickened with the thought that he might have to fight a trained soldier.

"Kill them! Do not let them escape!" shouted the knights who chased them.

Riordan spun, ready to face off with the Wyndhaven Forces. Adan ran into the main stairwell with Darych and Karyna. It stood empty except for a hooded stranger near the exit. Adan shouted for Riordan. The prince blasted several of the knights at the same time, holding them back with the incredible reach of his staff. Adan stopped. The stranger ahead of them stood statue still as he waited for their arrival. Riordan caught up to them halfway down the stairs. The stranger in black approached. Adan glared in fear, wondering how they were to escape. It was only one man, surely they could defeat him.

Darych pushed Karyna away and advanced with his sword drawn. Riordan, his face covered in sweat, walked to the stranger's left. Adan gripped his sword and moved to his right. They were going to attack him at once. "Prince Riordan," the stranger said. "You wouldn't believe my disgust when I heard you lived. After everything I did to make sure you were properly framed for the murder of your father, and then to find out it was a waste of time."

"I recognize your voice," Riordan said. "You are the one Sheldhan handed me to."

The stranger laughed. "If only your precious First Guard was harder to kill, perhaps you wouldn't be in this mess." Riordan screamed in frustration. The stranger dropped his robe. His long white hair partially covered a face that appeared as if it had been sewn together. Steel buckles hung off chains that wrapped his body. In his hands he held a long metal whip armored with jagged blades and a pointed tip. He cracked the weapon to the side and reached out with his other hand, motioning them to start the battle. "I am Demon Aramaz. Prepare to die."

Adan muttered in fear and thought of Myron.

Myron turned and pointed his bow at the knight. The knight leaned back in shock and Myron pulled the trigger. The arrow ripped through his neck. Myron sprinted up the stairs. As the knight's body hit the ground, an alarm sounded through the air. Myron cursed his luck; he had hoped to secure the wall before they realized what happened. Myron made his way onto the top of the wall and shot off another arrow. A knight grabbed his chest and fell off the other side. Several knights charged him at once. Myron stopped and loaded. He shot two in a row; both sank into their targets. The knights at the watchtower were struggling to load the massive steel tipped arrow. Myron ran and charged. He jumped at the knights, killing one with a shot and rendering the other unconscious by swinging his bow. He reached for the harpoon, but it wasn't ready to fire. He swore and sprinted for the next tower.

The dragon was up on his feet, Talin crouching in low behind him. Several knights attacked. The Andar apprentice shot out a blast of lightning. The blow left the knights running for cover. The dragon attacked.

Myron shouted at the knights that came up the stairs and charged him from both sides. He cleared his way to the next watchtower by firing several shots in both directions. The second tower had their harpoon nearly loaded. Myron took aim and fired. The arrow pierced a knight's helmet. He had his crossbow loaded instantly and fired again. He made it to the tower and pulled a body off the harpoon. The steel-tipped arrow was ready to fire and pointed at the dragon. Myron cursed, knowing it was a sign that the third tower surely had its arrow ready. Myron dropped his bow and reached for the knight's sword. Using it for leverage, Myron thrust the blade under the corner of the harpoon. He used every ounce of strength to turn the device. A knight attacked him from behind. Myron turned and countered with the sword.

Below, the dragon roared and swung its tail. Knights flew in every direction.

Myron fought off the knight, screaming with every thrust. After everything he had been through, he was not going to be defeated. He ran forward, almost crazed, and shoved his sword deep into the knight's chest. When he pulled it free blood sprayed into the air. Myron turned back to the harpoon, worried he was out of time. He prayed that the arrow was pointed where he wanted. He slashed the rope. The harpoon fired. The steel-tipped arrow whistled toward the third tower. Rock and brick exploded when the arrow hit. Knights were blown into the air. Myron cheered. He retrieved his crossbow and searched for his exit.

Down below the dragon charged.

Adan wiped the sweat off his brow. To live through the Stag of Waters, and then to die at Wyndhaven was a cruel fate. Demon Aramaz laughed and cracked his steel whip.

The castle walls shook. Zadryan crashed in through the front entrance. Rock and stone exploded on impact. Debris flew over their heads. Aramaz turned to face the dragon, but Zadryan belted him away with one of his claws.

Adan lowered his sword in relief. Darych and the others ran for the entrance.

"Adan, get out of here."

"Where's Myron?"

Zadryan roared. He arched his back and extended his neck. Adan heard a crackle and Zadryan released his fire. The blast ripped into the throne room, destroying those knights who still threatened their freedom.

Adan charged out into daylight. Darych and Riordan saved Talin from knights set to attack him. Zadryan backed out of the castle and destroyed the gate. Knights fell into the shallow moat and Zadryan crushed them down. Adan helped Talin to his feet. Together they staggered toward the center of the courtyard. Zadryan returned to them. *"Get him onto my back. I'll fly us out of here."*

Myron raced along the top of the outside wall, still fighting the knights that chased him. Adan screamed. Demon Aramaz climbed through the debris of the broken drawbridge and cracked his whip. He advanced on Darych and Riordan. Adan shouted a warning; they took it seriously. Aramaz was frightening and powerful. They would die if they fought him.

"Myron!" Adan shouted.

Myron fired a shot and a knight fell over the edge. A Wyndhaven flag flapped through the wind over the main entrance. Myron ran, gaining speed. Adan watched nervously as Myron leapt into the air, grabbing onto the flag. He fired his crossbow as he slid down the flag. A knight fell dead below and Myron landed safely on the ground. He loaded his crossbow. Aramaz turned to face Myron. Adan feared the worse. He charged with his sword in his hands. His war cry resounded as he lifted the blade over his head. Knights appeared in heavy numbers. "Adan, wait for me!" Darych screamed. Zadryan roared as an onslaught of arrows sank into his body. Darych dove to the ground as another stream of arrows blazed overhead.

Demon Aramaz heard Adan running for him. He sidestepped and cracked his whip, striking Adan across the top of his hands. He dropped the sword when he noticed his hands covered in his own blood. In that instant he thought Aramaz had killed him. Aramaz cracked the whip, aiming the sharp-bladed tip toward Adan. He dove for cover. Myron used his crossbow to deflect the whip off its mark. Aramaz backhanded Myron and knocked him down.

Zadryan roared and released his fire. The blaze flared behind them in the background. Knights ran for cover.

"Adan!" Darych shouted. The general was fighting his own men. Flanks of knights circled them, firing off arrows as fast as they could load them. Zadryan covered them, spraying his fire in different directions. Adan thought to climb to his feet, but the sight of Myron lying face down on the ground with his blood splashed across the dirt kept him frozen. Aramaz turned to look directly at Adan. The expression on his face was blank as he twirled his whip. His silver hair glimmered from the fire in the background; his eyes flickered in confidence. Behind Aramaz, Myron struggled to his feet. He loaded his crossbow and took aim. Aramaz stared intently at Adan. Adan held his focus, hoping that he was unaware of Myron standing behind him with his arrow loaded to release.

Myron pulled the trigger. Aramaz, faster than Adan could blink, spun around and cracked his whip. The metal fins connected with the arrow searing toward him, shredding it on impact. The whip kept moving, ripping into Myron's torso. Blood gushed on its impact. Adan screamed. Aramaz stepped up to Myron as he held his stomach. Aramaz reached for Myron's neck and threw him down to the ground. The demon laughed and turned back.

    Hatred welled in Adan. His sword lay on the ground, reflecting the sun. He reached for it. His bloody fingers wrapped around the cold scales of the Dragon Sword. As he lifted the blade off the ground, a seething rage awakened within. Aramaz cracked the whip. Adan stepped forward to meet him. Arrows missed Adan so closely the slight breeze tickled his skin, but not for an instant did he turn his gaze from Aramaz. Behind him he heard the others fighting for their lives. Zadryan roared and fire ripped across the battlefield. Adan rushed for the kill. Aramaz stepped forward and cracked the whip. Adan, not even aware of what he was doing, deflected the blow. He rushed forward and swung the Dragon Sword. Aramaz, his face frozen in disbelief, didn't have the time to use his whip. Instead he turned and drove his elbow into Adan's chin. The blow stopped Adan on impact. The sound of his jaw cracking was followed by the thud of his head on the ground.

    Zadryan finally cleared the area of enemy knights. The dragon charged at Aramaz with his jaws wide open. Aramaz threw his arms up in defense, screaming as Zadryan bore down on him. Zadryan took Aramaz between his teeth, but he didn't bite through. He shook his head back and forth until the sounds of Aramaz's screams stopped. Zadryan snapped his head to the side blasting Aramaz against the castle wall. His body hit the rock and splashed into the moat.

    Adan crawled to Myron on his hands and knees. Tears traveled down his face. Myron lay motionless on his back. Adan cradled his head and grimaced at the amount of blood. "I'm so sorry my friend."

    Myron's eyes opened slowly, the life in them distant and faded. They no longer had the excitement of life that Adan always admired. "Adan…I'm sorry," he said in a barely audible whisper.

    Tears dripped off Adan's chin. "Don't talk, Myron. Keep your strength."

    "Tell Maureen I love her."

    "No!"

"Adan...I'll be with you." His body seized and went still. Myron was dead.

As Karyna and Talin climbed onto Zadryan, Riordan fought off the remainder of the knights.

"Adan, we must get out of here," Darych told him as he tried to take Adan by his hand. Darych had an arrow deep into his shoulder. Blood poured from a wound on his leg.

Adan screamed, "We're not leaving him!"

Riordan ran to help them. Together with Darych they lifted Myron and carried him onto Zadryan's back. Adan grabbed Myron's crossbow and followed. Zadryan took to the sky. A handful of knights watched at the castle entrance.

They were all shocked that the King of Wyndhaven betrayed them. They were heartbroken by Myron's tragic death. Talin tugged on Adan's arm. "Ask the dragon to take us into the Angled Spine. We will be safe with my master."

Adan pounded his fist into Myron's chest. "This is my fault."

Zadryan turned north.

Demon Myra approached Demon Aramaz as he struggled to breathe. He clung to the edge of the shallow moat and hissed at his defeat. His chest had several punctures from the dragon's sharp teeth. When he noticed her he spat blood. "You're late. Where was Zar?"

"Zar was injured when he defeated Zalphyna. He is resting," she replied.

"That dragon son of hers should have been killed long ago. He has matured, and now he is another threat. Adan is becoming powerful. They both need to be taken care of."

"Don't worry about Adan; I will take care of him." She flicked back her long hair. She moved her arm so she could stare into the eyes of her pet, resting still on the silver clip. "Follow them."

The deamlon screeched and flapped its wings.

Zadryan landed in a small clearing shrouded with mountain evergreens and bushes. A small cabin was hidden on the edge of the clearing. It was an older building, withered and decayed. They dismounted and lowered Myron to the ground. The door to the cabin opened. A man dressed in gray and blue greeted them. He was an older man, gentle in his walk. "Welcome, friends," he said. His beard was long. The silver hair blended with the colors of his robes.

Adan wiped his eyes dry and turned to their hero. "Thank you, Zadryan."

The dragon nodded. *"Here, Adan, please take this."* Zadryan stretched out his left hind leg.

Adan shook his head, "Take what?"

"Do you see that horn protruding from my leg? Grab onto that and pull." Adan wasn't in the mood, but he owed Zadryan the respect to do as he was asked. His fingers wrapped around the odd-looking deformation. He could see his reflection in the blue scales. Adan pulled. Zadryan replied with a deep groan and Adan fell back, astonished. He released a long sword exactly like the one he wore on his back. *"Take this sword, Adan. It binds us together as friends. You saved me once; I returned the favor. This bond is our reward. I will always know where you are and you will know where I am. Keep it close, Adan. The swords strength is entangled with my own."*

"What do you mean?"

"I haven't the time to explain, Adan." Zadryan lifted his wings. *"I must mourn the death of my mother. I may be gone for some time, but I promise to return. Take care, Friend."*

"Take care, Friend," Adan murmured and watched his friend fly away. Behind him the rest of them stared at the lifeless body on the ground. Adan knelt before Myron. He stared at expressionless face. His friend would never wake and flash his trademark smile. Myron was gone. Adan collapsed onto his friend and sobbed.

Karyna walked in silence. So much was happening around her, one bad nightmare after the other. Her own father ordered her death. Had it not been for their escape, they would have perished. Her wrists dripped blood where the claws broke through her skin. Her blood was unusually dark and thick. She could still feel the power of the claws surging through her body. The image of the old man that appeared in her mind was clear. It was Jayntil. The old man that she envisioned was the Andar.

As she watched Adan grieve for his friend, she felt that Myron saved them all. She couldn't take her mind from Adan's grief. She knew she had to say something, but for now she thought it best to remain quiet. Poor Adan, she thought. Her heart went out to him. She knelt next to Adan and held out her arms. He accepted her gesture; they hugged and wept finding consolation in one another.

Chapter 40

After three days of mourning, Adan accepted what couldn't be changed. The Dragon Fire continued to burn with each passing day. It filled the sky with its doom. Together, the companions would watch from their viewpoint high in the mountains. They watched as the fire twisted and turned, destroying everything it touched. It moved as if it searched for something.

Jayntil welcomed them into his home. He helped clean their wounds and comfort their losses, though Myron's death was hard on all of them, especially Adan. Jayntil cremated the body. Adan insisted that he release Myron's ashes to the wind as was done through past generations. Adan remembered the ceremony when Myron's uncle died. The ceremony was greatly respected with their family. They believed that the release of ashes into the wind was a form of afterlife that allowed their spirits to be free in the wind.

The sun rose in the east on a new day. Adan leaned against the side of the cabin, admiring his new sword. He had named it *Death*. With all that was on his mind, he felt it was most suitable. The sword itself was remarkable. He compared it with his father's sword and found answers for many of his earlier questions. Zadryan told him that his father befriended Zalphyna. That must be where his father retrieved his sword. He remembered Zadryans' words; *"The power is entangled with my own."* It explained why his father's sword failed him. Zadryan told him he must go and mourn the death of his mother. If his father's sword came from Zalphyna, then its remarkable power died with her. It was an odd sword. The long handle curled back at the tip. Armored with scales, they faded softly as the handle touched the blade. At the base of the blade the metal was white as the color of bone. Gradually the tip turned into polished silver.

Jayntil appeared from around the corner of the cabin, walking slowly with his staff in hand. Adan admired the old man, more so than his apprentice. He remained quiet in his words and never really bothered him. He seemed to carry a remarkable power with him at all times. His grayish-blue robes billowed gently from the soft breeze. It was the Andar who saved them from Demon Vayle at the Stag of Waters. Apparently he also came to Riordan's aide during the traumatic events leading to the king's death. Adan was grateful for his aide, but he didn't help them at Wyndhaven where they lost Myron.

He stepped up to Adan and held out a corked cylinder. "Here are the remains of your friend, Adan. I am terribly sorry for your loss."

"I appreciate your help, Jayntil."

Jayntil nodded with a smile. "You have only begun to realize the help that you are going to need, Adan. The road here has been painful. Don't misunderstand your friend's sacrifice. Myron died to save you…not because of you."

Adan sheathed *Death* into its scabbard on his back and held the cylinder against his chest. It felt cold and heavy. His throat felt sore when he choked back the tears. "I miss him more than I thought possible."

Jayntil grabbed him firmly by his shoulder. "Listen to me now. You must fight your feelings. Take his death and become a stronger person. He died, but you live. You can avenge him. First you must strengthen your will. Harness your anger before it overcomes you."

"I don't know what I'm going to do now. My brother is still out there somewhere. I failed to find him. Wyndhaven turned against us. What hope is left?"

Jayntil nodded sadly. "Your story is troubling indeed. The powers of our enemies are much greater than I feared." Corrona and Wyndhaven were taken. Who was left to stand against the demon invasion? Jayntil spoke with fiery determination. "There is always hope when you are still alive, Adan. All but one of you escaped with your lives; we can counter. Remember that." He paused, "And Dex is still waiting to be found."

Adan shook his head, "I don't know where to go. Without Myron, I feel lost."

Jayntil sighed. "I will guide you. Faral wanted me to find you. Now that I have we must discover why you are so important. We must reason why these demons want to kill you. We must find out why, and use that information to aide us."

Adan nodded. Talin appeared and motioned Jayntil to walk with him. The Andar and his apprentice left him standing alone. He didn't know how Jayntil expected to help him, but for the moment he let the matter rest. A fallen tree rested on a gentle slope. He sat down between dead branches and thought about Myron. There was a time when they were children and they made a pact to be friends forever. Now there were only two of the four left.

One day he would have to tell Maureen; he dreaded the thought. He looked down at the cylinder. "I'm so sorry."

Darych entered the cabin searching for Karyna. The events in Wyndhaven had seriously disturbed her, but she had to understand there was still hope. It sickened him to think that Mel's betrayal came directly from his very mouth, but there was an explanation for it, there had to be. Mel would not order them killed unless he was forced to. She sat in the corner with her knees pulled into her chest. Her eyes were red from crying. Her wrists were covered in bandages. Blood soaked through and stained her clothes. "Karyna, the events at Wyndhaven may have been beyond your father's control."

She looked up at him. "Darych, I'm scared."

He sat beside her. "I know what happened in Corrona. The events are similar to our own. Your father has been twisted somehow, just as Riordan's mother when she accused him of murder. There must be a way to save your father and take back our home."

She trembled. "Darych, that's not the whole of it." She pulled away the bandages. "When these first appeared I had a vision of an old man. Now that I have seen Jayntil, I know that person is him. He is responsible for what has happened to me."

Darych sighed. "You don't know that for certain. There is an explanation for everything."

She bit her lip. "It is clear to me now. The only person I can trust is Rowen. I realized that when Race looked me in the eyes and told me how he yearned for my death. My own father ordered my execution. The two people I know loved me most are dead."

She left him alone. He felt cold and stranded. Karyna was the only connection he had to home, the only person that hadn't tried to kill him. Darych lowered his head. Karyna could trust him. Somehow he was going to have to prove that to her. It was his duty to protect her. Maybe one day she would open her eyes and realize how much he cared.

Talin knelt in front of Jayntil. They finally found time alone so they could speak in private. The Andar and his apprentice were downhill from the cabin where the others would not hear them. "Now, Talin, explain everything; do not leave out a single detail."

Talin did as he was asked. He told him how Karyna and the Armaments found him near death and the encounter with demons and their fight in the swamp. He told Jayntil Riordan's story and the events in Ruhln. He detailed what he witnessed with Karyna, and how they all managed to escape the Dragon's Fire. He explained to his master how they flew to Wyndhaven on the back of a dragon and how they were betrayed by the king they sought to protect.

Jayntil trembled. His ancient body quivered beneath his silver-blue robe. "Karyna has learned of her heritage?"

"Yes, Master."

"And how has she responded?"

"Not well, I believe."

His eyes misted.

"Master, Riordan has received Anemenitty's staff."

Jayntil gasped. "Are you certain?"

"Yes, Master."

"Why would Faral choose the Prince of Corrona for such a task? It doesn't make sense. Riordan is needed in Corrona. Even the greatest Warrior of Ches in our known history, Anemenitty Ches, died of a horrible fate. Why would Faral chance the fate of the future King of Corrona?"

"Anemenitty's staff is a powerful weapon. Perhaps Riordan is stronger than we believe. It is possible that Faral has chosen Riordan to become a Warrior of Ches. In everything that has happened, I have not had a chance to speak with him."

"Indeed." Jayntil ran his fingers through his beard. "We must watch all of them closely." He thought of Karyna, and when he felt tears in his eyes he looked away.

"Master, why do you weep?"

"One day, Talin, I may explain it to you. But first I must speak again with Adan. I didn't realize the extent of what he's been through. One important detail that I have missed was that Darren was his father. Darren was a great friend of mine, the leader of the Warriors of Ches twenty-three years ago. Adan is an extremely important person, Talin, and I must make him understand that."

"His brother is missing," Talin told him.

Jayntil nodded. "The Dryden must have his brother to awaken Granaz. Adan is the one to stop it, but he will need our help. If his friend's death affects him like it may, we will lose our only hope."

"You speak of the demon plague?"

Jayntil ignored him. Karyna stormed down the hill and through the trees, her face set in anger. "Leave us, Talin." His apprentice backed away and disappeared through the trees.

Karyna stopped abruptly. "Tell me who you are."

"My dear, Karyna, I am confused."

"Enough! Since I fell off of that carriage deck, every since these claws appeared"—she ripped away the bandages so she could thrust her wrists in front of his face—"you have been in my mind. Before I arrived here I didn't know who that person was, and since I've seen you I'm even more confused."

Jayntil shook his head "Please calm down."

She yelled, "I have no intention of calming down until I get the truth. Tell me who you are!"

His eyes welled with tears once again. "Please Karyna, not like this. I've waited my whole life for the right moment."

"Waited your whole life for what? My life is turning upside down. My own father tried to kill me. Tell me what is going on." Suddenly, the claws popped out of her skin. She thrust the tips of them close to his face. It dropped the Andar to his knees. "Tell me who you are, and what it is you're doing to me, old man, because everything points to you. You are responsible for this!"

"Karyna, no please, you must understand."

She grabbed his collar with her left hand, and raised her right claws into the air above his neck. Her eyes set with rage. "Explain yourself or die."

Jayntil dropped his chin toward the ground and spoke softly. "I am your father."

She loosened her grip. "What?" she asked with a shaky voice.

Jayntil stood and rubbed feeling back into his throat. "I am your father, Karyna."

"That's not possible."

He had waited his entire life to meet her, spent days deciding what he would say. Now that she stood before him with the truth, he was speechless. "You have my deepest apologies, Karyna. It was never my intent for you to find out like this."

"Then explain yourself."

He felt his aging heart beat as if it cried. "It's my fault your mother is dead."

Karyna stepped away from him. "My mother died of illness."

"What? No, my dear child, your mother was murdered."

Karyna groaned in disbelief. "That isn't possible. I watched her die of illness."

Jayntil shook his head. "Listen to me closely now. Your mother was murdered by Mel. This makes sense now, as he has now betrayed you. I've always known your mother had been murdered, but I never had proof until now. Mel killed your mother."

"No!"

"Karyna, listen to me. Your mother was a Warrior of Ches, like I was, many years ago. We were deeply in love, but a battle at the Pales of Nothingness caused concern, because we had been betrayed by one of our own. As an Andar, I was forced to seek the truth. I had to consider that it might have been your mother, even though I loved her. The Dryden are patient, cunning individuals who will never reveal their intent until their time arrives. The betrayal at Wyndhaven has me believing that it was Mel who betrayed us at the Pales of Nothingness; then years later killed Aylynna. It is the only explanation."

"Why did you say her death had been your fault then?"

Jayntil felt the tears resurface. "If I had given her my complete trust, she would still be alive."

Karyna appeared ready to throw a fit of rage. "What about the claws?"

"There is so much to explain," he said.

"Tell me!"

He gathered the information in his mind so that he could tell her flawlessly. "Your mother's ancestor was Spiral Ches, a warrior in the time of Anemenitty, and together they fought in the Dragon War. Anemenitty and Spiral were lovers, and it was said their love for one another was so great, not even death could come between them. During the final stages of the war, the enemy captured Spiral. Demons tortured her for weeks. They used the venom in their claws to poison her. They mutilated her by peeling off her skin. Her blood sucked in the venom, and of course it almost killed her. The weeks of torture and the demon's venom had a strange effect on her. When she awoke with new life, she could summon claws just as the demons could. She killed every demon that touched her. On the battlefield she reunited with Anemenitty; together they defeated the Dryden. Her unusual blood was passed down through generations. Your mother had the claws just as you have, Karyna. I helped you summon them so you could protect yourself. The claws are an unusual curse, but they are also a powerful weapon."

Karyna stared at the claws, her own blood dripping down from the cuts on her hands. "This can't be happening."

"My dear, Karyna, I'm here to help you."

She shook her head. "I don't trust you. I don't trust anyone. I must find Rowen."

Jayntil fell to his knees. "Please," he implored.

"I need some time alone."

Jayntil watched her leave. Once she disappeared, he sank to the forest floor and wondered what he would have to do to win her heart.

Chapter 41

Adan sat with Riordan outside of the cabin. They waited for the others to join them, for the time was upon them to say farewell to Myron. Riordan seemed heartbroken. "I don't know where to go from here, Adan."

Adan nodded. "I'm so sorry."

"At Wyndhaven I expected to receive help and return to Corrona. Now that will never happen. For the first time in my life I'm uncertain what to do next." Adan understood what he was feeling. There was no denying it. Southern Yannina had fallen, and somewhere in that tragedy, Dex was still lost.

Darych approached them slowly. "Want some advice? Stay clear of Karyna for a little while." Riordan was about to ask why, but something on Darych's face told them both to remain quiet.

Adan held Myron close to his heart in an attempt to harness his anger. Since the battle at Wyndhaven his hate for everything had grown. The Andar apprentice appeared. In the last few days, Talin had shown remarkable signs of recovery. Adan stood; his eyes flashed with anger. "Talin, at Wyndhaven, why were you not helping us?"

The Andar apprentice scowled. "I beg your pardon?"

"At Wyndhaven, as we all fought for our lives, you did nothing."

"When you were inside the castle, I used what power I had accumulated since the Stag of Waters. I used my power to help the dragon."

Adan felt his anger heighten. "I don't believe you. I haven't believed you since I first met you. It seems that everything you do is done to benefit yourself."

Now Talin was angry. He stepped closer to Adan. "Why do you wish to make an enemy of me?"

Darych and Riordan waited to intervene.

"Out of anyone here, you had the power to save Myron, and you didn't."

"I saved your life!" Talin shouted. "Why do you accuse me of such things?"

"Enough!" Jayntil shouted from behind them. "Have you forgotten we are on the same side? How will we succeed if we can't get along? Stop this now." Adan sighed and nodded. He would let the matter rest...for now. Karyna stormed up the hill. She stopped when she saw them all and ran into the cabin. She slammed the door behind her. Jayntil sighed. "Karyna will not be joining us, so we may as well leave." He took the lead and they followed. Jayntil led them down a twisting path through the high mountain evergreens. It didn't take them long to arrive at a ledge. From there they overlooked southern Yannina. The dark smoke stretched across the sky from east to west. Adan walked past Jayntil and stepped up to the edge of the embankment to see his world below. The dark, smoke-filled sky reminded him of his failure. He never found Dex. Myron, his best and true friend, died because Adan couldn't protect him. He failed to avenge his father when he had the chance.

"Do what you've come to accomplish, Adan," Jayntil told him.

Adan turned to them. He nodded to Riordan, Prince of Corrona, a friend with problems of his own. He silently wished him the best of luck in the fight for his people. He smiled at Darych Shade, the man who repeatedly saved his life. Talin, the Andar apprentice, watched him with a frown. Perhaps his accusations were wrong, but there was a feeling inside Adan that warned him. For whatever reason, the Andar apprentice was not to be trusted.

Karyna ran through the trees. She looked at Jayntil and then at Adan. "I'm sorry, Adan, please forgive me."

Adan gave her an approving nod. Karyna had no need to apologize. Surely she understood that Adan knew exactly what she faced. She shot Jayntil an odd look. There was tension between those two that he didn't understand.

He turned back to the ledge. "Thank you for coming with me," he said quietly. Adan held the cylinder and removed the cork. A gentle breeze blew through his hair. Tears trickled down his face. The ashes sailed into the wind, cradling Myron in a soft twisting whirlwind that spun off into the sky. Adan inhaled deeply, breathing in the clean fresh air. He told himself then, even though he had lost his father, his brother, and his best friend, that there must be hope out there somewhere.

The stranger burst through the doors of the old tavern, almost ripping the hinges off the wall. He collapsed hard onto the floor, knocking over a table as he fell. The drunken customers cursed at him for disturbing their drink. He lay on his back and stared at the ceiling. His short, coarse breaths came slowly. He reached upward with gnarled hands and pulled away at the long strips of black that covered his identity. The noises of those around him drifted away.

Memories of pain and torment flooded through his mind like a poisoned wave, memories that he no longer wished to have. He recalled a fire and explosion, and days of crawling through the forest, unaware of his own identity. It had been too late to remember. His brother was gone. He had found him once, but his voice was destroyed. It had come to a whisper, and he failed to hail him.

From the background came a song, a gentle song, like the one his mother once sang to him. He hummed along for awhile. His eyes were still locked onto the ceiling far above. As the song carried on, the room around him began to spin. Above him an image came. "Father, is that you? Mother, are you here too?" The room spun faster. The song continued to burn in his ears. A tear slipped slowly over his scarred face. "Adan, why can't I find you?" he whispered so softly.

Aren closed his eyes and prayed to live another day.

The End of Book 1
The Demons of Destiny

About The Author

Shayne Easson resides in Calgary with his wife Mandy, daughters Hailee and Kaylan and son Owen. He is a Master Electrician and co-owner of his own electrical company. Writing is his true passion. The seeds of writing were nurtured by a series of short stories he wrote in High School. The character Riordan was first developed in a short story titled The Guardian. Shayne credits that story as the inspiration for his Demons of Destiny series. Not all of his time is spent working or at the computer. When the weather is favorable, he and his family enjoy camping and fishing in the beautiful Canadian Rockies.

Watch for release of
The Resurgence of Granaz
Book 2
The Demons of Destiny

The hardships that Adan and his companions endured are nothing compared to the fate that lies before them. It is soon after their arrival in the mountains that Adan and the Andar apprentice mysteriously disappear. It forces the others to continue their plight without them. Karyna and Darych journey to Akhran to secure loyalty and aide against the growing forces of the demon army. Prince Riordan seeks the entrance to the Pales of Nothingness to unravel the Dryden's ambitions. Each must discover what it takes to fight alone and stare into the face of death, for in the haze of a terrible awakening, born in the den of Granaz's wake, a successor shall rise.

Other WestBank Publishing Books

The Chosen of Azar, book 1 of *The Fifth Age Chronicles* by Carol Kluz released April, 2007

Books Pending Release

The Hawk and the Wolf by Mark Adderly

The Commanders by Carol Kluz

The Resurgence of Granaz by Shayne Easson